Redemption's Road

Also by CJ Murphy

frame by frame

The Bucket List

Five Point Series

Gold Star Chance
Forever Chance

Redemption's Road

CJ Murphy

Desert Palm Press

Redemtion's Road
(Five Point Series – Book 3)

By CJ Murphy

©2020 CJ Murphy

ISBN (book) 9781948327640
ISBN (epub) 9781948327657
ISBN (pdf): 9781948327664

Desert Palm Press
1961 Main Street, Suite 220
Watsonville, California 95076
www.desertpalmpress.com

Editor: CK King, Raven's Eye Editing
Cover Design: Murphy's Law Ink

Printed in the United States of America
April 2020

Author's Note

I've been asked, several times, a question that has a complicated answer: "Which of your characters do you most resemble?" I think many authors will say that there are bits and pieces of their true selves in many of their characters. There is a good portion of me in Sheriff Chance Fitzsimmons with the fire and rescue incidents you read in the Five Points series. Readers have told me that the stories seem so real. The reason is that many are based on real-life incidents from my near thirty years in emergency services. The crevasse rescue in Gold Star Chance is based on an actual event, horses and all.

In this book, you'll be reading the first-person perspective of Pastor Rhebekka Deklan. This point of view was a new style of writing for me, but it also felt like that was exactly how I needed to write this story. It's intimate and familiar. Part of Rhebekka's past is also mine in fictional form. I'm talking about her upbringing as one of Jehovah's Witnesses. I'd wager a bet that you've encountered one or more of these evangelizing individuals when you've answered a knock on your door to find someone wanting to "share the good news" and talk about the Bible.

Her faith is another trait we share. Rhebekka's story gave me the opportunity to reveal an important aspect of my life. Despite negative experiences as a Jehovah's Witness, I gratefully accept God's grace and do my best to live out my faith.

From the age of four or five, I was a *door knocker*, trying to sell my magazines. I did so until the age of twenty, when I completely broke with them and their beliefs. What people saw of the witnesses that showed up at their front door was very different from what went on behind the doors of the Kingdom Hall. I experienced a closed society of male-dominated, brainwashing control. Recent investigations have revealed the abuses others have experienced within the Watchtower and Bible Tract Society.

In the middle of writing book two of this series, Forever Chance, a completely different story took control of my writer's brain. A character with a varied background developed in my head. Once I started writing Rhebekka's character, I realized her view of organized religion was coming from my own childhood and young adult experiences. What I lived was spiritual manipulation, as well as emotional and physical abuse as a female in a male-dominated, head-of-household ruled religion. From a young age, I suppressed the fundamental fact that I am a lesbian. In that society, acting or admitting that you were LGBT was automatic grounds for shunning, or disfellowshipping, from the organization.

Writing Redemption's Road was extremely cathartic, as I banished my demons into the world of a fictional book. I assure you, some of the details are anything but fictional.

I hope you'll enjoy Rhebekka and her family of choice, because there is so much more to tell from this group of characters.

Dedication

This book is dedicated to the many ex-Jehovah's Witnesses who have been forced to create a new family because they've been shunned by the one they were raised with. May you find the grace you've long been denied and the love you deserve with your family of choice. To the vilified sexually, physically, and emotionally abused who've been made to feel like it was your fault, you are not alone. No matter what they say, there is no time to remain silent on these things. Speak up, let no one take your voice *or* your choice.

"Three things cannot be long hidden: the sun, the moon, and the truth."
Buddha

Chapter One

I'VE LEARNED THAT CASTING your net in the right water is important. The fish won't come to you. Instead, you have to make your way to the river or the pond where they are. With that logic in mind, I sat there at the bar, applying one of my unconventional ideas about how to be what Jesus referred to as 'fishers of men.' This little brewpub had become the perfect place to spread a little grace, spiritual bait, in the pint glasses of the patrons. Not just any brew pub, Redemption's Road was secretly purchased with proceeds from my former career. I wasn't always the spiritual leader of a non-denominational church in Thomas, West Virginia.

The woman with the blonde dreadlocks, sitting beside me, was giving me a curious look. "So, you're really a preacher?"

A small sigh left my body. If I had a nickel for every time I'd heard the question Senna had just asked, I could be retired. With that kind of money, I'd be enjoying a sandy beach in the Caribbean with a tan that would be sure to mute the colors of my many tattoos. "I prefer pastor compared to preacher, but yes, I'm Pastor Rhebekka Deklan. One with more than just an online ordination to marry people."

My conversation with the newcomer took a sharp right turn, as the word pastor fell from my lips. The shocking revelation that someone wearing a Metallica T-shirt—whose tattooed arms were adorned with an angel wing down one and a demon's down the other—could be a minister, had obviously sent Senna into a contemplative trip down the proverbial rabbit hole. In reality, all five foot eight, one hundred and sixty pounds of me was, in fact, a minister.

"No shit?" She shook her head.

I held up my right hand as if giving an oath. "I actually have a degree in theology."

Senna's pint jar traveled back to her lips, as I watched her try to wrap her head around the latest tidbit. The taproom area was small and dimly lit. Most patrons sat in front of the hand-hammered, copper bar top on stools that resembled sawhorses with wide seat boards.

Her eyebrows went up. "Definitely a different kind of preacher. That's so fucking cool." Senna slapped her hand over her mouth, as her face turned crimson. "Sorry."

The woman standing beside me in a flannel shirt with baggie jeans tucked into Doc Martens, washed her warm gaze over me. Something about her screamed crunchy granola and had my gaydar needle pegged. As a pastor, I was always observant for subtleties in body language and demeanor.

"Don't worry about it. The word fucking is merely a present-participle adjective, unless you mean the verb. That is something totally different." I decided it was time for a subject change. "Karmen over there tells me you're new in town."

Senna took another drink and nodded. "I am. I'm a chef at her fresh food grocery store, three days a week." She pointed to her glass. "This beer is so good."

Karmen was the unofficial welcome wagon, as well as being one of my best friends. An invitation to one of my beer and Bible gatherings was on the tip of my tongue. "Total agreement there. Let me personally welcome you to our little piece of heaven. I'm sure, by now, you know most of the entertainment spots and places to eat?"

Senna lit up, and a wide grin graced her face. "I've devoured pizza at Sirianni's, had the best guac I've ever eaten from Hellbenders, and inhaled a mouthwatering corned beef sandwich from Big Belly Deli. Haven't I seen you play at The Purple Fiddle?" Senna finished the rest of her pint and looked toward the bartender.

I raised my hand and caught Tank's eye, motioning for her to get Senna a fresh beer on my tab. "I do a set once in a while, around town. You've already found the best beer."

"I can't believe how many craft breweries are in this one little area."

There was the crack in the door I'd been waiting for. "A small group of us do a tasting of the latest offerings, twice a month, at my place." My place meant House of the Rising Son, the church I created where saint and sinner were welcome as equals.

It was obvious that Tank had heard my lead-in, as she set the fresh pint in front of Senna.

"She's telling the truth. I provide our latest beers for the event. The reverend here provides the Bible trivia. A little bread with the wine, so to speak." Tank wiped at a water ring on the bar top and winked at me before she moved back to serve another customer.

Senna turned to look directly at me. "When do these epic beer and Bible soirées take place?"

God bless you, Tank. "The second Tuesday and the third Thursday of each month, six in the evening, right down the street from where you work with Karmen. It's in the old community theater. Look for the sign on the door that says—"

Senna laughed and nearly spit out her beer. "The place that says House of The Rising Son, the one with the big Jesus?"

Clever irony struck like lightning the day I decided on the official name of my church. The double entendre played to my advantage as much as it was tongue in cheek.

"That's the place. The giant Jesus was accidentally created when I placed a small fountain of Christ with outstretched arms in the courtyard. Once it got dark and the floodlight came on, the fountain cast a large shadow of the Messiah on the side of the building. It would have felt sacrilegious to take it down after that."

I'd endured a good bit of ribbing for it over the last few years, but it'd become something of an iconic place for tourists to visit. With one last drink, I finished up my beer and put the Mason jar back down on the counter. As my tongue snaked out to lift the froth off my lips, Senna's eyes were drawn to me like a moth to a flame. *Oh, yes, very gay.* "Senna, I've got to roll. It was nice talking with you this evening. Again, welcome to town. Feel free to stop in if you're interested in the beer and trivia night."

Senna nodded her head. "Shouldn't you be working on a sermon for tomorrow morning or something?"

It was close to ten o'clock. I laughed and was about to throw out one of my best lines, when Tank came to retrieve my glass.

The former Marine, built like a brick wall, winked at me again. She knew my shtick so well. She could repeat it with flattering imitation.

"The Lord can't do no savin' on Sunday without sinners from Saturday night. Be careful on that bike, Reverend. See you in the morning." Tank saluted.

Senna's eyes showed shock and alarm. "You rode a motorcycle in this weather?"

"Not a motorcycle. Tonight, my ride home is a Salsa Mukluk fat bike."

"That lime green one chained to the post out there?"

I nodded my head. "The very one."

She shook her head and laughed. "Radical. Shiny side up, Pastor."

I pointed up to the ceiling. "God willing."

I grabbed my helmet from the shelf, before pulling on my leather jacket and gloves. With a wave to everyone, I took a step out the door where the frigid night air stole my breath. I fastened my helmet in place. Eyes heavenward while muttering a small prayer, I expressed my gratitude that home was less than a mile away and that the snow wasn't too deep. After pulling my neck warmer up over my face, I unchained Marvin. I'd named my trusty steed after the Looney Tunes character, Marvin the Martian. I even ordered a sticker and secured it on the frame right after I bought Marvin. As I slung my leg over the bike and settled my right foot on the pedal, the wide expanse of midnight sky and stars that twinkled from a million miles away took me aback.

"Lift up your eyes on high and see: who created these? He who brings out their host by number, calling them all by name, by the greatness of his might, and because he is strong in power not one is missing." For the curious, that's Isaiah 40:26.

I pedaled my way down a back street to avoid the snowplows on the main road and the ill prepared tourists, who had mostly arrived on Friday night to take on the slopes. The streetlights illuminated dirt-streaked snow, piled high and packed with rocks and grime, left by the plows as they cleared the roads.

January had brought exceedingly low temperatures and steady snowfall, good news for the tiny mountain communities and their small businesses. They'd be able to pay their bills from the tourism dollars.

I avoided a section of ice and used a small snowbank as a ramp, launching myself slightly into the air before landing in softer snow that led into my courtyard. Jesus' shadow welcomed me home with open arms.

With my bike on my shoulder, the three ice-covered steps into the back door of the church weren't easy to manage. After a struggle with the door, I hung Marvin vertically on the hooks I'd positioned above a tray that caught the melting snow. My favorite low-top Chuck Taylors, without laces, replaced my snowy boots. Heading to my loft, I scuffed my way up dull stairs that had long ago lost their finish to thousands of footfalls.

"God, my fingers are freezing." I blew on my hands and sprinted up into my private sanctuary that sat above my spiritual one.

Senna was partially right; I had a sermon tomorrow, but my preparation was already done. With the flick of the switch, the loft's interior was bathed in soft, white light. Each step on the hardwood floor produced the creaks and snaps that had become part of my everyday world. Like a song stuck between the individual boards, they sang out with each footstep. A strong aroma of cinnamon drifted to me, a sure sign that Karmen had visited before stopping by the bar. Covered in glorious white icing, a plate of freshly baked sweet rolls sat on the counter. There was a note.

Bite me.

Joyous laughter bubbled up from my belly, along with a hungry growl. Karmen's wicked sense of humor inspired either love or hate.

I poured a cup of coffee into a small metal pan on the stove, to warm it exactly as I'd seen MaMaw do a thousand times. In fact, I was still using that exact pan that held no more than a cup or two. My parents bought her a microwave one year, and they never heard the end of it. I watched MaMaw use the pan every day of my childhood, all the way through until the day she died. It was one of the few things I'd asked for when the other grandkids were asking for money or her 1988 Oldsmobile. I also ended up with her recipe box. The chicken scratch-like handwriting on the scraps of paper was barely legible. It was decipherable only by those who'd spent years reading birthday and Christmas cards from her. Amazing that I could read them at all, as I'd never celebrated my birthday or Christmas until I was nearly twenty-one.

Having grown up as one of Jehovah's Witnesses, those occasions were for the others. Always *us* versus *them*. I nearly scorched my coffee reliving that feeling of separation. The God I'd come to know was very different than the one I'd prayed to for my first twenty years.

With a full cup, I pinched out one of the rolls and went to my small, soundproof studio in the corner of my loft.

Heather-gray acoustic tiles lined the walls and ceilings. I'd hired a professional to come in and build it for me. Writing songs and making music was like a drug to my system, the only kind I indulged in. I chewed off a giant bite of the roll and let my eyes flit back in my head, as the sweet sugar rush met my taste buds. *Bless you, Karmen.* Self-taught, true, but the most incredible chef I'd ever run across. In my travels around the globe with the band, I ate in the finest restaurants staffed by French chefs and still had never found anything as decadent as Karmen's creations.

The steaming cup of coffee drew me in with its aroma. I'd never been a coffee snob by any means. For me, Maxwell House beat a thirty-dollar bag of organic beans any day.

A swallow of coffee washed down the rest of the sweet roll, and I pulled my grandfather's 1956 Gibson L7C Sunburst off its stand. The story was that the organ, at the Baptist church they attended, had died. He decided to learn how to play for the choir. MaMaw had a voice like butterfly wings that would land on your ears so gently you weren't sure you'd actually heard it. They were quite the pair.

I strummed a few chords of Grandpa's favorite hymn, *It Is Well With My Soul*. The melody poured from my fingers and transported me right back to that rickety wooden porch, where he taught me to play the instrument I held in my hands.

"Grandpa, when will my fingers stop being sore?"
"When the music is something more than what you're playing."
"Huh?" My twelve-year-old brain couldn't understand.
"When the music reaches here"—he poked a finger over my heart—"and not just here." He touched my forehead before urging me to continue.

It took years for enough callouses to build up on my fingertips, while I learned to play at Grandpa's knee. My sister and I were proud of the source of our musical talents. None of our other cousins had inherited the musical gifts, but Grandpa sat on the porch with us on hundreds of occasions. He taught us the verses to every hymn he knew, much to my mother's angst. Dad, on the other hand, couldn't have cared less. His conversion to becoming a Jehovah's Witness was merely a ruse to get my mother to remarry him after he'd strayed one too many times. He was my own personal version of the devil.

I walked out of my studio as I sipped my coffee, then strummed through *Here I Am Lord*. I was feeling introspective. Senna's innocent question hadn't shocked me, only pointed out the obvious—that she saw me as anything but a typical pastor.

My phone rang. As if I'd conjured her up with the notes I played, the name of the woman who'd changed my life appeared on the screen. I answered the call in a way I knew would make her smile.

"Peace be with you, Pastor."

"And also, with you. How are you, Rhebekka?"

I pictured the woman on the other end of the line, all five foot five of her. "I'm good, Naomi. How's the weather out there?"

"Freezing, how about your neck of the woods?"

"The same. Fresh layer came down last night, a good eight inches."

She was beautiful no matter what time of day it was. If I tried hard enough, I could smell her perfume.

"Ha, not more than a skiff then. Try seventeen here."

Reverend Naomi Layman lived in Colorado and Open Door Ministries was an unconventional church much like my own. As their spiritual leader, Naomi accepted saint and sinner to join her in worship.

That was how I ended up sitting in the back row, hungover and watching a very sexy woman drop wicked riffs on a Fender, as she espoused the grace of God. At that point, I didn't think God existed and certainly not for someone like me. Naomi's voice pulled me out of that memory.

"Dusting the cobwebs?"

"Huh?"

Apparently, I'd missed something in my thoughts of a woman in a short leather skirt, boots, and a leather jacket.

"I asked if you have your sermon done."

"Sorry, got lost in a moment there. I do. Tomorrow, we're examining the issue between love and lust."

"Ah, as if you aren't lusting right now."

The sound of my laughter bounced off the plaster walls of my loft. She knew me far too well. "Guilty as charged. I was thinking about the first time I saw you in those boots."

The returned laughter over the line was like water in the desert. It'd been far too long since I'd held her, something I knew I'd likely never do again.

"Wow, you really did step into the way-back machine. I'm way past the miniskirt."

"You could still rock it. I've seen you, remember?" Oh, the memories.

"I'm almost old enough to be your mother."

"Given my mother was sixteen when I was born, that's not saying much."

Naomi grew far too quiet for my liking, and I knew the thoughts running through her mind. "I'll behave. Now, to what do I owe this honor?"

"I'm coming to Pittsburgh. I know you got an invitation as well, so don't bullshit me."

Eyes closed, I focused on her voice, smooth like aged bourbon, with a burn at the end that left my nerve endings raw and exposed. At fifty-one, she was still the sexiest woman I'd ever met.

"I did. I looked at the schedule, and I can't make it. I didn't know you'd be there. I'm playing that evening."

"At your own bar. Find someone else. Put your ass in that rust bucket you own and drive north."

God, how this woman knew me and how to work the internet. The little shit had checked the entertainment schedule on the Tucker County live-music web page. I was sure of it.

"It's not that easy." I strummed the chorus to Eric Clapton's, "Wonderful Tonight," our song.

"It is that easy. You're making it difficult."

I heard her join in on the Fender I knew she still played during her services. I could feel her long fingers stroke my skin, as I visualized them strumming the harmony. I more than lusted after this woman; I still loved her with all my heart. "I probably am. Doesn't mean it's going to change."

"Not until you're ready for it."

There was silence between us, only the notes of the melody drawing out in a long cry. We reached the point of the song that epitomized the crux of our relationship, the lesson we'd learned the hard way. The chords we played blended like honey melting into hot tea. They became one, inseparably joined. As the final note drifted off, we sat silently with thousands of miles between us.

"I need to go to bed." My jaw ached from holding back what I really wanted to say.

"You're a terrible liar, Rhebekka. You forget, I know that you never go to bed before four in the morning. Peace be with you."

"And also, with you." I heard the click, then the endless silence that indicated she'd disconnected.

I raked my pick across the strings angrily, frustrated at my inability to forgive. I was a minister who spoke of God's grace, the forgiveness of sins paid for by Christ. Yet with all of that, I was unable to forgive...myself. My mood was on a downward spiral. If I didn't reverse course, the morning's sermon was headed for an iceberg bigger than the one that sunk the Titanic.

I stripped down to my black jog bra and jeans, then carried my guitar back to the stand. I stepped into my recording room. After I chugged the rest of my cold coffee, I picked up my Strat and plugged in the amp.

Sometimes, I would sweat out my frustration in the gym or on a long trail ride. Other times, I exorcised my demons with vibrating strings on that black-and-white electric guitar. At heart, I'd always be a musician. That night, I channeled Stevie Ray Vaughn, until I'd cast the demon out. I launched into *Voodoo Child* and prayed to the God of peace and mercy.

Chapter Two

I HEARD RUSTLING IN the seats as I slowly paced across the small stage with my guitar slung across my back. I'd read to them from the Bible, my well-worn, leather-bound companion, which held the message I'd tried to impart. There's a difference between love and lust. I gave my small congregation examples from both the New and Old Testaments to show the destructive side of desire, if not channeled properly. They sat on a mishmash of secondhand furniture, sipping from teacups and mugs of coffee as they listened.

The previous year, a stalking incident had nearly cost the lives of the local veterinarian, Jax Fitzsimmons, and her assistant, Lindsey. More recently, there'd been an incident in the newspaper where a young man had refused to take no for an answer. He stalked the girl so mercilessly that she'd been forced to get a restraining order against him. It was a high-profile case, because he was a commissioner's son.

"King David lusted for Bathsheba to the point he committed adultery with her, then had her husband killed to hide the child they'd conceived. There are consequences to destructive desire. Having desire isn't wrong, until you turn it into something ugly, hurtful, or deceptive. Desiring to be a better person isn't wrong; desiring to pay your bills or make a good grade isn't *wrong*." I made air quotes as I said this, to drive home my point. "Lying about who you are and catfishing someone, writing a bad check or cheating on an exam, is. God wants us to be happy and have the things that will bring Him honor and glory. It's up to us to find the path that can do that, while still honoring our commitment to being good people. It's by His grace we can do that, and by His grace alone. Amen."

Their faces lit up with anticipation, as I pulled my guitar from my back. "Turn in your hymnals to page 499, *Come Thou Fount of Every Blessing*."

I played through the first verse my way. The melody stays the same, but admittedly, I like to change the tempo and intensity a bit, always a rocker. They came for my message, but they also came for this, the moment when they became part of the music.

As I led my congregation into the first verse, the energy in the room was palpable. By the time we hit the last verse and "I will sing" poured from my mouth, Johnnie in the back was jumping straight up and down and singing with me at the top of his lungs.

My group of believers was small but mighty. Sermons were intentionally short, then I'd sit down on the edge of the stage and strum my guitar, while I opened the discussion portion of my service. Someone would throw out a topic, and it was my job to find the question in the suggestion. And an answer.

Laura, a young nurse at the state orphanage in Elkins, was the first to throw something out. After the night I'd had, I was grateful she threw a softball.

"Faith," Laura suggested.

I looked around the room and nodded. "Faith has different connotations. Trust or belief in something. Confidence that something is true. Then there's the parallel with those thoughts, such as belief in God, religion, or ideology." I stopped and looked at each of the eager faces and silently asked God for direction, as I continued to strum. "We have faith that tomorrow will be a new day. We can believe in this, because we've seen it time after time, without fail. We trust that it will happen. Our faith tells us that God created all things, and thus, He makes the sun come up in the east and set in the west, without fail. We have faith this will happen, because we have witnessed His ability in our everyday life, over and over. The question comes in when the belief, or faith that we've held to, is shaken somehow. We know the sun is there, even if the clouds cover it. The belief that if I live a good life, God will reward me, hangs on a thin line of faith in what we can't see. None of us have seen heaven, but our faith tells us that by His grace, we will see it. We can strengthen that thin line by studying His word and the plans He has for us. We are all children of God, and He knows our hearts. He was there the day we were born, and He'll be there the day we take our last breath. Faith helps us believe that, even when our fragile human thoughts doubt it. He walks beside us. Isaiah 41:10 says, 'So do not fear, for I am with you; do not be dismayed, for I am your God. I will strengthen you and help you; I will uphold you with my righteous right hand.'"

We recited the Lord's Prayer together, and I closed the service with my usual thoughts. "Go in peace. And next week—" I waited for them to finish the phrase.

"Bring a friend!" the voices sang out in unison. That never failed to make everyone smile.

I shook hands and hugged each of them. This was a beer and Bible study week, Salvations and Libations, as it had come to be known. "Those of you who can, join us Tuesday at six. If you will, please sign up, so we have enough for everyone."

Tank sat down on the stage beside me. "Nice sermon, Rev."

"It had its moments." I looked around at the vacated furniture. "I need to fix the leg on that chair. I thought Karmen was coming out of it during the sermon."

"I almost did." Karmen sat on the opposite side.

Tank stood and wiped her palms down her jeans. "Let me see what it needs."

Seconds later, I watched her pick the heavy chair up as if it was nothing. "Glad she's on my side."

Karmen cleared her throat and averted her eyes. "Did you get the cinnamon rolls?"

"I did. There's only one left that's not in here." I patted my gut.

"I talked to Senna after you left last night. You can add her to the list for beer and bullshit next week."

"That's beer and Bible study, you heretic."

She tipped her head from shoulder to shoulder. "You say tomato, I say tomahto."

"You can't tell me you don't have a good time."

Tank came back with the broken leg in her hand. "The damn screw's broke off. I'll get my tools and fix it later this afternoon."

"I'll pay you in beer."

Everyone had gone but the three of us, and I kicked my arms back and rested on my palms.

Tank snorted. "I work at a bar."

"True and you are an excellent barkeep." I nodded. She was much more to me, but few people knew. Tank had been my shadow for the majority of my rock 'n' roll career. She hated the terms bodyguard or security agent, so we'd settled on shadow. Tank had saved my life many times, in numerous ways.

Karmen elbowed me. "What's going on in that bucket up there?" She touched my temple. "You've got bags under your eyes, which means you didn't get your normal three hours of sleep last night."

I shrugged it off and looked around the former theater. Thick, red velvet curtains still hung at the edges, and dark wood accents sucked up every bit of natural light. The wooden floors popped and creaked like my loft, a sound I found more comforting than creepy. "The songwriting

13

bug hit me. I put together a few things for Ellie."

Ellie was my superstar sister. Once I stepped back out of the limelight and into a silent partner role, she turned up the wattage on her star and became the lead singer of my former band. EllieAnna McNally was a bonified rocker, and I loved her even more for it. She'd put in the hours to keep the band relevant, when everyone in the music industry wanted to write them off after I left. Regal Crimson is still in the top one hundred every year, when they talk about bands with staying power.

Ellie inherited MaMaw's butterfly soft voice. When we sang together, she smoothed out my gravel. For twenty years, Regal Crimson had held court in the rock world. Just over five years ago, I personally hit bottom and walked away. EllieAnna let the horses run and surprised even me with the power she could generate.

"Anything we can hear yet?" Tank beamed.

"They're still pretty rough."

"When's she coming by again?" Karmen kicked at one of the rugs that had flipped up. I watched Tank straighten a bit and move in toward us.

Like half the world, Tank had a monster crush on my gorgeous sister. Ellie is feminine where I'm butch, soft where I'm hard, and bisexual, which I am not. Tank had pined for her since the first night they met. I'm sure they hooked up at least once, but neither woman has ever said so. It wasn't my business.

"I talked to her last week. The time difference is killing us. They're touring in Europe, right now, and coming back to the States next month."

Slumped shoulders showed Tank's impatience. I was sure she wanted another shot at trying to catch the wind that was my sister.

Karmen touched her index finger to her lips and pointed at me. "You know, you could always go to her. I know she's offered you tickets more than once."

The conversation was headed down a dangerous road. "I'm aware. That would only lead to the belief I'm coming back, and that isn't happening." That was why I'd stopped using the name I was born with, McNally. Deklan was MaMaw's maiden name. The attention that came with the name Bek McNally was more than I wanted ever again. When I walked away from the band, I took the formal version of my name, the one Naomi preferred. I became Rhebekka.

"Come on. I'm cooking, and you're supplying the beer." Karmen

14

pointed to Tank.

"If you're good, maybe I'll give you a sneak peek of what I've been working on." I stood and dusted off the back of my pants. If only Tank saw that Karmen had a thing for her. I could see it as plain as the nose on my face.

With Grandpa's guitar safely in the case, we climbed the stairs and stepped into the warmth radiating from the fireplace in my loft. My home was comfortably furnished with big, soft leather couches and chairs. Wooden end tables and a coffee table with slate accents finished it off. I didn't struggle financially, between my income streams and investments. I'd spared no expense in the kitchen. My kitchen would make any serious chef drool. I didn't cook much, but I knew someone who did. More than one someone, present company included. Karmen made her way behind my counters and went about fixing a meal that I had no doubt could be served in a five-star restaurant. She'd started on the basics before services began.

Tank dug a growler out of a cooler and poured two Mason jars for us, before confiscating my leftover coffee for herself. From the color of the liquid inside that Kerr jar, I could tell she'd brought the stout I'd been drinking the night before.

Karmen pointed a wooden spoon at me. "I'm thinking spicy chicken noodle. That way, you have enough for lunch this week."

Her constant need to mother me made me smile, even though she was ten years my junior.

"Thanks, Mom. If I run out, I know where I can check out the daily specials."

"Oh, by the way, I'm making your favorite this week." Karmen grinned.

I perked up at that. "Broccoli cheddar?"

She nodded. "That'd be it. Get there early, or it'll be gone."

I walked over to the studio area and grabbed the Strat, along with the score sheets I'd been working on. Tank camped out on the couch, while I took up residence in the window seat overlooking downtown Thomas. Streams of people made their way into the coffee shop next door. The sight brought the memory of the first time I took my skeptical, coffee-snob sister there. Ellie swooned and made me swear to send her the house-roasted beans wherever she was on the road.

"You know you can order this online. Having me personally send this to you is like demanding I give you all my green M&M's when we

were on the road."

Ellie's eyebrows rose. "And hearing from you once in a while would be so bad how?"

"Ellie, I call you every week."

"It's not the same."

I pulled her hands into mine across the table. Ellie, for all her bravado, was still my little sister, a beautiful young woman full of insecurities. Petite and shapely, she sat there playing with the neon blue streaks in her black hair and staring at me with her pale blue eyes.

I nodded and sighed. "No, I know it's not. I can't go back, Ellie. I'll send you pounds of coffee and call you every day if you need me to. My days of standing barefoot on a stage, with the Strat on my shoulder and sweat dripping off me, are over.

"But you'll do that for ten people while you talk about faith?"

"I don't do it in my jog bra"—I pointed at her with my spoon—"And there's more than ten, I'll have you know."

Ellie dropped her head. "I miss you. I can't get it right without you."

"You've gotten it right every night without me for years. I've seen it. I've heard it. The audience goes crazy for you. Regal Crimson sells out every show. You can do it."

"I don't write the songs, Bek, you do."

That was a fact. Ellie couldn't write music to save her soul. Her gift was bringing a song to life with vocals that couldn't be matched.

"Well then, I'll write the songs, and you give them a voice. Every time you sing one of my songs, I'm right there beside you." My sister needed to be grounded, and I knew how to do it. "Close your eyes." When I let go the first few notes of "Amazing Grace," Ellie relaxed and joined in on the harmony. By the time we finished, a slow clap had begun around the room from the six other patrons and the staff who'd stopped to listen.

That last time we sang together had been over a year ago. Ellie's schedule had been too crazy for her to visit, and I hadn't gone to her. My only sibling knew she could call me day or night, at any hour. I tried to be cognizant of where she was in the world and the time zone. Sending her a text before she hit the stage was my way of telling her I was right there with her, in spirit.

The loft smelled of the soup Karmen was fixing. I tuned my guitar and stopped to make a small adjustment. "I have no idea what this one is called yet. It's not done, but I've got the chorus." Pick against the strings, I launched into the melody. Tank tapped her foot and bobbed her head, while Karmen danced in the kitchen. Both were good signs for the unnamed composition.

Tank sat up and clapped. "She's going to love that."

"I'm not really happy with the bridge yet."

Tank tilted her head. "Did you write with her voice in mind, or just write the song?"

"I put down what came to me for this. No one in mind, though." I shrugged. Tank joined me in the window seat. She picked up the score, and I could see her pulling it apart, note by note.

She pointed to the second line. "Here. Make that a flat and draw it out into this note." She handed the score back to me. I looked at what she had suggested and strummed through the bridge again, adding a few other adjustments.

"I like it. Thanks, Tank."

"You just make sure you let Ellie know I was thinking about her when I made it perfect."

Tank didn't mean anything by it, and I was sure she wasn't considering how words like that cut Karmen to the bone. I heard metal clatter into my sink and looked up to see my best friend's back turned to us. A glance over at Tank confirmed that she was oblivious to Karmen's pain or her affection. I wanted to shake both of them. I could see how they fit together, one too afraid to say anything and the other too afraid to let go of something unlikely to happen. Ellie was a free spirit with zero intentions of settling down. Karmen lacked the courage to tell Tank how she felt about her. And there we sat.

Even with her back to us, I could picture Karmen's expression as well as if I were standing toe to toe with her, sullen with a hint of defeat. If I only had a way to pull the blinders off Tank. You can lead a horse to water...

"That smells fantastic, Karmen. Is that your green curry recipe?"

"It is. Perfect for these sub-zero temperatures. Another ten minutes and we'll eat. The bread should be done about then as well." Karmen stirred the soup, grabbed a small, metal spoon, and ladled up some for me to sample.

Blowing across the hot liquid, I tasted it and laughed when a bit dribbled down my chin.

She shook her head. "You're worse than my five-year-old niece."

Karmen handed me a towel. The spill had made it all the way to my black T-shirt. "Guilty as charged. That soup is spectacular, and I'm likely to eat an entire loaf of bread myself."

"Good thing I made extra then. Tank, can you grab the butter?"

Tank rounded the corner and grabbed the glass dish off the sideboard. "One of my favorite things in the world is home-baked bread slathered with Amish butter." She held it up. "Butter that isn't kept in the fridge and melts, well, like butta."

My phone pinged, and I swiped the screen to see the incoming text. That simple message meant everything and tore at my heart, exactly as the woman who'd sent it knew it would.

1 Corinthians 13. And in case you've forgotten, I'm a patient woman, Rhebekka.

No one in my life had been more patient with me than Naomi, not even my grandparents. It was one of the reasons I would always love her, even as I couldn't let myself be with her again. The large grandfather clock in the corner told me what time it was in the Rockies. I knew she'd be getting ready for Sunday services. My reply was even shorter.

Patient and persistent. Peace be with you.

"Soup's on." Karmen moved around the kitchen, setting out bowls. From our local artisan potter, each was unique and beautiful. I'd handpicked a different color for each bowl and plate, not satisfied with having a bland matching set. I wanted eclectic, and Rhen produced some beautiful pieces that I took great pride in.

When the hot bread was pulled from the oven, my stomach told my friends exactly how hungry I was. Karmen clicked her tongue. "Holy cow, if you're that hungry, I might not have made enough."

"Jesus fed five thousand with two fish and five loaves. I think we've got plenty. Karmen, thank you for cooking." I hugged her and kissed her forehead, whispering against her skin. "You're worth the chance. Either she'll see someday, or you'll let someone else in."

She clutched me tighter and patted my back. That conversation was over for the time being.

Chapter Three

MONDAY'S TASK WAS PREPARATION for game night with my youth group, the after-school program I'd started. Some evenings, we dug through the massive trunk and pulled out various board games. Once a week, during the second hour, we played ArchAngel, a virtual-reality game. Daniel, formerly Daniella, was the electronics tech from my tour days and the game coding wizard who'd built the virtual world of good versus evil that I used in my youth ministry.

The main character, ArchAngel Michael, wore a long, white leather duster and the helmet of salvation, while wielding the sword of the spirit. The other armaments mentioned in Ephesians, could be garnered during special challenges. Michael would vanquish foes while bringing light where there was darkness. The clever coding allowed me to program in lessons each week. Participants wore virtual-reality headsets and could play individually or in teams if I chose. The lesson I'd prepared delved into the topic of temptation.

The bell over the door chimed and the herd poured in. I looked at my watch. "Right on time."

Seven bedraggled teenagers, laden with bookbags of every shape, made their way to the snacks. I high-fived, hugged, and fist-bumped each with their chosen greeting.

"Get something to eat, then get that homework out." That was the rule, no games until the schoolwork was done. With the prospect of ArchAngel on the horizon, it was easy to convince them to finish up. "If you need help, shout hallelujah, and I'll be around."

"Pastor, I have an essay I need help with." Alton Britton opened his bookbag.

"And how do we ask?" I smiled at the gangly teen with hair in his eyes.

A sigh left his lips. "Hallelujah?"

"Are you asking or telling me?" I quirked my mouth as if I was puzzled. Every meeting, one or more of the participants did their best to get under my skin. If they knew that only my parents or Naomi could accomplish that, they'd realize how futile the effort was. For everyone else, I had infinite patience.

Alton smiled and shouted, "Hallelujah," with his hand in the air.

"Excellent." I made my way to him, as he opened a jug of chocolate milk and poured a generous glass.

"I have to write an essay about something." Alton drained the glass before filling it again.

I straddled a backward chair to sit beside him in our recreation room. "Tell me something you feel strongly about."

He ran his hands through his hair in deep thought. "I don't know."

"Okay, let's look at it another way. What's something that pisses you off?"

Titters went around the room at my language. I was dealing with kids who had issues, and I connected with them on their level. I'd sat down with the parents of the participants, and they knew who and what I was. They knew how I interacted with the kids, and I respected their parental limits. I could see the wheels spinning in Alton's head. He cracked his knuckles.

"It pisses me off how people treat my brother."

"Okay, that's something we could work with. What do you want people to know about Darren?"

"He has autism; he's not stupid. He knows when people make fun of him. People hear the word autistic and think they can catch it or something. That's stupid. Darren's just different. He's really smart. He can do math problems that I can't, and he's nine."

"Then I think you've found your subject. Myths and facts about autism." I waited and watched the idea take form in Alton's mind. When he let out a small smile, I knew he had it.

Alton pulled a notebook from his bag. "My mom did tons of research after he was diagnosed. She still does. I could talk to his doctor. This will be easy."

"Get on it." I held my fist up. We touched and pulled back with the explosion motion.

Five tables were set up around the room. Each had at least one or two of the kids ensconced in a chair, most with some form of homework out. My job was to walk around and see if anyone needed help or to validate an answer. In the process, I also evaluated the mood and attitude of each. I had my sensitive kids and my tough ones. A motley crew of emotional hurricanes—my hurricanes.

A few were actually working on their homework, while others scrolled on their phones. I tapped my watch. "Twenty minutes, minions. Tonight's ArchAngel night. If you want to play, you've got to pay. And

don't try to BS me. You know your teachers send me your assignments."
While I poured a cup of coffee, phones clattered to the table and books
slapped open. No one wanted to miss one minute of life as a virtual
warrior angel.

I sipped and walked around, correcting where I could and
rewarding them when they got it right on their own. Amanda, one of my
tougher nuts to crack, was broody.

"There's a new Metallica video out." I frequently used music as a
conversation starter with her.

Amanda shrugged, not uttering a word. Her mom had recently
been deployed back to the Middle East. Sixteen and full of fear, she
turned her distress inward. Never much one to discuss her feelings, she
shared her thoughts with me through her journal. We'd come up with
this idea together. She would free write her thoughts without fear of
judgment from me over grammar, spelling, or prose. She would leave it
for me to read while they played games. I would read and comment on
her thoughts, attempting to direct her anger and fear toward something
positive she could focus on. Sometimes it was a line of scripture or a
poem I found that related. Sometimes it was nothing more than
acknowledging the unknown. I would leave the journal on her book bag
for her to find as she left.

"I heard you're helping direct the school theater performance.
That's cool."

Amanda looked up to me with surprise. I had her.

She quirked a sideways grin at me. "Mrs. Hambrick said she
thought I'd be good at it, since I catch things better than most."

I watched her spin her pen on the table. Talking about herself was
another thing I'd discovered she found uncomfortable. "I think Mrs.
Hambrick is right. You'll do a good job of keeping track of the timing and
marks the performers will need. Unless I miss my guess, you already
have the dialogue memorized." Another grin and a nod from my
impressionable lamb.

That was really all I needed to say for her to know I cared about the
everyday things she had going on. I could, and would, help her deal with
her anxiety over her mother's deployment without making a big deal
about it. Her thoughts would play out in a bold and angry blue script on
the lined page. My responses would be returned in my chicken scratch
with a black pen. I touched the cover of the black and white
composition notebook, and she nodded.

With a slight roll of my arm, I glanced at the watch I wore on the underside of my wrist. It made it easier for me to keep track of time without appearing like I was watching the clock during my sermons. I clapped my hands.

"Okay, five minutes to finish up. Meet me in the VR arena."

Seven teenagers yelled, "Hallelujah," as I left the room.

The VR arena was nothing more than an empty, twenty-by-twenty space backstage that I'd set aside when I renovated part of the old theater. It'd likely been the green room in the past. Ten pairs of headsets and gloves hung from hooks that once held costumes. I fired up the state-of-the-art computer server that housed ArchAngel and waited, while everyone burst into the room and donned their equipment. My avengers had arrived.

"Okay everyone, when we left off last week..." I oriented everyone to the particular lesson I wanted to emphasize, temptation.

I donned my own VR headset, which allowed me to see the actions of every player. My focus wasn't to participate but to facilitate and watch the decision-making process of each participant. The players could gain another piece of armor each week. In this session, they were working toward the breastplate of righteousness.

Ten minutes into the game, I pressed a key that initiated a challenge and uttered the words they both loved and loathed. "Boss fight!"

They pushed up their headsets and sat on the floor. I opened *The Message*, the version of the Bible that put scripture into contemporary language the kids could relate to. I read to them from the fourth chapter of Matthew. When I'd finished, the boss fight began. The players stood and put their headsets back on. My character, an ancient, winged book with ribbons tucked between the pages, appeared in their world.

"Jesus faced three temptations by the devil. What were they?"

The beauty of this game was that each individual player chose their answers without the others seeing if they'd gotten it right or not. There was no shame in getting it wrong, only a teachable moment. I watched the seven small boxes pop up on my computer screen. I was pleased that they'd all gotten the right answers: creating bread from stones, bowing down to Satan, and throwing himself off a cliff to see if angels would catch him.

"Jesus knew that nothing the devil could offer him was worth turning his back on God. The rewards would have been temporary. In the end, God's chosen one would have lost out on the ultimate prize, thus costing the entire human race their salvation. Enter code, the test."

I watched with pride, as each of the seven ArchAngels on my screen took up the breastplate of righteousness while wielding the sword of the spirit.

After another ten minutes, I hit pause and ended play. I chuckled at the groans of frustration. "Next week, same place."

While the kids fought with the foes in the game, I'd read through Amanda's short entry.

What if she's afraid?

My response was slightly longer, but still short and to the point. *Then we pray for her with this thought, Psalms 27. So, with Him on my side, I'm fearless, afraid of no one and nothing.*

The kids grabbed their bags and made their way to the door, where their parents waited to pick them up. I saw Amanda's mother, Lynn, and lifted my pinky and thumb to the side of my face to symbolize a phone call. She nodded discretely and put her arm around Amanda as they went through the door. The teenager had two mothers, something that made her stand out in our small community. I kept a close eye on her and communicated frequently with her parents. Amanda showed every sign that she too was gay, or at least bisexual. The family regularly attended Sunday services, and both mothers had approached me about her. Yesterday, they'd been busy putting the major on a plane to defend our country.

Stay close to them, Lord.

***

Later that evening, when I made my call to Lynn, I told her my plan. We agreed to keep a close eye on the sullen sixteen-year-old. Lynn struggled with parenting on her own while she managed one of the local resorts. Sydney had been in the Air National Guard for decades and had recently been promoted. Several deployments, each up to six months, had strained the relationship between Lynn and Amanda. I worked with them in family counseling to help them develop coping skills. I wanted to do something special for them, so I sent Daniel a text to call me. An hour later, my cell rang.

"Daniel, oh sentinel of God, good to hear from you. Any news in your world?"

"Your sister dumped the dickhead."

I could hear the sneer in Daniel's voice. He never liked any of the men, and very few of the women, my sister dated.

"I need to call her, huh?"

"That would be a thought, but you didn't contact me for that. What can I do for you?"

"I need you to create a face lens for me."

Daniel's laugh belted out from my speakerphone, as I poured coffee into my pan to heat.

"Seriously? I'm working the stage scene for your sister's multimillion-dollar tour, and you want me to turn you into a bunny rabbit?"

Though he couldn't see it, I rolled my eyes. "No techno-whiz, I need you to recreate the helmet of salvation, and the breastplate of righteousness, like you have in ArchAngel. It's important."

I heard voices and things moving in the background. A loud noise, like a pipe dropping off the stage support, pealed through the line.

Daniel yelled. "Hey watch it, fucker!"

Accidents could happen when setting up for a show. "You, all right?"

"Good help is impossible to find. I'll see what I can do. Lucky for you, I'm a damn genius."

Relieved, I continued. "And that's why I call you. The kids loved the last session. When they chopped the head off that giant serpent, they went nuts."

He chuckled. "Did they figure out the head could still bite them?"

I couldn't help but laugh. For all his bitching, Daniel liked knowing the kids enjoyed his work. "Poor Alton jumped five feet in the air when it moved as he walked by. He drove the sword right between its eyes. Oh, and the explosion associated with that? Outstanding."

"All right, all right, enough smoke up my ass. I'll work on it later tonight."

"Love ya, man. I'll call Ellie. Keep an eye on her for me, will you?"

"With a body like that, I'll take that job any day of the week." Daniel let out an ear-piercing whistle. "Hey, jackass, how about turning that screen around so people can actually see it? I gotta go, Bek. Take care of yourself and don't worry about Ellie. I got her covered."

Despite his reassurance, I would worry. I thought about Ellie's schedule and knew she should have a few hours of downtime. I walked up to my loft, while I hit the video chat. My sister's face popped up and made me smile with pride. "Hey, stranger."

Ellie narrowed her eyes. "Oh, you're one to talk."

My sister's tongue was as sharp as her intellect. Defensive was her normal modus operandi. It would take extraordinary measures to drop the walls around Jericho. I grabbed my guitar and began to strum. "I know I haven't called since last week."

Ellie rubbed her temples and didn't respond. That worried me. "Got a headache?"

She shook her head. "No."

I knew she was lying to me. I'd witnessed too many of her migraines not to know she was on the brink of one. This was the last thing she needed right before a show. Ellie stopped rubbing her temples and sat up straighter. She looked directly into the camera. I could see the dark shadows under her eyes. With each note I strummed, the tension rolled off her. A few more chords, and she was bobbing her head. Her index finger waved back and forth, as I started to sing about a little light.

Ellie started to sing along. We sang the first song Grandpa ever taught us to harmonize. With each word, she seemed lighter, and the tightness around her eyes eased. I blew into the camera and watched her move her flame to keep me from blowing it out, just as she'd done when we were little. By the time we'd reached the last verse, a smile made its way onto that beautiful face. "Better?"

"See? This is why I need you with me." Ellie stuck out her lower lip in a pout.

"I'm always with you, baby girl. You know that. Now, word on the street is you've scraped off the barnacles."

She sneered. "Let me guess, Daniel had his trumpet out?"

"I never reveal my sources."

"Tre was an ass, pretty, but a real ass. I think I'm done for a while. What's up with you?"

"Still standing on the soapbox."

"Has to be better than knocking on a door, trying to sell a magazine."

My sister was referring to our childhood spent "going out in the service." We spent every Saturday in a different neighborhood, talking to perfect strangers about God and pushing the latest *Watchtower* publication. Growing up as one of Jehovah's Witnesses had given me a skewed view of religion and left a bitter taste in my mouth. Only after meeting Naomi had I realized the true gift of God's grace.

"Amen, baby girl. Nice to see that smile." Ellie rubbed her eyes just like she'd done when she was five and tired. I wanted more than anything to wrap her up in my arms. "You need more sleep."

"You know the saying. I'll sleep when I'm dead." She yawned. "I miss you."

"I miss you, too."

"You know you could fix that. I sent you an invitation."

Tickets had arrived for the twentieth anniversary of Regal Crimson's debut in July, the same invitation Naomi had mentioned.

"Ellie, I—"

She held up a hand. "Don't say no. Think about it. You know what it would mean to me. To all of us."

God as my witness, I wanted to make her happy. I wanted to be there for a concert in the city where we'd played our first big show. I just didn't know if I could.

"Promise me you'll pray about it." Ellie winked.

"Oh, you little sneak." My sister knew what buttons to push. She knew I'd never refuse to pray about things that were important to her.

"You've left me little choice. I want you there. You don't have to sing or play. You don't have to do anything but be there, for me. Please, Bek?"

I sighed. "I'll pray on it. I love you, baby girl."

"Love you too."

I hung up the phone and looked to the heavens. "Lord, help me."

Chapter Four

DANIEL WORKED FOR A week to create my surprise for my sullen, yet sensitive, student. After reading Amanda's journal entry filled with concern for her deployed mother's welfare, Lynn and I had arranged for Sydney to video chat from her base. We made sure it timed with Amanda attending the after-school program.

I was reading from *The Message* and saw the silent reminder on my watch. Out the window, I noticed Lynn making her way to the back door, where Tank would let her into my office to wait. We had five minutes to get set up.

"Amanda, can you help Tank and me with something in my office?"

Suspicious eyes met mine, but she shrugged and got up to follow me. It was a standard procedure not to be completely alone with any of the kids to avoid any question of impropriety. Tank was ahead of me in the hall.

Amanda stopped beside one of the counseling rooms. "Did I do something wrong?"

With a smile plastered on my face to relieve her worry, I shook my head. "Not a chance. I've got a surprise for you." Tank held open my office door.

Amanda's brow knit in confusion. "Mom, what are you doing here?"

Lynn stood by a chair. "Come sit beside me, and you'll see."

Amanda slowly walked to her mom. I sat down at my desk and activated the large monitor on the wall. A private chat window appeared on my laptop, and I typed.

You ready?

The reply was instant.

And waiting.

With a single keystroke, pure delight overtook Amanda and Lynn when Major Sydney Parker appeared on the large wall TV.

Amanda yelled and jumped out of her chair.

"Mom!"

Tears ran down Lynn's face, as she looked at her wife in battle fatigues.

Sydney put her hands against the screen as her family did the same. "I only have about fifteen minutes, but Pastor Rhebekka wanted me to show you something. Hang on."

We watched, as she typed something with the keyboard. The moment she looked back at her wife and daughter, Amanda and Lynn stared at a woman wearing a white helmet adorned with an ornate gold cross that ran over the brow and down her nose. On her chest was a breastplate with a shepherd's crook crossing over a staff. Sydney stood and took a step back to allow her family to see that she held the sword of salvation and the shield of faith the book of Ephesians talked about. Everything looked exactly like it did in ArchAngel, the game Amanda played with the youth group. Credit was due to my friend, who'd created a masterpiece. *Daniel, you've outdone yourself.*

Amanda smiled from ear to ear. "Whoa, Mom, that's so cool!"

Lynn wiped away tears and wrapped an arm around Amanda. "See, she's got plenty of protection."

I moved around to the door, intent on letting this family have some private time. I stopped short when I heard my name.

Amanda held out her hand. "Pastor Rhebekka, will you pray with us?"

Choking back a sob of my own, I nodded my head. Lynn took one of my hands and Amanda the other. Both of them reached out to cover Sydney's outstretched palms with their own. It was my honor and privilege to speak to the Almighty with them as we bowed our heads. "Dear heavenly Father..."

***

By Thursday, I was ready for some adult time. From the sign-up sheets, we'd counted about ten that would be joining us for Salvation and Libations. By my calculations, Karmen would be arriving any second with the pepperoni rolls. Right on time, she walked in with a stack of her homemade deliciousness on a platter.

"Bring it on, Pastor!"

I held up my Bible. "No problem."

Tank walked in with three growlers of beer in her long fingers. "And I've got this."

Karmen pointed to the leather in my hands.

"And that book is why you facilitate and aren't allowed to play."

The next few minutes were spent setting up the tables. My

preferred u-shaped configuration allowed me to pour beer and interact easily with each participant. We dressed the surfaces up with red tablecloths and put the game's answer sheets at each seat. Our game closely resembled pub trivia, Jeopardy style. Participants would wager points in the categories they felt strongest in. Subjects ranged through biblical heroes, Jesus' parables, women in the Bible, and many others that opened doors for discussion. This was one of my favorite nights. It was the best of all my worlds. I could pick at my guitar, teach faith-affirming lessons, and drink beer with friends.

This activity appealed to a variety of people. Some didn't attend regular services anywhere, including House of The Rising Son. With Naomi's example as my guide, I'd set up activities that most traditional churches would have frowned on. When I first moved to Tank's hometown, I was an outsider, even among the mishmash of other transplants. The area was home to a collective group of families who had been around these parts for generations and others who had migrated for the unique way of life. A considerable percentage of the land was part of the Monongahela National Forest and offered outdoor recreation in its wooded areas and rivers. Two ski resorts, two state parks, and close proximity to Baltimore and Washington D.C. made it a perfect weekend getaway.

Chimes from the entrance alerted me that players were starting to arrive. I greeted my regulars and welcomed newcomers. Senna walked in the door and made a beeline for Karmen. I'd wait a few minutes before going to say hi and allow her to settle in.

"What kind of categories do we have tonight, Pastor?" Tom Roland sat in his normal spot.

The seventy-five-year-old former forester had a passion for the environment. He was a trivia master. He always brought his own beer stein that he'd found in a secondhand shop in New Zealand on one of his travels.

"Oh, I think you'll find tonight's subjects of particular interest." The list of questions related to different types of wood and wooden items from the Bible.

He pointed a finger to my forearm. "New ink?"

I smiled. Tom always noticed when something new adorned a part of my exposed skin. My latest was a replica of my Gibson guitar head. The frets on the neck burst out of my forearm toward my palm. "Yeah, got it done last week."

"Your artist is very talented. Looks like you could play it. That 3D is incredible."

I ran my hand over the ridges the needle had made when it embedded the ink. They were still slightly raised. "It took me a long time to find someone with Roman's talent. Now, I wouldn't trust anyone else. You ought to go see him."

He grinned. "This skin is too old to start drawing pictures on it. I'll just live vicariously through you. Someday, when you finally get that back piece done, I'd like to see it." He held his hands up. "Don't take that the wrong way, I meant a picture or a rendition. The little bit I can see of the angel and demon wings is so detailed."

"No offense taken. Roman is working on a painting of it as well, no worries." I changed the subject, knowing Tom meant no harm and was looking for a polite exit out of the conversation. "I think you're going to like tonight's beer offerings. Go see Tank for a full description."

He stood and held up his stein. "Excellent idea."

I liked the man. Tom had been one of the first people to join when I proposed this activity at Redemption's Road one evening. Naomi had been doing something similar for years. On one of those nights, I'd become so intrigued with her, I'd asked her to dinner.

"Pastor Naomi, would you do me the honor of accompanying me to dinner? I'd like to continue the discussion from tonight." I watched the startlingly beautiful woman gather Bibles from the tables. She looked at me with those ice-blue eyes, so light they were nearly white, and smiled. The magnetic pull made it difficult not to run directly to her.

"That depends." Naomi moved to another table.

Collecting used red cups, I watched her gather the books. Her calf-length, high-heeled boots clicked across the tile floor. "Depends on what?" Every move she made was captivating. The sway of her hips, the turn of a hand, and the slight tilt of her head as she looked at me. Her gaze created bore holes straight into my soul and made my center clench.

"On where you suggest we go."

Straight to my bed if I had my way. Chill bumps danced up the back of my neck and forced a shiver down my spine. "Anywhere you'd like. Someplace we can talk." Her auburn hair fell around her shoulders. I wanted more than anything to sink my hands into those soft, wavy curls and run them through my fingers. I accidentally crushed one of the cups and rushed to throw them away.

"What kind of food do you like?" Naomi stacked the Bibles on the

shelf. She leaned against it with her hands behind her, her chest presented front and center as she stretched and slightly arched her back.

That position had to be unintentional. She was far too classy to try and use her body to seduce me so blatantly. Regardless of intention, my eyes were glued to the most beautiful breasts I'd ever had the pleasure to admire, even fully covered. My mouth watered, forcing me to swallow or drool.

"I like just about anything." I raised my index finger. "Except organs or innards."

Naomi's laugh was rich and resonated around the room. It was like hearing my sister sing harmony, filling in all the blank spaces around us.

"No liver and no scrapple, got it. How about I cook for you? I promise to abide by your peculiar dislikes and come up with something you'll enjoy. That way, we can talk without feeling the need to clear out for anyone waiting to be seated."

My world spun backward on its axis. She was inviting me to spend an uninterrupted evening with her and offering to cook for me. My eyes dropped to the top of her boots and followed her gorgeous legs all the way up to the tight skirt that hugged her hips. I tracked that same line up her body to the open collar of her pale-yellow blouse that showed me enough cleavage to make me lick my lips. She caught me and flashed a knowing grin, as my face burned with embarrassment. Heaven help me.

"That sounds great." The voice I'd used to sing my songs to thousands of people failed me, coming out in a squeak. I cleared my throat. "Lead the way."

That night, Naomi had worked hard to convince me I was worthy of grace, though everything about my previous experience with religion had reinforced how undeserving I was. My entire life had been measured by an unattainable standard that left me feeling unworthy of Christ's sacrifice. What she said to me completely turned my world upside down.

For years, I'd sat uncomfortably on a stage, going over my talking points and counterarguments, all while being graded on my performance. These practice sessions, in front of the entire congregation, served as a measurement for our ability to persuade others that we were the only ones that had the truth when it came to God. All others offered false hope. For thirty cents, you could have your very own latest, greatest issue of the truth according to us.

I will say that being a Jehovah's Witness gave me all the practice I needed to talk in public and be on a stage. That was my only positive takeaway. According to my mother, when I left behind those beliefs and found a different point of view, I lost my chance at eternal life. It took me years to understand that, in that loss, I'd gained my soul. I turned my thoughts back to my gathering.

"Senna, good to see you. Are you going to play individually or on a team with Karmen? I'll warn you, she's a ringer if you go up against her."

Karmen brushed her knuckles along her chest and blew on them in smug agreement.

Senna pointed a thumb to her boss. "Think I'll stick with her then. I know plenty about beer. The Bible, on the other hand, I'm a little rusty. Last time I sat in a church was at my cousin's wedding over five years ago. I don't exactly fit in." Senna pointed first to her dreadlocks then to her attire.

"Remember who Jesus hung out with. It wasn't the rich and famous or even the most popular or pious. He hung out with the poor, the outcast, and even the unclean. All are welcome here." I indicated for her to have a seat at Karmen's table.

I made my way around the room, greeting everyone and catching up with a few people who hadn't been around in a while. The new Unitarian minister, a man in his twenties, had joined us for the last few weeks. Rev. Mathew's presence at our gatherings was well accepted. He was a favorite that the others fought to have on their team.

"Okay everyone, let's get started. I'm sure Tank has given you the lowdown on tonight's offerings of Brimstone Stout, Threshing Floor IPA, and Eden's Amber. For anyone partaking of tonight's liquid refreshments, Tank is your bartender and driver of Elijah's chariot. Drop your keys in the fishbowl over there, and we'll make sure you get home safe and sound. Round one's categories are the following." I wrote on a large whiteboard.

The Tree of Life

H^2O

It's a Miracle.

Each short round included five questions in varying in degrees of difficulty. "Anyone have any questions as to how we play?" I looked to Karmen to confirm Senna understood the game. She nodded back at me.

"Here we go."

***

Three hours later, Tank and I'd dropped off the last of our charges along with their vehicles. Black coffee was the refreshment of choice for me to keep the score and my pronunciations correct. Tom and Rev. Mathew had wiped the floor with the other teams, as expected. The group made them solemnly vow to not play as a team again and to give everyone a fighting chance. The pepperoni rolls and brownies had been devoured, but enough beer remained for me to enjoy a few drinks when we got back. Letting Tank drive the van was an easy decision. I rested in the passenger seat with my eyes closed. Lately, I'd been suffering from an exceptional bout of insomnia, even for me, wandering my loft and writing songs with alarming frequency. I rubbed my eyes.

Tank adjusted the heat. "You going to talk to me about it?"

I tucked my hands in my leather jacket and yawned. "Not much to talk about."

"Bullshit. I've been with you too long. Only two other people know you as well as I do. If they were here, both would call you on it too."

She was right. I was throwing out a line of crap to avoid talking about what was keeping me up at night. "It's nothing, Tank. I'm just not sleeping well."

"No shit, Sherlock. On a good day, you only sleep three or four hours. I'm betting a catnap at best, not sleeping even a solid hour."

"You ought to become a detective with those skills. Don't give up your day job though." I was being snarky, and she didn't deserve it. "I'm sorry."

"Don't be sorry, tell me what's wrong."

I turned my head to the window and watched the darkened scenery pass by. Snow-covered trees and indistinguishable objects lay under a thick blanket of white. Once we made it into Davis, there were streetlights to illuminate the sidewalks and building fronts. A few people rushed around, exiting doors to find their car or apartment. We passed the massage therapy and acupuncture business, reminding me that my elbow was acting up from the amount of playing I'd been doing.

"I need to call and make an appointment," I mumbled.

"I can't hear you when you turn away from me. A decade or so of standing off stage did a number on my hearing. Speak up."

"Just reminding myself to make an acupuncture appointment."

Tank waved a group of pedestrians across the street in front of her. "You've been playing a ton and likely have tendonitis again. What's got you rattled? No bullshit this time."

I let out a long sigh. Tank would keep dogging me until I either snapped at her or told her what she wanted to know. "The concert in Pittsburgh."

Tank nodded. "Thought so. Easy decision, go."

Another few minutes and we'd be home. Tank would drop me off and go back to her apartment in the back of the brewpub I owned and that she ran for me. "No matter what you think, it's not that easy."

"Oh, it's that easy. You get your ass on the interstate and drive north. Easy peasy, lemon squeezy, kind of easy."

I flipped her the bird.

"My, my, Reverend. Good thing you're a new age pastor, or you'd have to do some penance like sacrificing a pineapple or something. The only thing stopping you, Bek, is you. If Ellie asked me to come, I'd crawl on my hands and knees with a mouthful of saltine crackers, whistling The Star-Spangled Banner. Dammit, it's a Saturday concert. You schedule one of your lay speakers to do the sermon on Sunday, and you get your ass to Pittsburgh. Be there for your only sister. Get off the cross, Bek, someone needs the wood."

Tank pulled up to the giant Jesus and let me out without saying another word. When I shut the door, she left. I looked up to the shadow with outstretched arms and prayed.

Chapter Five

IT WAS ONE IN the morning, and I was still pacing around the apartment, strumming my guitar. Everything I tried to write was total crap. After reading my Bible, planning the next month's activities for the after-school program, and riding twenty miles on my stationary bike, no new music would come to me. The beer was long gone, and I'd switched to chai tea hours ago. Hell, the loft was even clean. Nothing would let my mind rest.

Even Grandpa's guitar wasn't bringing me the peace it normally offered, as I played through a variety of hymns and Regal Crimson songs. My phone pinged with an incoming message. Swiping the screen brought a smile to my face.

You up?

My sister wouldn't call just in case, by some miracle, I'd started to go to be before four in the morning. Needing to hear a friendly voice, I called instead of texting back.

"Hey, little songbird, how are you?"

"Tired, Bek. So tired."

"This is a down night for you, isn't it?" Her voice didn't sound right to me.

"Thankfully, yes. I don't think I could hit the chorus of *Sacred Scream* tonight if I tried. I think I'm getting a cold."

I was worried; Ellie never got sick. "You want to text instead, rest your voice?"

"No, please. I need to hear your voice. Tre showed up at my hotel and tried to get past Marlon."

The thought of that jackass getting anywhere near my sister after she'd dumped him boiled my blood. "Did you have his ass thrown in jail?"

"Didn't have to. He was high as a kite when he hit Marlon. The Police Service of Northern Ireland escorted him away. I imagine a jail cell that is less than accommodating for his six-foot-two frame. Not sure how his ego fits in the cell with him."

I had half a mind to give Tank her greatest wish and put her on a plane with orders to become Ellie's second skin. "Is Marlon okay?"

"He's got a monster bruise on his shoulder, but he's fine. Trust me, Tre got the worst end of it. He looks a lot like a raccoon."

"He never laid a hand on you, did he?" I felt my gut clench. We'd had an abusive childhood at the hands of our father and spent most of our life on the sour end of his temper. I stayed at home until turning twenty. The minute my sister turned eighteen, we walked out together and never returned. That was the last time a man ever hit me without me fighting back. I'd be damned if one would abuse my sister without me doing anything about it. She was hesitating too long. Ellie had never directly lied to me, but she'd tap dance more than Shirley Temple to avoid a topic. "EllieAnna Leigh McNally, I'm asking you a direct question. Did Tre ever lay a hand on you in anger?"

"Yes," Ellie answered in a voice as soft as a feather.

My mouth stayed silent while my head exploded. "I'm getting on a plane as soon as I can."

"Bek, I'm all right. It only happened once. That's why I broke up with him."

I walked over near my stationary bike and punched my speed bag so hard I was sure the knuckles on my right hand would be bruised and swollen by morning.

"What was that?"

I winced at the panic in Ellie's voice. "Nothing but me putting my fist through Tre's face."

"You punched your bag instead of the wall, I hope."

"Lath and plaster will break bones, and I can't afford to do that again." I closed my eyes and tried to bring my blood pressure back down. My jaw was so tight, I was sure I was going to crack a molar.

"I remember when you punched the wall near that jackass that kept trying to put his hand up my skirt. You scared him so bad, he pissed himself. You broke three bones in your hand and could barely play for a month."

"Which is why I put the bag in." Ellie's laugh lifted my spirits even as my hand throbbed. "I wasn't going to let anyone treat you like a piece of meat."

"Always my hero."

"Is Marlon pressing charges?"

"He is, and I have a restraining order on Tre now. He can't come within five hundred feet of me. I'm okay, Bek. I promise."

I closed my eyes and breathed in through my nose and out through my mouth. What I should do was get my ass to the nearest airport and jump on a plane to Ireland. *Maybe Tank would be the next best thing. She is a trained bodyguard.* "Ellie, do you want me to send Tank to be with you until Marlon is one hundred percent? You know she'd be more than happy to do it."

"No. I'm alright. All that will do is get her hopes up that there's a chance for there to be an us. She wants to be more than my bodyguard, and that's not what I want."

"Have you decided you aren't bisexual anymore?"

"Oh no, I'm still very much interested in both men and women. Gender doesn't matter to me. Tank's very sweet, just not aggressive enough in bed. I might be small, but I'm not fragile."

I shut my eyes and tried not to think about my sister having sex, period. "Say no more."

Ellie chuckled. "For someone who's had as much sex as you've had, you can't stand to even think about what I do in the bedroom. You'd die if you knew the conversations that Naomi and I have."

I loved the fact that she and my ex still talked. What they talked about, not so much. "I don't even want to imagine." Imagination had nothing on reliving the memories that played through my mind and ignited my body. I'd never lived until the day I touched Naomi, and I'd died with pleasure every time she kissed me. "So, tell me where you're headed next."

Chapter Six

THE DOOR TO THE brewing room always stuck in the winter. I pulled hard on the handle and winced in pain from the punch I'd thrown the night before. The knuckles were bruised, and the swelling prevented me from making a fist. The aroma of hops and wort hit me the minute I stepped onto the concrete floor among the giant brewing tanks. I'd managed to get two hours of sleep, right after the sun came up, making me feel listless. This morning was brew day, and it was time to make beer.

Tank moved past me without saying a word. She carried a large bag of malted barley over her shoulder that she threw in the area of the brew tank. Time to perk up and get moving.

"Morning. What do you want me to start on?"

She walked back over to retrieve another bag. "You're the fucking boss, do whatever you want to. I'm setting up for another round of Brimstone. That's been really popular."

From her tone, I could tell she was still pissed at me. "Okay, then the boss says you need to put that down and follow me into the office for a minute."

"I'm in the middle of something, boss. Can it wait until later?"

Her eyes glared at me, and the bite in her voice would only get sharper if I didn't put a stop to this. "No, it can't. This won't take more than a minute, but the longer we wait, the more stewing you're going to do."

I heard her mutter several curse words under her breath, as she grudgingly followed me to our shared office. The coffee smelled heavenly. I picked up my mug and blew into it to remove any dust, before filling my cup and hers. I plopped down in the chair off to the side of the desk. She had no choice but to sit in the office chair. She ran this place, and I wanted no questions about that, regardless of ownership.

Tank rhythmically tapped her fingers on the desk. "Bek, I don't have time for this. You know it's brew day."

Sipping my coffee, I wrapped my fingers around the cup and let the warmth soothe the ache in my knuckles. "I'm sorry for being short-tempered last night and apparently inconveniencing you now. Deciding to go to Pittsburgh has to be my decision, not made out of guilt from anyone, including you. There's very little about me you don't know. But, Tank, some things truly are more complicated than just showing up. Naomi will be there too, which brings up a lot of things I still can't deal with." I sat up a little straighter and put my coffee cup down. "I walked away from Regal Crimson for a reason. Coming here with you to build this place allowed me to put that part of my life behind me. Everything could be steered in a new direction. The one thing you have no right to ever question is my love and devotion to my sister. I stayed in a horrible situation for two years longer than I had to, so I could protect her. There's nothing I wouldn't do for Ellie, including taking beatings to keep her from being subjected to them. I've got the scars to prove it."

"Bek, you don't have to—"

"Apparently, I do." I stood and paced to the other side of the small office, running my hand through my black hair. "I know my sister better than anyone. This is the twentieth anniversary of Regal Crimson, and what she wants is more than moral support. I've built a quiet life here, where they know me as a minister. They don't know me as Bek McNally, only Pastor Rhebekka Deklan. There's a reason this place and The Purple Fiddle get my guitar but not my singing. It's the one thing that keeps this community from putting two and two together. I let my hair grow back into its natural black, so it's completely different from the crimson it was during those years."

Tank dropped her head. It was time to take a breath and bring it down a notch. "Tank, I like who I am now. Living in the town you grew up in has given me a sense of who I was always meant to be and to become comfortable in my skin. Showing up in Pittsburgh is more than being there for Ellie. I'm sorry for last night, truly, I am. Now if you'll accept my apology, we can go brew some beer. If not, then we'll go brew anyway, but expect to throw out the whole batch." I held out my left hand to bring her to her feet. I waited to see what she'd do. When she reached out her hand to grasp mine, relief washed over me.

She nodded. "Let's go brew some beer."

We were going to be fine, and we were going to create some killer beer together.

***

Friday night, I plugged in the sound system and adjusted my stool and mic. Tank made sure a pint of Brimstone Stout and a shot of Macallan sat beside me. The crowd was good for February, and much of that had to do with the fresh snow that kept falling.

Tank put another few logs on the fire, then stepped to the mic to make introductions. "Evening, everyone. Thanks for coming out. Tonight's cover charge and tips go to the Blackwater Food Bank. I'm happy to announce that we have a local favorite on the musical tap tonight. Please give a warm welcome to our house musician, Rhebekka Deklan."

A loud whistle pierced the room. Only one woman could do that. Karmen sat in the front row, with Senna beside her.

I waved. "Good evening, everyone. Welcome to The Confluence here at Redemption's Road. Thank you for coming out. The food we'll be able to purchase from your cover charge and generous donations will go toward feeding those who need a little extra to make ends meet. I'm going to start out tonight with a song that was perfected by one of my absolute favorite guitarists, Stevie Ray Vaughn. Let's hope you enjoy my interpretation of "Little Wing.""

For the next seven minutes, I lost myself in every note and finished with a final downstroke on the Strat. Milliseconds later, the room erupted with whistles and applause. I can fully admit I was holding my breath. Most people wanted to be entertained by someone singing and not purely an instrumental offering. Over the years, the crowds had been understanding, and the warm reception tonight settled my nerves. After raising my hand in appreciation for the applause, I led in with an iconic opening from another popular song. Thunderous applause started within moments of the opening riff, dragging the audience along with me on a musical rollercoaster. We rolled through twenty minutes worth of music before we took a break. Karmen made her way to the stage, as I downed my shot.

"You're on fire tonight." Karmen handed me a fresh pint.

"It feels good to play. The swelling in my hand went down a few days ago, or I'd have been in trouble."

Karmen crossed her arms. "That's why you're supposed to tape your hands before you work out on the speed bag."

I'd told Karmen the story of what happened after she cornered me about my fingers looking like sausages. "Thank you, Captain Obvious."

She rolled her eyes. "Good crowd tonight. There's a jackass in the back that keeps saying his five-year-old could play better. He's ruining the show for a good many of us."

This perked me up. "There's always one. Think I need to shut him up?"

"Pull out the big guns, sister. I'll request a classic."

I grinned at her knowing exactly what she wanted me to do. A few more people, including Senna, stopped by. My interest was piqued by how closely she stood next to Karmen. My friend might not have been able to see, but to me, it was plain that Senna had a crush on her boss.

"Hey Senna, how are you this evening?"

Senna's eyes were twinkling, and her smile genuine. "Stoked. Great set with some excellent song choices. You can really play."

I held my pick in the air and showed my calloused fingers. "Years of practice."

She held up her own hands. "I get that, play a little bass myself. Maybe some time we could jam."

I loved talking with other musicians, professional and amateur. "That can be arranged. You bring some of that incredible chicken salad by my place, and we'll bust the plaster."

Senna's face pinked at my compliment. She was personable, if not a bit on the shy side.

"I can do that. You getting ready to start again?"

I settled the Strat's strap on my shoulder. "I am. Karmen told me about the ass in the back, so I'm about to shut his trap for him."

She put her hands together as if in a prayer of thanks. "Thank God."

Once settled back in my seat, I looked out into the crowd. "Okay everyone, let's mix this up a little."

Karmen cupped her hands around her mouth. "Play a classic."

"Ah, a request for a classic. Let's see, how about this?" I rolled through the first few notes of a popular cover song and watched my audience begin to nod their heads. Minutes later, I played Eric Clapton's "Layla," then finished with Stevie Ray Vaughn's "Pride and Joy." When I'd struck the final notes, I held my hand in the air and flipped my guitar pick. Senna reached out and grabbed it with a huge smile. "How was that for classic?"

Karmen shook her head, as I took a drink.

"Good, but not quite what I meant. Got anything else, classic wise?"

I'd seen the great Eddie Van Halen play "Eruption" in public and practiced until my fingers bled, until I could play it flawlessly. The true guitar aficionados in the crowd made themselves known with claps and whistles growing louder and louder. My fingers flew over the frets, tapping out the notes and drawing out the unique sounds in my recreation. Sweat ran down my back as I jammed through the piece. At the finish, the roof nearly came off the place. I looked at Karmen. "Well, how about that?"

My friend sat back and crossed her arms. Her grin was subtle, but she wasn't done.

"You've played some classic *rock* songs, but I think you missed my point. Maybe I need to rephrase my request. Can you play me something classical?"

Tank set a glass of ice water beside me. I guzzled it.

"Demanding fan out there, Rhebekka. Think you can find something that will meet her expectations?" She refilled my glass from a pitcher.

I shrugged and turned back to Karmen. "Classical, huh? I tweaked a few tuning pegs and winked. "Let's see if this falls into your wish list." The third movement of Beethoven's Moonlight Sonata opened like a prayer. *Heavenly Father.* The familiar sounds resonated through my hand, up my arm, and into my chest with each note. This was one piece of music that I enjoyed hearing no matter what instrument was being played. My head fell back slightly. I sent my music heavenward, and the prayer continued.

To me, playing guitar was a conversation with God, a prayer of thanks for the gifts I'd been given. In the six minutes that my fingers tapped, strummed, and picked the strings, God and I spoke of all the things yet to be done. When I slid my fingers down the fretboard for the final refrain, it was like standing in front of my congregation. I uttered the words that closed my prayers, "in Jesus' name..."

I hadn't looked at my audience through my entire performance. The room was silent for several seconds before timber-rattling applause filled the room. I caught Karmen's huge smile and shrugged my shoulders. She walked forward and hugged me.

"Show off."

I lifted a shoulder. "You asked. I assume I shut the asshole up?"

"The jackass hasn't said a word since you channeled your inner Stevie Ray. Well done, Reverend."

"Amen."

Chapter Seven

WITH THE WEEKEND AND my Sunday services under my belt, I turned my attention to one of the lay speakers I'd been working with. Once a month, we'd work on speaker presentation for Bible study. This time, our focus was delivery. He was the only one in my congregation who used music the way I did, the same way Naomi had taught me.

Franklin Meyers was a twenty-four-year-old philosophy graduate, considering a career in ministry. Tall and gangly, he'd been born with a gift in his ability to play any instrument he picked up, some better than others. He carried a harmonica everywhere. After we'd finished our sermon preparation, we spent at least thirty minutes jamming to anything he wanted to play.

Franklin tapped his harmonica against his leg. "Let's see if you can keep up." He brought it to his mouth and played the first few notes of *House of the Rising Sun*.

Grinning, I picked up Grandpa's Gibson. "Oh, now you're just sucking up." I fell into the introduction, and soon our instruments were crying with a bluesy rock version we'd played together many times. Playing with Franklin was more enjoyable than most people I'd ever jammed with. The one exception was Naomi. When our two guitars lit up a room, little was left standing.

When we'd finished, I clapped. "I want you to come to play with me some night at Redemption's Road. Seriously."

"I don't know, Rhebekka. I'm comfortable playing with you here. I have no idea how to play in front of an audience like you do."

"That's why we'd do it together. Think of it as outreach."

He grinned his baby-face smile. "I'll think about it."

Groundwork for another idea needed to be laid. "I may need you to cover for me in July. I'm not sure yet if I'm going out of town. In the event I do, someone will need to lead Sunday services for me."

"That's no problem. I need the practice, and HRS is the best experience I could get if I'm serious about having my own church someday."

"More details will be forthcoming after a bit more of the logistics become clear. Do me a favor and keep this close to the vest. I don't want to disappoint anyone if I change my mind."

I laughed, as he mimicked stuffing the thought into his shirt pocket. My phone chimed. I pulled it from my pocket to silence the alarm before I rose. "I've got an appointment with Roman this afternoon, so I need to get moving. I'm playing the brewery next week. Plan on joining me for a set. I know your talent, and we'll play the songs by ear as we go. We can feed off each other."

He nodded his reluctant agreement. "Let me check and see if this is the weekend I'm supposed to pick up my sister at the airport. She'd enjoy listening to us play."

"Deal. See you later." Franklin offered to close up downstairs, while I went up to retrieve my keys. I wanted to run by the food bank before I headed to Morgantown, to see if they needed me to pick up anything while I was over there. Patting my back pocket, I felt for my wallet and closed the door behind me. My restored 1970 Toyota Land Cruiser sat in the garage. I'd put on tires with tread so aggressive I could climb trees with the royal-blue, white-topped beauty. I used the beat-up Tacoma if I needed to haul anything in town. For trips longer than twenty miles, the Land Cruiser's five-speed transmission and a V8 engine gave me all the power I could want. My brand-new Indian Scout Bobber and a vintage 1948 Indian Chief Classic sat idle, waiting for warmer weather and roads without ice and snow.

Blackwater Food Bank was run by a group of socially conscious community members who wanted nothing more than to make sure needy families never went hungry. Their fearless leader was a woman in her late seventies we all called, "the general." Victoria Start was a retired army nurse with a get-it-done attitude and the determination of an ant carrying a boulder. She was a force to be reckoned with and someone you wanted in charge when something needed to be done. I walked in and stood at attention; my arm snapped at a forty-five-degree angle. "Private Deklan reporting for orders, ma'am."

Vikki smacked me on the arm. "At ease, Reverend. You headed over for your shot of ink?"

"I've got a late afternoon appointment." I smiled at her reference to my tattoo work. "Is there anything you need me to pick up for the food baskets?"

Vikki clapped her hands together. "Excellent. Stop by the day-old store and pick up as many loaves of bread as you can bring back. We'll be delivering soon, and the bread will be a welcome addition. I called earlier, and they said they have plenty on hand."

"That's an easy request, anything else?" I made a mental note to move a few things around in the Toyota.

"That'll do for now. I might need you to help me go get potatoes next week. Danny Trader is giving them to me at a discount, so I want to get as much as possible."

"Let me know. All right, if that's all, peace be with you."

"And also with you, Reverend. Safe passage."

***

Two hours later, I was face down on a table with my shirt off. A tattoo gun buzzed along my skin. Roman was working on the area where the angel and demon wings burst forth from my spine. We had something special planned for between the two wings that would come later. We'd worked on this design for the last five years, and it was finally coming together. Roman Talon's artistry could have hung in any modern museum, if his medium wasn't someone else's skin. Looking at the feathers of the angel wing on my right arm, I could imagine their downy softness.

In contrast, I could feel the rough, scaly texture of the demon wing that adorned my left arm. Tonight, we'd do a three-hour session that would result in more fresh ink on my back, as well as the final touches on the inside of my right forearm. This would complete the body of Grandpa's Gibson, with an amp cord plugged into my skin at my elbow.

I flinched as the gun found a particularly sensitive spot.

"Tickle or hurt?" Roman held the tattoo gun away from my back.

"A little of both, I think." I willed myself to be still and not mess up Roman's work.

"Ah, pain and pleasure. If only you were a man, I'd marry you."

"A pipe dream, my friend, since I lack certain equipment. Five bucks says your husband might object as well. Sorry, I'll try to lay still. That place right near my spine is sensitive."

"Understandable. Let's take a break on this area and work on your arm." He put his gun on the stand and waited for me to sit up. He completely wiped my back down before sitting in front of me.

It had taken a while for me to be comfortable bare-chested around him. Nothing phased me anymore. Not that I had much in the way of breasts. My sister and I were shaped from two different molds. Roman was the ultimate professional. He'd seen nearly every inch of me, as we'd cleansed my soul of demons by impregnating them into my skin.

He cleaned my forearm with antiseptic solution before he started again.

Roman was a tight-muscled man in leather pants and a black tank top. He had more tattoos than anyone I'd ever met and was the ultimate master when it came to technically difficult work. Sporting elaborate full sleeves, he was as much of a machine as the steampunk design on his right arm. Gears, levers, and rods worked under windows of riveted, framed glass and broken skin. Near the clavicle of his left arm, a large scar played directly into the tattoo's broken chainmail that ran under damaged shoulder armor. Renditions of metal plates layered one over the other, all down his arm, until they covered his hand. I could see the scars that ran its length. In various places, the scar was surrounded by more damaged armor and shattered links of chainmail.

The tattoo was created by Harlan Talon, Roman's father and mentor. In his twenties, Roman suffered a motorcycle accident that nearly cost him that arm. When he'd healed and regained the use of it, Harlan rewarded him with the three-dimensional tattoo to celebrate his survival and recovery.

Roman went back to work. "So, what's new in your world?"

I sat fascinated, as the needled gun embedded ink under my skin. My trust in Roman allowed more than going au naturel in his presence. The first time I walked into his shop, he recognized me for exactly who I was. He saw not just the rendition of my current life as Rhebekka Deklan, but also Bek McNally from Regal Crimson. He respected that Bek was my past and Rhebekka was my present and future. My chimera was symbolized in the angel and demon wings we were pulling from beneath my skin. Every once in a while, we revisited my past together, when I needed a friendly ear. I needed that now.

"Regal Crimson's twenty-year reunion concert is coming up in a few months."

His hand stilled for just a moment. "I've told you I was there the first time you played in Pittsburgh."

His words made my heart ache. He wasn't talking about our first big arena concert. He was talking about a small club my sister and I played at, as we were trying to make our way.

We ran away from Virginia the night my sister graduated. We'd spent weeks secretly packing my beat-up Subaru station wagon. We drove all night and slept at a rest area outside of Morgantown, on the West Virginia state line. The entire time we drove, we were sure the devil that was our father was right behind us. Our plan was to get lost in the city and make music.

I smiled at Roman's memory. "That seems like a hundred years ago. A little dive club so dark, I could barely see where my foot pedal was. Ellie kept her hand on her mic stand so she wouldn't lose sight of it."

"You two were so good back then, raw but so good. I had no doubt you'd make it big."

"You were trying to get through art school. When I saw that sleeve on your arm, I knew I'd want you to do my work someday. You learned from the best."

Roman stopped and pointed to an old, black-and-white photo of his dad working on the ink that covered Roman's damaged arm. "Watching him cover up my stupidity, I knew I had big shoes to fill by trying to be even a tenth of the artist he was."

I covered his hand with mine. "I know you still miss him."

Roman nodded and got back to work. "Every day. He loved me even when he found out I was gay. He never agreed with my leather lifestyle, though I never doubted he loved me or how he felt about Andre."

I arched my eyebrows up and down. "Who wouldn't love your husband? The way that man can cook is an art form in itself."

Andre owned a tapas restaurant in Morgantown. Those fifteen tables were the most sought-after food entertainment around. He'd set it up to allow the diners to watch him cook.

Roman licked his lips and grinned lasciviously. "He is beautiful to watch. I collared him as quickly as I could."

"Like he was interested in anyone else." I'd witnessed their courtship, as I passed through many different music venues, the leather clubs included. Once Regal Crimson signed a record contract, I lost touch with Roman. I looked him up during a tour stop in Pittsburgh one year, and we began our own journey with skin and ink.

He peered up from my arm through long lashes. "You're avoiding any elaboration about the anniversary concert."

I sighed and tried to relax. "Every year, Ellie asks me to come back to the band."

"And you don't because?"

"It's not who I am anymore."

He shook his head and barked a laugh. "Oh, you're still the best damn live guitarist I've ever heard. A born rocker exists under your nonexistent clerical collar." He pointed to the artwork he was detailing. "This guitar has always been an extension of your body, Rhebekka."

I nodded, knowing his words were true. I'd had a guitar in my hand from a young age. It felt strange when I went more than a few hours without playing. I'd learned at Grandpa's knee and with a Glen Campbell beginner's book. I watched *Hee Haw* with MaMaw and tried my best to learn every song I heard. "I won't argue."

"I get why you don't want to go back to Regal Crimson. The bigger question is, why don't you want to be at the anniversary gig? I think you need to find the answers to what you're truly avoiding."

As much as I wanted to argue, he had a point. Thinking about it wasn't on my to-do list. I wanted the natural high from the endorphins running through my body. I'd think about his point on another day.

Chapter Eight

IT WAS FRIDAY MORNING, or at least I thought it was, when my phone rang at an ungodly hour. I hadn't been asleep more than a half hour. No one called at this time of the morning with good news. I couldn't see the display through my bleary eyes.

"Rhebekka Dek—" I coughed, cleared my throat, and started again. "This is Rhebekka Deklan."

"Bekka?"

Only my mother still called me Bekka. My brain whirled. I sat straight up and tried to flip on the lamp near the bed. The sheets were tangled around me, and I fell out of bed, cracking my foot on the chair beside me. "Ow. Hang on." I rubbed my foot and hopped to the wall switch. "Mom? What's going on?"

"It's your father, he's had a stroke."

The hand I scrubbed over my face stripped some of the sleepiness away. "A stroke? How bad?" I could barely make short sentences.

The stilted cry on the other end of the line sounded strangled. "Bad. Get here within the next twenty-four hours, if you want to see him. After that, you might not get the opportunity. He's at the University of Virginia Medical Center, in the critical care unit."

"Is anyone there with you now?" I was wide awake and packing a duffle bag to head to Virginia. Not for him, but for her.

"Brother and Sister Raymond are with me. The elders are arranging friends to come."

"I'll be there as soon as I can. It's pouring down snow here. It will take a while for me to get to you." Mom didn't know exactly where I lived. I wanted it that way for a reason. "Have you called Ellie?"

Another sob, accompanied by a muffled cry, came through the line. "I tried. Her number is apparently different from the last one I had."

"I'll take care of it and be there soon." *What the hell do I do now?*

The phone clicked off without anything else being said. There would be no niceties, not with other members of her faith beside her. I'd been disfellowshipped years ago and shunned for being unrepentant. They considered me a false prophet, an apostate, one of the most loathed terms used for a former Jehovah's Witness. It meant

I'd been indoctrinated from birth with their version of the truth, only to turn my back and abandon the teachings when I was old enough to make decisions for myself. A defector who, by their own terminology, could tempt others into becoming a deviant. I was treated like an infectious disease and ostracized from the community that once claimed to love me.

Ellie was in the same boat, other than that she hadn't formally adopted another religion. My sister had chosen to skirt the edges, only speaking to me or Naomi about things within the realm of religion.

Ellie, I've got to call Ellie. While still packing, I hit the speed dial for Marlon's international phone. It was four thirty in the morning, which meant it was nine thirty her time. She'd still be in bed, and I didn't want her to hear this news when she was by herself. After talking with Marlon, I waited until he handed her his phone.

"Bek, what the fuck? What's wrong?" Ellie's voice trembled.

"Dad's had a stroke. From what little I got, it doesn't look like he's going to survive. It's up to you, but Mom said if we want to see him, we need to get there in the next twenty-four hours. I'm headed out as soon as I hang up with you."

"Why are you going?"

Ellie's question stopped me in my tracks. I hadn't seen my father in almost twenty years. I'd not laid eyes on him since the day Ellie graduated. *Why am I going?*

I sighed deeply. "I don't know, Ellie. Trust me, it's not for him. Maybe for Mom, to show I'm not the monster I've been made out to be."

"She's not going to talk to you, she's not allowed. The elders won't let you anywhere near her."

"That may be. I guess I'll find out after I get there. For now, she called and asked me to come. Maybe I see that as her way of reaching out. Maybe it's nothing more than me needing to see the past finally put to rest." I needed to shower quickly and grab a thermos of coffee. There was no way to do this on less than a gallon of strong, brewed java. "It's okay if you don't come back, Ellie. I called so you would hear it from me."

"Marlon is making the arrangements. We finished up over here last night. I'll call you when we land, most likely at Richmond. If I can get a commuter flight closer, I will. If not, we'll have to drive it."

I could hear Ellie's tears over the phone, in her quiet sniffles. I wanted to hold her, to tell her that the monster who was our father couldn't hurt us, ever again. I knew what to do, so I let the first words leave my mouth in song. "Amazing grace…"

***

Three hours later, and only with God's protective hand, I pulled into the hospital parking lot. The weather had been atrocious on the drive. Twice, I'd stopped because of whiteout conditions that made it too dangerous to continue. Along the way, God and I had a long conversation. To me, prayer was exactly that, a conversation with God as someone who knew me before all others. I'd always loved a particular verse from Galatians and used it frequently when I questioned my path.

He who had set me apart before I was born, and who called me by his grace. Along the trip, I'd asked God for strength and the conviction to offer what comfort I'd be allowed to give. I prayed for my father's peaceful transition. I didn't know where the man who had a hand in my birth believed he would end up after he died. His tin-plated faith covered a body and soul that had never truly believed the way my mother did.

Hospital Volunteer, embroidered on the pocket of her pink smock, identified the petite woman in the reception area.

"Excuse me, can you tell me what floor the Cardiac Care Unit is on?"

Her face showed compassion, as she pulled a black-and-white photocopied map from a stack. She circled the reception desk and drew an arrow. "We're right here. Follow this hallway to the bank of elevators, then up to the third floor."

"Thank you." I took the map and followed her directions. Standing in the elevator, my finger hovered over the button that would deliver me face to face with my past. As I stood there, another individual entered the space.

"Miss, are you all right?"

I looked up to see a man wearing a white lab coat. "Oh, sorry. Yes, thank you, I'm fine. What floor did you need?"

He squinted with a clinical eye. "Five, please. You look a little pale. Are you sure you're okay?"

"My father is in the Cardiac Care Unit, and I've been driving in a snowstorm for almost three hours. Just trying to settle my nerves."

"I'm sorry to hear that. Do you know where you're going?" The man pointed to the map I held.

"I do, thank you."

We rode the elevator until it stopped on my floor. "Peace be with you, sir." I'd started to step out, when he touched my arm.

"And also with you."

I smiled at him, bolstered by the words I'd needed to hear. I stepped into a hallway with an institutionalized tile floor. I looked at the map again, before turning right and walking toward a set of double doors at the end. To the left, there was a waiting room. My mother and two people I hadn't seen since I was much younger sat toward the back.

Irene McNally's hands worried what was left of a tissue she held. My mother looked much older than I remembered. Her brown hair had lost much of its sheen, though it was still cut in the same style she'd worn since I was a child. When our eyes met, a tear ran down her cheek and off her jawline.

"I'm here, Mom." I didn't know what else to say other than the obvious. As a minister, I was supposed to be able to talk to people about any subject. In that moment, I found that I could say little more than the three words I'd uttered. Her shoulders slumped as she stood, as if she'd been carrying the weight of the world on them. My mom didn't hug me or make any move to even touch me, as she smoothed back her hair. She stepped toward the door of the CCU. She motioned for me to join her.

"We shouldn't wait." Twenty years had passed between us, and those were the first words she said to my face.

"I'll follow you."

Sister Allen stood. "Irene, do you want me to come with you?"

I turned and stared hard at her, unable to pull any compassion for the woman I'd once considered a friend. "I think we can handle it. I'm not here to subvert her for heaven's sake."

My mother's hand stopped near the intercom, as she whispered to me. "Please, Bekka?"

I took a deep breath and nodded. Once she'd requested entrance, we stepped into an area where each patient lay inside a glass cubical. A cacophony of repetitive beeps accompanied the sound of ventilators pushing air into bodies incapable of breathing on their own.

Beneath bleached white sheets and a pale-pink thermal blanket, tubes and wires snaked out like tethers holding him to this life. His cheeks were sunken, and deep hollows around his eyes made him look much older than he was. His hands bore dark lines, where grease and oil stained his skin as permanently as the tattoos on mine.

I shook my head. "His hair has really gotten thin. He looks more and more like his dad." I moved farther into the room, behind my mother. Some irrational fear that he'd come out of his unconscious state kept me from approaching the bed. I wasn't expecting my mother to answer me, sure that she would still abide by the rules of her faith.

The hand that held a wadded-up tissue was at her lips, as she kept her eyes tightly closed. "He'd hate to hear you say that."

The fact she'd said anything to me made me jump slightly. My reaction to seeing my father was merely me thinking out loud, not expecting her to acknowledge my assessment.

"You're probably right."

I leaned against the metal railing that ran along the glass wall, unable to go any closer to him. As a child, I both loved and feared the man who'd given me my olive skin and hazel eyes. I strived every day for an elusive word of praise that rarely left his lips. Over the years, before our departure, many people told me how proud my father was of me. I often wondered how it could be so easily said to someone else, but not to the *source* of said pride. I'd heard the man say he was proud of me twice. I held on to one of those memories like a precious heirloom. The last time I held a sliver of a belief that I mattered to the man in the hospital bed happened in my senior year.

I came down the stairs dressed for school. Ellie was tagging behind me. In the kitchen, Mom was getting ready to go to work. "Can you drop us at school today?"

Mom turned from the coffee she was pouring into my father's thermos to look at me. "Is that what you're wearing to school?"

The exchange struck me as strange. She hadn't answered me about the ride but was questioning my clothes. I looked down at my jeans, striped shirt, and paisley suspenders. Nothing about it was immodest or inappropriate. "I'd planned to. Is there something wrong?"

I could see the gears grinding in her head but was unable to read her mind. She turned back to her task.

"No, I'd think you'd dress a little nicer. Remember, you're always representing Jehovah, no matter where you're going."

I plucked at my shirt, confused. She'd been with me when I bought the shirt and the suspenders. The jeans were nothing special. The entire conversation baffled me. "So, can you drop us at school? If not, we need to catch the bus."

"Not today."

Ellie held her hands up in confusion and mouthed that she had no clue.

A few hours later, the entire student body sat in the auditorium. This was induction day for the newest members of the National Honor Society. I sat with a pad and pencil in hand, to take down the names of the students for my article. The school newspaper was one of the few activities I was allowed to participate in. My religion kept me from any sports or school clubs that met in the evenings. Most of my nights were taken up with going to the Kingdom Hall for various Bible studies.

Our principal, Mr. Smith, stepped to the podium. "Good morning, everyone. As you know, today is a special day." He relayed the method used for selection. Some were nominated by fellow students, and others by teachers. As I scribbled notes, current members made their way off the stage to retrieve the individuals who would be awarded the golden, silk sash to be worn at graduation with their cap and gown. Selection was supposed to be secret until revealed at the ceremony, though it was easy to tell who already knew. They'd positioned themselves on the outside of the aisles and were dressed for something other than hours of classwork. Two expected names had made it to my tablet, when I heard my own name. I looked at the end of the aisle. A friend of mine, grinning from ear to ear, spoke my name and curled a finger at me.

"Me?" I managed to squeak out.

Sherry chuckled and waved me to her side. When I made it to the stage, I stared in disbelief at my parents standing in the back of the room and clapping wildly. It finally struck me why my mom had questioned what I was wearing that day, though she had resisted the urge to make me change. For the first time in my life, I let the feeling of my father's pride wash over me. The honor bestowed on me paled in comparison to even a glimmer of his approval.

I startled from the memory, as my mom walked by me sobbing as she made her way to the other side of my dad's bed. She quietly slipped her hand in his. As I'd expected, there was no reaction to her touch. Any more than perfunctory affection was rare between my parents. They went through the motions and held hands as they walked together in public. Natural affection, out of love and devotion to each other, was never part of the equation.

I shook myself. That line of thinking was not helpful. The one thing I knew was that my father wasn't the reason I was there. In truth, neither was my mother. The reality was I came to say goodbye to years of abuse, anger, and rejection. After this moment of crisis, I had one goal. I was going to take back the piece of myself I'd left behind on my parent's porch the night Ellie and I drove away under the cover of darkness.

CJ Murphy

Chapter Nine

HOSPITALS HAVE NEVER BEEN my favorite place. I provide pastoral care for members of my congregation and community without trepidation. Spending time in a hospital for my own family was different, especially this member. It wasn't my place to offer words of hope for where my father was heading when he passed. My mother held to her own beliefs and had no need for that kind of comfort from me.

His doctor, a man who looked in his late fifties or sixties, came in to talk to us. He asked that we step into a small conference room with a table and a few well-used and abused chairs. He held his stethoscope in his clasped hands on the table. I wondered if the unconscious barrier offered him a shield against the bad news he was going to deliver. I'd spent enough time in hospitals to see the signs.

"Dr. Varetti, this is my daughter, Bekka McNally."

I nearly startled when she laid her hand on mine but caught the emotion in time to stifle it. The doctor dipped his head in greeting.

"I'm sorry we have to meet under these circumstances. I'm your father's neurologist. As you know, Mrs. McNally, your husband suffered a severe stroke caused by an embolism in his brain stem. This is the area that controls a great deal of function required to support life." He swiped at a computer tablet, waking the screen. An enlarged, 3D image of my father's MRI appeared. "The stroke has affected his ability to breathe, control his heart rate, and even his blood pressure. Without the life support he's currently on, he won't survive."

"Is there any cognitive function at all?" My voice came out in a rasp, as if it came up through gargled glass. I knew the answer to my question; my point was for my mother to hear it.

"His EEG shows no brain function." Dr. Varetti squeezed his stethoscope.

My mother's grip tightened on my hand, as the sobs overtook her. I pulled her into my arms. Since the time my mother was sixteen years old, the man lying in a hospital bed had controlled her life as much as the machines he was attached to now controlled his. He'd gotten her pregnant and, in the tradition of the day, married her. I knew my mother loved him, though I struggled to find even the smallest bit of sympathy for him.

Dr. Varetti shifted in his seat. I watched his trepidation as he started to speak.

"I'm sorry to say that Mr. McNally won't recover from this. I understand this is a difficult time. In no way am I saying we have to make a decision right now, but you need to consider your options. Nothing in our records indicates whether Wesley is an organ donor. Would you consider—"

My mother sat up and pulled herself from my arms. I braced for what I knew would be her answer. Though organ donation was a matter of personal conscience for Jehovah's Witnesses, most did not look upon it favorably. My mother was no different.

"Thank you, Doctor, for your explanation. I'm waiting for my other daughter to arrive. We'll make a decision about what to do next when we have time to be together and search our hearts. I can tell you now, as his medical power of attorney, I'm opposed to donation."

He nodded. "I understand. I'll leave you now. If you have any questions, don't hesitate to have one of the nurses call me."

I nodded at him "Thank you, Doctor. Mom, I'm going to check on Ellie's progress. I'm sure she's in the air by now, and I need to make some calls back home. I left without any notice."

We stood and made our way back to the waiting room where the delegation from Mom's congregation had grown from two to six. I caught the eye of one of the men. Twenty years ago, Sam Daily had been a ministerial servant in the hierarchy of the congregation. He was also my former fiancé. By the way he was clutching his Bible and holding out his hand for my mother, I was sure he'd risen to the level of elder. His disdain for me was obvious.

I noticed the gold band on his hand. I'd worn his diamond ring my entire senior year. Though I had grounds, breaking the engagement hadn't been easy, and I'd been pulled before the elders to explain myself. Only by laying out my justification on a scriptural basis, did I avoid disciplinary action. Sam had either changed a great deal about himself or had sharpened his ability to hide his true personality. Either way, I shuddered to think that he now controlled the spiritual wellbeing of others.

Judgmental much? I chastised myself and walked to the end of the hall, where I could make calls in private. I tried to reach Ellie and got her voicemail. After giving her the basics, I called Tank. Hearing her voice was a relief. "Hey."

"Where are you? I stopped by the loft with a plan for next month's entertainment spots. The Land Cruiser's gone, so I assume you had a pastoral care emergency. This weather is brutal."

"My mom called me a little after four this morning." I knew those words would land like a grenade going off.

"Holy shit. Has Armageddon been scheduled?"

I loved Tank. She knew when to try and bring me up, and she succeeded in making me laugh. "Well, that very well may be true, because I'm positive hell's frozen over. It's my father. He's had a massive stroke."

There was silence on the line for a few seconds.

"Damn, Bek, I wish I could say I'm sorry and mean it."

"Trust me, I understand. I'm here for me, no one else. Ellie's on her way back from Ireland. That's the only reason he's still among the living, if you can call it that."

"And your mother?"

"Currently in prayer with about six Bible-holding congregants."

"Has she actually spoken to you?"

"A few words. She's let me hold her when no one was around. I really don't know what to say to her."

"I'd let her make the moves. When Ellie gets there, I'm sure there will be less tension. At least you can share it. She wasn't disfellowshipped, right?"

"No, she left before she became a baptized Jehovah's Witness, so the terminology doesn't really apply. She's still shunned, because she left." I heard Tank sigh over the line.

"What can I do? Need me to come down there for moral support?"

"No, I need you to keep things running there. Call Franklin and ask him to fill in for me on Sunday. We worked on a sermon the other day. Tell him to use that. Let the foodbank know I won't be there today. Other than that, there isn't anything you can do."

"Are you sure? I hate for you to be down there by yourself."

"Ellie will be here at some point. I've got Aunt Dinah and few cousins who aren't Witnesses, if I need something. I'll stay wherever Marlon puts Ellie up."

"Think Ellie could use some more company?"

I knew where Tank was going. It wasn't my place to tell her the chances she had with Ellie resembled the Pittsburgh Pirates' chances of winning the World Series, slim to none.

"You'd have to ask her that question, but honestly Tank, I wouldn't get my hopes up."

There was a long pause, then I heard Tank let out a slow breath.

"Okay. I'll tell Franklin he's on deck and let Victoria know you'll be a no show. I'll give Karmen a call too. You know her. She'll have your favorite comfort food waiting on your return."

"Thanks, my friend. I have no clue when I'll be home. I'll keep you as updated as I can."

I hung up and walked back down the hall. The group was huddled together, hand in hand. I listened, as they prayed for my parents to feel the love of the heavenly Father around them. Words I'd heard a thousand times and said myself to those I was comforting during moments like this. As I heard the murmured amen, my phone rang. I saw Ellie's name on the display and stepped away. "Hey, you."

"So, she actually spoke to you?"

I sighed. "Briefly, as long as no one else was around. She's surrounded by several elders and their wives, including Sam."

"You've got to be shitting me?"

"I wish I was. Seeing Dad, that was shiver worthy. He's hooked up to every machine known to modern medicine. The stroke was catastrophic. In practical terms, he's gone. It's only his body that doesn't know it yet."

"Why are they keeping him alive?"

"I think Mom's waiting for you to get here."

"Like I give a fuck about him."

I closed my eyes. "Easy little sparrow, I'm right there with you on that. If I know Mom, it's all about respect and appearances. For me, it's about taking back something I left behind. You'll have to search your own heart as to why you're making the trip."

"I came close to canceling my flight. I couldn't find a good reason to come other than I need for us to be together."

I smiled at my sister's words. I was well aware she was coming for me, as I would have done for her. We were still healing from my perceived abandonment when I left the band. There was only one person who knew how close I'd come to permanently abandoning life itself. "I'm with you on that. How long before you get here?" I looked at my watch. It had been nearly five hours since I'd first called her.

"I'll get into Dulles around five thirty. There weren't many flights available, so we took what we could get into an airport on the east coast. I've got a charter flight to get us to Richmond. Marlon booked us the executive suite at Omni. I've got your name on the list, so you can go over there anytime you want."

"Thanks, I'm going to try and hang in here for a few more hours."

"Bek, I don't want you to sit there at that hospital by yourself all day. I know what's going to happen. They'll all fawn and pray all over Mom, while giving you the great cold shoulder to make you pay for your sins. That's not fucking happening on my watch. I'll be damned if I'm going to let you take any more beatings, literal or figurative. I mean it."

I leaned against the wall. "Ellie, I promise, I'm fine. Their shaming tactics only work for someone who wants what they have to offer. That straight and narrow path they guide their followers along is paved with broken glass that bleeds away free will, while they dangle eternal life in front of you like a carrot on a stick. They aren't the gatekeepers for my salvation. Add in that I'm an unrepentant lesbian and irrevocably doomed to the second death. Amazing what freedom feels like when you recognize you've already been to hell and found redemption's road out."

Ellie sniffled into the phone. "You know what I consider the greatest moment of my life?"

A tear escaped the corner of my eye and ran over my cheek. "I have an idea."

"The minute we passed that Charlottesville, Virginia city limit sign. It was as if someone pulled a cold, soaking wet, wool blanket off me. Even though it was pitch dark, I felt the warmth of the sun for the first time."

As she spoke, one of the brightest rays of sunlight I'd ever experienced broke through the clouds. Warmth poured in the large, plate glass window and heated my skin. At that moment, I felt love that didn't know the bounds of earth's orbit. In a few simple words, my sister had described my own experience.

"Me too, Ellie. Me too."

Chapter Ten

THE KEYCARD SLID INTO the door lock. I was frustrated when I got a red light and tried again with the same result. Exhausted from the day, I shut my eyes and leaned the top of my head against the door. With the square of plastic between my thumb and forefinger, I rotated the card until the magnetic strip was on the left side instead of the right. The green light allowed me to push the heavy door open with my hip. I carried my duffle bag and an acoustic guitar inside. The suite was pleasantly furnished, though it wasn't as big as some we'd shared over the years. I laughed when I saw the king-size bed. Those first few weeks after we'd run from our parents, we stayed in the cheapest motels and slept in a double bed. I held Ellie when she cried and promised her it would be all right. The outside world, beyond the sheltered one we'd grown up in, was terrifying.

My phone rang, and I answered it without looking at the display.

"Rhebekka Deklan."

"How are you?" That voice had wrapped around me in my darkest hours and now sheltered me in its comfort from hundreds of miles away. I sighed into the warmth she poured over me, like standing in front of a blazing fire after being lost in a blizzard.

"Naomi."

"I hope it's okay I called. You sound exhausted, Rhebekka."

I let her words blanket me. "It's more than okay. You were always good at needling the truth out of me, so I won't even try to lie. I'm shaken and worn out. The reasons for both are a bit more complicated than the lack of sleep. Twenty years is a long time."

"I'm sure it was hard to be there. Did your mom speak to you at all?"

I told Naomi about the early morning call. I suspected Ellie had filled her in on the rest. Personally, I was grateful to hear her voice and for the comfort she offered. We spoke for twenty minutes about ways to handle my time around the people who had left such a negative impact on me.

"I'm waiting for Ellie to get here. Mom went home, and we'll meet back up at the hospital tomorrow morning. Hopefully, I'll have Ellie chilled out by then." Between the two of us, Ellie was slightly more volatile when it came to our father. She'd never been what most would consider rebellious. It was that she was more vocal about her feelings than I was. This led to violent exchanges that put me between my sister and our father's belt, more than a few times.

"He can't hurt either one of you now, and unless you let them, neither can the people surrounding your mother."

"I know. The hard part will be the visitation services. Ellie and I will be allowed to stand with Mom, but while everyone is paying their condolences, none of the Witnesses will speak with me. Ellie is their wild card. They could try bringing her back into the fold or treating her as disfellowshipped. People from our neighborhood and family from outside the Kingdom Hall will be at the funeral home."

"No matter how many times we talk about this, Rhebekka, I still don't understand. The God I know is one of love. He doesn't want his children to suffer. Your former religion's attempts at bringing people into compliance speaks of anything but love to me."

"It's all mind control. They isolate your whole life in every way they can. You're dependent on them for your social structure, your relationship with God, and your worth within the isolated community they build for you. When you do something they don't like, you're relegated to the back of the hall to exist with no contact beyond what is necessary within the family. Until you show a level of repentance they find acceptable, you sit starving and looking in the window, while others feast at a full table. It's soul-wrenching. I watched husbands unable to speak to their wives and children expected to shut out their fathers. The society talks about wanting strong families, when what they truly want are mindless followers who question nothing."

I ran my hand through my hair, exhausted. The day had been incredibly draining. I heard a click from the door and looked up to see my beautifully bedraggled sister push into the room.

"Our little songbird just flew in. Ellie looks like I feel. Naomi?"
"What, love?"
"Thanks. You always know what I need."
"It comes from loving you. Now, hug Ellie and call if you need me."
"I always need you. Never doubt that."
"Love bears all things, believes all things, hopes all things, endures all things."

Every time she brought up that scripture, another piece of the guilt I felt cracked and fell away. "Love never ends. Call you soon."

I put my phone down and held out my arms, as Ellie melted into them. "It's good to see you, baby sister." I succeeded in making her laugh.

"How old do I have to be until I'm not a baby? I'm well into my thirties, Bek."

"Sorry, El, I've only got one baby sister, and you're it. How are you?"

"Exhausted."

I took her wheeled bag from her and pulled it farther into the room. "I see you at least upgraded us to a king size." I nodded toward the bed.

Ellie's smile let me know she understood my reference to the past. She pulled off her coat and hung it up.

"I figured we left this hell hole to sleep in a car, so we deserved to come back and enjoy a little luxury."

"It made me smile, and to be honest, I haven't done much of that today."

As she emptied her suitcase, I took out Grandpa's Gibson and started to strum go-to songs. Ellie jumped on the bed beside me.

"And that is why you're my favorite sister."

I rolled my eyes at her and snickered. "As I pointed out earlier, I'm your only sister, you nut case. How was your flight?"

"Long. The storm was still raging when we got to Dulles. We had to circle forever, while they attempted to clear the runways. I was afraid we were going to get diverted. It's a good thing we got in when we did. I wouldn't be surprised if later flights were canceled. Have you eaten?"

"I grabbed something on my way here. I'd had all the hospital coffee I could stand."

"Want to go grab a drink in the bar?"

"I think that's an excellent idea. Is Marlon here too?"

"He's like a second skin after what happened with Tre." She ran a hand through her long hair. "If Marlon had his way, he'd have someone in the room with me. The only reason he isn't freaking out right now is he knows you're here."

"I can't say I blame him. I might even give him a big hug, after I put a boot up Tre's ass. Promise me you won't ever let anyone do that to you again, Ellie. Honestly, I don't want to go to jail, but if anyone ever touches you like that, I'll be asking God for a great deal of forgiveness. Trust me, I already have enough to atone for."

She crossed her heart. "I promise, you've taken your last beating for me."

"Let's go get a drink."

We spent the next few hours catching up and slowly sipping our beers. I'd missed her more than I could have imagined. Ellie knew me well, all the forms and renditions of myself. After our second beer, we both admitted we were exhausted and made our way back to the room. I took a shower, then slipped into a pair of loose boxers and a Redemption's Road T-shirt. Once Ellie had done the same, I moved over into the lounge area to say a few quiet prayers before bed. Ellie let Marlon know we were tucked back in the room. We crawled into bed, and I wrapped my little sister in an embrace. I held her tightly, the same way I had every time she was stressed. Ellie had frequent nightmares her whole life. They intensified once we'd broken away.

"Remember when we were little? You used to sneak into my room dragging Peppy the rabbit?"

"I hated sleeping by myself. There were monsters in my room, and you were the only one who made me feel safe, Bek."

"It was my favorite job ever. Go to sleep, El. Tomorrow's going to be rough, trust me."

"At least we'll be together."

I squeezed her tighter and kissed the top of her head. "Yes, at least we'll be together."

Chapter Eleven

AFTER BREAKFAST IN THE hotel restaurant, we left my vehicle in the lot. The service Ellie had hired allowed us to steel ourselves against what was to come instead of stressing about where we should park. Marlon would stay close to us. It was always possible Ellie could be recognized as the lead singer of Regal Crimson. I'd already witnessed several people discretely taking cellphone pictures of us at breakfast. My departure from the woman I'd been when I was with the band shielded me in many ways. It wouldn't take long for people to put two and two together.

"You ready?" I wrapped an arm around her shoulder, as we made our way to the hospital elevator. I could see tears on the brink of spilling over her lashes. "It's going to be okay. He can't hurt either of us, and neither can any of the others, if we don't let them."

She didn't speak, nodding her agreement, as we stepped inside the metal cage that would carry us into the lions' den. I knew the reception we were likely to receive and could only hope there wasn't a huge delegation waiting with Mom. It was Saturday. Many of them would be out in the service, knocking on doors and questioning the resident if they wanted to talk about God. I hoped they hadn't met their monthly quota. I prayed that supporting my mother in her time of need wasn't as important as the chance to convince someone that only Jehovah's Witnesses had the path to salvation. I'd always found their belief that God Almighty favored only them incredibly egotistical.

"Here we go." I grabbed Ellie's hand, and we stepped into the waiting area. I was grateful to find only my dad's sister, Aunt Dinah, sitting with my mom. They rose, and I watched as Ellie stood rooted in place like a statue, her jaw clenching and releasing. Aunt Dinah approached and gave us each a hug. Ellie clung to her like she was a small child again, while our mother watched us.

"You look good, Bekka. I like the hair." Aunt Dinah was a beautician. She mussed the layered cut that faded from black to burnished copper near my neckline, pulling a strand or two where she wanted them. My hair always looked casually windblown and was intentionally a mess.

"Glad you approve. It's good to see you." I grinned.

She pulled me into another embrace. I had a fleeting feeling that, just maybe, Mom understood what it felt like to be the outsider. I would need to talk things through with God for enjoying that karma moment.

"Hello, EllieAnna. I wasn't sure when you'd be arriving." My mother approached the group.

I stood and watched the stare down between Ellie and the woman who gave birth to us. We both felt she'd chosen to turn her back on us. I was sure she would say it was for our own good, though Ellie and I were unable to find anything good about what had happened to us. Only after we were no longer tied to a set of ridiculous ideals had we found peace.

"Bek said that there are decisions to make and that you were waiting for me to get here. Well, I'm here."

Mom nodded and looked around. She went back and withdrew her phone from her purse. Her thumbs tapped slowly across the screen.

Aunt Dinah scrunched her brow and scowled at her. "Irene, who are you texting?"

"I need to let the elders know I'm going in to talk to the doctor." She tucked her phone back in her purse, then slung it over her arm.

Aunt Dinah put her hands on her hips. "Do you have to tell them when you take a shit too?"

"Dinah, language!" It was my mother's turn to scowl.

This might get interesting. I caught a smirk on my sister's face, and we stood back from our mother. Aunt Dinah turned to us and pulled our hands into hers. "I'm right here girls, and I'll still be here when you come back out, no matter how long it takes. Someone should be, and I think she's got her own support. You two were the best thing my brother ever accomplished in his life, even if he had no clue."

Ellie and I watched our mother walk to the door to request entrance. I held my gentle sparrow around the shoulders, and we followed behind her. As we approached his room, Ellie stiffened. I stopped, not forcing her to move forward. I'd had my moment of shock. She could have hers in the safety of my arms. We could see him through the window, lying there. The same noises of life support filled the air, met by the pungent smells of sickness and antiseptic.

I leaned my head against hers and whispered into her ear. "We're as free as the sparrow that sings in the wild. Everything that made him the monster he was died days ago. Now, only the vessel remains. Psalms tells us when their spirit departs, they return to the ground. On that very day, their plans come to nothing." I hugged her hard before holding out my hand. "Together."

My beautiful sister wiped her eyes and placed her hand in mine. "Together."

* * *

We'd spoken with Dr. Varetti and asked that life support be discontinued. At six that evening, my mother stood with Sam, as well as Brother and Sister Raymond. Bibles in hand, they prayed for my father.

A muted click silenced the machines, and Wesley McNally's body joined his spirit in death. Ellie and I left the room and walked out of the intensive care unit without a word. To us, he'd been dead for years. There was nothing left to say to a mother who'd made her own choices. Not even his memory could hurt us anymore.

Aunt Dinah caught up with us as we passed the waiting room. She and Dad hadn't been close since he'd followed my mother into the world of being a Jehovah's Witness. The male hierarchy of the religion appealed to him. The order that women be submissive to their fathers and husbands was right up his alley. He'd also keep doing whatever the hell he wanted behind their backs.

"I'm sorry my brother never followed the example our own dad set. Daddy loved my mother and never treated her as anything other than his equal. He certainly never treated me the way Wesley did you. I want you to know, I understand why you never came to me. He'd have dragged you back. Just know I love you both, and you are always welcome in my home."

One more obstacle fell away as Aunt Dinah held our hands. She'd always reminded me a great deal of MaMaw. "Thank you. We won't lose touch again."

Ellie gripped our aunt's hand tighter. "That goes for me, too, Aunt Dinah. Now, I could really use a shot of Jack Daniels Black Label. You know this isn't completely over. She's going to want us there."

I straightened my back. "I will not walk in that Kingdom Hall under any circumstances. I'll go to the viewings at the funeral home, but I've subjugated myself enough to their dismissive looks and disdain. It's her faith and her beliefs, not mine. There will be no comfort in the words of the message they peddle. He can go back to the ground or straight to hell, as far as I'm concerned. I'm done."

***

Over the next few days, Ellie and I traveled through parts of our old hometown. We walked by our high school and the ice cream shop where Ellie worked. We'd escaped there whenever we could. We stopped by the restaurant where I'd waited tables from the time I was sixteen until we left. I squirreled away every penny I could to buy my Subaru and give us starting money. The management had changed, and no one knew me in the Mexican cantina that took its place. In twenty years, much about the area had changed, both good and bad.

Ellie kept in touch with her band, and I helped her rehearse by playing for her while she sang. They planned to play a concert in a small venue in Vienna, Virginia, on the edge of Washington, D.C. soon after the funeral. No flashing lights or smoke machines. Just Ellie's voice, John's guitar, and Adriane on the keyboards would grace the stage. Intimate and low key, it reminded me of playing at a much larger Redemption's Road. I knew she was looking forward to it, and I was truly enjoying playing for her. More than once, she'd coaxed me into singing along. She'd smile and drop into harmony, forcing me to take the lead. I did miss singing with her, but I didn't miss the road or the pain it brought. That life had cost me the greatest love of my life. In truth, it wasn't the music or the road's fault, but my own doing. A drunken night and my own excesses had cost me my one great love. The blame sat firmly on my shoulders.

We'd just finished lunch when Mom called and asked if we could come to the funeral home to finalize our father's service.

"I'm meeting with the director at one. Can you and your sister meet me there?"

I had her on speakerphone. I watched Ellie take a face-first dive onto the bed and beat her fists against the mattress. I completely understood her frustration. I always knew this wasn't going to be easy.

"Is it going to be just us, or will you have your entourage?"

My mother nearly growled her answer. "The brothers from the Kingdom Hall are not an entourage, Bekka. You will be civil."

Ellie sat up and vehemently flipped my phone the double bird, while never saying a word. I nearly snorted coffee out my nose. I coughed.

"Mom, very soon you'll be able to immerse yourself completely in all things your Witnesses want from you. But for the next few days, can you remember that, at one point in your life, we were important to you? Dig into your memory bank and pull out the file that has our birth certificates with your name on them. Sometimes, I feel like I'm beating my head against the wall and talking with you is about as productive as that." I remembered she was grieving and stopped to take a deep breath. "We'll be there." I caught Ellie rolling her eyes as I hung up.

"You're too fucking nice to her."

"I'm trying to remember the scripture that says honor your father and mother. Trust me, it's not easy for me."

Ellie moved about the room, pulling on her faded Indigo Girls sweatshirt. I couldn't help but laugh. "That thing is almost as old as you are."

She fingered the ragged cuffs. "You bought this for me in a secondhand store in 1999."

My guitar rested across my lap, and I moved it into position. I grinned at my sister and watched a smile appear like the sun pulling from the earth's horizon to rise into the sky. Within a few seconds, her honeyed voice was wrapping itself around mine, as I rolled into the chorus of the Indigo Girls' "Secure Yourself." It was the anthem of our escape into a world where we didn't have to listen for footsteps behind us. The song put to words the feeling of our worth in this new life. I rarely pulled this one out. As much of a balm to our open wounds this song had been back then, it brought up a really rough time for us. Freed of the oppression we'd grown up in, we quickly found out how terrifying this new-found freedom could be. We swam like guppies in an ocean of sharks.

When we finished the last chorus, I put the guitar to the side and grabbed my jacket. "It's going to be okay, Ellie. If you believe nothing else, believe that."

Chapter Twelve

IT WAS SNOWING THE morning of my father's funeral. Outside the window of our hotel, a blanket of white had been thrown over everything to hide the ugliness we'd see that day. We knew a painful piece of our lives would be buried under six feet of earth and marked with a piece of granite as a memorial to a wasted life.

"Ellie, we need to leave soon." I stood outside the bathroom door, giving her ample warning. Living in this hotel room with my sister for the last few days had taken us right back to the time we shared a tiny apartment in Pittsburgh. Her clothes were strewn everywhere, while mine were in a neat pile. Her makeup occupied every flat space, and her pillow was squished up into a tiny ball on the bed. I buttoned my black shirt and tucked it into the pants I'd purchased a few days ago. I'd packed in such a hurry and hadn't thought to bring any dress clothes. Ellie had taken great pleasure in picking out the dark, silver-gray suit for me. I'd just tried to button the cuffs and was failing miserably, when there was a knock at the door.

"I think Tank and Karmen are here. Make sure you're decent before you step out," I called out before I pulled open the door.

A rush of coffee beans and vanilla met me. I nearly cried. I'd given her many bottles of that scent as an expression of my love. Despite all my protestations and shields, the one woman who still clawed and flowed into all my secret spaces stood before me. Her name came out like a whispered prayer floating on a feather.

"Naomi."

She said nothing, as she strode into the room dressed in a long wool coat and drew me into her arms. For the last few days, I'd jammed every painful emotion I'd experienced down into a glass jar and screwed the lid down tightly. I'd planned to bury that jar in the grave with my father. The minute she tucked me into her arms, the jar slipped from my fingers and shattered all around me. The tears poured out of the container and pooled around my feet. I nearly collapsed, but Naomi held me tightly in her arms.

"I'm right here, Rhebekka. It's time to let it out. Let it go, my love."

Unable to hold back great howling gasps, I was held in the arms of the woman whose touch could strip me bare and whose heart could wrap me in the safety of her love. She moved us to sit on the couch in the lounge area and just held me. Ellie came out of the bathroom, leaning tentatively on the door frame and biting her thumbnail. I stretched out an arm to her and she ran to us, tears pouring down her own face. Naomi held us tighter and spoke the words we needed to hear.

"I've got you both. We'll get through this together. You're not alone, and you never will be."

***

It felt like hours, as we cried and finished getting dressed. Naomi ironed out the wrinkles we'd put in my shirt and buttoned my cuffs for me like a hundred times before. I still couldn't believe she had flown in to be with us. I guess I shouldn't have been surprised. She and Ellie were still very close, regardless of my situation with Naomi. With her right in front of me, it was harder and harder to remember why we weren't together. I'd never stopped wanting her, needing her, and certainly never stopped loving her.

Ellie wore a simple black dress and boots, nervously flicking her middle finger against her thumb. I wanted to remove the frown from her face. She was a beautiful mess, and I wanted nothing more than to rub away the worry lines that marred her gorgeous face. I sighed deeply, as Naomi ran her hands down my chest, smoothing the shirt. As tense as I was, I wished for a few solitary minutes to center my thoughts but quickly dismissed the idea. I couldn't imagine being without her for a single second now that she was there.

I reached out a hand for Ellie and brought her to my side until we formed a circle. Naomi said a prayer with us, and I felt a peace come over me.

"Amen."

Naomi reached for my jacket and helped me slip it on over my shoulders. She held my face in her hands.

"My God, you are still so damn handsome."

Her fingers adjusted my collar, and she leaned in to softly kiss my lips. She smirked, knowing exactly what she was doing to me. I let a smile break over my face. "You're pretty damn beautiful yourself." I helped her slip into her coat and admired the black, suit dress she wore. The double-breasted placard, buttoned at her hip over a white shell, was elegant. The knee-high black boots she wore with it were doing pleasant things to my insides.

"Come on, girls, let's do this." Naomi's smile lit up the room.

I grabbed my guitar case. I had something planned for after the visitation that had nothing to do with my father's burial. We met Marlon in the lobby, and he led the way to the car.

Naomi sat in the middle and held our hands as we drove. I watched my sister fidget restlessly.

"I don't know if I can do this, Bek. Why are we going? It feels wrong. We had nothing to do with that bastard for the last twenty years. Why do we need to show respect now that he's gone?"

I rolled my head from shoulder to shoulder, trying to buy time to formulate an explanation that would make sense. "I can't speak for you, Ellie. Honestly, if you don't want to do this, I understand. For me, this is burying the past, letting go of the disappointment and abuse."

I ran a finger in the condensation on the window, drawing four connected squares on the glass. "Each pane contains a snapshot of my self-worth. The window of my life." I drew a challis in one and pointed to it. "For years, I never felt worthy of God's love. I was told the price was total submission. The whole time, I fully knew I'd never attain the promised reward, because I was hiding who I really was."

I drew a circle in the next pane. "In this one is a record. I spent years singing for the approval of others, searching for acceptance and success." In the third one, I drew a cross. "This pane holds the symbol of the grace I am freely offered, while still struggling to understand that I am worthy of the sacrifice that guaranteed it." I tapped the last empty square with my knuckle. "This panel is for what I will be when I bury those feelings of inadequacy with the man who was our father." I reached for her hand. "Your windowpanes are different than mine. Your journey is your own. The reason I'm going is so that when I leave, I can walk past that city limit sign, not run."

***

The funeral was difficult, to say the least. People came through to pay their respects. My mother took her position by my father's head. We stood slightly past her, uncomfortable facing the raised eyebrows of those who veered off before they got to us. Some of our relatives, people from the community, and a few classmates continued through the line with their condolences for us.

Aunt Dinah stopped and hugged us. "How are you holding up, girls? Don't think, for one second, I don't see what's going on here. I'm not buying that this is God's compassion in action. You know where I am, and I'm here for you."

"We're doing all right. What comes next will be the worst, this we can handle."

Ellie crossed her arms. "She's right, wait until they get to the service part of this charade."

Two hours later, we'd endured a memorial service that had been more like a rebuke. Brother Raymond took the opportunity to subtly remind us how far from their favor we'd fallen. The God he spoke about fell well short of the loving Father I'd come to know. Naomi rubbed her thumb across the back of my hand, subtly reminding me I wasn't alone. Ellie clung to me, the rage rolling off her in waves. When the internment was over, Ellie and I made our way out.

When I reached for the car door, a loud voice accosted our backs.

"Can't you two put something other than yourselves first for once?"

I kept Naomi's hand in mine and turned to face my mother. "No, Mom, not this time. We spent more than enough time ignoring our own self-preservation. For once, how about you pray God forgives you for letting that monster leave marks on my back and legs? Pray that God understands why you let our father berate and emotionally abuse us. You were supposed to protect us. I wish you well, Mom. You're now completely free to become the perfect Jehovah's Witness without any encumbrances. At the end of your days, I hope it will all have been worthwhile."

For twenty years we'd been estranged. Until she had her own epiphany, it would be the last time I would ever speak to her. I had no illusions that she would wake up one day and realize that her children had been a gift from God, born with the right to make our own decisions, whether she agreed with them or not. We were adults, and she wasn't responsible for either our salvations or our sins, nor were we tied to her own.

***

Naomi walked beside me up to my grandparent's grave. I held my guitar in one hand and Ellie's hand in the other. Tank and Karmen trailed behind us. When we reached the simple gray stone with a cross down the middle, I wiped a tear away. The names on the smooth surface recalled two people who'd lived a full life and raised a family with love, though they had little else. I asked Tank to hold my case while I removed my guitar and slid the strap over my head. As I ran my hand over the strings, soft snowflakes floated in the air.

MaMaw had enjoyed winter's slower pace of life. No garden to tend, no flowers to water, and the promise of spring when the cycle would start all over again. Flakes landed on my lashes, as I started one of her favorite hymns. "In the bleak midwinter…" My alto voice was joined by Naomi's powerful soprano and harmonized by my sister singing tenor. We'd sung together so many times, it was as if we'd spent hours practicing just that morning.

We moved into the hymn Grandpa taught me without the benefit of any sheet music. Our voices blended and rolled over each other in beautiful harmony, and it was well with our souls. I knew our grandparents had to be smiling from heaven. The weight of the last few days dropped away and melted into the ground. When we finished, I let the tears come. Great wails wracked my body. I tried to hold back the floodgate with tightly closed eyes, to no avail. I felt the guitar removed from my hands. Arms surrounded me, and soft lips kissed the tears away. A second set of cries joined mine, as Ellie moved into the small circle with us. We cried for every moment of our past. I fully intended to leave all the sorrow right there on that hallowed ground. My grandfather had worked this farmland to feed his family and had eked out a meager living. I wiped my eyes.

"When we fled, one of the things I took with me was a small tin of dirt from the top of these graves. I wanted to be grounded in the love and gifts they gave us. I wanted to remember their humble beginnings and the love that served as our foundation, not the pain of the house we grew up in."

I held my hand out for my guitar case and pulled back the velvet pocket inside to reveal that small tin that had once held MaMaw's peppermint balm. When we stayed with her, she'd rub it on our lips before we went to bed.

The tin sat in my open palm. "In each ounce of dirt, there are pieces of things that have broken down and turned into something else, just like we have."

These people were much more than a sister, a lover, and two friends. This was my family, the people I'd built my present and future on. I put the tin back inside and laid the guitar in its velvet protection. I closed the lid and flipped the clasps back in place, before I reached for the handle. I saw Tank reach out for Ellie's hand, and winced as my sister stepped to my side and slid her hand into mine instead. Tank took the case from me and started back to the car, leaving the rest of us standing there. Naomi wrapped her fingers in mine and reached for Karmen's. Slowly, we made our way to the car. The four of them climbed in, while I turned for one last look. I took a deep breath, pulling in the scent of crisp winter air and pine, then repeated the first verse of *It Is Well With My Soul.* For the first time in a very long time, I realized it truly was.

Chapter Thirteen

BACK AT THE HOTEL, I packed my belongings as I talked with Ellie. She was going to have to deal with Tank's unrequited love. Tank was my friend, and I didn't want to see her hurt, though I knew it was coming. It wasn't Ellie's fault, but only she could be the one to tell Tank it was never going to happen.

"You're going to have to be straight with her, Ellie. She's going to brood for months."

Shrugging her shoulders, my sister packed the last of her makeup. "What more do I have to say? I've told her, more than once. Poor Karmen, I saw the tears in her eyes. Can't Tank see she's crazy about her?"

"Unfortunately, no." I shook my head. "I've done all I can to get Tank to let this go, and I've told Karmen she deserves better."

Naomi was folding one of my shirts. "Sometimes, people can't see what's right in front of them."

Ellie smirked and cleared her throat as she backed toward the door. "I need to check on something with Marlon. I'll be back in a little while."

I shook my head at Naomi. "You're about as subtle as a foghorn."

"And your sister is perceptive." Naomi hugged Ellie before she walked out.

We were alone. It'd been a long time since we'd confronted the elephant in the room. Sweat formed on my upper lip.

"It's time we talk, and I don't mean about your parents, or Ellie, or the weather."

Seeing her that morning had been God's answer to a silent prayer in the form of a beautiful woman who'd taught me how much I was worth and loved me in spite of myself. I closed my eyes. I'd been dreading this all day.

"Naomi—"

My argument couldn't even get started. She shifted her weight onto one booted heel and crossed her arms over her chest.

"Don't Naomi me. I'm going to talk, and for once, you're going to listen."

She pulled out a chair and pointed. I sat obediently.

"I'll wait for you until the end of days, Rhebekka, but that's a lot of wasted time we could be using to make love and hold each other every day we draw breath. I've given you the time to flog yourself. I've allowed you to deny yourself in penance, but we're done with that. You slept with someone else. I get it. I've forgiven you, even if you haven't found a way to forgive yourself. I know every gritty detail of what happened and exactly why it happened. There's no need to rehash it. You were angry at me. Trust me, I was just as pissed at you. I said something that hurt you, and you retaliated in a way another woman might not be able to get over. I'm not excusing what you did, but you don't get to decide for me if I can get over it or not. I want you to get the fuck over it. I don't ever want to talk about it again. It's over and done. Dead and buried, I'm hoping. I'm not giving up on what we have. Yes, *have,* present tense. You're still mine, and I'm still yours, unless you're going to tell me you've moved on with someone else."

The chair bounced on the floor, as I hastily stood. "I haven't!"

She walked over, righted the chair, and pointed again. "Sit."

Holy shit, she was turning me on. From the day I walked out of the house I'd grown up in, there'd only been one person I'd willingly let control even a small part of me. The captivating woman before me held more power than she knew. The mortar in my brick wall loosened beneath her delicate hands.

"I know that, Rhebekka. It was a rhetorical statement. I have no doubt you've been more celibate than a hermit in the Alaskan wilderness or the Catholic nuns who take a vow."

I couldn't help but laugh, and I saw her smirk. I started to speak. She raised a finger tipped with a blood-red nail.

"I said, it's my turn. Since you've become a pastor, how many people have you counseled? I'd bet more than you can remember. Have you ever told a single one of them they were unworthy of grace or forgiveness? Let me answer that for you, since I was not only your lover but your mentor."

She brought her fingers to her thumb and formed a zero. Again, I chuckled. She was so good at this. Hard like steel when she needed to be and as soft as a newborn chick when the situation called for it. I'd seen her work many times and been on the receiving end of both sides of her gift. It was just one of the reasons I loved her so damn much.

"None. Zero. Zilch, Rhebekka. I know this as much as I know that God forgives me for all the mistakes I make, daily. Not just once, but daily."

She pulled her earlobe. This was one of the things she did when she was trying to calm herself and formulate her next words. She'd already won. She just didn't know it yet. I was tired of being without her.

"In the same way you buried all the pain from your childhood today, I'm asking you to bury that horrible night alongside it. I was angry at you for a long time. I felt betrayed and inadequate. It's time for that day to be relegated to our past and forgotten. You've hated yourself over this for too damn long. Proverbs says hatred stirs up strife, but love covers all offenses. I love you, dammit. I love you, and I've forgiven you for this years ago. Your choice to deny yourself forgiveness is denying me a love I deserve. If I had a nickel for every time you told me you were sorry, I could feed every hungry child in America and beyond. I...forgive...you."

My tears had welled up the minute she said I'd betrayed her and made her feel less than enough. I was so wrong for denying her. At that moment, I understood how the thief who hung beside Christ felt when he was forgiven. Unworthy of grace but granted it in spite of himself. The weeping grew from a place deep inside me. Each tear ripped away the guilt that clung to my soul. For the thousandth time, her scent completely filled my senses and washed over me like the smell of MaMaw's coffee cake, warm and comforting on an elemental level. I leaned forward resting my head in my hands. Arms full of feminine grace and strength wrapped around me and held me, as my remaining bricks crumbled into a pile of useless rubble. Naomi rocked me. My head rested on her soft breasts, while her hand sifted through my hair. A million sensations coursed through my body, the strongest of which was desire. I turned my head and kissed the exposed skin above the shell she wore. I felt her press my head tighter to her chest, before the fingers tightened in my hair and pulled my lips away. She bent down until her mouth was a fraction of an inch from my ear, so close the warmth of her breath made me shiver.

"If you think I've waited this long to have your touch, only to have it last the few minutes Ellie will be gone, you'd be dead wrong. When we come together again, we won't be getting out of bed for hours."

She traced the outline of my ear with her tongue, and I shivered uncontrollably. "You're killing me." I grabbed her face and kissed her with a hunger I'd been suppressing for years. She met me with the same intensity and nipped at my tongue as it parted her lips and entered her mouth. I tasted cinnamon and sweetness from the latte we'd stopped for on the way back to the hotel. I pulled her to straddle my lap, which was no small feat given the restrictions of her dress. I ran my hand up her thigh, feeling the top of her stockings and the garters that held them in place. I wrapped my arms around her and pulled her tightly to me. I wanted to devour her with all the repressed need I'd kept bottled up, deep in my body. She surged her hips into my pelvis, and I groaned into her mouth. When I shifted my hand between us, she once again pulled my hair.

"Rhebekka, I wasn't kidding. As much as I want you"—she nipped my lip—"and I do want you, I won't settle for less than I deserve. That isn't a quickie. Put this on simmer." She stood and straightened her clothes.

There was a knock at the door. She raised an eyebrow at me as I growled in frustration. "Just a minute." I needed a few more seconds to get myself together.

Naomi stood and walked over to her bag and pulled her Bible from it. She opened to a marked passage and laid the Bible in my hands.

From the book of Ruth, I read aloud, "'...Don't urge me to leave you or to turn back from you. Where you go I will go, and where you stay I will stay. Your people will be my people and your God my God.'" I looked up at her, as she took it from my hands and put it away. "Naomi, what are you saying?"

Naomi looked at me with those piercing, ice-blue eyes. I held my breath.

"I didn't buy a return ticket, Rhebekka. Where you go, I will go. Where you stay, I will stay. I'm in this for the long haul."

The knock at the door came again. "Bek, I have to pee."

Naomi doubled over with laughter, as I wiped at my face on my way to the door.

"You are such a pain in my ass, Ellie. Get in here."

Ellie strode in with her hands in the air. "I've been standing in the hallway for thirty minutes. I can't help I have a small bladder." She pushed past me to the bathroom.

"You said you needed to check with Marlon." I saw Naomi pull on her ear again. I crossed my arms. "You two planned this moment, didn't you?"

Naomi planted her hands on her hips and shifted into the 'you are about to step in it' pose. "And your point is?"

Doing all I could to hold back my grin, I narrowed my eyes. "My

84

point is—" I cut off my own words and strode across the room. I swept Naomi into my arms, dipped her back, and pressed my mouth to hers in a bone-melting kiss. When I let her up for air, I finished my sentence. "Thank you for never giving up."

She kissed me softly, and the only thing that stopped us from continuing was the clearing of Ellie's throat.

"Do I need to go back into the hallway again?"

"No, you damn brat. Get over here." I pulled my little sparrow into my arms and kissed the side of her head. "Thank you for being so damn sneaky."

She whispered into my neck.

"I needed my family back together, Bek. It's the only thing that ever felt safe and real." She smacked my shoulder. "Now, don't screw it up."

"Not a chance."

CJ Murphy

Chapter Fourteen

I GENTLY TOUCHED NAOMI'S shoulder. "Hey, sleepyhead. Wake up." I watched, as those eyes I loved so much blinked awake. She stretched and smiled at me.

"Are we here?"

I shook my head yes, as I leaned over to kiss her. "Welcome home."

She cupped my face with both hands. "Do you have any idea how long I've been waiting to hear you say that?"

"Too long, I know." I pointed to the giant Jesus. "Welcome to House of the Rising Son. Jesus says, hi."

I watched her reaction as she looked up at the giant Jesus shadow.

"You weren't kidding me, were you?"

I reached for the door handle. "Nope. Watch yourself. The ground is likely icy, and your boots aren't exactly made for trudging through a foot and a half of snow."

Naomi rolled her eyes at me and pushed open the car door. "Again, you forget, I was born in the Colorado Rockies, honey. I think I can handle what you call deep snow."

"My bad." I pulled our bags out of the back of the Land Cruiser and pointed to the small set of steps to the left of Jesus. I handed her the keys. "Can you unlock the door?"

"That I can."

We made our way through the courtyard, and I marveled that she was there with me. I truly thought I'd missed my chance, and yet, there she was, sliding the key in the door as if she'd done it a thousand times.

"The light is there to the left, just inside." She fumbled for a moment, until she found the right switch and turned the hallway light on. I nodded with my head up the steps. I was struggling with our bags. She took the guitar case from me, and I walked up behind her. Even though her coat hid her shapely ass, I knew exactly what it looked like.

"Quit staring at my ass, Rhebekka."

I laughed and nearly fell down the stairs. Naomi pushed open the door to the loft and stood a foot inside the darkened room. I hit the lights.

"Wow, this place is beautiful." She set the case on the floor and pulled off her gloves.

"Let me take your coat." I helped her slip out of it and watched her take everything in. "I'll get a fire going in a minute. There's wine, whiskey, and beer in the kitchen. Glasses are in the cabinet above the sink.

After I'd moved around the room turning on two torch lamps, I wadded up a few pieces of newspaper and put them in the fireplace. With kindling covering that, the fire easily lit off. I held my hands up to the flames and turned to watch her beautiful form moving around my kitchen, our kitchen, if what she'd told me held true. I caught her smile more than once and realized, even without the fire, the entire loft was warmer. As the flames grew, I added a few larger pieces of wood and closed the glass door. I wanted to call Karmen and check that they'd made it back. To be honest, I wanted to check on both of my friends, that ride home couldn't have been pleasant.

"I need to see if the girls made it back. Feel free to look around."

She walked over and handed me a tumbler filled with a few ice cubes and two inches of amber liquid. "Go ahead, give them my love. Where's the bathroom?"

I pointed back to the small hallway. "First door to the right." When she was out of my sight, I called Karmen. After two rings, she answered.

"Did you make it back all right?"

"We did. Tank went to the bar to make sure everything was running smoothly. Senna had everything well in hand at the store when I called her earlier today. I decided I just wanted to come home."

"Thank you for being there. I know today was hard on you."

"Only because I let it be. I think it's time to stop wishing for something that's never going to happen."

I sighed and ran my hand through my hair. "I'm glad Naomi didn't do that."

"I'm so happy for you. Naomi seems like a keeper. What did she think of your place?"

"We just got in." I looked up to see Naomi in a pair of leggings and an oversized Colorado sweatshirt. "She's making herself at home."

"Good, now maybe you'll get some regular sleep and eat more than what I drop off."

A barefooted Naomi made her way to my stereo system and browsed through my CD collection. She made her selection and I heard the first strains of Jason Mraz's "I Won't Give Up." I swallowed hard and fought back the tears. "Right now, sleep is the last thing I want." I was so grateful she hadn't given up, no matter how hard I pushed, no matter how stubborn I was, no matter how withdrawn I'd become, she'd never given up.

"And that's my cue to go. I love you, Rhebekka. Bring Naomi by the store when you come up for air."

"Will do, just don't expect that to be any time soon."

"Go get it, girl. 'Night."

I hung up the phone and added large chunks of split wood in with the pieces that blazed like the desire within my center. My call to Tank could wait. "Karmen sounded resigned but surviving." Naomi pushed her hair behind her ears.

"Did they have any trouble on the way home?"

"Karmen didn't say. Tank went to the brewery and her apartment is attached. I'm sure she's in for the night as well." I picked up my drink and took a swallow. My mind undressed the woman I never thought would be standing there in my home.

Naomi walked up to me and took a sip from my glass before putting it down. "Then I'd say I'm done talking for the night." She wrapped her arms around my neck and started to dance with me.

Without her boots, she was a few inches shorter than me. I pulled her close and swayed with her. No longer able to stand even that distance, I picked her up to hold her in my arms. She naturally wrapped her legs around my waist, the same way she'd done hundreds of times before. She put her lips on mine. Her mouth tasted of the Jack Daniels lingering on her tongue as it slid across my own. My need for her hadn't been this all-consuming since the first night we'd made love. In those days, my pursuit of her had been relentless, overcoming every argument she gave me. The lyrics cut right into me, as the realization of how close I'd come to losing my entire world came crashing in. I held her close to my body and slid a hand under the back of the sweatshirt to find warm skin. Groaning into her mouth, my other hand roamed under the fabric and up her back. She wore nothing underneath.

"I want you."

She didn't say a word, only nodded, as I carefully knelt. I laid her down on the soft rug in front of the fire warming the room. With one swift motion, I pulled the sweatshirt over her head to reveal beautiful breasts, perfect in every way. Leaning over her, I took one of her taut nipples in my mouth. Her fingers made their way into my hair, pressing my lips hard to her skin. Her body arched beneath me. I slipped her leggings off. I held myself above her and marveled at the beauty beneath me, adorned only with a small, gold cross on a chain.

Her hands tugged at the T-shirt I'd changed into after the funeral. I sat up and quickly pulled it off. She smiled as she pushed up the jog bra and ran her hands over my small breasts before relieving me of the offending piece of fabric. Naomi drew me closer to her by tugging on the burnished wooden cross adorning my neck on a braided leather choker. She'd given it to me the day I humbled myself and took communion for the first time, accepting that I was worthy of the sacraments for the first time in my life.

When our bodies met, she rolled me over onto my back and stared at me. She flipped open the button on my well-worn Levis. I lifted my hips, and she pushed the jeans down. Her expression was priceless.

Wearing nothing beneath those jeans was my small rebellion against society's expected norms. Naomi ran her fingers through the coarse hair at the juncture of my legs. Watching her eyes flutter closed as her fingers brushed my obvious sign of desire was delicious.

"Off."

One simple word spoke volumes and I obeyed. When we came back together, skin to skin, I knew I would never be without her by my side again. This was where she belonged and the only place I'd ever want her to be for the rest of my life.

"I love you, Naomi. I love you so much."

She answered me with a kiss, before she rolled us over again and allowed my body to blanket her entire length. My hands roamed her flesh, reacquainting myself with all the places that made her arch, gasp, and moan. I kissed down her neck and bit gently on the tendon that joined at her shoulder. I licked her pulse point and softly kissed all the way down to her breasts, before taking a puckered nipple into my mouth.

I knew I'd taxed her patience long enough, when she grabbed my wrist and pushed it between us. Leaning on my left elbow, my fingers parted her center, sliding through liquid silk. She was so wet that, when I pulled my fingers away, I felt her desire run down my hand. She growled at me, and I watched her eyes turn from melted arctic ice into black embers the moment I brought my fingers to my mouth and sucked off her passion. I leaned down and kissed her, allowing her to taste herself, as I slid my hand back down her body. She parted her legs for me, and I plunged three fingers into her without hesitation.

I groaned as her body clenched tightly around my fingers, nearly preventing me from pumping into her, as I simultaneously drove my tongue in her mouth. My knee between her parted thighs slammed against my hand, driving my fingers hard into her center.

Slow and sensuous would come later. What we needed now was to throw gasoline on glowing coals too long starved for fuel. We needed hard and fast. Her mouth fell open in a pant, as she pulled desperately on my shoulders, our foreheads pressed together. I moved my thumb to her clit and stroked it with every hard thrust. We were both nearly out of breath and using that blazing fire to forge our souls into one.

I felt her stiffen in my arms. I squeezed my center against her thigh, while her body convulsed against my hand. Her orgasm grabbed onto mine and pulled me over the edge of the cliff with her as we released together. I was lost in the bright rainbow colors behind my eyelids. I was unable to make out anything but the intense pleasure of our shared climax. My heart nearly burst, as I realized I'd never really lost her. The only person who had been adrift was me. Naomi was my lighthouse, the sun, moon, and stars wrapped up in a love so big it swallowed me whole. My heart was hers, and always would be. I gave thanks that she'd refused to give up on this stubborn soul, literally and figuratively. Oh, how I prayed, that someday I would be worthy of her. The truth was I'd never stop trying to be.

***

It was after midnight. I wrapped her in my arms and carried her to the bedroom on a natural high, softly placing her on my rumpled sheets, still mussed from my abrupt departure. *I could have lost it all.* Endorphins raged through my body like cocaine. I'd been clean for years. I hadn't touched drugs since I stopped touring with Regal Crimson, not since the night I destroyed my life. Naomi had told me touring was going to kill me or destroy us. I was pissed. A woman I didn't know offered me two lines of blow on a compact. That night, I'd been so high I imploded my entire life over a face I, still to this day, couldn't remember. It was hard to reconcile that my guilt was what had nearly destroyed us in comparison to my infidelity. The woman lying naked in my arms, above my church, had forgiven me before I'd been able to forgive myself. I'd thrown myself into my religious studies and seminary, completely shielding myself in theology, while looking for answers and redemption.

I traced the skin of her arm with my fingertips. She was completely exhausted and, as was my norm, I wouldn't fall asleep until four. I'd tried herbal teas, supplements, and even meditation. The pattern was still the same. The only thing that exhausted me enough to sleep was music. I couldn't bring myself to leave her arms even to play.

She stirred and pulled me tighter before she kissed my chest.

"I was right, this hasn't changed."

I settled my cheek against the top of her head. "What?"

She pinched me lightly. "You know what. Your four in the morning bedtime. I'm completely wiped out from making love with you, and you still can't wind down until that magic hour."

"Years of touring routines cemented into my DNA."

"Do you ever miss being in the band?"

I shifted her until she was lying completely on top of me. "Singing with Ellie, yes. Everything else, no."

"I can still see you jumping around that stage in your bra, playing *We're One Step Away*, on the Strat. You were so fucking sexy in those leather pants."

"I wrote that anthem to get us through until the day we finally walked away."

"Why did it take you years to perform it on stage?"

I rubbed my hands down her bare back before resting them in the dip where her hips met her beautiful ass. "Honestly, the song was almost too personal. We were still looking over our shoulders for him to come after us."

Naomi sighed. "I've had to ask God's forgiveness for many murderous thoughts over that man."

I rolled over on top of her. "Is that so?" I smiled when she nodded and kissed her with all the restraint I could muster. "Well, I'm glad I don't have to answer to the Almighty for his sins. He's gone, and I want him to stay gone. The looking over my shoulder is done. A Jehovah's Witness song says, 'I'm keeping my eyes on the prize.' The prize I'm currently eyeing is naked in my bed. Am I detecting a second wind blowing in?"

I felt her tongue snake up my throat and along my jawline. She grabbed one of my hands and sucked my fingers in her mouth. I shuddered, as her tongue delved to the juncture of my index and middle finger. She moved her hands and pulled upward on my hips.

"Oh, fuck." I followed her directions, knowing exactly what she wanted. As I moved up her body, she kissed her way down my chest and over my abdomen until my center hovered above her. A devastating gleam stared back at me when I looked down. I'd desperately missed that stare.

Naomi grinned with pure lust in her eyes. "I've been waiting so long to have you exactly like this, to reclaim you in every way. To touch..."

She ran her hands over my hips and back down my ass.

"To see..."

Molten eyes devoured my sin with each gaze.

"And to taste you."

Her lips found my flesh and sucked it into her mouth. Instinctively, my hands latched onto the rail of the headboard, knowing I needed to hold onto something solid. Fully aware of her plan from our previous years together, I knew she'd entwine her hands with mine and hold my hands behind my back on her final assault.

Her tongue licked down each side of my clit, until she darted her tongue in and out of my body. The vibration of her mouth hummed against my skin. She licked and sucked me until my legs began to quiver. I knew the minute she was ready for me to flood her mouth. She made a quick lift of her left eyebrow, and I released the headboard. She clasped my fingers in hers and crossed my hands behind my back. Her tongue glided around my clit then flicked it in rhythmic strokes until my entire body was vibrating like a guitar string. I threw my head back and arched my body, staring at the wood planks of my loft's ceiling. My body shuddered through the strongest orgasm of my life as I screamed Naomi's name.

I had no recollection of her laying me down and tucking me against her breast. My last conscious thought noted red digital numbers that read two thirty-seven.

Chapter Fifteen

I WOKE AND REVELED in the warm body curved into mine. I'd always been the big spoon to Naomi's smaller frame and waking like this caused a small prayer of thanks to fall silently from my lips. "I'm such an idiot." I'd whispered this into the skin of her shoulder, believing she was still asleep. When her arm pulled mine tighter to her chest, I knew I'd been mistaken.

"You're not an idiot. We all make mistakes, Rhebekka. The question lies in what we learn from those moments. Do they become lessons or habits?"

She pulled my hand to her lips and kissed my fingers. I wouldn't ever disappoint her again. "It's a lesson I don't intend to repeat, ever."

"Then let this moment be the last we waste talking about it. Let it be a lesson of the past, and let's enjoy everything ahead of us." She bit my index finger. "Like breakfast. Please tell me you have something in this place that resembles bacon and eggs."

"I'll have you know, I've gotten much better at cooking. It's not something I have to do very often, because Karmen keeps me fed. With that being said, I do have bacon and eggs. More importantly, I have coffee."

"If you didn't, it would be a deal breaker. Get up and make me breakfast, woman." She sat up and turned to look at me over her shoulder, the sheet pulled up to her chest. "We burned a few calories last night, and I'm famished."

After all the energy we'd expended the night before, it was no wonder she was starving. "Yes, mistress." The phrase earned me a raised eyebrow, and I laughed out loud. Oh, how I'd missed her.

***

A perfectly folded omelet slid onto her plate, with a pile of bacon beside it. Naomi eyed it suspiciously, and then completely melted my heart with her smile. She sat there in one of my button-up shirts with the sleeves rolled up. Her legs were bare. Her perfectly painted toenails matched her fingernails.

"Voilà!" I refilled her coffee to finish off my masterpiece.

Over the rim of her cup, she narrowed those eyes at me. "Who are you, and what have you done with my Rhebekka?"

I skirted around the bar and sat beside her. "This is the new and improved Rhebekka."

She leaned over and whispered in my ear, causing a shiver to run completely through me.

"Your cooking might have improved, but the way you make love? Still perfect."

"Why mess with a good thing?" I took a big drink of my own coffee, cursing when I burned my tongue.

Naomi wagged her finger in a disapproving scold. "Careful now, I have plans for that tongue later."

That devilish grin was making it impossible to tame my libido. I had things that needed to be done, and I was using all the restraint I possessed to not throw her down and make love to her again, immediately. Our time apart had been far too long, and I was glad those days were behind us. How had I survived without her touch, without touching her? No matter how many times I'd been tempted, I'd never given in. My infidelity betrayed her and going without intimacy had been the penance I'd given myself. I shook my head.

She leaned over and kissed my cheek. The love of my life drew my face into her hands and looked me directly in the eyes.

"Let...it...go."

Naomi could read me like an open book. I'd do well to remember that. *Time to put your money where your mouth is.* I'd promised we'd put this in the past, and it was time to do just that.

"How long can you stay? Is someone covering Open Door for you?" I chewed on a piece of bacon.

She grabbed her napkin and wiped her mouth. She pulled on her ear. I waited. I'd watched her do that a million times, when she counseled someone or answered a child's question. A thoughtful person, Naomi was always conscious of what she said and how she said it.

She pressed a few stray salt grains onto the end of her finger, before rubbing it off over her omelet. "Ashley Kingman is covering Open Door Ministries."

"Ashley's outstanding. You couldn't pick a better stand-in. I'm surprised she doesn't have her own church yet." I took a bite of my omelet and wondered why Naomi was so apprehensive in answering me. *What is she not telling me?*

"She does have her own church. Ashley's the new pastor of Open Door. I told you...I didn't buy a return ticket."

I inhaled at the wrong time and choked, coughing violently at her declaration. I tried to suck in a breath and couldn't, the coughs barking out across the kitchen. Naomi jumped off the stool and came to my side, rubbing my back. I sucked in a big breath and found a way to suppress the next cough.

"Why did you give up your church? What the hell happened?"

She rubbed my back, moved in, and wrapped her arms around me. I followed suit and held her tight, as she laid her head on my shoulder.

"You happened, Rhebekka. You stumbled into my church, hungover and still a little high. I looked up, took one look at you, and started singing—"

"*Beautiful Brokenness* was the first hymn I ever heard you sing. Even as fucked up as I was, I took notice. I realized later you'd changed what you had planned."

"That's what I saw in you. At that time, the depth of that despair was beyond my comprehension. All I knew was that I was drawn to you, completely oblivious that I'd just found my soulmate. The one thing I didn't miss was how gorgeous you were and still are."

"How you could have possibly thought that still baffles me. I was dressed in the previous night's clothes and smelled like cigarettes and Scotch."

"A diamond in the rough, with a desperate spirit clawing at your insides trying to reach the light."

"Come on, let's eat first, then tell me everything."

She nodded against my shoulder and brushed my lips with a chaste kiss. For all its softness, it made my nipples hard as rocks. While we ate, I asked questions about mutual friends and the organizations I still supported in Durango. These discussions were side dishes for the meat of the subject. When we'd finished the kitchen cleanup, I refilled her coffee cup and led her by the hand to the couch.

"Okay, Naomi Rainelle Layman, spill."

She sipped her coffee and settled with her back resting against the arm of the couch, while she entwined her legs with mine.

"About a year ago, I started seriously talking with Ashley about taking over Open Door Ministries. Over the last fifteen years, my church has acted as an alternative to mainstream, traditional religion lost on an entire section of the population. Those first few years, it was a good week if four people showed up for Sunday services. Eventually, word got out that I was anything but the typical preacher." Naomi made air quotes and shuddered when she said the word preacher.

She still hates that word. "You don't preach to people, you never have."

"I started the evening Bible study program because I realized if you want people to talk about living their best life, then show them that moderation for that life could happen at church as well as in a bar or their living room. That's why they could bring their own liquid refreshments. You know the rest, Rhebekka. Now, Open Door is one of the most regularly attended houses of worship in Durango. It's not that there aren't souls still to seek, or that I'm bored, trust me. What I am is a fifty-one-year-old woman who misses you like a piece of my body is gone. I've left everything there in good hands. Ashley's been leading for the last six months. I've been stepping back, doing more of the behind-the-scenes work and preparing for my eventual exit. I want to give us one more chance. To give myself one more try at showing you that I love you beyond measure. Your father's passing sped up my timetable. I hadn't planned to leave in winter, but here I am. For the first time in five years, I'm not doubled over in grief from missing you. I guess what I'm saying is, I'm yours and here forever if you want me to be."

I grabbed her coffee cup and set it on the high table behind the couch. I slid her down until her back was against the cushions and hovered above her, staring into translucent blue.

"If I want you to be? The only thing I ever wanted more was to get Ellie out of harm's way years ago. I didn't think I deserved you, and I'd vowed to never love another." I set my resolve with a deep breath. "I want you to do something for me."

"Anything."

"Stay right here. Don't move. I'll be right back."

With a look of incredulity, she grabbed me by the front of my T-shirt.

"Where are you going?"

"Just into the other room." I kissed her. "Be patient for two minutes. It'll be worth it."

"Really, you're going to get up right now?"

I rolled my eyes at her. "Yes, Miss Impatient. Sixty to ninety seconds, I promise."

Naomi narrowed her eyes, grabbed the back of my head, and crushed her mouth to mine. She drove her tongue past my lips until I groaned.

"Shit, forty-five seconds, no more." I held up my hand in an oath.

"One, two, three—"

I launched off the couch and nearly fell trying to make the corner into my bedroom. I grabbed my sock drawer and dumped it on the bed. She continued to count from the other room.

"Ten, eleven, twelve—"

I mumbled under my breath, as I threw socks everywhere until locating the orange pair Tank had given me as a joke for Christmas. I hated orange, and she knew it. I struggled to pull the roll apart.

"Twenty, twenty-one, twenty-two—"

"Fuck, I'm coming, I swear. Count slower!" I bent a fingernail back and cursed in pain, as I sucked it into my mouth. I shook the blue velvet box out of the toe of the sock and ran back to the living room.

"Thirty, thirty-one, thirty-two —"

The corner of the breakfast bar caught the little toe of my left foot as I tried to get back to her while she continued her infernal count down. I yelped and hopped on one foot, before crumpling to the floor in a spectacular heap. That was apparently enough to stop her. In seconds, I found myself face to face with her on the floor. With my throbbing foot in one hand and the velvet box clenched tightly in the other, I winced in pain.

Naomi's hands were all over me.

"Oh, Rhebekka, I'm so sorry. Are you alright?"

I rolled onto my back and gasped. "No, I'm not fucking all right."

"What can I do to help? Oh, baby. I'm so sorry."

I could hear the panic in her voice. I'd be damned if I'd broken my toe for nothing. By my calculations, I still had a few seconds left. I held the box up and pushed past the pain in my foot. "You want to know what you can do to help? Marry me. Marry me and fill the holes in this Swiss cheese life I've made for myself. Marry this pig-headed fool, who's never stopped loving you. Marry me and stay by my side for the rest of our days." I flipped open the box with my thumb, wincing about my foot but looking intently into her eyes. "I love you, Naomi. Marry me?"

She knelt there between my legs, her hand over her mouth, as she stared at the diamond ring nestled in the velvet. When she brought her eyes to mine, the tears were spilling over. I had about five seconds left. I shook the box at her.

"Well? I'm running out of time here to make the deadline you set. Not quite the romantic gesture I'd planned all those years ago, but I'm sober and head over heels in love with you. Five, four, three." I put my index finger on the lid. "Two, o—"

"Yes, you damn idiot! Yes, a thousand times, yes!"

I pulled her on top of me, the pain in my foot completely forgotten, along with the one in my heart. She smothered me with kisses, and I melted into her. Something occurred to me.

"Do you know what today is?" I pushed a strand of her hair behind her ear.

A broad grin spread across her face.

"I do. It's the day you asked me to be your wife."

"That too, but, it's also Valentine's Day. I'd say that's a mic drop." I smiled at her and the one she returned to me was brighter than the sun.

Naomi stretched out on top of me and kissed me with the passion of all our missed hours, minutes, and seconds. I pushed my fingers into her auburn waves and pulled her so close, she could have been implanted in my skin like my tattoos. When we came up for air, I grinned at her.

"If only you'd been able to experience the proposal I'd planned before I fucked everything up."

Naomi pressed her fingers to my lips. "My love, nothing you could have planned would have made your proposal any better, unless we could go back and erase the years and your broken toe. This was so us. Grand gestures never have meant that much to me."

"Says the woman who left her entire life to come here. I'd say that's a pretty grand gesture in comparison to me putting a ring on your finger." I smacked myself in the forehead. "I haven't even done that yet." I rolled us over and found the box I'd dropped when she'd accepted my proposal. I fumbled to pull the platinum band from the box. She held out her left hand, and I slipped the brilliant-cut, princess diamond I'd waited too long to give her on her third finger. In my life, I'd never experienced the level of joy that washed over me. "So, do I take your name, or do you take mine?" I watched her grin.

"I think Naomi Deklan has a nice ring to it."

I sat back and interlaced my fingers. "I don't disagree. Are you sure?"

She ran a finger over my lips.

"When I first met you, the glassy-eyed, barely conscious woman sitting in my pew looked so lost...until I grabbed my guitar."

I growled slightly. "I'd never seen anything so sexy. There you stood in a black miniskirt, pirate boots, wearing a clerical collar over a black silk shirt."

She nodded. "Over the next few months, that same woman kept showing up. Her eyes weren't glazed anymore, and she sat up a bit straighter. I watched your fingers work through every chord I played. I knew it was important to learn your name. Over time, you introduced yourself as Bek."

"You asked me if Bek was short for something." I kissed her softly. She pulled me from the floor and over to the couch, where I covered her body with mine.

"Rhebekka Lynn McNally. I loved the way your first name rolled off my tongue. I couldn't spend enough time with you. Every moment you weren't on tour for the next four years. Right before things went off the rails with us, you told me you wished you could completely reinvent yourself. I'm guessing the person you imagined was Rhebekka Deklan. Now, every part of you is the strong, beautiful woman I fell for, cocky grin and all. The only difference is you're not running flat out to avoid your past."

She stopped to kiss me again and rested her hand on my cheek.

"So, that's the woman I'm marrying. Your last name is the one I want to carry with me for the rest of time, because it's a name that brings you no pain and no bad memories. Layman isn't the name I was born with anyway."

I stared down at her, as she shifted my bangs out of my eyes. "You know none of that would have been possible if I hadn't met you."

"Oh, I don't know. This woman was inside you all along, hidden among the chords and amplifiers."

"Maybe it took someone like you to unplug it all and hear the notes underneath."

My phone rang, and I let my forehead fall to hers, cursing under my breath. It was Tank's ringtone.

"Duty calls, love. Life isn't going to stop because we want to cocoon ourselves away from the rest of the world. You get that, and I'm going to shower."

I reached for my phone. "Hang on one minute, Tank." I sat up and watched her crawl out from under me. "Feel free to look around and use anything you want."

The diamond I'd put on her hand glinted, as she made the okay sign before disappearing into the bedroom.

"What's up?" I caught the time and saw it was a little after ten.

"I take it the reunion went well?"

I couldn't help the grin that formed. "You could say that."

"Then I'm guessing you want me to cover the after-school program?"

I rubbed my eyes. "Shit. No, the kids count on me. It will be a good time to introduce her to everyone."

"Naomi sticking around for a while?"

I flashed back to my proposal and realized my toe was throbbing. "More than a little while."

"Huh?"

I got up to grab a bottle of water and some Advil for my toe. "Naomi's here for good."

"Wow, that must have been some talk."

"Oh, we did a little more than talk. I asked her to marry me."

Tank's yell forced me to pull my phone from my ear. I laughed with true joy.

"About damn fucking time. What about Durango?"

"I'll fill you in later. Right now, there is a beautiful woman in my shower, likely completely naked."

"I'd hope so, taking a shower with clothes on makes no sense. Congratulations, Bek, I'm happy for you."

"Thanks. Keep that under your hat for now. If Ellie finds out you knew before she did, there'll be hell to pay." I downed the last of the bottle of water and cringed. Bringing up Ellie right now probably wasn't the kindest thing I'd ever done.

"I'll see you this afternoon. Tell Naomi congratulations for me."

"Will do."

I hung up and limped into the bedroom, stripping off my shorts and T-shirt on the way. I could hear her singing. As she washed her hair, I slid in behind her and swayed with her body, harmonizing to a song that spoke of everlasting love. I kissed her naked shoulder and nuzzled her neck, as I pressed myself to her back. Her right hand reached into my hair. I held her left hand, so I could admire the symbol of my devotion on her finger.

"You're going to make a beautiful bride."

She tightened her grip on my hair.

"This time, for the right reasons."

Naomi had married when she was young and divorced several years later, which was likely why she wasn't attached to her last name. Coming of age in a traditional home, she was expected to marry and have children. She'd done the marrying part and spent years teaching music. She found her true calling by starting Open Door Ministries.

She turned and slid her arms around my neck. I wrapped mine around her waist and pulled her as close as I could while I kissed her. The hot water poured over us, and I rubbed my lips over the simple dove image on her shoulder.

"I promise, unless you want to renew these vows twenty years from now, it's the last time you'll ever have to do it."

She pulled back and looked at me. Her fingers began to travel over my arms. Some of the tattoos she'd never seen.

"Halleluiah to that. I can tell you've been spending a lot of time with Roman. Turn around so I can get a better look."

It hadn't escaped my notice that she'd been eyeing my ink, likely catching glimpses of my body while we made love. Something told me she hadn't noticed the full detail in the dim fire and lamplight. When I turned, I heard her audible gasp.

"Oh my God, Rhebekka. This is stunning."

"Roman is an unbelievable artist. I started this right after...well."

She kissed both sides of my back, giving equal treatment to the angel and the demon that resided on my skin. I felt her fingertips trace the outlines of the demon's wing. I wondered when she'd see the intricate script woven there.

"You have the twenty-third Psalm around this."

"I do. Keep looking, my love. You might see something else."

It was obvious when she found what I was referring to. It wasn't her fingers that traced the scripture outlining the angel's wing. Her lips caressed my skin before she uttered each verse with care.

"Love is patient and kind; love does not envy or boast; it is not arrogant or rude. It does not insist on its own way; it is not irritable or resentful; it does not rejoice at wrongdoing but rejoices with the truth. Love bears all things, believes all things, hopes all things, endures all things. Love never ends."

Naomi turned me, then pressed in close and kissed my chest near my heart, where the skin was raised. "You have my name branded on your skin."

"You were branded into my heart years ago. I wanted a permanent reminder of the only woman I'd ever love." I turned and held her face in my hands. "You are the only woman who ever saw me. All of me. The sinner"—I kissed her left eye—"and the saint." I let my lips linger gently on her right eye. "You, Naomi. You saw all of me."

"But you had that done after we were apart." Her brow was drawn.

"We were always together here." I placed my hand over my heart. "No one touched that. You were the first person to peel away every one of my masks to find the real Rhebekka. You were also the last."

We stayed in the shower until the water grew cool, our tears mixing and mingling with grapefruit-scented body wash until all of the sorrow of the past swirled down the drain. I couldn't get back those years we'd been apart and refused to lose a second more. I pulled Naomi from the glass and tile enclosure. Once she was wrapped in a plush towel, I kissed her again and held her hand bearing my ring to my lips. I was so in love, and I had things to show her that I hoped would demonstrate the person I'd become.

We dressed and headed downstairs, where I could introduce her to the space I'd created to spread the word about God's grace. I watched her eyes roam over the wooden stage. I'd chosen this space because of how much it reminded me of the place where I'd found my own redemption. Naomi's sanctuary was different than mine, though I'd worked hard to recreate the atmosphere where I'd experienced the grace I felt so undeserving of.

"This place is extraordinary, Rhebekka."

I took a deep breath of relief. I watched Naomi touch every chair, before she stepped up onto the stage and picked up one of the guitars I kept there.

"How are the acoustics?"

"Well, this place used to be an old theater, so not bad. I enhanced it a bit, added a few things to project and reflect the sound. Try it out. Play for me." I loved to see her dimples appear. Everything about her was beautiful. My heart pounded every time the light caught her ring. She started to play, and I pulled my phone out and snapped a photo. I'd recorded numerous videos of her in the past and watched them obsessively since we'd parted. I was captivated by her voice and found myself completely lost as she sang.

I watched her pace and sway around the antique wooden stage. It wasn't hard to envision her sharing her words of grace and love with my congregation. More than that, I could picture a lifetime with her. The thought brought a peace to me that I hadn't experienced in a very long time. When she'd quietly ended the hymn, I clapped with appreciation and watched her take a slight bow with a smile.

"The sound in here is great and, as always,"—she held up my guitar—"your instruments are superb."

"Want to see the rest of the place? The kids will be here around

104

three thirty."

"How many kids?"

"There are about seven teenagers who come in for two hours, sometimes longer, depending on what we have planned. Do you remember Daniel?"

"Ellie's geek?"

"That's him. Let me show you something he created for me." I held out my hand to her and was pleased when she put hers in mine. In the video room, I put a set of headgear on her and booted up ArchAngel.

"Holy shit, Rhebekka. Warn a girl, would you? This is so cool!"

"Daniel is a genius when it comes to programming. The kids have to earn the armor."

Naomi pulled off the headgear and walked over to yank me into a passionate kiss.

"You are so amazing. Did you dream this up?"

"I did. I was trying to come up with a way to incorporate the things their generation thrives on with what I wanted to accomplish. I brought you back here for another reason. Hang on."

I connected the screen to my phone and called Ellie. Naomi moved in front of me and pulled my arms around her. We stared at the call screen displaying a photo of Ellie in full Regal Crimson costume. Within seconds, a live video chat connected, and my sister smiled back at us.

"Hey, you two, how are things? I didn't think you'd be out of bed yet."

Naomi tilted her head and shook a finger at my sister. "Behave."

I loved the relationship between the two women I cared about most.

"Hey, little sparrow. We're fantastic, and vertical because I have kids coming here in about two hours. But..." I paused to build suspense. "We have news."

Ellie bounced up and down. "She convinced you to come to Pittsburgh?"

I didn't want to break her heart, but I was sure the news I was going to share would soften the blow. "I asked this beautiful woman to marry a fool like me, and she said—"

"Yes!" Naomi held her hand up and displayed the ring.

Ellie's hands went to her mouth before she started jumping up and down. She made the screen bounce all over, and her squeals were deafening. "Oh my God, you guys, it's about fucking time!"

Naomi bent forward and laughed. "Amen."

"I wish I were there to celebrate with you. Honestly, Bek, I was worried you didn't have the guts. I guess calling Naomi was one of my better ideas, if I do say so myself." Ellie buffed her nails on her chest.

I shook my head at her and kissed the back of Naomi's head. "I won't disagree with your diabolical plans, but don't think I don't know you two have been in cahoots for a long time."

Ellie put a hand on her hip. "A long damn time, trust me. I knew how you felt about her. I just needed you to get out of your own fucking way. God, you are so stubborn. Be glad you have a saint for a fiancée."

I pulled Naomi closer. "I won't disagree. Now, look at your schedule, because it's your tour dates that will likely screw with any plans we make. I intend to do this soon, like within two months, no longer."

I felt Naomi nod as she spoke. "I'd do it tomorrow if we could get you here. I've been waiting a long time to get Rhebekka this far. I'm not giving her any wiggle room to back out before we get to the altar. Besides, my Colorado driver's license runs out this year. If I'm doing an address and name change, we can kill two birds with one stone."

Naomi stretched an arm up so that it cupped the back of my neck. I melted into her touch, even as I laughed at her task combination skills. Ellie had her hand over her heart, with tears glistening in her eyes.

"Seriously you two, if there ever was an answered prayer, it's the one I've been asking for more times than I can count. Let my sister be happy, and let it be because Naomi will be my sister-in-law. I'm so completely over the moon for you two. I'm finding the first date I have an opening. Hell, I'll cancel an event if I have to, because you two are getting hitched pronto!"

I gave my sister a big thumbs up. "And with that, your future sister-in-law and I have a few more calls to make before my kids get here. Call me when you can."

Ellie blew us several kisses. "Will do. I love you guys."

When the screen went blank, I turned Naomi around and picked her up until she slid her legs around my waist. "Anyone you want to call with the news?"

"A few friends and Ashley. I'm sure she'll want to make the trip. I assume you want to do this here? I don't care where we have it, but small. Small and intimate, my love. I've shared you with the masses for years."

"I agree, close friends and family. Hell, I wouldn't care if it was just the two of us, but that would likely lead to a need for a lot of hospitalization. Trust me, Ellie can throw a hell of a punch."

"Okay, enough of this for now. We'll make my calls later. We have your kids to get ready for. What are you going to tell them?"

"Well, they'll be pretty surprised, for sure. I've never hidden my sexuality with any of my congregation. If I want them to know there isn't anything wrong with it, then I'm not going to make it weird for them. I'll introduce you, confess that I've been an idiot for too long, and by the grace of God, you've forgiven me. Grateful isn't a strong enough word to describe how I feel about the fact you didn't give up on me." I held her and thanked God for answering Ellie's prayer and mine.

***

Introducing Naomi to the kids went smoothly. She could immediately put anyone she met at ease. The kids knew me well and didn't hesitate to question why they'd never heard of Naomi. I sat on the edge of a table, dangling my feet, with her at my side. "I've loved her for a long time but didn't think I deserved her, because of a monster mistake I made."

Naomi rubbed my arm and threaded her fingers in with mine.

"On top of her bad decision, she wouldn't forgive herself. She did hurt me, but I forgave her the way God forgives all of us. She didn't repeat that mistake."

Listening to her gently use our situation to show God's love and forgiveness was just one more example of what a wonderful pastor she was. Talking about it still wasn't easy. It made my heart bleed over the pain I'd caused her. With her hand in mine, I had the strength to endure anything.

"I also wouldn't make the mistake of walking away from her again. I did what I should have done a long time ago." I held her diamond-clad hand up to the broad grins and claps of my young flock. From the surprising joy I saw in their faces, I knew they'd already accepted her as part of my life. The minute she dropped my hand and pointed to their schoolbooks, they also accepted her as a leader.

"Okay, show and tell is over. Get that homework done so we can go play ArchAngel. Let's see how good you guys are."

Backpacks were emptied and books slapped open, as they enthusiastically got to work. With the promise of ArchAngel, their acquiescence was easy. Naomi grinned with a raised eyebrow in my direction.

I leaned over and whispered in her ear. "Lion tamer. And the promise of ArchAngel? You are brilliant."

"It never hurts to offer a little incentive. It seemed to work on you."

"That it did, that it did."

Chapter Sixteen

WE SPENT THE NEXT three weeks reacquainting ourselves. Not a day went by when I didn't kick my own ass for the time we'd missed. It was comforting to see her coffee cup beside mine in the morning and the refrigerator containing more than a six-pack of Brimstone Stout and a takeout dish from Karmen's. Naomi flowed into my life like rain on parched earth. I soaked her in.

Her melodious voice called me from the other room. "Breakfast is ready."

"Coming." I ran a hand through my damp hair and tucked my T-shirt into my jeans. She placed a plated Belgian waffle topped with strawberry preserves on the bar, and I stopped to show my appreciation. When I bent her back during the kiss, she was forced to wrap her arms around me or fall down. "Good morning." I pecked her on the nose.

"Good morning to you, too. What was that for?" She steadied herself against the counter and fanned her reddened face.

"Expect me to surprise you for the rest of your life, as many times as I can, because I can."

"Is that so?" She moved around a kitchen that was no longer mine, but hers. Naomi's ability to turn simple ingredients into a gourmet meal was nothing short of miraculous. She set a mug in front of me and kissed my lips, before straddling my lap to bring us face to face. She moved the plate so she could cut a piece of waffle and feed it to me. Holding her in my arms, I was completely filled with love. I watched her eat a bite and sigh in obvious pleasure.

Every small joy she experienced here with me increased my appreciation for how brave she'd been to break through my stubborn walls. I gathered her hair off her shoulders and held it back out of the way.

"Karmen makes the most incredible preserves. The strawberries are grown on a U-pick farm over in the next county. Last year, we took the kids over for an outing. They brought some of their younger siblings, and I swear they ate more berries than they ever put in their baskets.

Everyone came home with red-stained fingers and full bellies."

Naomi swallowed another bite, and I noticed a small drizzle at the corner of her mouth. With my index finger, I spread it across her lips and watched her shiver. I kissed the preserves off her lips and smiled against them.

"I love you so much."

She tightened her hold on me. "I love you, too."

***

After breakfast, there was work to do on a song list for a set I'd play at The Confluence. All around me, minor changes were reminding me Naomi now shared my home. Small additions of color and texture started to make their way onto the walls and surfaces. A box of her personal things had arrived. Looking at those photos of us could have pained me, but they just reminded me of how she'd known we were meant to be together. More of her belongings from Durango would follow in a moving truck I'd arranged.

Mementos sat around our home, paying tribute to the fact she'd loved me through it all and had photographic proof. I picked up one of the frames with a picture of us singing at one of her casual church gatherings. My eyes were glued to her face. Her eyes were closed, lost in the song. I put the picture back and moved to the couch.

I was scheduled to play at Redemption's Road for Saturday night's entertainment. Naomi had become my most loyal groupie, and I wanted her to do more than sit on the sidelines. As far as I was concerned, she'd done that for far too long. Tank had a suggestion box near the cash register, with more than one request for someone to sing while I played. I wrote down a few of Naomi's favorite songs. There was little doubt my selections would draw her to the stage with me. I picked up my guitar and began to strum a few bars to test my theory. Sounds from the kitchen told me she was in there cleaning up. As soon as I made it to the chorus, she sat down beside me and began harmonizing through each verse. I leaned over to kiss her and remind her how beautiful her voice was.

"I've missed singing with you."

Her hand slid into mine, while her other hand caressed my cheek. "I know what you mean. You can still sing with the best of them, retired from Regal Crimson or not."

My phone rang, and I squinted at the screen. *This can't be good.*

"Sheriff, how can I help you?"

"I'm calling to see if you can do some organization for pastoral care."

A call from my friend Chance was always welcome, but I could hear the tension in her voice. "Chance, what's wrong?" I hit the speakerphone icon, so that Naomi could hear the conversation.

"We've had a student pass away. Xander Gardener overdosed yesterday. We got word from his parents an hour ago."

"Oh, no. Chance, I am so sorry. I'll do whatever you need. I'll make calls and get in contact with the community grief counselors and pastors. I assume you're working with the principal. Do you want us to come to the school or arrange something for the next few days?"

I grabbed the notebook I'd been writing my song selections in and started to take notes. I could hear the distress in her voice.

"This one is going to be difficult for everyone. There's nothing we'll formally be able to do today, but we can set up a general assembly for tomorrow morning. After that, we'd like to offer an area for counseling with whomever you can bring. Xander was popular, a star athlete, and was on the student council. No matter how we try to prevent it, this is becoming part of our everyday reality. The school is keeping Narcan at the nurse's office. They've had to use it on more than one occasion. The opioid epidemic gets worse every day, and I've been working with the school to develop action plans. Unfortunately, they won't help Xander."

My heart dropped at the mention of Xander's name. His grandmother worked with Victoria at the foodbank. He'd even come in a few times to help when they'd received a truckload of potatoes or some other heavy item the older women were unable to handle.

"I'll get to work making the notifications."

"Let me give you some numbers, in case you need to touch base and I'm out of cell service."

When I hung up, I let my head fall back on the couch. *Lord stay close. I'll need you.*

Naomi reached for my hand, and we prayed together. I was incredibly grateful to have her by my side.

***

After a few hours, I'd managed to reach six pastors who promised to call the other religious leaders I didn't have direct contact with. It wouldn't be easy trying to work together. As accepted as I was with many of the ministers on the mountain, the lowland pastors tended to be more conservative and less forward thinking. There was only one high school in the county, so every congregation likely had someone who knew Xander or his family. Naomi and I worked on a few remarks for what I'd say when we met with my after-school group. They'd be coming through the door in minutes. Seven teenagers would be looking to me for comfort and explanation.

Naomi and I met the red-eyed, solemn group at the door and took the time to hold each of them tightly. Holly, a sixteen-year-old, sobbed uncontrollably. Xander was her brother's best friend. Ian was away at college, and they'd called him to deliver the bad news. Naomi gathered her into her arms and led her to one of the couches. When everyone was inside, it was time to talk with them.

"First, I want you to know that Naomi and I are here for you, as long as it takes. I knew Xander and I've worked closely with his grandmother for years. Over the next few days, the pain you're feeling won't get better. It's likely to get worse with the intense focus of the school assembly and his memorial. Nothing that you feel is wrong. What I don't want to do, and won't do, is preach to you. Each of you knows that isn't my style. I won't have all the answers that will suddenly bring everything into clarity. What we can do is offer you God's love and whatever comfort you need." I made eye contact with each and every one of them. "Is there anything we can help you with?"

Over the next few hours, the kids asked questions about death and what happens. Where would Xander's soul go? Why doesn't God stop bad things from happening? Beyond grateful for Naomi's many years of pastoral care, I was comforted watching her put the vulnerable teenagers at ease. The answers they wanted weren't always easy to hear.

Tension built in my shoulders. Without asking, Naomi began to rub my neck when the kids started working on their homework.

"I'm so grateful for you."

"This is a tough one. Believe it or not, you're handling it beautifully, Rhebekka. They trust you. That's a difficult feat when it comes to teenagers. It would be nice to say they'll find some greater message in this. The reality is it hurts. They've lost a friend, and there's no rhyme or reason for it other than poor choices with devastating consequences. Your own life experiences will help you explain it to them. The best that you can hope for is that you keep even one of them from trying a drug that will kill them."

A moment of clarity came over me. I realized that the glass I'd crawled through on my journey was so that, in this moment of tragedy, I could tell them they would survive this and all the other tribulations to come in the future. I looked over my tiny, brokenhearted, adolescent flock. They needed to love and respect themselves enough to walk away from the things that would hurt them. Maybe it was my example that could help them avoid the same fate as Xander.

"Hey guys, can I get you all to head into the sanctuary?"

Naomi put her hand in mine. Together, we followed my seven charges, who chose their favorite landing spots. I took the stage and put my guitar around my neck, while sitting down on the edge of the stage. Naomi sat beside me with a small keyboard in her lap. I absent-mindedly played, as I opened myself up in a way I'd never done with them before.

"Years ago, I was very different from the woman you see before you now. I was anything but a pastor."

For the next hour, I laid bare most of my former life. I left out the part about being the lead singer in Regal Crimson. I didn't want to tie Bek McNally into my new life. I'd always told them the truth, and their trust allowed me the freedom to be ambiguous when it came to how big a rock star I'd been. I knew they'd have more questions. Someday, when they met my sister, they'd figure it out on their own.

"Naomi can tell you, when I met her, I was as close to rock bottom as I could be. She offered me redemption through God's grace. I wasn't ready to see the path through and nearly lost it all by chasing that high." I felt her hand at the small of my back. She'd moved closer at some point in my confession. That silent support was just one of the many reasons I'd fallen in love with her.

Amanda stood and pushed her hands into her jean pockets. "Did you ever overdose?"

I shook my head. "Fortunately, no. I probably should have. I'm not going to lie to you and say I had it under control. It had more to do with luck and the people I'd hired to look after me. More than one of my security guards pulled pills out of my hand or physically removed me from danger. There are nights I don't remember how I got home. If I didn't have people looking out for me, regardless of my threats to fire them, I might be on one of those dead rock star shows. There were people who believed in me when I didn't. Eventually, I found the one person who could offer me something drugs couldn't."

Amanda looked puzzled.

"A reason to stop." I kissed Naomi's hand. I started singing "She Talks to Angels," from The Black Crowes.

I let the music take me back to those feelings of desperation. Back to a time when, no matter how hard I flailed trying to swim to the surface, the weights tied to my ankles dragged me back. Complete exhaustion had overcome me. I'd stopped struggling and let the cold numbness take over and pull me to the bottom. I looked up to the surface one more time and saw Naomi with her hand out, ready to pull me out of the water. She'd saved me from myself. Like a fool, I later let a stranger coax me to dive back into that black water. That relapse had nearly cost me the love of my life.

Every chord melted it all away, like an icicle in the bright sunshine. All I had to do was close my eyes and hear Naomi's sweet harmony to realize it was all behind me. No one knew the deplorable person I'd been, not even Ellie.

When I finished the song, my kids were sitting completely still. I'd never sung anything to them that wasn't out of a hymnal. I knew, for the first time, they could truly see the musician in me and not just the pastor who offered them a path to find their faith. A slow clap started, then a thunderous stomping on the tongue and groove floor. The small sanctuary filled with enthusiastic appreciation. Their applause lifted my spirits and reminded me there was a time when the joy of singing outside of church was something I'd looked forward to.

"That was awesome. How come you've never done that with us before?" Alton asked.

I laid my guitar beside me. I rested my elbows on my thighs and scrubbed my hands down my face, before I looked at them.

"Years ago, I left my old life behind." I turned to look at Naomi. "At least most of it. I had to decide which was more important, living only for myself, or for something much greater than me." With Naomi's hand in mine, I raised them. "I had an amazing example of what was possible if I used my gifts in a way that helped others to find their faith. I've never regretted my decision. In the end, the blessings that came back to me have been a hundredfold."

Holly fidgeted nervously in her seat. "Pastor Rhebekka?"

"Yes, Holly?"

"Do you think Xander went to heaven?"

I walked over to the frail girl and knelt before her, taking her hands in mine. "I had the chance to meet Xander on more than one occasion. I'm not God, so it's not my place to stand in judgment of him. Xander wasn't evil. He made a mistake. I, for one, am very grateful the God I serve is one of love and forgiveness. In my heart, I believe Xander is in heaven."

I looked at each and every one of the young minds and hearts I was trying to reach. I hoped I was getting through to them and offering them the comfort they needed. Turning my head, I saw unshed tears glimmering in Naomi's eyes. I hoped they were tears of pride. The smile she gave me relieved all my fears. "Bring it in, everyone."

The kids joined me in a circle, our arms around each other as we prayed.

CJ Murphy

THE REST OF THE week, the other pastors and I offered grievance counseling to Xander's fellow students and teachers. His funeral on Saturday morning was a large affair. My friend and fellow pastor, Pegi May, presided. Naomi and I stood behind my tender flock of Xander's classmates and tried to support them. I listened to Pegi offer words of comfort. She urged those in attendance not to be angry at him but to vow to set an example for others. She asked that they do things that would honor his memory in positive ways.

When the service broke up, I gathered the kids off to the side with their parents.

"I'd like us to do something in Xander's memory, if you're up to it. Next month, we'll be doing a major food drive and distribution at the food bank where his grandmother volunteers. Xander used to help out occasionally. I'm telling you now, so you can look at your schedules and put it on your calendar if you want to participate. I'll give you details at our next after-school meeting." My heart was breaking for them. I watched as Holly held onto her brother, Ian. I still considered him one of mine, even though he was now in college.

"Ian, you're welcome to join us if you can. I'd be proud to have you."

He nodded and pulled Holly closer. I knew in my heart, none of them were invisible in the Father's eyes. Naomi pulled closer to my side, and I opened my Bible to Isaiah 43. "Do not fear, for I have redeemed you; I have summoned you by name; you are mine. Since you are precious and honored in my sight, and because I love you…" We prayed together, before each of them made their way back into the world. I hoped I'd sent them off with something to cling to. I felt Naomi's arm tighten on my waist.

"You're so good with them. Don't ever think you aren't making a difference. You get to those kids on a level I've rarely seen."

I kissed her temple and the scent of coffee beans and vanilla both calmed and excited me. "I had a very good example to follow."

She chuckled and pinched my side as we walked. "I never had a relationship with the youth the way you do. I had a few kids, but you reach them on an elemental level. You may be twenty years their senior, but you see things through their eyes."

"Probably because I was never a kid when I was their age. I was already thrown into adulthood by the time I was thirteen."

Naomi nodded. "That might be part of it. The rest is purely your ability to relate."

I turned and looked at the freshly dug grave where the body of a promising young man would return to dust. "That could have been me."

I heard her quick intake of breath and felt her clutch me tighter.

"It could have been."

Sheriff Chance Fitzsimmons approached us. "Rhebekka, I'd like to talk to you two if I could."

"We'd be happy to. Why don't you stop by our place? Naomi makes killer coffee, and it will offer us some privacy."

"Excellent. Twenty minutes be all right? I need to check in with my office."

"The steps at the bottom of my loft are unlocked. Come on up when you're ready."

The sheriff and her dog strode back to her vehicle, as I looked to Naomi.

Naomi's brows knit together. "Wonder what that's all about?"

"I'd say we'll find out in twenty minutes."

Chapter Eighteen

SHERIFF FITZSIMMONS AND HER K9, Zeus, sat in our dining area. Naomi offered her a sandwich and coffee, since it was lunchtime.

"Sorry for the short notice on speaking with you. Thank you for the coffee."

I waved off her apology. "Not a problem, Chance. Now, what can we help you with?"

"I can't talk about the specifics of Xander's case, but I have concerns he won't be our last funeral. Every county around us is experiencing issues with an influx of heavy drug trafficking, and we aren't exempt. If you remember, during Run For It last year, we had several overdoses in a single day. Though we made some major arrests, I'm a believer in the old saying that an ounce of prevention costs less than a pound of cure."

She wasn't the only one who believed that. I nodded. "What do you want to do?"

"I watched you with those kids today. That's not the first time I've seen you connect with the younger generation on a different level. They trust you, regardless of your profession, or maybe because of it. All I know is, in my law enforcement experience, it's rare to find someone who connects the way you do. I think that has a lot to do with your background. What I'm proposing is a community task force to try and prevent what happened to Xander from becoming a regular occurrence."

The dull thud in my head that had become a constant companion over the past few days roared back into a painful pulse. I'd attended enough funerals for friends and acquaintances over the years. I was in agreement with her about trying to get ahead of the problem. "Okay, how do you want to proceed?"

Naomi offered a suggestion. "If we had more assistance, we could expand the after-school program. Maybe, one day a week, we could meet in a larger forum? There are subject matter experts out there in community awareness and prevention we could tap into."

Chance nodded. "I know someone like that. Kathleen Redar is the fire chief in one of West Virginia's southern municipalities. Her city has been devastated by epidemic drug trafficking and dependence. I'll give her a call and see what she suggests. Maybe she can come up here for a community forum and help us set up a task force to better combat this."

"We also have to offer alternatives and solutions." I knew this from my own experience and was determined we'd get it right. "We can talk a problem to death and never see any action. This can't be one of those situations. Our kid's lives are on the line, and there are those who will prey on their vulnerability and need for acceptance. Someone will try to profit by selling the escape drugs appear to offer. What comes along with those dealers is more violent crime. You've felt the reach as much as anyone."

Chance's knowing eyes met mine. She explained for Naomi. "That's what happened when I was shot at and Jax's uncle was kidnapped. One of our local dealers almost killed Jax and her vet tech. It's one of the major platforms I'm running on in my reelection bid."

"I can tell you that my vote is yours, Chance. I remember visiting her and Lindsey in the hospital after it happened. It shook us all."

"I realize you started a new life when you came to live here. You've been an incredible asset to the community. With your experiences on both sides of this issue and what you've seen in our community, you are uniquely qualified to help with this. It's why I called you when it first happened. Momma Dee suggested I come and talk to you after several in-depth conversations with Holly about how you helped your group deal with Xander's death. Holly is on the basketball team Dee coaches. You've got a gift, Rhebekka. That gift and your life experiences give you particular insight on the direction we need to go. Naomi, I appreciate all you've done to help our community through this ordeal. I'd be honored if the two of you would help me develop and implement a youth plan."

Naomi squeezed my arm, giving me her permission to speak for both of us. "Whatever you need, Sheriff. We're at your disposal."

***

After the sheriff left, Naomi and I had a few quiet hours before we were supposed to head to the brewery. Both of us felt equally drained by the funeral and uplifted by the prospect of the community-based prevention efforts.

"You and the sheriff seem to know each other pretty well."

"We do. I was the officiant at her wedding. Her wife is a veterinarian who left decades ago, then came back to take over her uncle's practice. They apparently never fell out of love. I'll introduce you sometime. Occasionally, they come to hear me play at The Purple Fiddle or The Confluence. They've even been to a few services over the years."

"Imagine that. Being apart for years and still loving each other. Sounds a bit familiar, doesn't it?"

I grinned at her. I couldn't disagree.

"Nice segue. Chance also got me involved in the county's disaster-relief efforts. I offer pastoral care to her search-and-rescue group during tragic incidents. I'm not a formal chaplain but someone they can call in times of need, for the family or for the rescuers. I've taken several critical-incident, stress-debriefing classes to be able to help them deal with difficult circumstances. Sometimes I work with the other disaster agencies, if they have a fire and the family needs temporary lodging."

The crooked grin on Naomi's face slightly lifted one corner of her mouth. "You are a woman of many facets, each and every one more revealing than the next."

"Is that so?"

Naomi moved into my arms. "It is, and I'd like to explore the one that kisses me senseless."

I put her hand in mine and led her to our bedroom. "A request I'm happy to fulfill."

***

Later that evening, Karmen picked us up and took us with her to Redemption's Road. The place was buzzing when we got there. I stood mesmerized, as my fiancée made her way around the room. She'd quickly ingratiated herself with the locals, and I'd begun to think they liked her more than me. That was okay, I liked her more than me too. Our wedding was set for the twenty-fourth of May. We'd decided this was where we'd hold our reception. Ellie had threatened to cancel a tour date to make it happen sooner. Naomi nixed that idea. She didn't want my sister to go right back on the road the next day. If we waited until May, Ellie would have well over a month before the big anniversary gig in Pittsburgh.

"Can I get two Brimstones?" I stood at the end of the bar looking over the people milling about.

Tank set two Mason jars in front of me. "Looks like it's going to be a good crowd for your show."

"I can still pack 'em in occasionally."

Tank chuckled. "If they only knew."

I leaned back and looked toward the stage. "Were you able to set that up?"

"I did. There's a mic and stand ready to go. Are you actually going to sing?"

I grinned and raised my eyebrows. "Not exactly. I'm putting a five down that I can get Naomi to."

Tank rubbed her hands together. "I'll take that action. She's a pretty tough cookie."

I picked up the drinks. "I have my ways."

"What? You're going to get naked?"

Senna was sitting at the bar and turned her head so fast, she nearly fell off the bench. "You're going to get naked?"

"Very funny, you two. Real comedians. Nobody's getting naked, at least not in public." I sipped my beer and walked back into the performance room. Naomi took her glass, as I made my way to the stage. Grandpa's Gibson sat waiting, as did the 1965 Martin D-18 I'd found in a secondhand store in Tacoma, Washington, years before. The pick guard was heavily worn and the finish nearly gone where the neck and the body met. I'd had this dream that the strings and the wood could tell me the stories of its travels and the life it had led. That never happened, but I knew that night Martin and the woman I loved were going to make some beautiful music.

I went through my tuning routine and adjusted everything around me, before I started into my first instrumental offering. A few lines of the song reached inside my body and pulled at the strings of my heart. I'd designed the warm-up for getting my future wife up on stage with me. I knew she'd recognize the tune quickly.

"Evening everyone. Welcome to The Confluence here at Redemption's Road. I'm Rhebekka Deklan, the house musician." I waggled my hand back and forth. "Sort of. Feel free to get up and dance or work on your moves from the comfort of your chair. Tank, there at the bar, will serve cold brews while I do a little picking." I grinned at Naomi, who was shaking her head at me. "I'm going to start off with one I hope you'll enjoy from a true master of the road."

The claps quieted down, as the first few chords spread out into the room. I could see the smiles and head bobs throughout the crowd. Naomi swayed off to the side. By the time I made it to the chorus, several people were dancing, and more were singing the lyrics to my instrumental version. Three songs later, I was ready for a small break and a fresh beer.

Naomi moved to my side. "Nice selection. I see you've been into my playlist again."

I pointed to my chest. "Who me?" We liked the same music, with a few exceptions. "Not just yours. Our playlists are eerily similar."

"That's true. What's up next?"

I raised a wicked eyebrow at her. "You'll see." I turned back to the crowd after a few drinks from my beer. "Okay everyone, now I'm going to switch over to one of my lovely fiancée's favorites. Most of you know that I'm the pastor down at House of the Rising Son. What you don't know is that the gorgeous creature who agreed to marry a shmuck like me is also a pastor and an incredible musician in her own right."

I slipped my glass slide on over my finger. "One of Naomi's favorite songs is by an artist who reminds me very much of her. For that matter, the words to the song remind me of us."

Naomi's head shook slowly from side to side. She started mouthing the words, and I nodded in the direction of the mic. She declined, while I continued to play. She rolled her shoulders. The music was getting to her, exactly as I planned. When she walked across the stage and slipped the Martin's strap over her head, I knew I had her.

She leaned in close and fished in my back pocket for my spare pick. "You're such a shit, my love. Good thing you're so irresistible."

Karmen moved to put the mic in front of her. I caught Naomi's eye and mouthed *I love you,* as we started into the chorus. Her voice had always reminded me of Bonnie Raitt's, like gravel washed in warm whiskey. Years before, we'd made an incredible vocal team. With hard lessons learned, we were even better. Playing together felt magical. When we finished our first number, I didn't give her even a second to think. I moved into another of her favorites that Bonnie did, "Angel from Montgomery." The moment her voice started into the bluesy chorus, the hair on the back of my neck stood up. The urge to join her in quiet harmony was too overwhelming. I couldn't have stopped myself if I'd tried. I was grateful I didn't have a mic. Even without anything to amplify my voice, our audience heard me. My voice was powerful, and there were no other instruments to mute the sound as it mingled with Naomi's.

The tables had turned. Together, we rolled through each movement and verse. I heard the whistle from the front row and knew it had to belong to Karmen. Her joy at hearing me sing was unmistakable. Even Tank moved from behind the bar and into the main room. This crowd had never heard me utter a single vocal line outside the church. Put me beside Naomi, and it was as natural as breathing. As we brought the song to its close, there were a few seconds when I drew out the final notes without vocal accompaniment. The house erupted in loud appreciation, and I pointed to the love of my life.

"Naomi Layman, everybody."

She dipped her head in appreciation for the applause before she pointed to me. "Yes, ladies and gentlemen, she does sing! Rhebekka Deklan."

The room pulsed from the claps and stomps that echoed off the walls. I finally waved for them to sit down. "Thank you all. What can I say? She brings out the very best of me."

Naomi took over. "Every once in a while, you find a song that fits someone as if it was written about them. That's what this song is to me. The lyrics, written by an incredible artist, peel back the curtain just a little on how I feel about Rhebekka. Few of you will ever see all she is. I'm grateful I've seen so many sides of her."

A snicker went through the crowd, and she pointed her finger at them. "Behave. Although trust me, that side of her is pretty spectacular."

The crowd laughed, and my blush was strong enough to melt the snow outside. The woman was so good at leading a room right where she wanted them to be.

Naomi leaned over and touched my cheek. "Honestly, folks. I know how very lucky I am. I get to see all of her true colors." Naomi touched my cheek.

The lead-in was beautiful. Had she not chosen the path of ministry, Naomi could have been an incredible performer. Her song choice cut deep. I was willing to follow her anywhere. What she saw in me was so much more than I believed possible. As we played, each word wrapped around my healing heart. She was a master at being a balm for the soul, my soul in particular.

After the week we'd experienced, I wanted to cancel the night's performance. I couldn't imagine putting in the needed energy to entertain. With the intimate knowledge Naomi had of every part of me, she encouraged me to continue. It wouldn't be the first time she'd watched the neurosis of my grief. Had she envisioned me prowling around our loft, playing the Gibson until I expelled every soul-crushing emotion? Instead of playing to four walls that gave no feedback, she wanted me to share my gift, my grief, with those who were also grieving.

When we finished two more songs, I called for a break and spotted Franklin in the crowd. I needed a favor and hoped he'd help me out. Naomi was talking with Karmen. I touched her lower back and leaned in. "I'm going to get us a few more beers. Want anything else?"

"More of what I witnessed tonight."

I kissed her on the forehead. "We'll see."

She held my hand a moment longer and mouthed *I love you*. There was no doubt about it, and I was the most fortunate person on the planet because she did.

On my way to the bar, there were enough pats on the back and hugs to bruise me. I'd never intended to sing with my sets. When I'd been the lead for Regal Crimson, Ellie had added the harmony. We'd produced some memorable offerings to the throngs. Singing with Naomi was completely different, in every way. I relished my role in providing the harmony, letting her draw me along, exactly as she had in our relationship. I found Franklin and pulled him aside.

He was glowing. "Rhebekka, that was incredible."

"Isn't she though?"

He rolled his eyes at me. "Not quite what I meant, but yes she is. What can I do for you?"

"I know it's a lot to ask, but I want to dance with her to something specific. Do you think you can handle it?"

"I'll try. What is it?"

Franklin wiped his hands down the front of his jeans after hearing my explanation. I could tell he was nervous. Franklin needed confidence in front of a crowd. If he truly was to be a pastor, he needed experience. The people in the audience were his friends and wanted nothing more than to be entertained. His ability to deliver a spiritual message had to be paired with the ability to connect to the people. After a few more words of encouragement, and his eagerness to play my Gibson, he agreed.

I let a cheesy grin slip past my lips, as I stood at the bar and signaled for Tank. She set two Brimstones and a five-dollar bill in front of me while shaking her head.

"Naomi really does have magical powers."

I pushed the money into my pocket, before I sipped my beer and nodded in agreement. "That woman has the power to get me to do many things I never thought I would."

Tank shook her finger at me. "You're just whipped. Don't worry, it's a good thing. I wish someone would see me the way she does you.

Anyway, it's a good night. I've already had to change out the kegs twice."

If you'd only open your eyes, you'd see there already is someone who sees you that way. "Anyone we need to find rides for?"

"I'm keeping an eye on a few. Senna's going to have a hell of a headache tomorrow. I know she's walking home. I've got someone who's going to help make sure she gets to her place. Not sure what's wrong, but she's hitting it pretty hard."

Senna was parked up against the fireplace on the wide, stone hearth. Her eyes were shut, and she held tightly to a bottle of water. I delivered Naomi's beer before finding a spot beside Senna. I touched her hand.

"Rough night?"

She pinched the bridge of her nose. "Self-inflicted, though I've stopped now."

I looked around the room and saw Karmen still talking with Naomi. "Would this have anything to do with a mocha-skinned woman with chocolate-brown eyes, who can cook like nobody's business?"

Senna twisted the cap off the water bottle and drained the last of it. I saw her lock on Karmen's form.

"Could be."

"I see tonight's conversation is going to be all about practicing the principle of brevity. So, I'll sum up what I think. Karmen's been waiting on Tank longer than you've lived here. If you want something, tell her. Stop waiting on Karmen to figure it out. Yes, you might get your heart broken. It's a gamble. Weigh the cost, then step forward, or step away for the sake of your own survival."

I patted her on the shoulder and got up without waiting for her to answer. This was something she'd need to figure out on her own. No matter what she decided, there might very well be pain involved. I nodded to Franklin, letting him know I was going back in. Two more songs from my set, and he'd come and take over for one.

Back on stage, Naomi joined me. She took another sip of her fresh beer. The leftover froth on her upper lip was doing wonderful things to me. She wiped it away, grinning.

"What are you up to?"

"I guess you'll have to wait and see. You ready to start again? I promise, everything I have planned is something you know the words to."

"I'm trusting you."

"I'll always be worthy of it." I watched those blue eyes twinkle, as she settled her guitar strap. With the Gibson on my thigh, I attached my capo to the first fret. I strummed a C chord, then an E minor, F, and a G, before I repeated the notes. The little smile and headshake told me she had it, and we started into *Midnight Train to Georgia*, changing the pronouns as we went. The crowd joined in with a gentle sway and a well-timed clap. We worked our way through one of the Empress of Soul's hit songs. I loved listening to the woman who'd captured my heart and refused to let me go. She'd been so patient with me and loved me through it all. We spiraled right into another of her songs, and the crowd joined us. This was the most fun I'd had playing in a very long time, and it was all because of her.

The kiss I gave her at the end caused a bombardment of applause and whistles. I signaled for Franklin. I took the mic and faced the crowd. "I've wanted to dance with this beautiful woman all night. If you all will indulge me one dance, I promise, our last song will be the audience's choice. Okay?"

The crowd clapped and whistled, as I took Naomi's hand. She gave up her seat in front of the mic to Franklin. I handed him my Gibson and took the most gorgeous woman in the world out onto the dance floor. It took her less than three notes to recognize our song. Franklin's rich, baritone was perfect. "Wonderful Tonight" hit all the buttons for me and Slowhand himself was one of my guitar heroes.

We swayed together, and I held her tightly in my arms. She rewarded me with a delicious kiss. It took everything I had not to throw her over my shoulder and walk the few blocks to our loft. I'd have gladly trudged barefoot through four feet of snow to make love with her the way we had that afternoon. It was an incredible honor and privilege to be hers. I spotted Senna looking at Karmen and encouraged her to get moving with a jerk of my head in Karmen's direction. Naomi and I watched her muster courage, as she made her way to the object of her desire.

Naomi ran her hand in my hair. "Is that a good idea?"

"I guess we'll find out." Where this would go, I wasn't sure. What I did find intriguing was the expression on Tank's face, as Senna took Karmen's hand and led her to the dance floor. I held Naomi even closer and prayed for a peaceful resolution for my friends and their unrequited love. Whatever direction the road might fork for them, I wanted it to end in love. In my own life, there was no doubt where the path would lead me. Wherever Naomi was, that was where I'd be.

Chapter Nineteen

AFTER A QUIET SUNDAY service that was heavily attended, we fellowshipped with our congregation. Close to thirty people, some regulars and some not, had joined us. With Xander's death still weighing on us all, Naomi and I crafted a sermon that would offer hope. To be able to give comfort in the face of such grief took a light touch and a great deal of prayer. Naomi had dealt with this type of incident far more times than I had, so I deferred to her experience.

When my parishioners walked out that day, they looked lighter. I hugged Holly, then Ian.

"You call me if you need anything, even to talk. Promise me that?" I was holding him tightly to me and could feel the tremble in his upper body.

"Thank you, Pastor. I promise."

Naomi and I were joined in the loft by Karmen and Tank, for our weekly after-church meal. Before the service, our resident chef had placed a beef roast with carrots and potatoes in the oven. The night before, Naomi baked a chocolate, raspberry-mousse cake for dessert.

The loft smelled like heaven itself. Tank and I left preparations to the experts. As was my Sunday routine, I pulled out the guitar and headed to the window seat. I'd been working on a few power ballads for Ellie.

The last note faded, and I looked to Tank for her critique. "Well, what did you think?"

"Can't wait to hear her sing it. You may not be in the band anymore, but you keep Regal Crimson on the charts. The Confluence's crowd was buzzing the other night. You know you won't be able to get by with only instrumental anymore. If I were you, I'd keep your partner in crime ready to go."

"The nightingale will remain happy if I have anything to say about it. Life is so much better with her here."

"She's always been so good for you. You're blessed my friend. You're aware of that, right?"

Naomi moved around the kitchen with the grace of a dancer.

"With every breath."

Tank sighed deeply. "I keep hoping, someday, I'll find my one."

"How do you know you haven't already met her?"

Tank sighed. "Ellie blew me off at the funeral, when I tried to be there for her."

I shook my head, frustrated that Tank couldn't, or wouldn't, see what was right in front of her. "What you saw as supporting her came off as trying to be something she didn't want. She needed a friend, Tank, not a lover. I've never pried into what happened between the two of you, whether it was once or more than once. The truth is, I didn't want to know and still don't. It would force me to take some side between my sister and my best friend. Instead, I tried to let the two of you work it out. Now, I'm going to throw my two cents in. Ellie is an adult, fully capable of making choices about what she does or does not want. You've been holding this torch for someone who's had at least four significant relationships since your brief affair. Doesn't that tell you something?"

I stopped my diatribe to take her hands in mine. "Our lives are tiny in the stream of time." I pointed to the kitchen. "I nearly missed out on so much happiness with that incredible woman, because I refused to forgive myself and believe I deserve to be happy. I watch you continually hope for a future that isn't going to happen, while completely missing out on what could be today."

Her brow wrinkled. "What the hell are you talking about?"

I narrowed my eyes and dropped my voice. "Tell me you didn't feel anything when Senna asked Karmen to dance last night."

"I—"

"Here, let me help you with your answer. You did, because I saw your reaction. Don't lie to yourself. Karmen's had her heart set on you for the last four years, while you barely gave her the time of day. You want to know why Senna got toasted last night? She's got a monster crush on Karmen, and she knows how Karmen feels about you. Knowing all that, Senna still took a chance by asking her to dance."

Tank put her head in her hands. "What the fuck, Bek? What do you want from me?"

"I don't want anything from you, except for you to acknowledge what's right in front of you. You're about to let an incredible woman slip through your fingers. Karmen deserves to be happy, and she's not going to stay single for the rest of her life. You have two choices, continue to paddle upstream, or put your sail up and catch the wind. Your window is narrowing my friend. I can't make this picture any clearer."

It was never my intention to push Tank into something she didn't want. My only goal was to force her into taking off her blinders. The decision was hers and hers alone. Karmen deserved to be more than a consolation prize, and she'd been patient long enough. I'd talk with Karmen privately at a later date.

Tank had been my friend and shadow for a very long time. She'd taken care of me when I didn't deserve it, and I owed her in ways I would never be able to repay. My honesty was something I could and would give her. What she did with it was completely up to her. My phone rang and brought Ellie's sweet voice into the room with the ringtone of her singing *"Ain't No Road Too Long."* I watched Tank perk up and caught Karmen's shoulders sag.

I answered and told Ellie I'd call her right back. When I disconnected, I watched Karmen fold the dishtowel she'd been holding and place it on the counter.

"I just remembered I have something I need to do. You guys eat without me." Karmen walked over to the door and put on her coat. "I'm not very hungry anyway."

Naomi moved to the door and hugged her. My heart broke, when Karmen wiped a tear away as she slipped out.

I shook my head at Tank and moved into the studio to call Ellie back. After two rings, she picked up. "Morning, little sparrow. How are you?"

"Exhausted. The European tour zapped me, then we came right back here and hit it again. I think Stuart is trying to kill me."

Her voice was raspy. When I'd last seen her for our father's funeral, she'd looked tired. The attempt to conceal the dark shadows under her eyes with makeup had barely hidden the bruised look. She'd been thinner than I'd ever seen her. Her shrugged response to my gentle questions had left me more than a little concerned. Ellie never complained about her touring schedule. It was time for me to call Regal Crimson's manager and advise him to lighten up.

"Speak up, Ellie. The sled track you've been on for the last three years is unsustainable. You can't draw from an empty well. It's not good for your health."

"Please, no lectures right now. I won't deny what you're saying is true. After the Pittsburgh show, I'm taking a long break. I promise. I've been talking about it with Stuart and the band for the last six months. They swear to me I haven't been giving them anything less than my A game. My opinion differs greatly. Trying to hit the high note in 'Craving

Your Midnight' has been difficult, to say the least."

Ellie could hit that note in her sleep. The fact she was admitting to difficulty worried me. "Ellie, have you been to the doctor lately?"

"Last year for my checkup, why?"

I ticked off my list of concerns, adding her self-admitted fatigue. "Make an appointment, or I'll do it for you and drag you to it."

"Bek, I don't have time."

"Make time, Ellie. Your health is nothing to mess with. Promise me?"

"You're such a pain in the ass."

I rubbed my brow. She was fighting this too hard. That worried me even more. "Ellie, what aren't you telling me?"

"Nothing. Stop worrying. I'm fine. Please, Bek. Let it go."

Now I was pacing, and that had Naomi's attention. My next lap in the ten-foot area was obstructed by her hand on my forearm. She mouthed *what's wrong*. I pointed to my ear, indicating for her to come closer and listen.

"I'll be damned if I let it go. Something's wrong, and you're not telling me. You get to the doctor, or I'm on the next plane. You hear me?"

"All right, all right! Stop hounding me. I'll make an appointment tomorrow. There's nothing wrong with me. I've just been on the road for too long. I need to sleep in my own bed and eat food that doesn't come in a Styrofoam box. Can we please drop it for now? How's my almost sister-in-law?"

I punched the speakerphone. "Ask her yourself. She's right here."

Naomi leaned over and spoke. "Hey kiddo, what's up? Why is your sister frothing at the mouth?"

I scowled at the woman I loved for no other reason than she was always able to make me smile when I didn't want to.

"She's got her worrying mother hat on. I'm fine."

I pulled at the hair on the side of my head. If she said she was fine one more time, I was going to scream. All indications were that her answer was anything but the truth. The problem was that I was too far away to be able to prove it. My gut coiled like an agitated snake, ready to strike out in fear. Ellie was everything to me. I'd protected her for years, until I'd left Regal Crimson. When I'd walked away, I was sure she was fully capable of looking out for her own best interests. Had I been wrong? Had I been so distracted at our father's passing that I'd missed something?

I tried to imagine her face, to examine each conversation, each interaction we'd had in those few days. *My God, what have I missed?* I was so caught up in my musing that I hadn't even noticed I'd handed Naomi the phone, stripped off my shirt, and grabbed the Strat. I was absent-mindedly picking out an agitated melody, when I felt Naomi touch me. She hung up the phone, kissed me gently, and walked out of the room. It wasn't the first time my body had separated from my mind and moved of its own accord.

I plugged in the amp and let go with several technically difficult songs that I tended to lose myself in. This type of music challenged the technician in me, and I needed to channel my fear. Completely losing myself in the gift I'd been given was a form of prayer.

I had no idea how long I'd been playing. I felt Naomi's hands on my hips and her lips on my back. Seconds later, she unplugged my amp and removed my guitar.

"Enough, honey. You need something to eat. You've been in here for four hours. I promise you, if you come and eat with me, then I'll come back and play with you."

I picked up my shirt and wiped my face and arms. I drank down the glass of ice water she handed me. A tremor started in my hand, and I clenched it into a fist, wincing at my sore fingertips.

"Oh, baby. Come here."

Naomi pulled me into her arms, as the tremor worked its way up my arm and into my entire body. I felt my legs give way, and we crumpled to the floor. She cradled me, rocking gently. The tears poured out in great gasps, stealing all the air from my lungs. I was terrified.

"Rhebekka, listen to me. We don't know that anything's wrong. You have to take her at her word right now. Ellie's never broken a promise to you, and I made her make that same promise to me. We have to trust that it's nothing more than tour fatigue until we know otherwise."

"I left her on her own, Naomi. I walked away and made her fend for herself."

"That's bullshit, and you know it. Ellie is no child. Regal Crimson's had a long run, and I won't be surprised if she's had enough. I really think that's why the concert in Pittsburgh means so much."

"I didn't see this coming. I talk to her every fucking week, and I didn't notice a thing. Am I so self-centered that I couldn't tell something was wrong with my own damn sister?"

Her hand stroked my hair as she kissed my head, one arm firmly holding me to her. I held on to her as if she could anchor me, while the maelstrom of emotions washed over me. She pressed her lips to my temple. She sat me up and pushed my sweaty hair out of my eyes and off my forehead, melting me with her touch.

"Honey, there was a time I might have said yes. There was a time that you couldn't see things that were right in front of you. Those days are long gone. You don't see her every day, and you did notice something was wrong. I was there when you told her she was too skinny and not sleeping enough, when we were in Charlottesville. You can't force her to tell you what she doesn't want to. That's part of growing up; you get to make those choices."

I wiped my eyes. "I don't like it."

Naomi's laugh was as resonant as a bow drawn across the strings of a cello, rich and warm. "Of that, I have no doubt. Think I can get you to come and eat now?"

I nodded and helped her up after I stood. Everything in my life was better with this woman beside me. I thanked God every day for her patience and persistence. The desire to marry her grew stronger every second. I pulled her left hand to my lips and kissed each knuckle.

"I love you, Naomi."

"I love you, too. Now, come on."

She led me from the studio and into the kitchen where she sat me down at the bar. Resting my head in my hands, I watched her fill two plates.

"I see Tank left, too."

"I tried to talk to her, though I'm not at all convinced she's going to let go of the Ellie fantasy. Poor Karmen, the minute you said Ellie's name, Tank lit up like a Christmas tree. It had the exact opposite effect on Karmen, who was shattered when she left here."

"I've come to the conclusion Karmen needs to move on. I don't think Tank is going to change. Ellie told me herself, there isn't anything between them and Tank can't accept that."

Naomi set our meals on the bar. "Karmen is young, and Tank isn't the only fish in the sea. I have no doubt Senna will gladly offer to mend her broken heart."

"That's the thing. I know Karmen's type, and Senna isn't it, at least not long term. She's not exactly settled. That's what Karmen wants more than anything, stability. Growing up, they were incredibly poor. Her mother constantly moved them around downtown Cleveland, from one shit hole to the next. Her nomadic childhood was more than enough incentive to escape and find security. She wants to put down firm roots and have kids, not play house for a month or two."

Naomi poured two glasses of tea, put the pitcher back in the refrigerator, and joined me at the bar. "From what I've heard, Senna hasn't stayed in one place longer than a year. I saw her looking at a culinary school brochure from San Antonio the other day."

"I know, Karmen's encouraged her to go. The other thing is Senna drinks a little too much for Karmen's liking. Her mother was strung out most of her childhood, and she won't live that way. All I know is I want her to be happy. It's up to her to find it." I bit into a piece of roast, allowing a moan to pass from my lips. "Either way, she's one fantastic chef."

Naomi raised her tea glass in a toast. "Agreed."

Chapter Twenty

THE FOLLOWING WEEK, WE met with Salvations and Libations, imparting a bit of fun with our message. Naomi and I were becoming one in so many ways, feeding off each other in the ministry. I loved watching her in everything she did, from playing ArchAngel with the kids to kicking Tom and Rev. Mathew's asses in Bible trivia. As always, Tank brought the latest offerings from the brewery, and we'd snack on the treats Karmen dropped off.

For the first time since I'd started the twice-monthly gathering, Karmen didn't stay. She came to visit us in the loft but seemed to be making a conscious decision to avoid Tank. We checked on her frequently, and she told us she was fine, though reevaluating a few things in her life. Tank was becoming surlier by the day. By Friday, I'd had enough.

I rode to the brewery early in the morning, knowing Tank would be getting things ready for the weekend. I found her in the back, taking inventory of the peanuts, potato chips, and other snacks. She had one pencil in her hand and another stuck in the adjustable band on the back of her ball cap.

"Can't talk now, I've got to make a store run." She pointed to our pretzels. "We'll never make it through the weekend."

I pulled the clipboard out of her hands and walked away from her toward the bar. "Stockholders' meeting, now. The store run can wait."

She resisted at first, and then I heard her boots thudding behind me. I pointed to one of the stools and let the clipboard clatter to the copper bar top. I poured us each a cup of coffee. "Sit."

"Bek, honestly, I don't have time for this."

"You'll make time. You're more foul-tempered than a possum being shooed out of the garbage. It's not just me that's noticed. You were so condescending to Franklin last night. He made up an excuse to leave early. Not to mention you about snapped Senna's head off. Now if you want to yell at someone, I'm right here, but you're going to get this out of your system."

I watched her jaw jump, as she ground her teeth together. If she didn't talk about whatever was gnawing at her, it would eat her up.

"Ellie called me."

I was pretty sure what my sister had said to her, but I wanted a verbal confirmation from Tank.

"And?"

"I took a chance and sent her flowers the other day. All I was trying to do was let her know I was thinking about her."

"None of that tells me why you're so cranky."

Ellie's reaction had obviously rattled Tank. One of the strongest women I'd ever known had a tremble to her hand when she took a sip of coffee. The mug clattered hard against the hand-hammered surface.

"She told me there would never be a chance for us. Said that if I was waiting on her, I'd be alone for a very long time. I begged her, Bek. I begged her to give me one more chance to be the woman she wants. I've never groveled in my life, but I did. Ellie turned me down flat." She threw her hands in the air. "Go ahead, tell me I told you so. I know it's killing you."

"In all the years I've known you, have I ever been purposefully cruel, drunk or sober?"

"No."

"Thanks for passing judgment, knowing it wasn't the truth. I'm sorry, Tank. I truly am. I've always considered you family, and I want to see you happy. My sister's a grown woman who knows what she does and doesn't want. No one has a right to dictate anything about her love life. You worked with her long enough to know she won't be pushed into anything. The torch you've been holding has burned down to the quick. You're letting it burn your hand off instead of letting her go."

She was quiet when she replied. "I always thought, if you loved something, you were never supposed to give up. Where would you be if Naomi had completely walked away?"

I put a hand on her shoulder. "There's a difference between those two scenarios. I still loved Naomi as much as she loved me. I was stuck in a darkness of my own making for a while. Thank God, she was patient enough to let me go through it and come out the other side. Ellie isn't in darkness and certainly not unsure of herself. None of us has a right to dictate to someone else who they should love. Is it really love if you have to force the issue? In that same regard, I wouldn't think about turning to Karmen, because you know what? She deserves someone who believes she's more than a consolation prize. Your head is stuck so far up your ass, you didn't even notice how much your reaction to Ellie's call on Sunday affected Karmen. Nor did you recognize why she didn't come to trivia the other night. You sent a clear message to her where she stands with you. I'm going to tell you this as a friend, Karmen's letting go of the idea of a relationship with you. She's leaving the shop in Senna's hands for a few weeks and flying out to see her sister in Michigan. Naomi and I are driving her to Pittsburgh tomorrow. If you aren't interested in her that way, then so be it. My suggestion is that you try to salvage the friendship, because she's worth it."

I drank the rest of my coffee and walked to the door. Tank would need to sit with everything to weigh it out. I'd known her a long time. She'd break everything down to the core argument, to its most basic pieces. She wasn't one I could minister to in the typical way. We were too close for that, and the subject was too personal. I slid my helmet on and rode my bicycle back home. I'd done ten miles on Marvin before I'd stopped in to see Tank.

A shower and some lunch were what I wanted. Most of the snow had turned to a slushy mess, as I made my way home down the back streets. The thought that Naomi was there waiting for me had become one of my favorite things in the world. I bounced the muck off the bike and carried it up the stairs and into the hallway. I changed my shoes and took the stairs two at a time. The aroma of minestrone filled the space.

"That smells so good, and I'm starving." I kissed Naomi on my way through the kitchen.

"You smell like you rode twenty miles. Shower now and put those muddy clothes directly in the washing machine." Naomi pointed her wooden spoon toward the bathroom.

"You'd have made an awesome mom, you know?"

"Between our after-school kids, you, Ellie, and Tank, I've got plenty of kids. Go."

I waved my hand, as I stripped off my muddy riding clothes and placed them, as instructed, in the washing machine. Steam quickly filled the bathroom, when I turned the shower on and stepped in. I planted my hands on the tile wall. Hot water poured over my head and down my body. I wasn't shocked when I felt hands slide over my hips. Naomi would never pass up the opportunity to see me naked.

"Took you long enough."

She kissed my shoulder. "I had to take the bread out of the oven."

"Ah. Have I told you how much I adore your cooking skills?"

"Once or twice."

She loaded a loofah with grapefruit-scented body wash and went about systematically removing the stench from my workout. I washed my hair and enjoyed the feeling of her hands gliding sensually over my body.

"I love you, Naomi, with all my heart."

She hung the loofah up and wrapped her arms around me. Her lips touched my collarbone with such tenderness, it nearly melted me. I was putty in her hands.

"I'm incredibly happy to be here with you and more in love than I've ever been."

I'd been so stupid, though I refused to go back and wallow in that sorrow. It only served to steal more time from us. I moved my hands to cup Naomi's face and kissed away all the hours and days I'd been without her. Her passion and desire matched my own. I moved a hand over her breast and squeezed lightly at first and rolled the nipple in my fingers.

"Oh my God, Rhebekka."

"You're so beautiful, Naomi. Not a day goes by that I don't realize how incredibly stunning you are." I bent and kissed her chest, taking the other nipple in my mouth, sucking gently at first. When she groaned in pleasure, I grazed it with my teeth. Her fingers tightened on my biceps, her deep-red fingernails leaving small pinpoints of pain and pleasure on my skin.

"You taste so good." I lavished her other nipple with my warm mouth and felt her tremble beneath my lips. Needing more, I slowly kissed down her body until I knelt in front of her. I carefully pushed her flat against the tile. I lifted and bent her right leg over my shoulder and parted her silken folds with my fingers, kissing her clit before sucking it into my mouth.

"Rhebekka!"

Her left leg tried to buckle. I braced it with my body to keep her from falling. I needed her so much and wanted her to feel the devotion of my love down to her very core. My tongue explored and drank her in as I savored her unique flavor. Nothing in the world ever felt like making love to this woman, the only one I'd ever trusted with my heart, and more importantly, my soul.

I slid two fingers into her swollen depth and enjoyed the tug as her hands tightened in my hair. She moved against me in the exquisite throes of passion, head thrown back, eyes closed tightly, and lips parted. Her auburn hair hung in wet ringlets, cascading down her chest and curving around her breasts. Naomi had been made for me, and I was going to claim her with my mouth, tongue, and fingers.

I felt the telltale tightening, as I increased the intensity of my strokes. I concentrated on sucking her clit in a way I knew would send her over the edge into bliss. It only took seconds before her body went rigid, forcing me to slip my free hand around her waist to support her through her climax. My mouth filled with her essence, and I drank her in as if my life depended on it. Naomi was an oasis in my desert. Never again would I be without her. She slid down the wall into my arms, and I held her to me. The water grew cool on my back, so I reached up to turn it off. I pillowed my head against her breast.

"Holy shit, Rhebekka. What was that?"

"Proof of how much I love you."

Naomi kissed me and clutched my body to her. "You never need to prove that to me, love. I know that here."

Her left hand covered her heart. I kissed her fingers, then her lips. "No one else in the world knows me like you do. There are only two people in my adult life who believed in me with conviction, you and Ellie. The two people who taught me what love really is. Somehow, by the grace of God, I was given two people to walk this life with. I'm forever grateful."

She shivered, as she pushed my hair out of my eyes. "I love you, Rhebekka."

We stayed like that for several minutes. Naomi kissed me and smiled.

"How about we get dried off and go have lunch? Then we'll head over to the food bank. Tonight, I'll cook dinner for us, and we can curl up on the couch for a movie night. We can even play *Name That Tune*."

This woman always knew what I needed. A night at home watching cheesy movies and playing guitar with her was the best idea I'd heard in a long time. *Name That Tune* involved losing pieces of clothing when we got it wrong. As far as I was concerned, there were no losers in the game at all.

***

The bell on the door of the storefront jingled as we pushed inside. The weather was milder than the last few days. The temperature was slowly coming up, melting the last of the winter slush. Naomi and I both stomped our boots on the textured, industrial rug right inside the door. Victoria's stern, yet cheerful face met us.

"About time, you two made it in. Time's a wasting." Victoria passed a large box of bananas to the older gentleman beside her.

I looked at my watch. "I thought we agreed on two this week. Did I miss something?" My mischievous side couldn't help but dig a little at our fearless leader. We were an hour early and somehow, still late.

Victoria pinched me on the arm. "Don't sass me. Naomi, how in the world do you put up with her?"

"With God's help, Vikki. Now, how can we help?" Naomi took off her coat and headed to the large tables with boxes arranged all over the surfaces.

With hands planted firmly on my hips, I scowled at both of them. "Hey, wait a minute here. I don't need both of you ganging up on me."

"Shut your pie hole and get to work. These boxes won't fill themselves." Victoria handed me a case of macaroni and cheese.

Beyond the gruff exterior beat a heart of gold. Before I could be accused of sandbagging, I shook my head and got to work.

For the next few hours, we put food items in each box to be delivered the following day. When we were done, we stowed the extras in the storage area. Victoria's delivery army included kids from local youth groups. I had plans of getting my group involved soon and on a regular basis.

Victoria hugged both of us when everything was cleaned up. "I know I give you the devil, but we couldn't do this without you. Thank you both."

Naomi held Victoria's hands in hers. "It's our pleasure. If you need anything else, let us know."

"I'll do that. Now you two run along. I've got things to do." Victoria shooed us out into the sunlight.

"She's tough. The community wouldn't know what to do without her." I opened Naomi's door for her, then shut it before walking to my side of the truck to climb in beside her.

"She thinks the world of you. That's why she gives you such a hard time."

I winked at Naomi. "Duly noted. Let's hit the grocery store before we leave and stock up on some junk food. I want some cinnamon-and-sugar pretzel nuggets for our movie night."

"That sounds good. How about we grab a pizza from Sirianni's for dinner? I'll call it in, and we can pick it up on our way home."

"Sounds like a plan."

***

We snuggled on the couch, gorging ourselves on a vegetable loaded pizza and a growler of Ascension Ale, one of Redemption's Road's lighter brews. I'd let Naomi make our movie selection, and she'd chosen a movie we always enjoyed, no matter how many times we saw it. We loved the soundtrack. Eventually, both of us had our guitars, singing as loud as we could while jamming along. This, of course, led to our version of *Name That Tune*. We turned to face each other, legs entwined.

"This song's inspiration was the lighting director for an iconic band." Naomi waggled her eyebrows in challenge.

Knowing her musical favorites was my greatest advantage in this game. She loved seventies music and bands with female vocalists in particular. I thought for a few moments. I was a winner, regardless of whose clothes came off. "I can name that tune in six notes."

Her head dropped. She strummed G minor, F, then E. I could have named it in four, but I wanted a little cushion. I enjoyed her clothes coming off more than mine. I strummed the next few lines to prove my prowess. "'You Make Loving Fun,' Fleetwood Mac."

She strummed through the first few bars and touched her nose. "Okay, winner's choice."

"Well, since you aren't wearing any socks, and I can already see those adorable painted toenails, I'll say your yoga pants." I was almost positive she was wearing some very sexy lingerie for the occasion.

Naomi put her guitar down and slowly drew the leggings down and off. Her bare legs were beautiful, each muscle defined from her daily runs. I could see a pair of lace bikinis.

"Like what you see?"

"I surrender now!" I sat up and tried to climb across the couch to her but was stopped with a hand to my chest and a soft kiss on my lips.

"Oh no, we see this through. I promise it will be worth the wait." Naomi kissed me again.

I growled but quickly came up with my offering. "The song was inspired by an Emily Bronte novel."

"Oh, nice clue. Sadly, it's going to cost you an article of clothing. I can name that tune in three notes."

Laughter bubbled up. "Like I said, I love this game." I hit the first three notes and watched as she eyed my body.

"'Total Eclipse of the Heart,' Bonnie Tyler. Off with the shirt." Her grin was sinful.

With the guitar lying on the floor, I stood and slowly pulled off my turquoise Henley. I let it drop beside me, revealing the fact that I wore nothing underneath.

"Oh my, I like when you skip a few rounds." Naomi stood and walked around me, trailing her fingernails across my skin. Their starry glitter caught the light with each movement. Soft lips found the juncture of my neck and shoulder and kissed a path to my back. Each sensation nearly brought me to my knees and flooded my center with liquid desire.

"My God, woman, are you trying to kill me? One more touch like that and I'm calling it. It's your turn unless you'd like to declare a draw right now and take this to the bedroom?"

"Oh no, I'm betting you aren't wearing anything under those jeans. I'm about to see if I should bet the bank or just a single article of clothing." She snaked her fingers around the front to the metal buttons and pulled the fly hard to the left. She slid her fingers down the open front and into the curls at the base of my belly. Her fingers dipped lower and parted my folds. She withdrew and walked back in front of me, with a deliciously wicked smile on her face. She sucked her wet fingers into her mouth and proceeded to lick her lips. "Confirmed."

I groaned from an intense pulse at my core and picked up my guitar. There was nothing I wouldn't give her. "Let it ride, baby."

"Recorded in 1964 by the Big O and Billie Dee, this song is also the title of a movie."

"I'll say, I can name that tune in six notes." As badly as I wanted to get my beautiful fiancée into bed, I wanted to see the matching bra to her exquisite lace bikinis, while she held the Strat.

"Oh, come now, surely you can do better than that? I've likely given you too much information as it is."

Naomi's tongue snaked out and lightly licked her upper lip. *Oh, she knew that would send me reeling.*

"Three, I can name it in three," I croaked.

She drew her thumbnail across the E string and moved her right hand onto the fourth fret and strummed again. Her left eyebrow drew up in a sensuous arch.

I knew the lick she played as well as I knew the chords to every song I'd ever written. I would soon see her standing before me in nothing but that deep-scarlet intimate apparel. I repeated what she'd played, then added the rest of the iconic riff to Roy Orbison's "Pretty Woman." She threw her head back and laughed, as I continued to play.

She placed her guitar back on its stand and slowly began to unbutton the dress shirt she'd claimed from me. The burgundy shirt just happened to match her lingerie. *No one in the world is this sexy.* She moved with such grace and revealed so much more than skin to me. On display was her heart wrapped in a delicious package.

The shirt slid off her shoulders and caught on her bent elbows, as it draped her waist. If I could capture one image to look at for the rest of my life, it would be this one. She was perfect in every way to me. Sensuous, captivating, and untamable, she was all those things and so much more. She let the shirt flutter to the ground. Before me stood beauty made flesh. I was done with *Name That Tune*.

"Game Over." I needed her without delay. My Gibson joined the Strat, and I bent to put an arm behind her knees and one around her back. When she wrapped her arms around my neck, I carried her to our bed. I would give her anything she asked of me. I would lay down every care and worry. I would surrender to her desires in every way and fulfill my own in the process. She would own me in body, mind, and heart. I was hers.

Chapter Twenty-One

LENTEN SERVICES TOOK THE place of the Salvation and Libations gathering. Ash Wednesday had been well attended. On Thursday, Naomi and I took time to stop by Doggy Sods to help walk and play with residents large and small. Maddie and her partner, Allie, did a great deal for living creatures with fins, fur, and feathers. They'd asked if Naomi and I could transport a cat and dog to Morgantown to their new "furever" home. I made an appointment with Roman to continue his work on my back. It would be the first session for Naomi to watch in a long time. The last was a tour stop in Pittsburgh, years before we separated.

Naomi changed the radio in the Land Cruiser and stopped on a classic rock station.

"Maddie is incredible at finding homes for odd pairings. That Great Dane and calico were adorable together. "

I nodded in agreement. "Maddie rocks. That pair we just delivered came from the same home. Their owner passed away with no family to take them. Maddie scooped them up and made sure they would be rehomed together. I met her the same year I moved to Thomas."

"You know, we should really think about getting a cat, maybe a dog, someday."

I grinned and tried to concentrate on the road. What my body wanted was to pull over and kiss her. "Sure. You want to go to the shelter this week?"

"Yeah. I think we need to help out an older cat. Kittens have a much easier time getting adopted. Maybe even one with special needs."

"I'll talk to Maddie and see if she knows of any that are having a hard time being adopted. We'll take them down to Jax for a thorough checkup and make sure they have everything necessary." I extended my arm and laid my hand on her leg, palm up. She entwined our fingers, while I drove us to Roman's.

Naomi caressed my hand with her thumb. "I can't wait to see Roman again. Don't let me forget to give him his wedding invitation."

The last few weeks had seen a flurry of activity surrounding our simple nuptials and the St. Patrick's Day celebration we'd had at

Redemption's Road. We'd decided to move the wedding up. Ellie had called saying she would be with us sooner than originally expected. The ceremony was now planned for the weekend after Easter, April 27. The plan was to hold the wedding in our small courtyard beside House of the Rising Son.

Snow at Easter wasn't unusual for our area. Even if it snowed, the ceremony would be held outside. If it rained, we'd move inside on the small stage of our church. We'd ordered four outdoor heaters to make the space comfortable for our guests. Most of the people attending were from our church and a small group of friends and family. We had friends coming from Colorado, as well as the few remaining members of the original Regal Crimson.

Though I bugged her every day, Ellie had yet to let me know what steps she'd taken to slow down. I'd called Stuart and made him promise to stop pushing so hard. I wasn't sure whether I'd gotten through to him or not. When you were up close and personal with someone, you could occasionally miss signs. Seeing Ellie at the funeral had given me a pretty big dose of reality on what the constant touring was doing to her.

A simple sign hung over an unassuming door. Sessions at The Acropolis were highly sought after and by appointment only. I ran around to open Naomi's door and took her hand to help her through the gravel lot beside Roman's tattoo studio. Her high-heeled leather boots turned me on but weren't the best choice for this surface.

Roman greeted us at the counter and quickly came around to hug Naomi.

"It's been too long, woman. You look fantastic." Roman held her at arm's length before pulling her into a tight hug. They caught up with each other, and Roman waved me back to his salon.

Naomi took the chair close to the table. "So, what are we doing tonight to my beautiful bride to be?"

I removed my jacket and shirt before I lay face down on the cushioned black surface that smelled slightly of disinfectant. "I think we'd planned to put more detail into the wings and add the cross."

I heard Roman roll his chair close to the table and turned my head to look at him for confirmation.

"That's what I have written on the schedule." He pulled on a pair of nitrile gloves, before he cleaned my back with an antiseptic solution. He traced a few lines on my shoulder and chuckled. "You two will have to go easy for a bit while this heals. Don't fuck up my work, okay?"

It took me a few seconds to realize he was tracing fingernail scratches. The second I understood his meaning, I felt my face heat. Naomi laughed, and I turned to see her grinning with both hands in the air.

"I'll do my best to, uh, hold onto something else." She shook her head and put a hand over her mouth. She was incredibly adorable when she blushed.

"Okay, okay, you two. Let's get busy. Naomi, I know you are aware of how to care for these, so I'll skip that lecture. I won't ask how you were cleaning it before that beauty busted her way through your thick head." Roman's tattoo gun buzzed. "Ready?"

"Let's do it." I lay with my face pillowed in the circle, with my arms resting at my side. I felt the bite of the needle. Within minutes, endorphins flooded my system.

I enjoyed listening to the banter between them, as Roman worked his artistry into my skin. I didn't know if he could capture exactly what I'd talked about. I never brought Roman any pictures. We'd talked through the design, and I trusted him. He was working on the center of my back, and the buzzing I felt into the base of my skull told me he was working near my spine.

I completely lost track of time in my hormone-induced haze. Roman turned off the gun.

"Let's take a break. You want something to drink?"

"That'd be good." Standing to stretch, I wobbled, slightly light-headed. Naomi caught and steadied me with both hands.

"Easy there. Lean against this for a minute." Naomi rubbed my arm and pointed to the table.

"How long have we been at it?"

Roman handed me an orange juice. "About two hours. It's looking really good, don't you think, Naomi?"

Naomi turned me so that the light was fully on my back.

"It's outstanding. What you do with ink is what Michelangelo did with paint. It looks so real."

I rolled my neck back and forth. "When Roman started specializing in the 3D look, I was hooked. We started on this, what? Five years ago?"

"That's when we first put ink to the idea. We've been kicking this one around since you met her." Roman pointed to Naomi. "You've always been her inspiration for this, you know."

Naomi put her hand to her mouth, as if she finally understood everything. "The saint within the sinner."

Years before, Naomi had taught me that within each of us, there existed both. We were imperfect and yet longing to do the right thing. Thus, a saint existed within every sinner. It was also why the angel wing was more detailed and slightly larger in size.

I took another drink of juice and smiled at her. "All have sinned and fall short of the glory of God, and all are justified freely by his grace through the redemption that came by Christ Jesus. You read that to me years ago, from the book of Romans."

"I also read to you from first John. If we claim to be without sin, we deceive ourselves and the truth is not in us."

"I am who I am today because you believed in me enough to remind me that the saint existed inside the sinner. This tattoo is the representation of my redemption, though both still reside within me."

Naomi took my hands, kissing each one. "And God loves them both. One just needs a little more work than the other."

Roman sat back down on his stool. "Come on, I need to add a little more shadow to the cross. Another thirty minutes or so and we'll quit."

I handed my empty cup to Naomi and returned to my prone position on the table. I could hear them talking to each other, but I was lost in the endorphins.

Naomi held my hand. "You used the cross she wears around her neck as the model?"

"That was her request, down to the small imperfections from years of wear."

I felt her lean over me and kiss my neck. She whispered close to my ear. "You were never really without me, were you, Rhebekka?"

I didn't dare turn my head, even though I wanted so badly to kiss her. All I could do was mumble. "No, not for one second."

***

Later that night, with her spooned up tight to my front, I lay there listening to her rhythmic breathing. The feel of her skin on mine was like nothing I'd ever experienced. The first time I touched her, it was like I absorbed her into my flesh. It was a miracle that I found her at all. Our touring schedule was crazy, and Ellie and I were either on a bus or a plane over two hundred days a year. I'd purchased a small studio apartment in Durango. I wanted to be away from LA and New York. Pittsburgh felt like home in many ways, but I was too well known there and couldn't disappear into a crowd. I loved snow and craft beer, so Durango became a place to roost when I wasn't on tour. Those were dark times for me, and the memories weren't always clear. This one was.

I woke up, still wearing my clothes from the night before, minus shoes. "I need coffee." I jammed my feet down in the motorcycle boots and threw on my leather jacket and sunglasses. There was a coffee shop three blocks down. I could get something to eat that might soak up some of the Scotch still swimming around in my stomach.

"Shit." I pulled up the zipper on my jacket and jammed my hands into the pockets, as I stepped out of the lobby door into the biting January wind. There was fresh snow on the sidewalk. I made my way down to Black Gold, a local café that played up to the gold rush days of old. I'd come to know the baristas pretty well.

Tegan gave me a thumbs up. I ordered a breakfast sandwich and hoped I could hold it down. I still felt queasy, so putting the highly caffeinated coffee in my empty stomach wasn't an option. I stared at the bulletin board full of telemarketing job openings, sale advertisements, and available housing. I saw a bulletin for someplace called Open Door Ministries. There was a color photo of a woman with auburn hair, wearing leather, with a Fender hung around her neck. I was pretty sure there was a Bible in her hand. The welcome line caught my eye. "Saints and Sinners Welcome."

It literally made me laugh. That a church would invite sinners intrigued me. I slid up my sunglasses and examined a list of dates and activities a little closer. "Beer and Bible Study? What kind of preacher advertises that? You've got to be kidding me."

Tegan walked up and handed me my coffee. "No, it's for real and awesome. Naomi Layman is the coolest pastor you'll ever meet. Her services are full of hymns that sound more like a rock concert. Just don't call her a preacher; she hates that. You should come later. Her service doesn't start until four in the afternoon, so everyone who partied too hard on Saturday night can sleep in and still get their Jesus on."

"I don't think so. I've had all the Jesus I'll ever need." I walked to the counter to get my sandwich.

"You're missing out, trust me. Pastor Naomi is fucking amazing. Your loss."

I thanked him for the coffee and stopped briefly in front of the flyer again. I mentally took note of the address and pushed out the door.

Later that afternoon, I was still hungover and slightly high, as I paced my apartment. Something was niggling against my skull wall. I knew what it was and looked at the clock. "Still have thirty minutes. What do I have to lose?" I called a cab and met it downstairs.

The cab let me out in front of an obscure storefront, with a glass door bearing the words Open Door Ministry, along with a list of times. I hadn't stepped into a church in nearly ten years. Walking across that threshold meant I was missing something. It certainly wasn't the people who'd given me a skewed version of who God was. No, it was something I couldn't explain.

I walked down the street and away from the door. "This was a bad idea." I kept walking for several more blocks, before I turned around and went back. When I looked at my phone, it was fifteen minutes after four. I hesitated. Someone stepped to the door and opened it. A gentleman, who had to be in his seventies, looked at me. His rainbow bow tie proudly peeking out of his overcoat.

"Come on, I'm always late. Pastor Naomi won't care. Trust me." He held the door for me, and I stepped inside.

I could smell cinnamon and cloves as he guided me into the sanctuary. I sat in the back near him. The woman I'd seen in the flyer paced the stage, reading from Ephesians 2.

"'For it is by grace you have been saved, through faith—and this is not from yourselves, it is the gift of God—not by works, so that no one can boast. For we are God's handiwork, created in Christ Jesus to do good works, which God prepared in advance for us to do.'" She looked out into the crowd, looking at each one of us, and briefly stopped on my face before she continued.

"'...that Christ may dwell in your hearts through faith. And I pray that you, being rooted and established in love, may have power, together with all the Lord's holy people, to grasp how wide and long and high and deep is the love of Christ, and to know this love that surpasses knowledge—that you may be filled to the measure of all the fullness of God.'"

I sat up straighter, captivated by her beauty and the honeyed gravel of her voice. She set her Bible on a lectern and pulled a pick from the pocket of her short, leather coat. I didn't recognize the song at first, the arrangement completely different, until the first few words left her lips. I definitely wanted to hide the cracks in my soul.

For the next four minutes, I sat transfixed, watching her play through a hard rock version of the iconic hymn, Beautiful Brokenness. She bent the strings and tapped out a melody that pulled deep on my insides. I leaned forward and watched how she completely captivated the congregation of mostly twenty-somethings, save rainbow tie guy. I glanced at him and watched his hands play the same chords as the pastor. The ends of his fingers had thick callouses. The dude was a serious string player.

I had no idea how much time had passed while I listened to the beautiful woman. She reached into my body and found my soul. Before I knew it, she was closing the service. For the first time in my life, I didn't feel like a wrathful God was being jammed down my throat. The message Pastor Naomi Laymen had offered was that I was worthy of God's grace, freely given.

***

Naomi stirred in my arms and rolled over, tucking herself under my chin.

"What are you pondering so hard on? I can hear you thinking."

Placing a soft kiss on her forehead, I sighed. "Just remembering the first day I met you."

I felt Naomi smile against my neck.

"Did I ever tell you I recognized you immediately?"

The dim glow of the streetlight filtered through the window, and I leaned back to see her. "How is it I've never known that fact?"

Her arms tightened around me. "I didn't want to freak you out. When you told me your name was Bek, no last name, I realized you wanted anonymity. I was willing to let you have that. Durango's pretty small, but remember the day I told you I'd seen you in concert?"

"Yeah."

"What I didn't tell you was that I'd been to more than one of your shows, a few before Regal Crimson even hit it big. You played an armed services concert in Colorado Springs, a few years before you walked into my church in Durango."

"Weren't you married then?"

"I was. Aaron was in the Air Force and stationed at NORAD. We saw you together."

"He tracked Santa?"

Naomi chuckled against my chest.

"Every year. God, we were just kids, trying to make our parents happy."

"Have you heard from him recently?"

"About a year ago. He's retired. He and his wife, Denise, own a ranch in Wyoming." She laughed, "They have six kids."

"Wow, busy guy."

Naomi kissed me.

"According to him, he's happy as a lark. So am I."

"You know who else came to mind? Alfred. I can still remember him opening the door to your church for me."

"Oh my, Alfred. What an incredible man. Did you know he played violin in a symphony? That man was a serious rock and roll fan. I can't tell you how many Metallica concerts he'd been to. He's the one who helped me rewrite the hymn arrangements with a rock theme."

"I'd never heard anything like your rendition of *Fountain*."

"We worked on that together. Alfred was in his early seventies when you met him. I was devastated when he passed away."

I pulled her close, remembering how hard it had been for her to write his eulogy service. "Alfred adored you."

"I'll bet he's incredibly proud of you, too. He never got to see you as a pastor in life, but I'm betting he hangs out to hear your sermons now."

"I wonder if God let him keep his rainbow tie. It always made me smile, knowing he was wearing it for you."

"Few people knew he was a straight ally. His wife passed years before he did. I never got to meet her. That tie was also a tribute to his son, Roger, who died of AIDS. Alfred told me he wasn't as supportive of his son as he should have been." Naomi leaned up on her elbow. "Enough reminiscing. What time do you want to leave to pick up Ellie?"

The morning sun was slowly overtaking the streetlight. We had things to do. Ellie had chartered a plane that would bring her into a neighboring town that had a small airport. She'd be staying with us through the wedding and into her long break before Pittsburgh.

Finally, I'd get real answers about her health. Stuart had managed to cancel the last few small concerts at her request. That was as much information as I could get out of him. When I'd pressed Ellie about what was going on, she told me it was nothing to be concerned about. Her excuse was that she was suffering from exhaustion and the doctor wanted her to rest for Pittsburgh. I wasn't buying it, and neither was Naomi. I was worried, but there was also nothing I could do until she was in front of me. "We need to be over there by eleven. We can take her to lunch before we come home."

Naomi's eyes lit up. "Oh, can we take her to Beanders?"

I kissed Naomi. "It'll cost ya."

Naomi slid her hand down my abdomen toward my center and caused my back to arch into her touch. Her fingers sought out my clit and grazed across the tip. Her eyes locked on me.

"I'll be more than happy to pay the cost. How's your back feel?"

"Still a little tender."

"Well then, let's get a little creative."

The grin on her face sent a shiver up my spine. When she rolled onto her back, she let her tongue snake out and flick her upper lip. She drew me in with a crooked finger. I knew what she was proposing, and I loved her that much more for it. I climbed up her body and straddled her face. Her hands found my center and spread me open. The first touch of her tongue against my skin made me buckle forward, forcing me to grab the wrought iron headboard to keep myself from falling.

"My God, Naomi!"

She continued her assault on me, moving her hands to my hips and digging her fingers into the flesh of my ass. Her tongue lashed through my center, pulling a cry from my throat. I looked down at her and nearly laughed, as she arched an eyebrow at me before settling on my clit, sucking and circling it with her tongue.

We entwined our fingers, and I felt my orgasm rush toward me. I struggled to hold myself up and not crush her beneath me. My legs trembled with the effort, and still she held on, pulling my hands behind my back. When blinding white pleasure washed through me, I felt her swallow and begin to gentle her mouth against my skin. I was completely spent. With near boneless movements, I found my way to her side.

"Damn, woman." I was panting. "What was that?"

She ran her fingers through my damp hair. Her touch nearly broke me out in a fever every time we made love.

"Me, showing you how much I love you and relaxing you so you won't fixate on Ellie. Working yourself into a lather before we pick her up will only lead to you interrogating her in the first five minutes. Whatever it is, Rhebekka, we'll handle it. She's coming to us, and that means we help her in whatever way she needs. If it's rest, then that's what she'll get. The guest room is all ready for her. I have a big pot of her favorite chicken gumbo waiting in the refrigerator, and we'll spend some time together as a family. Simple as that, okay?"

No one could read my inner thoughts the way she could. It was as if I had a billboard on my head, flashing my thoughts across a rolling screen. "I'll try, I really will. If I go all protective big sister, I'm sure you'll wrangle me in."

"That's my job, honey. Now, how about some breakfast? What would you like?"

"More of you."

"I'll have to check the menu and see if that item is still available."

I laughed against her chest. "It's not a permanent offering?"

Naomi pulled up her left hand and twirled her engagement ring. "Soon, very soon."

I grabbed her hand and pulled it to my lips. "Not soon enough for me."

Chapter Twenty-Two

WATCHING MY SISTER STEP off the plane offered me a modicum of relief. It was Saturday, the third week in March, and I was thankful that she didn't look any thinner than the last time I'd seen her. Her smile rivaled the sun. I put my arms around her and sighed deeply. From this point on, I could, and would, protect her.

"It's good to see you, little sparrow."

She melted into me. "It's so good to be here. I've missed you."

Naomi got in on the group hug and pulled my sister to her as well.

"Hey, you. Welcome home. We've been looking forward to this all week. How was your trip?"

I waited by the plane's cargo area for her bags, listening to the two of them talk like girlfriends who hadn't seen each other in years. I was extremely grateful the two of them got along so well. Even if Ellie wouldn't open up to me about her health, she could never escape Naomi's gentle interrogation.

"I'm starved, where are we going for lunch?" Ellie hooked her arm in Naomi's elbow.

Walking beside them, I made my suggestion. "I think we need some pulled pork nachos, an order of onion rings, and a dozen hot wings. How does that sound?"

"Like I'm not going to be able to fit into any of my performance outfits when it's time to hit the road again." Ellie groaned and held her stomach. "Make that two dozen wings and you have a deal."

If I had my way, she wouldn't be hitting the road any time soon. I wanted to know exactly what was wrong. If her doctor wanted her to rest, then rest she would get, along with some of Naomi's home cooking. My plan was for us to spend time together, finalize everything for the wedding, and nurse my sister back to health. She was with us, and that was half the battle.

***

Ellie rolled her eyes back in her head. "These nachos are to die for."

A local beer from Big Timber Brewery sat in a frosty glass in front of me. The place boasted a dozen taps from West Virginia breweries. "No arguments from me."

A tall, dark-haired woman walked up with a menu. "Can I offer you some dessert?" Her Irish brogue grabbed our attention.

Ellie nearly choked on her beer. She took a good look at the woman, while attempting an answer. "What would you suggest?"

"Have ya been here before?" She handed Ellie a small menu. Intricate Celtic knots decorated leather cuffs on her wrists, scuffed and battered from what appeared to be years of wear.

My sister melted in front of me, right into the server's coal-black eyes and thick accent. This woman had many of the things I knew would push Ellie's buttons. Toned forearms and sculpted biceps, all topped off with a killer smile. The accent was whipped cream with a cherry on top.

The woman glanced at us and sheepishly dropped her gaze. Ellie quirked a smile that could melt stone. "I haven't, but these two have."

"Have ya tried the cinnamon pita chips?"

Naomi's eyes went wide. "Oh my God, they're heavenly."

The black eyes twinkled. "They're baked right here every day, and I make the creme fraiche by hand."

Naomi pointed to her. "You make that?"

"I do. I wanted a simple bar fare dessert. The creme fraiche adds a bit of class."

"I'm Rhebekka, and this is my fiancée Naomi. This beauty"—I pointed—"is my sister Ellie."

The woman dipped her head in greeting. "It's a pleasure. Now, can I bring ya a few orders? One won't be enough, trust me."

"I think that's a fabulous idea." Ellie spoke for all of us. "By the way, you know my name, what's yours?"

"Siobhan, Siobhan O'Broin."

Naomi squeezed my knee, catching my eye, and tipped her head in Ellie's direction. I felt a little tug in my stomach. My sister's eyes were locked on the dark onyx of Siobhan's. She was positively glowing. What I was witnessing was worth every calorie I was about to consume. My head told me Tank would soon witness the reality of Ellie's rejection play out right in front of her. I could hear her heart shattering an entire county away.

***

We left Beanders completely stuffed, with a sugar rush from our dessert. Ellie was buzzing with something else. The small business card in her hand provided Siobhan's phone number.

Naomi wrapped her hand under my arm and around my elbow. My free arm slid around Ellie's shoulder. "So, are you going to call her?"

Ellie looked at me like I'd lost my mind. "Well, duh." She pointed back to Beanders. "Siobhan ticked off every box I have in a fantasy woman."

I couldn't help but laugh. "She did seem to have all the things I consider your kryptonite."

"And she plays the fucking bagpipes."

"You're shitting me?"

Ellie held up her hand in oath position. "According to this card, she's in a bonified Irish trad."

"Wow, I don't get over here to the Celtic music scene much. We'll have to check that out."

"Oh, I plan to check her out from head to toe, if I get my way." Ellie nearly snorted her laugh.

Naomi chuckled so hard, she nearly lost her balance and pulled harder on my arm to steady herself. "Oh, honey, I'm pretty sure from the looks she was giving you, she has plans of her own."

We made our way back to Thomas and got Ellie settled in. We spent the rest of the evening vegging out on the couch, watching the original Jesus Christ Superstar. When it ended, I sat up and moved close to Ellie. "Okay, sparrow, it's time to sing. I want you to tell me exactly what the doctor said. I've been very patient. It's time to tell me what's wrong."

Ellie's eyes welled up. Now I was scared.

Naomi got up and settled on the other side of Ellie.

"I have Papillary Thyroid Cancer. It's a small tumor that we've caught very early." Ellie took the tissue Naomi handed her and wiped at her eyes. "It's also why my voice has been a bit rougher."

Alarm bells went off in my head, sending my heart into a terrifyingly quick rhythm. If Ellie said anything else after the word cancer, I didn't hear it. The vibration in my ears reminded me of standing too close to a concert speaker as blood rushed through my ears. The room was starting to spin.

"Rhebekka, breathe." Naomi's cool hands held my face.

The pale blue eyes in front of me weren't quite enough to focus my mind. Panic welled and sent bile into my mouth. I jumped up and stumbled to the bathroom, where I lost what was left of my lunch. I heard water running, then felt a cool cloth on my forehead. Naomi's sharp whisper clipped my ear.

"Rhebekka, pull yourself together. This is important. We need to hear the rest of this before we drop into an abyss that we may not need to. Come on, stand up and wash your mouth out." Naomi pulled me up and wiped my face with the cloth again.

My sister has cancer. Ellie needs her big sister. I grabbed onto that anchor to stop the room from spinning. It was time for me to get my shit together. My own fears needed to be relegated to the back burner. I nodded and rinsed my mouth with water from the tap. Naomi handed me some mouthwash, and I gratefully replaced the taste of bile with the mint. I splashed my face with water, dried off, and made my way back.

Ellie sat in the living room, chewing on her fingernails. I cupped her cheek. "I'm sorry, Ellie. I lost it there for a moment. Forgive me. This isn't about me, it's about you. Tell me everything and what the plan is."

"I need surgery. To give me the most favorable outcomes and best remission chances, that thing has got to come out. It'll mean lifetime thyroid replacement therapy, along with blood tests to monitor my levels and adjust as needed. There may also be complications."

I furrowed my brows. "Such as?"

"Long term vocal changes. Small chance, but given my profession, bigger than I'd like. With the anniversary concert coming, this was the worst time to find this." Ellie wiped tears away.

Naomi settled on her other side again. "No, it's not. Finding it now means we can get it taken care of before it spreads, honey. You found this early. If you'd waited, the tumor might have grown larger. Will it require chemotherapy or radiation?"

"They really won't know until they get in there and take it out. It's possible. The doctors will schedule a full pathology work up."

I pulled my fragile sister into my arms. "Whatever it takes, I'll be right beside you. No matter what, we'll get through this as a family. You'll have the surgery as soon as possible and be on the road to recovery. Is it scheduled yet?"

Ellie nodded. "Friday at Sloan Kettering."

"Okay, then we make plans. Until we get on that plane, we enjoy this time. When we get back, we have this wedding and start living the life we're all meant to as a family." I stuck my right hand out, palm down. "Deal?" I waited, as Naomi put her hand on top of mine.

"Deal!"

I looked at Ellie and used my faith to channel all the strength and determination I could. Her eyes glinted with the tears perched on her lashes. I knew my sister was terrified behind the mask she bravely wore for me. Gently, she put her hand on top of the pile.

"Deal."

Naomi moved nearer, and I held the two most important people in my life close as I closed my eyes. "Heavenly Father..."

Chapter Twenty-Three

THE NEXT FEW DAYS were a blur. Ellie's doctor had her scheduled for surgery Friday morning. We planned to go up and stay Thursday night.

I checked in with Karmen and found her voice surprisingly chipper. Being with her family was doing her a world of good. She had nieces and nephews who were soaking up her attention. She mentioned someone named Zandra more than once. My last stubborn obstacle was Tank, and I had no idea how to deal with that situation.

We'd gone down to the coffee shop. Ellie had invited Siobhan over, and they sat in a cozy table near the window. I stood at the counter, ordering, and turned in time to see Tank stop abruptly and stare through the glass. I followed her gaze and saw Siobhan move a lock of Ellie's hair off her forehead. There was no misinterpreting the intimate gesture. I tried to make it to the door to intercept my former bodyguard. "Tank, don't."

Tank pushed me aside and approached my sister's table. There was no doubt she was zeroed in on Siobhan. "Who the fuck are you?"

I'd had several conversations with the Irishwoman about growing up on the tough side of Dublin. This wasn't going to turn out well.

Siobhan stood up. "I don't know who ya are but move along. This conversation has nothing to do with ya. This is none of your business."

Tank got in her face. "Ellie's my business, and you've got no right to touch her." Tank swung without warning. Siobhan threw up an arm, blocking Tank's blow, before sweeping the former Marine's legs from under her.

Tank's head bounced off the hardwood floor, causing me to wince. This was going from bad to worse. "Siobhan, let me handle her."

"Rhebekka, watch after Ellie!" Siobhan grabbed Tank by the leg and started dragging her out the door of the coffee shop. "Name's O'Broin. I'll ask ya the same question ya asked me. Who the fuck are ya?"

Pushing out of the coffee shop, I stepped between them. Unfortunately, Tank had made it to her feet. Her roundhouse caught me in the cheek and knocked me to the ground. Balancing on one knee, I grabbed my injured eye. With the good one, I watched the horror register on Tank's face. Ellie raged out the door.

"My God, Tank! What the fuck's the matter with you?" Ellie pushed Tank with both hands and went after her again before Siobhan grabbed her.

"Come on, lass. It's yer sister that needs lookin' after." Siobhan led Ellie to me.

"Bek, your eye!" She spun on Tank. "You fucking asshole!"

A siren in the background drew my attention. I shook my head as a large, black Suburban pulled up with lights flashing. Chance rushed out of the vehicle, a hand on her gun and Zeus right beside her. I waved. "It's okay, Sheriff, just a little misunderstanding."

"A little misunderstanding seems to be the understatement of the year. Rhebekka, are you all right?"

"Honestly, Chance, I'm okay.

Siobhan pointed to Tank. "Sheriff, this git came in the cuppa shop and started swinging. I don't even know the gobshite."

Sheriff Fitzsimmons looked at my best friend, who sat with her hands clutching hair on the sides of her head. "Tank, would you like to tell me what the hell is going on? The comm center reported an altercation. I really didn't expect to find Pastor Rhebekka on her knees with the beginnings of a shiner."

As if the situation couldn't get any worse, Naomi came tearing down the street from home. *Someone must have called her.* There would be little I could do now to keep Tank from getting the ass chewing of her life. I stood, wobbling a bit. Ellie grabbed my arm to steady me. "I'm fine. My face got in the way of Tank's fist."

The sheriff pulled Tank up with a strong hand on her bicep and walked her to a bench a few feet away. "Why don't you come over here with me and let's talk for a second. Let things cool down a bit."

I tried to focus my eyes. When I reached up to my face, Naomi pulled my hand away.

"Oh God, honey. The wedding pictures are going to have to be profile shots. What happened?"

I painfully tested my jaw and found it worked fine. I looked over at Chance and Tank. Only one of them was doing the talking. Tank sat, shaking her hand and her head.

Ellie was pacing close to them, fuming. She flipped Tank the bird. "I'll tell you what happened, she has some fucked up idea that she owns me and decided to piss on her territory when she saw me having coffee with Siobhan." She turned and yelled at Tank. "We were never a freaking couple, ever!"

I put a hand out to calm Ellie. My face hurt, and my head was splitting. "Calm down, there's been enough loud and obnoxious behavior."

Ellie's eyes were livid with fury. She was as fired up as I'd ever seen her. "Don't tell that to me. Tell your best friend! I didn't start this. Siobhan, I'm sorry, I really am."

Siobhan grabbed Ellie's hands in a futile attempt to calm her. "You've got nothin' ta be sorry for. You didn't accost me."

The owner of the coffee shop brought me an ice bag. "Thanks, Arty. I'm okay. Sorry for the disturbance."

Arty shook his head and fiddled with his barista apron, as he looked down the street. "No, problem. Luckily, it was only you guys in the shop. What's got into Tank? Never seen her like that."

"People do things they wouldn't normally do when they're stressed out." I turned back to Siobhan and my sister. "Siobhan, do me a favor and please don't press any charges. I'm not planning to. I can promise you Tank will regret this more than you'll ever know. Ellie, don't antagonize her. Let me handle this. After all, I'm the one sporting a shiner."

Naomi remained quiet, holding the icepack to my face.

Chance walked back over to us, Zeus at her side. "I've known Tank for a long time. What the hell happened here? I've got her version of events. Care to tell me your side, Rhebekka?"

How was I supposed to explain this without revealing that Tank and my sister slept together and that Tank had never gotten over it? "I got between Tank and an innocent person, who has nothing to do with this other than having coffee with my sister. I'm not going to press any charges."

Chance turned to Siobhan. "How about you? My understanding is that she accosted you without cause. I can charge her with assault if you'd like. There are enough witnesses around to back up that your reaction was self-defense."

Siobhan's chest rose and fell with a few deep breaths exhaled through wide nostrils. Ellie had her hand on her forearm. Siobhan covered it with her own. "I think enough damage has been done. I won't be pressing any charges either."

I sighed in relief. "I need to go talk to Tank. Thank you, Chance. I think we can handle it from here. I promise you, there won't be any more misunderstandings."

Chance adjusted her Stetson and nodded to me, as she loaded Zeus in the vehicle before climbing in herself. She rolled down the window.

"By the way, I've set up that meeting with Kathleen we talked about. I really want to get our community action group going. Jax said to tell you hi and that you and your bride to be need to come for dinner."

"Send me the info on the dates, and we're there. I'll have Naomi call Jax about dinner."

Chance nodded in Tank's direction. "If you change your mind about pressing charges against Tank, let me know. You might want a doctor to look at that eye, it's swelling pretty badly."

"I will. Thanks again, Chance. I'm sorry for the disturbance. Take care, Sheriff."

I watched her drive off before looking over at Tank. She still sat with her head down, elbows resting on her knees. I went and sat beside her. "In the book of James, it says everyone should be quick to listen, slow to speak, and slow to become angry. Anger does not produce the righteousness that God desires." I put my hand on her back. "And it fucks up my wedding pictures. No one's pressing any charges, Tank. What in heaven's name were you thinking?"

Tank scrubbed her face. Her cheeks were wet.

"I wasn't. When that woman touched Ellie, I saw red. I don't even know who the hell that is."

"It doesn't matter who she is. You stepped way over the line, my friend. Ellie doesn't belong to you. You're turning into some psycho stalker. My sister's made it very clear she isn't interested in a romantic relationship with you. At this point, she isn't even interested in having you as a friend. You keep this up, and she'll go after you legally for harassment. I really don't want this to go there. You've been my best friend for years. I want that to continue. Ellie's my sister. If you can't handle that she's going to be with someone else, then we need to figure something out. There is no middle ground on this, Tank. When we started the brewery, I made you a shareholder. We're business partners and more. As far as I'm concerned, we're family. I forgive you, but this," I pointed to my face, "can't ever happen again. You can't go after someone interested in Ellie. That will be the end of us, Tank, period. I don't want that." I rose and made my way to Naomi. Ellie and Siobhan were walking toward the loft.

The sympathetic look Naomi gave me let me know she understood my struggle to cope.

"How's your face?"

I took her hand and moved my jaw sideways, while I blinked hard.

"It hurts like hell. Tank can throw a hell of a punch. It was why she was so good as my bodyguard. Apparently, her jealousy clouded her long-practiced control. Ellie was ready to kill her."

"Oh, you're right about Ellie. She's pissed. I think I'd be more worried about Siobhan. She has a few specialized skills of her own. She was an officer in the Irish Army for longer than Tank was a Marine. I think she could have truly hurt Tank if she didn't possess incredible control."

I tried to calm my mind as we walked. Tank would stew about this for days, and I didn't have the time or the energy to worry about her. Ellie's surgery was less than forty-eight hours away. My sister had cancer. Tank would need to do her own soul searching. My priorities list had all the concerns I could handle.

Back at the loft, Ellie was tending to Siobhan's hand. I hadn't seen her throw a punch, only block one. Naomi slid her hand down my arm.

"I'm going to get you another ice bag, hon."

I nodded and walked over to my sister and pointed to Siobhan. "I didn't see you get a shot in. What did you do to your hand?"

"I scraped the knuckles when I drug that eejit outside. Ellie here has insisted they need attention. What the hell was her problem anyway?"

Ellie answered the question with brutal honesty, as only my sister could. She wasn't ashamed of anything. "We slept together, once, a long time ago. Apparently, one of us thought it was more than a way to blow off the stress of a long tour."

Siobhan grinned. "Well, ya do seem to be pretty special, so I can't blame her."

Ellie blushed and continued to dab peroxide on Siobhan's knuckles.

Naomi grabbed my hand and led me to the couch.

"Sit."

She handed me a few Advil and a glass of water. I swallowed dutifully and gave her no resistance when she urged me to lay back. She pulled the boots from my feet and sat beside me, as she put a wrapped icepack on my face.

"Ow."

"Sorry. This is going to leave one hell of a black eye, Rhebekka. I think the sheriff's right. We might want to go to see the doctor. Your eye is swelling shut, and there's a cut on your cheek."

"I'm fine. This isn't the first black eye I've had." The first was from my father, when I put myself between him and my mother. He'd told me it was my own fault for sticking my nose in where it didn't belong. I was seven.

I'd watched him drag my mother across the porch by her hair. She screamed at me to get Ellie in our car and lock the doors. I put my five-year-old sister where Mom told me and ran back to defend my mother. I'd hung from his arm, doing all I could to keep him from swinging at her. He shook me off like a rag doll and backhanded me. My mother let out a blood-curdling scream and went after him with a snow shovel. She smashed him over the head and knocked him out cold on our trailer's cement patio. She picked me up, and we drove to my grandparents.

Cool fingers brushed along my uninjured cheek. "Hey, where'd you go?"

I tried to focus on Naomi's blue eyes that I knew and loved. "To the day I got my first black eye."

Naomi knew the story. Mom divorced him after that but remarried him less than two years later. He'd faked becoming a changed man who'd seen the light. The light he'd seen was the pinpoint of freedom from court-ordered support of an ex-wife and two kids. As one of Jehovah's Witnesses, he found his true power over us. The beatings were subtler after that, in places where inquiring eyes couldn't see. I closed my eyes, remembering how our lives got worse after the monster had been given his biblical head of household title. He was granted permission to do whatever he wanted to control his family for the honor and glory of God.

Naomi leaned over and kissed me, forcing my eyes to hers. "That's all in the past, Rhebekka. He can't hurt you ever again. I know Tank didn't mean to hit you, and I'm betting she feels lower than dirt for it. Right now, we need to concentrate on getting Ellie through what's coming. After that, I want to put that platinum band on your hand to match the one I've mentally installed on other, more intimate, parts of you." She winked.

I snorted then winced. "Don't make me laugh; it hurts too much. When Tank decides to turn to someone, it may have to be you. I'm a little overloaded right now. Honestly, probably too close to the situation. Tank is imploding her life over something that isn't going to change. If Ellie had any doubts, today put the nail in the coffin."

Naomi nodded. "I'll call her later. Maybe she needs to stew for a bit. Every action has a consequence. It's time for her to do a little reflection about the direction her life is headed. I was talking to Karmen when the call from Arty came in. I'm starting to think Zandra may be coming back with her. Zandra illustrates graphic novels with her sister. Karmen's apparently known her for years."

"I want Karmen to be happy, no matter who she's with. I've given up on Tank seeing what was in front of her. Karmen is too wonderful to be pining for someone who's too blind to see the forest for the trees. If Zandra comes back with her, then we do all we can to welcome her into the family."

* * *

Siobhan made no attempt to wake the fragile woman who'd fallen asleep on her. She tenderly held Ellie as they lay on the couch. Naomi went down and handled our after-school program with assistance from Franklin and later led the Lenten service while I recovered. She'd ordered pizza before we settled in to watch a movie.

When the credits rolled, Siobhan stretched and gently woke Ellie. "I need ta go home. I work tomorrow and have ta be in at eight for prep work and liquor delivery."

Ellie yawned and grabbed her hand. "I'll walk you out."

"Siobhan, despite what happened earlier, you're always welcome." I rested a hand on her arm as they passed by.

"I'll be back. The company is spectacular." She kissed the top of Ellie's head, towering over her as they walked out.

Naomi snuggled in closer. "I've never seen Ellie so smitten."

"Time will tell. Her track record is pretty shaky. She hasn't let herself feel anything beyond surface attraction. I shudder thinking about some of her past relationships, especially Tre. I'd still like to string that guy up by his balls."

"Now, now, remember you're a pastor who speaks about forgiveness. Enough about him. How's your eye feel?"

"Sore. Still can't open it all the way."

"Tank called me to check on you, when I was with the kids. She's too embarrassed to call you."

"I've already forgiven her. I might not be ready to talk about it yet, but I hold no malice against her. Is Franklin okay to handle services, if we run into complications at Sloane Kettering?"

"He is, but there won't be."

I was praying fervently for everything to go well. Ellie came back into the room, slightly flushed and running her finger along her bottom lip. Unless I missed my guess, a make-out session had taken place at the bottom of our steps. When she lay down on the couch and bounced her feet up and down, I could tell she was excited.

"I take it you like Siobhan a little bit?"

Naomi's laugh was enough to start me chuckling and stirred up pain in my swollen face.

"Ya think?" Naomi cupped my cheek.

Ellie put her hands on her hips. "Come on, you two. Cut me some slack, but yeah, I like her. I'm not sure I've ever met anyone like her. And that accent, holy shit. It cuts right through to my—"

I put my hands over my ears and started to chant. "Nah, nah, nah, nah. I don't want to know what happens to certain parts of you. I'm enjoying the smile on your face though."

"She put it there. Siobhan's different, Bek."

"Well, then enjoy it. Does she know about the surgery?"

My sister nodded. "She really wanted to come with me. The bar keeps her pretty busy. She's part owner with the other members of her band, The Trad Brigade. She showed me some of their stuff on YouTube, incredible. Siobhan's a talented musician. She plays bagpipes, fiddle, and guitar. She was eyeing your Gibson." Ellie pointed to the sound booth. "She's jealous of the in-house studio."

"It does come in handy. So, I take it you're going to see her again?" I raised my head enough to be able to see her clearly with my one good eye.

"I am. She's asked that you text her when I'm out of surgery. Will you?"

Naomi pulled out her phone. "Give me the number, and I'll put it in my contacts."

Ellie rattled off the number as she bit her fingernail. I knew what was coming. "Bek, what are we going to do about Tank?"

I sighed deeply. "I don't know Ellie. You two obviously need to have a sit down and establish some clear boundaries. I know you've tried, but you've done it from a distance. Let Naomi mediate if necessary. I'm too close." I pointed to my eye. "And I need one good side for pictures."

Naomi smacked my arm. "Smartass. Let me up so I can get you another icepack."

"I don't know what more to say to her. I've told her there's nothing." Ellie formed a zero with her thumb and fingers. "I have no romantic feelings for her, period."

"I know that, and I've tried to tell her the same thing. Everyone has tried to tell her she needs to let go. She thought she could keep waiting and eventually wear you down like Naomi did with me. She thought all that was a way to show you how committed she was, or so she's told me."

"Hell would freeze over first, especially now. I'm going to bed. I've got a ton of calls to make before we leave for the airport. You guys are still okay flying, right?"

"Yup. We need to be over there by noon. According to the pilot, we'll be in New York before we can drink a can of soda. We'll go get checked into the hotel then out to dinner." I snuggled my head into Naomi's lap when she came back and placed the icepack back on my face. "How's the swelling?"

Naomi twisted her mouth a bit. "Not much better. Without the ice, it'd be worse. It's a lovely shade of black and blue."

Shaking my head, I added to the misery. "And by our wedding, likely a gorgeous shade of green and yellow."

"I'll call in the best damn makeup artist in the business. I don't want your wedding pictures to look like head shots for *The Walking Dead*." Ellie came over and kissed us both. "Night, you two, and thanks for everything."

I held her hand. "It's going to be okay. Have faith. I do."

"Love you both."

When she was gone, I let go the breath I'd been holding. "I'm scared, Naomi."

"So is she, my love. The difference is, we don't have cancer. She's going to need us to be stronger than we've ever been. We have each other, and we'll be there through it all with her. No matter how long or what it takes. That's what family does."

"I wonder if she told Mom? I doubt it, but that popped into my head when you said family. Today's events stirred up a few things for me. I need to spend some time with the guitar to process all this."

"Want company while you work through those demons?"

I kissed her hand. "You know my system won't let me sleep for a long time. You're tired, and tomorrow's a big day. Go to bed. When I wear myself out, I'll join you." I stood and helped her up, drawing her into my arms. "I love you, Naomi."

"I love you too. How about some help pulling that shirt over your eye?"

"That'd be nice. Guess I need to pack button ups for the trip."

We kissed and parted ways near the soundproof booth. I walked in and plugged in my Gibson. Pulling my pick from my back pocket, I settled the guitar in place. I cleared my mind and channeled some of the guitar greats. I had one mission, make sure Ellie beat this cancer and lived a long life. I let the notes I played take me to another state of mind, one that told me anything was possible. It had to be, I would make it happen, no matter what I had to do.

Chapter Twenty-Four

ELLIE'S SURGERY WENT WELL, though she developed a fever in the recovery area. The complication caused a delay in her release. Instead of leaving the hospital Saturday, as we'd planned, we were still in New York. I wandered the hospital hallways drinking bad coffee until I finally located the chapel. That's where Naomi found me and told me they were releasing Ellie.

The doctor was in Ellie's room when I walked in. Ellie was pointing to her throat. The doctor pushed his hands into his lab coat. "I believe the hoarseness is likely from the intubation, as much as the thyroidectomy. We'll call with the pathology as soon as we have it, so we can make further treatment decisions if necessary."

Ellie nodded and thanked him with a rough whisper.

I leaned over and wiped a tear from her cheek. "It's going to be okay, Ellie. Let's go home."

***

Siobhan met us at the airport and carried Ellie to my Land Cruiser. She was already so frail in my eyes and further weakened from whatever she'd picked up at the hospital. "Thank you, Siobhan. Do you want to come with us?"

"I'll follow in my vehicle. I've booked a room at the bed and breakfast there in Thomas. I've taken the week off ta stay close."

The second her hands planted themselves on those lovely hips, I knew Naomi was about to change Siobhan's lodging arrangements. Naomi tilted her head to the side.

"You'll do no such thing. You'll stay with us. If Ellie doesn't want you in with her, there's another guest room. I'll let you two work that out. For now, let's all get back to Thomas."

I yawned and handed the keys to Naomi. I hadn't slept for more than a few hours since we'd left. "I'd listen to her, Siobhan, she's the most stubborn woman I know."

Naomi held up her hand with the engagement ring and bumped my shoulder, nearly knocking me down. "Siobhan, sometime ask me how long it took me to get this. Talk about stubborn."

I was exhausted. "Touché. For now, how about we head to the house?"

Siobhan followed us home and helped Ellie upstairs, while Naomi and I took care of a few things in the church. My congregation was truly amazing and always supported me when I needed it. I'd called everyone from our after-school program and found a few parents, as well as Franklin and Rev. Mathew. I was free to make sure Ellie was healing. I promised to be back no later than Wednesday for the next Lenten service.

All I really wanted to do was care for Ellie and get married, but everything seemed to be tunneling in around me. I had an amazing woman in my life who had waited long enough.

When I peeked in on my sister, Ellie was dressed in a T-shirt and yoga pants, lying on Siobhan's chest. One leg and foot was out from under the covers, exactly as I'd expected. She'd slept like that since we were kids. I got a thumbs up from Siobhan and smiled at the way she was taking care of Ellie. It was after midnight. My exhausted body was in direct opposition with my mind. Naomi tugged my hand.

"Come on, my love. You haven't slept in days. I know your internal clock hasn't struck four but come to bed with me. We'll watch television until you fall asleep. You're too tired to play, no matter what your head says."

I didn't argue. I walked into our room to get ready for bed. Naomi moved around the plush space, turning down the sheets while I stripped and went to brush my fangs. My mouth felt like I'd been sucking on cardboard, which was exactly what the hospital coffee tasted like. I climbed into bed and waited on Naomi. Once she was snuggled in my arms, I lay there watching the faint, yellow light from the streetlamp filter in. The weather was changing.

Recently, I'd noticed some bushes starting to push buds out. I silently hoped for snow on our wedding day. The pristine white would hide the muddy brown of prespring. The rains hadn't come to wash off the mud created by the constant plowing of the snow and sleet.

I nestled her closer to me. "It's good to be home."

"I won't disagree."

Her quiet sighs told me how tired she was. I kissed her head. "Go to sleep, baby. I won't be far behind."

"Yes, you will, but I want you here with me anyway. Night."

She kissed the skin on my chest, as I watched the shadows around the room. We were home, and that was all that mattered.

*　*　*

I had no recollection of falling asleep. When I woke, Naomi was gone. I could smell the coffee as I stretched. After a trip to the bathroom, I made my way to the kitchen. My favorite mug sat waiting for me.

"What time is it?" I slurped my coffee and looked at a fully dressed Naomi.

"A little before ten. I checked in on Siobhan and Ellie. I asked about breakfast, but they declined. I'll make sure Ellie eats something for lunch. Senna sent some chicken soup from the store. Oh, and Karmen's coming home early. She heard about the dustup with Tank. She's pissed."

"She'll have to stand in line on the pissed part. Ellie was still ranting about it in her fevered state. Have you heard from Tank?"

Naomi dried a few plates and put them in the cabinet. "Yes, she called to check on you and Ellie. She's really hard on herself. I told her it was something she was going to have to work through. My suggestion about prayer didn't go over too well, so I let it go."

"Talk about me being stubborn." I continued to drink my coffee.

"She's cut from the same cloth as you."

I followed Naomi, who carried a basket of laundry to the living room. I sat beside her and grabbed a T-shirt to help. "It took me a while to get out of my own way. I'm so incredibly thankful you didn't give up on me."

She snatched the T-shirt I held and threw it aside. She pushed me back and lay down on top of me. "You were worth the wait."

I wrapped my arms around her and kissed her. She met my lips with all the passion of a woman who'd waited years to be with the most stubborn woman in the world, namely me. "Do you have any idea what you do to me?"

Naomi nodded, as she pulled up my T-shirt and ran her nails across my stomach, just above the waistband of my sleep pants. "I do."

I groaned, as I pushed my hips up into her touch and watched a wicked smile cross her lips.

"And you're not the only one in need." She rocked her hips into me, as I ran my hands up under the back of her shirt. Her skin was fine silk on my fingers. I'd often wondered what the sensation would be like without thick callouses hardened by guitar strings.

Without prompting, she let me know how she felt about my hands. "I love the roughness of your fingertips. It brings your touch to an entirely new level. I especially like it when you brush them lightly across my cli—"

I put a hand across her mouth and jerked my eyes to the kitchen. Our company was up and pouring coffee in the adjoining room. I put a finger to my own lips and tried to keep her from laughing. We listened to a giggle that moved into a light groan. Naomi and I were doing all we could to keep from revealing ourselves or embarrassing my sister and the woman who obviously had her attention. There was more rustling in the kitchen followed by quiet conversation.

"Quiet, lass, they'll hear us."

"My sister doesn't go to bed until four am, she's still asleep. I have no idea where Naomi is."

Naomi couldn't hold back and started chuckling into my hand, which made me stifle my own laughter. The couch cushions absorbed most of the vibration, as I put an arm around Naomi to hold her below the back of the couch. I implored her with my eyes to get it together as we listened to Siobhan's rich accent.

"So, we're all alone in this kitchen?"

"Seems to me that's the case. Look around, it's an open floor plan."

"Then they won't mind if I put ya up on this counter, and run my tongue—"

Naomi popped up from my arms. "Wait a minute, not on my counters."

The laughter that came from near the kitchen was infectious. We sat up to meet the mischievous eyes of my sister and her accomplice. The two stealthy women had moved around the counter and had come to stand near the couch, coffee cups in hand. Apparently, they could see us even though we couldn't see them.

Ellie stood with a hand on her hip and an eyebrow raised. "We heard you guys a few minutes ago. Bionic ears over there told me where you were even when I couldn't see you." She pointed in the direction of Siobhan.

Naomi and I looked at each other, laughing. Together we said, "Busted."

Naomi crawled off me and sat up. "How are you this morning?"

I eyed the bandage on Ellie's neck. It no longer seemed to have anything seeping through. She wagged her hand left and right, a noncommittal answer.

"Still a little sore, but I don't feel so drained. Voice is still hoarse."

I watched her eyes. I knew all her tells, and those eyes held concern even if she didn't let the words pass over her lips.

Siobhan held the coffee pot in her hand. "Either of ya need topped off?"

My coffee was likely cool after our impromptu make-out session on the couch. Naomi moved to the kitchen to start something for brunch. It was way past breakfast, but a little early for lunch. I readjusted my position and held up my cup. "I could use a warm-up."

Ellie snickered. "I'm pretty sure that's what we busted up."

I threw a pillow at her that she deflected.

"Too slow, old woman." She sat down on the loveseat and curled her feet under her.

After Siobhan topped off the coffees, she took the pot back to the kitchen. I heard her ask Naomi to let her help, and the assistance was accepted. The woman I was marrying was getting to know Siobhan on her terms, in her way. She'd also get the low down on how Ellie was really doing while I distracted my sister.

"Slow my ass. Let's talk wedding. Did you want to have a part in any of it? Maybe a reading or something? You'll be making the maid-of-honor toast at the reception, but I want you to have more of a part than merely standing up with Naomi."

Ellie sipped her coffee and gazed into the kitchen.

"Is it okay if Siobhan comes?"

I reached over and grabbed my sister's hand in mine. "It's more than okay. Don't worry about anyone else. There won't be a scene, I promise. You really like her, don't you?"

Ellie nodded slowly, her eyes never leaving Siobhan's form.

"I do. She's different, Bek. Doesn't give a damn about who I am with Regal Crimson. Even as pissed off as I was about the stupidity of the situation, when she dragged Tank outside like a sack of malted barley, I got so turned on."

I rolled my eyes at my sister. Tank was no small challenge, and Siobhan had handled her as if Tank had no protective skills at all. There was more to my sister's new girlfriend than we knew. I was sure of it. I looked back at the tall, brooding woman standing with Naomi in the kitchen. She had the bracers on her arms again, as if she'd slept in them. I turned to Ellie and indicated with a nod of my head at Siobhan and touched my wrist.

Ellie discretely put a finger to her lips and quickly indicated for me to let it go. If it were something I needed to know, she'd tell me later. I nodded.

"She seems more than capable of protecting your honor."

Ellie's face blushed a bit. "When I get better, I've got plans for her. I just don't think I can do that with you around, and I'm not supposed to strain my voice."

I put my hands on my ears and mumbled, "TMI, TMI."

"You crack me up."

"Back to the wedding." I tried to change the subject.

"I do have something, but it will depend on my voice and…" Concern shadowed her face, as she dropped her head. I expected she was worried about the cancer that was supposedly contained to the small tumor the doctors removed through the three-inch-long incision on her neck. *Had it spread?* They'd sampled the lymph nodes closest to the thyroid. We'd get the report in the coming days. I reached out and grabbed her hand again.

"Give it time. Whatever it takes, you will get better. They caught this early, sparrow."

She wiped a tear away and stood. "Something smells good in here."

I followed her and helped carry items to our small breakfast nook. Naomi and Siobhan had created a feast of omelets, bacon, and crepes.

After we'd all settled, I grabbed one of Naomi's hands and one of Ellie's. Naomi and Ellie each held one of Siobhan's, as I said grace and silently asked for a good report for Ellie. When we finished, Siobhan automatically crossed herself. *Lapsed Catholic?* I was making an assumption based on the movements, so automatic I doubted she even realized she'd done it.

My first bite into the crepe had me moaning with pleasure. "Holy cow, baby. When did you learn to make these, and why have you been holding out?"

Naomi smiled and pointed her fork at Siobhan. "This morning, and you can thank our closet chef over there."

A wide grin brightened Siobhan's face, and she flicked a palm upward. "I like sweets." She took a bite of bacon.

I pointed down at my crepe. "You have an open invitation, with or without my sister's permission."

We all turned at a knock on the loft door. "I'll get it."

"Hey, Karmen, welcome home. Come in." I wrapped her in a hug.

"I'm not disturbing anything, am I? A cooler issue at the store cut my vacation short. I wanted to check in on everyone. God, your face looks horrible."

With a roll of my eyes, I waved her in. "Thanks for the compliment. You're never disturbing anything; you're family. Are you hungry?"

"It does smell wonderful in here, but lunch is waiting at the store."

Karmen followed me and walked into Ellie's arms for a hug.

"Hey, stranger, good to see you."

Ellie was considerably shorter than the dark, lithe woman who embraced her.

"It's good to see you, Karmen. I've missed you."

"Back at you. And who is this tall drink of water?" Karmen indicated Siobhan, who rose to meet her with an outstretched hand.

"Name's Siobhan O'Broin, pleased ta meet ya."

Karmen looked at Ellie. "Girl, where'd you get this one?"

Siobhan's face colored, as Ellie smiled and stepped to her side. "Elkins."

"Ha, I've been to Elkins. Never seen anything the likes of her. Damn."

I dropped my head and shook it side to side. "You two are embarrassing her. Try one of Siobhan's crepes, Karmen."

"Can't stay, just wanted to touch base and drop off some sweets." She held up a canvas bag. Zandra is over at the shop, redoing my website. Ellie, how'd the surgery go?"

Ellie's hand went automatically to her neck. "Not bad. No report yet. We'll see what happens after that. For now, I'm mooching off my sister and hanging out with some spectacular company."

"You're in the right place. Anything you'd like from the shop? Next Sunday, whatever you want after services. Okay?"

Ellie hugged her again. I couldn't hear what she told Karmen, but when I saw the embrace tighten, I knew it was about Tank.

Karmen looked good, glowing in fact. "I'll walk you downstairs."

Naomi rose and hugged Karmen as well, welcoming her home and making her promise to bring Zandra by soon. I took Karmen's hand in mine and walked down to the quiet of the sanctuary.

"Now, we're all alone. How are you, really?"

Her index finger traced the pattern on the fabric of the chair she was sitting in.

"Believe it or not, really good. Sometimes, you have to stop staring at the closed door long enough to see the window. Zandra is my window. She's opened a whole new world to me. She's kind, gentle, and so very sweet. We dated once before. It never went anywhere, then she met her wife. Leslie passed away in an accident a few years ago. Zandra and I reconnected at Akira's house, and everything clicked again. We've spent every day together since."

"And a few nights, if I'm reading you right."

She nodded slowly, with a huge smile on her face. "That too." She pointed to the ceiling. "So, Siobhan, wow."

"Ellie was gut hooked the minute we met her at Beanders. I've seen her with a lot of women, and men for that matter. That kind of connection, I've never seen."

"And Tank didn't take it well, did she?"

I pointed to my eye. "Like a bull seeing red. Tank's lucky Siobhan has the control she does. Unfortunately, I stepped in between them, trying to defuse the situation."

Karmen shook her head. "Have you spoken to her since?"

"No," I shook my head, "I've been too worried about Ellie to deal with Tank's shit. I know she's hurting. That doesn't excuse the fact she tried to assault Siobhan because she was touching Ellie. Tank used to be able to direct her emotions into something positive and protective. Now?" I held my palms up. "I have no idea how to redirect her, and I don't have time for it. I'm getting married in a little over a month. I assume you're still up to catering our reception?"

"You'd better not hire anyone else. It's my wedding gift to you two." Karmen glared at me through narrowed eyes.

"The labor, not the food." I pointed at her. "We agreed."

"You're not the boss of me." Karmen stuck her tongue out at me and stood. "Now, I should go. I'm afraid if I leave Zandra there alone too long, Senna will start swooning over her. Just kidding. Senna is leaving in a few months. She's headed to Austin for cooking school."

"I thought maybe she was headed to San Antonio. Austin seems more her style. So, nothing there for you, huh?"

"Senna is a great person, but she's not someone I can see settling down with. I don't know where Zandra and I will be next month or the one after that. Right now, we're in a good place."

I pulled Karmen into me. "I'm sorry for all you had to go through. I hope this works out." I welcomed her hug back.

"So do I, Rhebekka. So do I. Honestly, she's incredibly sensitive to my needs. I don't want to screw this up."

I held Karmen by her shoulders and looked in her dark, chocolate eyes. "You listen here. I know you. If anyone screws this up, it won't be you. Don't be looking over your shoulder for the dark cloud. Live in the moment and enjoy every freaking second. Promise me."

She wiped a tear away. "Promise. We'll see you at Wednesday's Lenten service. I love you, my friend."

"And I love you. Now get out of here. Go find your woman."

"On it."

I watched Karmen walk out the door, before I headed back upstairs. They'd put my plate in the oven, and Naomi retrieved it as I stepped back into the loft.

"Karmen okay?" She set the plate back down on the table and handed me a fresh cup of coffee.

"Yeah, better than okay. Karmen's pretty smitten. Where'd the girls go?"

"Ellie got really tired, so they went to lie down."

I looked up the hallway to Ellie's room. "Is she okay?"

"Ellie's going to be fine. She had surgery, honey. It's going to take a while for her to get her strength back." Naomi held her hand out to mine.

"I can't help but worry. You taught me how to pray, and I've been doing that with fervor."

"You're not alone, my love. How about we do that now?"

She took both my hands in hers, and together we prayed for Ellie's health.

***

Our kids were excited to see us. As each of them came in, I apologized for our absence over the last week. We sat everyone down to talk with them.

"I know you all have questions about what happened to my face." I pointed to the obvious bruises. "The truth is, I got between someone throwing a punch and an innocent person. The really sad thing is the person who threw the punch was a good friend of mine. Sometimes, you have to stand up for what's right at great cost to yourself. Now, I'm not advocating you step into something that you'll get hurt over. What I am saying is that some things are worth standing up for. Sometimes, that's going to cost you a friend. Other times it could cost you financially, and sometimes, it's going to hurt here." I pointed to my heart.

Amanda spoke up. "Like my mom. She's deployed because she's

fighting for something bigger than herself."

"Exactly, Amanda. It's why we ask God to protect her, so she can do what's right. In Isaiah, it says, learn to do good; seek justice, correct oppression; bring justice to the fatherless, plead the widow's cause." I looked at each of them. "Sometimes doing the right thing is very hard, but the rewards are more than worth it."

***

After the black eye conversation, the kids got involved in their homework, followed by board games. All except Amanda. She held her phone in her hands as if her life depended on it. I sat down beside her. "Not interested in a high-stakes game of Scrabble?"

She glanced down at her phone before sliding it under her leg. "Nah, my spelling sucks." Amanda's short reply oozed with a complete detachment to anything going on in the room.

"Is your mom doing okay on her deployment?"

She nodded her head. I noted the young woman was chewing the side of her cheek before she continued. "We video chatted the other night, for a few minutes. The connection was bad. She seems okay."

More chewing on the cheek. Amanda was going to bite a hole through her flesh.

"Everything okay at home?" Another nod. Something was eating her that she didn't want to talk about. Naomi walked by us, and I smiled all the way from my heart.

Amanda pointed to her. "She's pretty awesome, you know. Naomi, I mean."

"That she is. I came close to losing her until I came to my senses. They say God watches over children and fools. Since I'm no longer a child, guess which category I fall in?"

Amanda grinned and shrugged. "I was going to write this in my journal, but I think I want to talk instead."

I nodded. "You can talk to me about anything."

Amanda took a deep breath. "How did you know?"

That got my attention. Clarifying what she meant would be a delicate process. "That I was gay?"

"No, goof. I know how that works." She pointed to herself. "Duh, a kid of lesbians. My parents are all about talking through how it's okay if I am or not."

Ah, slightly irritated but more communicative. "Then you want to know how I knew Naomi was the one?" Head nod. *Bingo.* I held up a finger to indicate that I needed a moment. This should be Amanda's parents talking to her, but as we all know, every kid thinks their parents are idiots. We seek out some other source that will magically have all the answers our parents are too stupid to possess. In my case, I wouldn't have asked my parents about anything related to love, sex, or for that matter, anything else.

"I'm going to be honest with you, because I think you're mature enough to understand what I'm going to say and not need the gritty details. Cool with you?"

Amanda added a smirk to her nod.

This was dangerous territory. *Lord, help me.* I'd already spoken to each of the parents and had their permission to be frank with the kids about my life. The kids knew I'd be as truthful as I could, without fail. I'd answer any questions, within reason. This conversation definitely meant walking that line with all the balance of a tightrope walker. "I knew she was the one when something other than my libido told me so. Does that make sense?"

I watched her mull over that statement. She waggled a hand back and forth, and I took that to mean she understood a little but needed more clarification.

"When I met her, I was physically attracted to her right away. At first, that was all I could think about. All I could see was how beautiful she was. Over time, I realized that what I saw on the outside was just a fraction of the person she was on the inside. The way her mind worked, her kindness, and her compassion all turned her outward beauty into something stunning. Not to mention, she plays a wicked guitar."

I bumped Amanda's shoulder to lighten the mood a bit. "She could read my mind and frequently finished my sentences. Naomi could tell what I was saying, even when I couldn't clearly articulate it. It was like having the final gear put in place to make the motor turn. When I felt whole, that's when I knew."

We sat for several minutes, silently studying the room. Amanda's eyes stopped on some invisible point. Suspecting her focus was actually internal, I waited.

"There's a girl." Amanda stopped and cleared her throat. "A girl that I met through the STEM club."

"The science and technology group you belong to?"

"Yeah."

I probed gently. "Is she any good at technology?"

"Wicked good." Amanda's smile lit up her face.

I listened, as she told me more about the young lady she was interested in. This was the most I'd ever heard her speak, period. *Smitten without a doubt.*

Amanda's phone buzzed, and she pulled it from beneath her leg. Her hands shook so badly, she dropped it. I watched her out of the corner of my eye, as she picked it up and let her thumbs fly over the screen, tapping out some message that made her giggle.

Amanda closed her eyes and smiled shyly. "Sorry."

"I take it that was her?"

"Yeah, Kiersten. She goes to University High in Morgantown."

"Well, here is my best advice. Get to know Kiersten. Obviously, you already have some things in common. She makes you laugh; that's important. Find out what's important to her. Be good friends first, then be good to each other." I looked up to Naomi, who was walking toward us. "And above all things, be honest. It's always the best policy."

Amanda nodded and let a small smile creep onto her face. "Thanks. Really."

I held up my knuckles so she could bump my fist. "Anytime."

***

Siobhan and Ellie had dinner ready for us that evening when we came back. Siobhan was indeed a closet chef and had whipped up an incredible lasagna. Ellie took credit for the salad, and I gave her as much praise as I did the new love interest in her life. The two women moved around my home, already so comfortable with each other that it was easy to see the growing relationship. Siobhan was fiercely protective and caring, with just the right amount of obstinance to let Ellie know she was no pushover.

"Siobhan, how about we play together tonight? Did you bring your instrument to practice, or would you like to use something of mine?" I opened the small studio area and showed her the collection behind the soundproof walls."

"I brought my fiddle, but I would love ta try your banjo." Siobhan looked around the room and ran a tender hand over the head of my grandpa's guitar. "Maybe later, you'll let me try ma hand at this beauty."

"Deal. You lead for a while, then we'll trade off."

Naomi moved toward the instruments. Ellie started to carry the keyboard to the living room and was chided by Siobhan. "Yer not supposed ta carry anythin' heavy."

Ellie planted her hands on her hips. "Siobhan, the keyboard is hardly heavy. Calm your butch down."

"Ya are a terrible patient." Siobhan stuck out her tongue at my sister.

"Is that tongue a threat or a promise?"

I put my hand over my ears and repeated my na, na, na chant. "My ears, my ears."

Ellie rolled her eyes at me. Siobhan let out a hearty laugh, before she strode across the room to where Ellie sat down. She handed her the keyboard and whispered in her ear. Whatever she said caused my sister's face to blush immediately. Again, I didn't want to know.

I grabbed the Gibson and chose my seat with Naomi on my right, holding a mandolin in her hands. When Siobhan got settled, she nodded to us. She started into a tune that began slowly then picked up. She told us the song was called *Spancill Hill*. When we finished that, we rolled through several more traditional Irish folk tunes. The way she played reminded me of Dropkick Murphys, upbeat and quick. Siobhan was a versatile musician. She piqued my interest enough to make a mental note to pass her group's name around Tucker County for booking opportunities. When we finished, I clapped with appreciation.

Ellie looked at me with a sly grin and played the chords to one of our songs. "I've got one." She began to play "Highways and Skyways."

In some ways, this song was an ode to our touring days. Throughout our early years, we were all over the place. My trusty Subaru station wagon died on the side of the highway with 300,000 miles on it. We sold it for scrap and barely had enough money to replace it. After that road trip, I never ate peanut butter again. I shook my head at the memories and sang the words to keep Ellie from doing it.

"Dreams die hard out on the highways and skyways..." We ran through the entire song, accompanied instrumentally by Siobhan and Naomi. My sister and I had written the song together, as we drove away from Daytona Beach. We'd worked every club that would give us a chance and walked away with a new-to-us vehicle and business cards from a few producers.

Ellie smiled at me with knowing eyes. "Boy, does that song bring back memories." She looked at Siobhan. "Our car took a shitter on our way to spring break in Florida. We slept in a secondhand tent at a KOA campground for a month, because we couldn't afford a hotel." She turned to me. "How many flavors of ramen noodles are there, Bek?" She went bug-eyed and she turned back to Siobhan. "Oh, and I'll warn you now, don't ever make her anything with peanut butter." She drew her hand in a line. "Ever."

My stomach lurched a little at the thought of it, and I almost retched.

"Got it, no peanut butter"—Siobhan mimicked Ellie's gesture—"ever."

Ellie reached out her hand for mine. "Good times, huh?"

"The best." I gladly took her hand and squeezed. My cellphone chimed with a text. It was from Tank.

Can I talk to you? Please?

I showed Naomi the screen and excused myself to the kitchen to avoid the explanation. The three of them continued the impromptu jam session. I watched, as each time Ellie tried to sing, Siobhan quieted her with a gentle hand over her mouth. The woman was growing on me in ways I hadn't expected. She fit in beautifully with my family. I typed a response.

Are you sure you're ready to?

I watched the ellipsis stairstep up and down, indicating she was typing.

Please, Bek?

I looked into the living room and was satisfied that they were engaged enough for me to slip away. I sent my reply.

I know you can't leave the bar. Fifteen minutes, in the back office.
Okay.

I caught Naomi's attention, and she joined me in the kitchen. "Tank wants to talk. I know she only has one other server on tonight, so I'm going to meet her in the office."

Naomi wrapped her arms around my shoulders. "Paul told the Ephesians, be kind to one another, tenderhearted, forgiving one another, as God in Christ forgave you."

Sighing, I held her tightly. I'd already forgiven Tank. What I really feared was that she wouldn't be able to forgive herself.

Chapter Twenty-Five

I PARKED MARVIN OUTSIDE the brewery and punched in my code to the rear door. Tank was sitting in the office, forearms on her knees, her hands clasped tightly together. I took off my helmet and unzipped my coat. The silence was deafening as I waited for her to speak. Tank blinked first.

"Well, aren't you going to say something?"

I pointed to my chest. "Tank, you messaged me." I sat on the couch.

She ran her hand through her short brown hair and stood, pacing in the small office. I still didn't let her off the hook. She had to find this within herself. Absolution couldn't be granted unless the individual recognized their error and atoned in some way. Even an "I'm sorry" would have been a start. Tank wasn't even giving that. I crossed my ankle over my knee and waited, this was her show.

She continued to pace. "I don't even know where to start."

I leaned forward. "The beginning is always a good place."

"God, you aren't going to make this easy on me, are you?"

"No, I'm not. I'm here because you said you wanted to talk." I held up my phone. "That's what your message said. If you need forgiveness, apparently, you've forgotten that I gave it to you the day this happened. The rest is up to you."

Tank stopped pacing and leaned against the desk with her head bent, avoiding eye contact. "I fucked up."

Sitting back, I continued to wait for her. I knew putting this into words would be difficult for someone as bottled up as she'd always been. Normally, it was my job to help her articulate what she wanted to say. This time, I needed to help her find the root of the problem, so it wouldn't happen again. I ran my hand across the leather of the couch and flexed my foot. Time passed. I tilted my head and arched a penetrating gaze in her direction. "Are you waiting for me to dispute that fact, or what?"

Tank scraped a hand over her face. "For being a damn pastor, you can be a bitch."

"This is a waste of my time." I stood and grabbed my helmet. Jesus said that I was supposed to turn the other cheek. She'd taken advantage and slapped that cheek hard. She wasn't ready, and I was too tired to coddle her. It wasn't my job to be a punching bag. I had Ellie to worry about. I took a step toward the door before she grabbed my arm.

"Wait, just wait. Shit. Please, sit down." Tank's voice held desperation.

I wasn't a cruel woman, but she was pushing the limits of my pastoral patience. "I'm listening." I didn't sit down, electing instead to lean against the door frame, helmet in hand.

"Bek, you're the best friend I have in the world and the only family I have left. I'm so, so sorry I lost it. I was completely out of line."

"If you'd have hit Siobhan, your ass would be in jail, and that might have been the least of what happened to you. The object of your raging jealousy is a former military police officer. The sheriff was ready to arrest you with one word from either of us. I asked Siobhan not to press charges, and I didn't file any either. Siobhan was an innocent party in this, and don't get me started about what Ellie was threatening to do to you. She doesn't even want you as a friend at this point."

Tank nodded, biting her lip. She jumped up and started pacing again. "I know, and justifiably so. I don't know what to do to make up for this, to any of you. Naomi asked me to do some soul searching, and I've tried, Bek. I have. I can't forgive what I did, and I don't know how to ask it of any of you."

I came back into the room and pulled a chair directly in front of the couch. "Sit." She hesitated, and I used more authority in my voice. "Sit down, Tank."

As if all the fight went out of her, she slumped into the seat. "Help me, Bek."

Pure anguish beseeched me from her eyes. I sat in front of her and leaned forward. "I've been trying to help you. I've told you that you can't hold on to something that doesn't want to be caged."

Dark eyes flashed at me. "But a stranger can walk in and take her away from me?"

"Let me say this slowly." I raised a stentorian voice to slam the message home. "No one took Ellie from you. She. Is. Not. Yours, period. Never was. Tank, whatever you've had in your head that said she belonged to you, is delusional. Ellie is an adult who knows her own heart and mind. She can give herself as she sees fit, to anyone she chooses. You, have zero say in it."

Tank wiped tears from her eyes. "I love her."

"The way you're treating her isn't love. You covet her. No matter what you feel, this just isn't love. You're trying to treat her as a possession. She's my sister, and no one loves her like I do. That love lets me support her in the things that make her happy. She's had people in her life that I wanted to toss off Lindy Point, but she can date any person she wants. No matter how much you think you have a right to be, you aren't her choice."

I shook my head gently, trying to control myself enough to continue. "If you continue this line of thinking, then we need to find a lawyer to dissolve our partnership. You've been my best friend for years, and I owe you more than I'll ever be able to pay back. Right now, I don't know who the hell you are. The Tank that's been in my life for nearly twenty years would never have tried to punch out someone they didn't know without it being a matter of life and death. You're obsessed with Ellie and oblivious to everything around you."

I was on a roll. I raised my hands in question, before crossing them over my chest to hold in the anger. "This, I can't help you with. I can listen and counsel you. I can make suggestions for you, but you have to realize you are on a self-destructive path that won't ever lead to Ellie being with you. You're pushing her further away and the rest of us right along with her. Nothing, and I do mean nothing, is going to make her do anything that she doesn't want to. She spent years being under our dad's thumb, doing exactly what our parents told her to do. Now, if I tell her to sit down, she stands up. When I tell her to go to sleep, she'll make it a point to stay up all night watching TV. Point that hard head in one direction, and she'll do an about-face to go the opposite. Ellie was never allowed to make choices for herself until we left."

I was pretty sure my blood pressure was up with the way my eardrums pounded. "If she sleeps with one or a hundred people, it will be her choice. You've got to face the fact, you aren't what she wants, and you can't force her to make the decision that you should be. Take a step back and let go of something that was never yours. Be grateful you've had the chance to have her in your life at all." I stopped and took a deep breath. I tried hard to tamp down my anger and disappointment.

Tank looked up with actual tears in her eyes. "You're right, about it all. My head knows it. It's my heart that keeps telling me to hold on. How can I want something so badly that will never be a reality? Hell, Karmen's so mad at me, she walked out of the store today when I came in. Senna said Karmen just got back and brought someone with her. What the fuck? Why can't I be happy? What is it about me that isn't worthy?"

And there's the crux of it all. Tank had grown up in the foster system, right there in Tucker County. When she aged out, she had nowhere to go except the service. She found a home in the Marines. She was forced out in 2000, when "don't ask, don't tell," was still the rule. She'd walked in on her girlfriend having sex with one of Tank's superior officers. She'd thrown them both out of the apartment. Out of spite and revenge, the superior and the ex-girlfriend reported her. In possession of special skills, Tank immediately found a job in protective services. I'd hired her shortly after that, and we'd been close friends ever since.

"Tank, you are worthy of many things, particularly God's grace and my forgiveness. We can never find our worth in others. If we try, there is little truth in it. Our value isn't measured in who we love, what we own, or what we do. Our worth is based on how we live and how we treat others. There's someone out there who is looking for someone exactly like you. Ellie just doesn't happen to be that one."

Lord give me strength. I gathered my thoughts. "She's going to be with me for a while, and from the looks of it, Siobhan will be as well. That isn't any of your concern. You have to come to terms with it and find a way to move forward. Please Tank, before this gets any further out of hand." I pointed to my face.

Tank closed her eyes. "There isn't anything I want more than to be able to take that punch back, but I can't. I couldn't be sorrier, and I don't want to lose you and Naomi the way I've lost Ellie. Hell, if it hadn't been for Naomi telling me she was fine, I wouldn't even know the outcome of her surgery."

"Eventually, you'll have to find new footing with her. You've got to get your emotions under control, because she's going to be here for a while. She'll want to come to hear me play, and she won't be alone." I looked hard at Tank. "Find peace with her choices, before you destroy everything you have."

I strapped on my helmet. "I'm going home. I'll stop in tomorrow."

Tank nodded and grabbed my hand. "Thanks, Bek. I mean it."

I leaned down close to her face. "You're worth it."

***

The kids were in charge of the Wednesday Lenten service. We'd put together a small drama for the parents that was well received. I watched the kids soak in the praise and appreciation for their efforts. Friday morning, I found myself practicing with Naomi to play at The Purple Fiddle that night. It was right up the street from the house, and Ellie felt well enough to join us with Siobhan by her side. With only a few days of Siobhan's vacation left, the two of them were inseparable. Tank hadn't tried to stop by the house at all, though she had come to the midweek service.

Naomi handed me a piece of sheet music. "Do you want to go over that new song?"

I nodded. "Yeah, that'd be good. See what reaction we get. I know Ellie loved it. I'm still worried about that hoarseness in her voice. Did she give any indication about when the pathology report would be available?"

Ellie walked into the room, hand in hand with Siobhan. She held a piece of paper in her free hand. "Now."

I turned so I could see her clearly. "And?"

A smile that crinkled her eyes broke through. "Everything's negative."

I jumped up from my seat and knocked the sheet music to the floor, as I grabbed and hugged her tightly. Ellie grabbed a handful of my shirt.

"Hey, hey. I'm okay, Bek. Really, I'm okay. It's over."

Siobhan put a hand on my shoulder. "Best news ever."

Tears were streaming down our faces, as Naomi wrapped both of us up. I hugged them closer. "Thank God. I was about to offer a free keg to bribe someone to get the report done."

Naomi went to the kitchen and pulled a bottle of champagne out of the refrigerator. She handed it to Siobhan and pulled down flutes. "This calls for a celebration!"

Like a pro, Siobhan opened the bottle without putting anyone's eye out and poured the golden, effervescent liquid into the glasses that were passed out to each of us.

Ellie wrapped an arm around Siobhan. "Who's making the first toast?"

Siobhan tipped her head toward Ellie. "I think it should be you, lass."

"OK, here goes. Bek, through all the times in my life when I've been truly scared, I've had you by my side. I'm not afraid to tell you how scared I was when that doctor said I had cancer. And like always, you guys were right there for me. Somewhere along the way, God knew I needed something more and sent me you, Siobhan. So, here's to family of birth and choice, may we watch many years pass together."

We toasted, and I silently thanked God for Ellie's health and the continued happiness I was privileged to see. I thanked God for my blessings, great and small. "So, does this mean you're completely out of the woods now?"

"I'll always need thyroid medicine and monitoring." Ellie took a sip. "We'll do a cancer check every so often. From what my doctor says, I shouldn't have any problems, since there was no lymph node involvement."

"Best news ever, little sparrow." I toasted my sister. "If we didn't have this gig at The Purple Fiddle tonight, we'd go celebrate."

"I say we celebrate anyway. We'll buy the entire place a round in Ellie's honor tonight." Naomi held up her sheet music. "If we don't practice, we'll need them good and drunk, so they won't hear the mistakes."

"Would you be opposed to us playing with you?" Ellie held her hands up. "I won't try to sing, I promise."

"Fill in with whatever you want to. Here's what I'm planning." I reached over to the bar and handed the set list to my sister.

"I know most of these." Siobhan was looking over Ellie's shoulder. "Aren't some of these from Regal Crimson, lass?"

"Yeah." Ellie nodded. "Bek writes most of our stuff. Since I can't seem to tempt her back into performing with us, it's the next best thing."

"I'd love to play with ya some tonight. What do ya think, banjo or my fiddle?"

Naomi's eyes were dancing. "Oh fiddle, definitely. You are going to have to bring Trad Brigade over here sometime."

"I'd like ta do that. You let me know when, and we'll try to find a way."

Ellie snuggled into Siobhan's side. "It'll feel good to get out and watch these two play for a crowd. They headline up at Redemption's Road frequently, though I don't intend on stopping in there for a while."

My sister patted my arm, and I managed a small smile at Ellie. She and Tank had yet to speak. I didn't know when, or if, that would change. I grinned at both of them. "Well then, let's get practicing."

***

The eccentric music venue was packed with tourists, as well as locals. Snow lingered on the ski slopes, though the season was over for anyone other than employees taking their final runs around the melting patches. The area was beginning the transition into spring's fishing, hiking, and mountain biking.

Repurposed pews and vintage, wooden folding chairs sat around the performance area. Thousands of footfalls, dancing in time to the music, had scuffed the tongue and groove planks between the bar and the small stage. We'd started playing at seven and would entertain the crowd until ten. We were firmly into the second hour and enjoying crowd requests.

A woman up front yelled at us. "How about something from Fleetwood Mac?"

"Great suggestion." I turned to my fellow musicians. "Which one?"

"How about, 'Say You Love Me?' Do you know that one?" Ellie grinned at the tall Irishwoman who had her complete attention.

"I do." Siobhan grabbed the banjo.

I pointed to Ellie. "No singing. I mean it." I leaned in close. "Say it with your eyes, little sparrow."

"Play, you jackass." She bumped me.

The rest of the evening, we played requests that ranged from a variety of musical styles and genres. I thanked the crowd and told them we would be closing with one of my favorite songs from Halestorm. I opened on the ancient upright piano at the side of the stage that played surprisingly well. I knew it was killing Ellie not to sing. She loved this song as much as I did. When she was in top form, she could blow the lyrics away.

Since *The Strange Case of...*came out in 2012, "Break In" had been in my repertoire. It always made me think of how hard Naomi worked to break through my walls, both spiritually and physically. I connected so viscerally with the song that I was nearly in tears by the time we pulled out the final words.

The crowd had grown very quiet during the song, but when we struck the last chord, they erupted in raucous applause and whistles. Naomi came over, and I melted into her touch as she wrapped an arm around my waist. This woman was my whole life, and I would always regret the years we'd missed.

"We've got a lifetime left, my love. Let all that go. We can't change five minutes of the past, but I refuse to miss a single second of our future. Let's pack up and go home, so I can do unspeakable things to your incredible body."

Her lips were so close to my ear, I could feel the heat from her breath. Goosebumps covered my skin, and I physically shivered. "How do you read my mind?"

"It's all part of loving you."

"Thank God for that."

Chapter Twenty-Six

TWO WEEKS PASSED AFTER Ellie's surgery. We were settling into a comfortable routine of having Ellie living with us. Most things were finalized for the wedding, and I couldn't have been happier. Yet I anxiously paced the floor. Ellie had gone back to Sloane Kettering for a follow-up appointment. Unfortunately, I had a previously scheduled engagement, necessitating I stay behind as Naomi made the trip with her.

The Strat hung from the strap around my neck. I'd played every calming and positive song I could think of. I moved on to complicated chords and riffs that occupied my mind, including classical compositions and progressive scales. My fingers were starting to feel uncomfortably shredded. I'd have to stop soon or be unable to play for a few days.

My back pocket vibrated, and I heard Ellie singing. I grabbed my phone and answered with a desperate tone. "Ellie?"

"Whoa there, Reverend of Rebellion. Before you have an anxiety attack that leads to an aneurysm, I'm fine, Bek. The tests took a little longer than expected. There was a foul-up with the lab. I'm okay, big sister, I promise. Talk to Naomi for a second to confirm I'm telling you the truth."

My tired angel sounded a little gravely but still as sweet as honey from the comb. "Baby, she's fine. I have a full report in hand that says so. I am positive you've been playing nonstop, so put the guitar down and talk with your sister."

I ran a shaky hand across my face and did as she asked. The Strat was now on the stand, and I managed to sit down on a barstool, clutching my phone.

Ellie came back on the line. "Bek, I'm all right. We do have a problem, though."

My senses went back on alert. What wasn't she telling me? It didn't take long to understand.

"A storm swept in. All small planes are grounded."

I walked over to the windows in my loft and looked at the snow that was blowing sideways. March had come in like a lamb and gone out like a lion. We'd had a small break that allowed Ellie and Naomi to make the flight north. We'd known there was a possibility they'd have to stay another night or two, if they didn't get another clear window.

I closed my eyes and held the phone tighter. "I figured. It's pouring it down here. I can't even see into the courtyard. Stay there as long as you need. What did they say about your voice?"

The long pause made my pulse jump. I didn't like the silence. "EllieAnna, what did they say?"

"There's damage. No one seems to know how long it will take to heal, or if it will get any better. I'm calling a specialist for a second opinion. According to the doctors here, actual singing won't do any more damage, but the tone and quality have definitely changed. They don't have any answers why."

My heart dropped. "I'm so sorry."

Her voice sounded so small. "I wanted to be the one to decide when my career was over. This wasn't how I wanted to do it. We'll talk when I get home. Right now, I need to process everything. I love you, Bek. It'll be all right. We've had a good run. Maybe something is telling me there's more to life. All I know is we'll figure it out. Here's Naomi, she wants to talk to you again. I love you. I'll text when we can fly out."

"I love you too, little sparrow, with all my heart."

Naomi came back on the line. I didn't press, knowing my sister was close to her. I could hear the apprehension in my fiancée's voice. "What's it look like there?"

The woman I was so deeply in love with knew me so very well. She was trying to take my mind off Ellie, and I was grateful for the attempt. I played along. "We've probably got four inches, and it's still coming down like crazy. It's a near whiteout here. They're trying to keep up with the plowing, but you know how narrow the streets here in Thomas are. I'll head out to shovel soon. Victoria's driveway will need to be done. When it settles down a bit, I'll go over there."

"I thought she had someone doing that?"

"She did. Unfortunately, the guy isn't reliable. I know she has a food bank day scheduled for tomorrow. She'll try to do the shoveling herself if I don't."

"Be careful, Rhebekka. Call me later. We're staying at the same hotel we did when we came for her surgery. I'll text you the number to the room."

"Is she still beside you?"

"No, she went to soak in the tub."

"How is she really?" I could hear some shuffling, then a soft click.

"I stepped into the hallway. She's trying to come to terms with everything. I really think she was working toward winding her career back anyway. This is going to bring Regal Crimson to an abrupt halt, unless we can find someone who has a solution. The only thing she has scheduled is the anniversary concert in Pittsburgh".

Naomi sighed into the phone. "From our conversation the other night, when Siobhan was there, Ellie's been planning on taking a full year off. If she can't pull off the Pittsburgh concert first, it's going to put a real financial dent in everyone's pockets. She's got event insurance that will cover part of it. You know how this business is. The money that's already been spent is going to be down the drain. I know you haven't wanted to talk about this, but it's time. I want you to really search your heart for what to do about the anniversary concert. I'm not pressuring you."

"I know. I just don't know if I can."

"This has to be your choice. I know why you stepped away, and you had valid reasons. Think about it. I don't want to be too far away from her, so I'm going back in. I wish you were here. She really needs you."

I sighed. "I wish I could have been. The interment service for Rhett's mother couldn't be rescheduled. He specifically asked for me to help him with the service, and I couldn't refuse."

"I know. We'll be home before you know it."

I rubbed a hand over my face. "Give Ellie a hug and a kiss for me. While you're at it, add several for yourself. I miss you."

"I miss you too, every second we're apart. I love you, Rhebekka, with everything I am."

"And I love you with more than I'll ever be. Call me later."

After we hung up, I went to the closet to get my cold-weather gear. The snow seemed to have let up. Time to get the sidewalks shoveled and treated around my building before lunch. I'd show up at Victoria's after that.

***

Victoria was scowling and fussing over me. A plate of homemade, chocolate chip cookies sat on the bar, as I warmed my hands around a hot cup of coffee. We'd been talking for the last ten minutes about what was needed down at the food bank. I watched Victoria wringing her hands, as she looked out the window. Something was bothering her. I touched her forearm.

"What's wrong?"

Victoria stilled her hands. "I was hoping we'd seen the last of the snow. I'm worried about Mr. Slawbaugh. I know he's running low on fuel oil. When that happens, he tries to get firewood from around his house. He's eighty years old and has no family in the area. We try to take care of him."

"I could take out a few five-gallon cans to him. I've got the truck. He lives down off Red Creek, doesn't he?"

"He does. At the end of what they used to call Carr's Camp Road, where it crosses the river over into Randolph County. With what we are expected to get in the next few days, you won't be able to reach him if it gets much deeper. That old man is stubborn as a mule. I've tried more than once to get him into town when it gets bad. He just calls me an old worrywart and thanks me for the food. When I was there two weeks ago, he was banging on that tank to see what the level was. His gauge stopped working."

I put the last bite of cookie in my mouth and chewed as I stood, making my way to the door to pull my boots on. "I'll go get him twenty gallons and take it out. I don't want to wait. This storm isn't over. There's another six to eight inches forecasted."

"Are you sure, Rhebekka?"

"Yes, I am." I hugged her.

"You let me get you a thermos of coffee and some cookies. I have a cake I baked for him. Take that with you, will you?"

"I'd be glad to." I nodded and slipped on my Redemption's Road beanie.

She handed me a green metal thermos that had seen better days. Her other hand had a bag full of cookies and Mr. Slawbaugh's cake. I snuck a kiss onto her cheek. "I promise not to tell anyone what an old softy you are."

The woman, who stood no taller than five feet, smacked my shoulder. "See that you don't."

I trudged out to the truck and drove to my outbuilding, before going to the local fuel oil dealer. The snow was falling again. I needed to make tracks before I lost the daylight. The road Mr. Slawbaugh lived on was in an isolated hollow that ran along Red Creek and was better traveled by daylight. It took close to forty minutes to get there in good weather.

Fortunately, they'd called school off that morning, which meant no formal after-school program. My door was always open for the kids who still stopped by for something to do. I was supposed to be at Redemption's Road around seven, for a jam session with a few local artists. I looked at my watch. Plenty of time to get back, take a shower, and still make it to the brewery. I concentrated on driving and enjoyed the pine boughs bent with the heavy snowfall.

I'd already started down Back Hollow Road, when it occurred to me I hadn't called Naomi to let her know where I was going. I pulled over and tried to find a signal. Fat chance. Nothing. The area was notorious for poor cellular service. I tried to send a few text messages, each one failing. I needed to get going before it got any worse. I put the truck in low range and pulled back onto the road. I'd be fine and back home before anyone missed me.

***

Mr. Slawbaugh had been surprised to see me and extremely appreciative. I poured the fuel into his holding tank and handed him the cake Victoria had sent with me.

"I've got to go, but we'll try to get back here in a few days with a larger supply, compliments of my church."

He dropped his eyes from mine. "I'd like to be able to repay you somehow, I just don't have anything to do that with."

"Promise me a few trout this spring, and we'll call it square." I patted his shoulder.

His eyes lit up. "That, I can do. Be careful going back up out of here. That hillside gets slicker than goose shit on wet grass."

I laughed at his analogy and agreed. I climbed in my truck and rolled down the window. "Will do. See you in a few days." I waved as I made my way back up the narrow lane. Traveling alongside the creek, I could feel my back wheels slipping, even in four-wheel drive. I slowed, using extra caution as I chose my path.

I'd have been better off in the Land Cruiser. That vehicle was heavier and made for terrain like this. Then again, if the jug would have spilled, that fuel would be inside the vehicle instead of the truck bed. Somewhere after the second turn, I realized I'd started singing the twenty-third Psalm.

"The Lord is my shepherd; I shall not want." I hummed a few of the lines, as I inched my way up the road. "Even though I walk through the valley of the shadow of death, I will fear no evil, for you are with me."

Out of the corner of my eye, I saw a brown flash bolt in front of me.

I had no time to think. I tried to steer out of the whitetail's path. Large brown eyes locked on mine. I clutched the wheel, elbows locked. The lightest tap on the brake broke the rear end of the Tacoma loose, sending it into an uncontrolled skid. Attempts to counter steer failed, and the edge of the roadway grew closer and closer. I felt the rear tire drop over and realized there was no way for me to save it.

Surely goodness and mercy shall follow me all the days of my life.

Crunching metal accompanied the sound of my own heartbeat. My sister's face flashed in my mind, until everything settled on the one person who completed me, Naomi. *Baby, I'm so sorry.*

The truck barrel-rolled into the deep creek, the broken windows allowing frigid water to rush in. I finished the psalm as the blackness took over.

"And I shall dwell in the house of the Lord forever."

Chapter Twenty-Seven

I WAS HOLDING MY head as I walked up Seneca Trail to the door of Redemption's Road. Drenched from head to toe, my legs felt heavy from water-logged boots and soaked jeans. My vision was blurred from the blood that kept running into my eyes. I had no idea how I'd made it this far. I spat a streak of red into the snow in a futile attempt to clear the tang of copper from my mouth. I must have bitten my tongue when the truck rolled. I knew the fireplace would be roaring, and all I wanted was a tumbler of Fireball to chase the ice from my veins. The closer I got, the louder the music became. I recognized the soul rendering strains of B.B. King's, "The Thrill is Gone." Whoever was playing was incredible. *Franklin?* Couldn't be, unless he'd been practicing more than I knew.

I stood at the door, trying to stomp some feeling back into my toes. My left foot felt completely dead. *How long have I been walking?* Had to be hours from where I'd crashed the truck. I tried to turn the knob with hands that felt like blocks of ice. Thankfully, someone opened the door for me, and I gratefully stepped into the warm air that rushed out at me. I shivered, as I made my way to the fireplace that oddly seemed a bit farther into the room than I remembered. *Must be from where I hit my head.* I stood facing the crackling logs with closed eyes, letting the heat sink into my frozen body. I'd never been so cold.

"You look like you could use a drink. Here, get this down."

Someone I didn't recognize handed me the shot glass. I gratefully tipped it into my mouth, letting it burn all the way down. I shivered, grateful the cinnamon whiskey had washed the taste of blood away. I'd expected it to sting the cut on my tongue. When it didn't happen, I looked into the glass only to find it full again.

I swayed a little, as I turned to warm my back against the fire. I hoped I could catch Tank's eye to tell her about the truck, so she could call a towing service for me. *Who's behind the bar? Did she hire someone new I don't know about?* I sipped the liquid and turned an ear to hear those glorious sounds of guitar magic. The music had changed in the short time since I'd stood there. Someone was imitating Stevie Ray Vaughn, wailing away. *Wow, that even sounds like Stevie.*

I wanted to move into The Confluence, but I was loath to leave the warmth from the fireplace. I continued to sip on what I assumed was Fireball, though I couldn't remember actually ordering anything. It was strange. I looked around the bar, I didn't recognize a single local, though many looked extremely familiar.

At the end of the bar sat a man who eerily resembled country music royalty. He held a guitar on his knee, as he picked with another man. I tried to name the tune, filtering out the bluesy electric guitar from the other room and focusing on the man's hands. After a few seconds of putting together the notes and chords, I could tell he was playing *Galveston*. I'd learn to play Glen Campbell's song when I was twelve, from the book Grandpa gave me. I'd watched *Hee Haw* with my grandparents and enjoyed Glen's performance more times than I could count.

The man turned to me, and I nearly choked on the liquor I'd let pass my lips. He could have been Glen Campbell reincarnated. I was mesmerized, as I watched him play. I wanted a guitar in my hand, so I could join in to show how I'd mastered those gold-record gems. *It can't be Glen, he died years ago.*

I stepped to the bar, trying to shake the cobwebs from my head. I needed to call Naomi. *She'll be worried sick by now.* Tank was nowhere to be seen. A man I vaguely recognized stood behind the bar and spoke to me as if he knew me.

"Play something you wrote tonight, will ya?"

Those words were so achingly familiar. I put a hand on my stomach. "I didn't bring my guitar."

The man had a receding hairline and a beard. "No worries, it's in the other room. Now, what can I do for you?"

When he leaned his girth on the bar, a powerful feeling of déjà vu hit me. He reminded me of a young Art Callahan. I knew it couldn't be him, because I'd read the man had died last December. Art allowed almost anyone to play at his bar in Wilmington, Delaware. He'd eventually been forced to close The Barn Door. Fortunately, before that, he'd given Ellie and me a chance. I was forever grateful. I even sent him an invitation one time to a gig we were playing in Connecticut. He'd declined but had ordered me to do exactly what the man in front of me had asked seconds before. "Play something you wrote tonight, will ya?"

At this point, I was sure I'd bumped my head harder than I'd thought. "I need to talk to Tank, where is she?"

"Not here yet. It's not her time."

"What do you mean it's not her time, she's always here."

The man wiped the bar top. "Exactly what I said, not her time to be here."

"This is ridiculous. Can I use the phone?"

"You can, but I'm not sure you'll get through." He set an ancient rotary phone, attached to a long cord, on the bar.

"What the hell is this thing doing here? Did we break the cordless?" I was starting to get pissed. I didn't know what the hell was going on, but I was going to find out.

He shrugged and walked away from me. I dialed Tank's number, only to hear a rapid beep. "Lines must be down. It's not like Tank not to be here." Something was wrong, definitely wrong. I needed some air. I stepped back outside and turned to stare at the sign above the door.

At first, it didn't look any different, until I noticed the t in *Redemption's Road*. The vertical line of the large cross was much longer and wider than we'd designed and lit up with an almost unnatural golden hue.

I heard voices behind me and turned to see two women wearing winter dress coats and heels, each with a pillbox hat. The two mocha-skinned women looked like they were from a completely different era, down to the completely impractical 1940s Cadillac convertible. One of them carried a white, electric Gibson SG. I rushed to hold the door for the two women and followed them back in.

The man behind the bar threw up his arm in a greeting. "Rosetta, Marie, nice to see you both."

I gasped at the names and turned back to the two women. The one holding the guitar handed it to a man sitting in a chair near the fire and drew off the white coat decorated in rhinestones at the collar. The other woman took her coat off, and both garments disappeared. Both women were stunning in their throwback elegance.

Guitar back in her hand, one of the women walked to me and used two fingers to close my gaping mouth. "Better close that flytrap, honey. Welcome home. I'm Sister Rosetta, and this is my companion Marie. We've been waiting for you for a long time."

I began to think there was more than just a bump on my head. Someone had put my brain in a blender.

"Come on, child. We've got some playin' to do."

She reached for my hand and pulled me into what should have been The Confluence. I'd designed and built that small music hall and played there almost every month since we'd opened.

Instead of my hall, there were four small stages surrounded by people sitting as if they were at a concert listening to the performers. My head was swimming, and the cinnamon liquor was obviously distorting my perception. When I was walking up to the building, I'd heard B.B. King's music. Now, right in front of me, were two of my guitar heroes playing side by side. Stevie Ray Vaughn stood at the mic, wearing his signature plateau hat, complete with a white foxtail draped down his back. He held his "first wife" Stratocaster. Off to his right, was the Beale Street Blues boy himself. Mr. B.B. King held Lucille, his iconic guitar.

I stood completely speechless, unable to form the words to ask questions or give testimony to my appreciation for the music. Two greats performing side by side in my bar. *Or is it my bar?* I looked around. I'd watched several documentaries on the Godmother of Rock 'N' Roll. Sister Rosetta Tharpe had influenced the infancy of rock 'n' roll.

Reverberations of two powerful guitars rocked the house. Turning around, I nearly fainted at seeing Jimi Hendrix and Prince, belting out *All Along the Watchtower*.

Sister Rosetta drew me to the front of the stage. My fingers formed the chords, and I could feel the strings beneath my fingers, vibrating through my hands. How it got there I didn't understand, but a familiar weight settled around my neck. My grandfather's Gibson materialized in my hands. When they finished, we started right into *Purple Rain*.

"Come on, darlin', we've got more to see before you decide which set you want in on."

We walked around, and I stared at two long-dead southern rock icons tearing up the stage. I had to be dead; there was no other explanation for what I was seeing.

"Am I dead?" I didn't know what was happening to me, but if this was heaven, it was exactly where I wanted to be.

"We all gotta die sometime, chil'. Whether this be your time or not, I don't know. Someone waiting for you over at that booth. Go on now, plenty of time to play with us in a bit. I'll be over there with Elvis. You come find Marie and me when you're ready to go. If you stay, we'll play as long as you want. For now, I need to teach that boy some decency and to get that hair outta his eyes."

"Elvis?" I choked out. She waved a hand at me, rolling her eyes as she pointed a thumb over her shoulder. I watched her go, playing that white SG and singing *This Train* with Marie at her side. A stunning young man with an arched lip waited for the pair. Rosetta shook a finger at him when he shimmied across the stage and swung his dark hair down into his eyes.

He looked at me and pointed. "Thank ya, thank ya very much."

"God's a music fan, there's no way around it," I mumbled to myself, as I looked around the room, completely transfixed. I fully expected to see Jesus leading a choir somewhere. *The booth.* Rosetta said someone's waiting to see me. I couldn't imagine what music great was asking for a minute of my time. I stopped dead in my tracks. I saw the scuffed leather boots from my childhood seconds before I spotted the overalls with the crisp, white shirt underneath. In front of him sat a glass bottle of Coca Cola with a straw in it. I could see peanuts up against the side of the glass. The shock strangled the breath in my chest. His grizzled face was lined with years of hard work. Not a single thing had changed about him. He was exactly as I remembered. Grandpa McNally stood and opened his arms.

The tears came like the Cheat overflowing its banks, pouring down my face as I walked into him. I melted into the strength I hadn't felt for more years than I cared to think about.

"Shhh...it's okay, Rhebekka. Everything is going to be okay." He held me for an eternity, before he ushered me into the booth. He took the Gibson and set it on the bench beside him. "Now, no more tears."

"What is this, Grandpa? Is this heaven?"

"In a way. For now, let's look at this as a stopping point. You rest a spell here before you choose a fork in the road."

"My choices being heaven or hell?" I wiped at my eyes, so desperate to see him clearly. I was afraid he'd disappear.

"Not exactly, more like today or tomorrow." He rubbed across sandpaper stubble with his palm. That sound always made me think of him. Grandpa could shave three times a day and still have a five o'clock shadow.

"MaMaw doesn't make you shave here?"

"Oh, she does, trust me. I bartered with her to let me have it when I came to see you. Wanted you to recognize me."

He smelled of hay and sunshine, mixed with motor oil. A scent so uniquely my grandpa I'd have recognized him in the dark if he was anywhere within twenty feet of me.

"This isn't where you stay?" I furrowed my brow as I looked around.

"Land sakes no. This is a special place. I visit when I can, just to listen. Can't say I care for every kind of music here, but just like with life, you learn to take the good with the bad."

I knew he was talking about Jimi and Prince, at the very least. "What am I doing here?"

He tilted his head a bit. "You gave this place its name. Why do you think this was where you landed for your in-between?"

The greatest garage band ever faded around us into muted tones that didn't compete with each other. They settled into *Amazing Grace*, and I blinked hard. "I don't even know how I got here."

"Don't you? Life wasn't easy for you when you were little. Your daddy, well, wasn't much I could do with the boy or the man. You seemed to find your path, you and Ellie. Then you lost your way for a bit."

I nodded, unable to look at him. He'd had a front-row seat in heaven to see it all. The nights of drunken or drugged stupor, the promiscuity, I'd turned my back on God.

"Can't change five seconds ago, Rhebekka, just the next five. Let the past stay buried. I like that girl of yours. Your MaMaw does too."

That brought my eyes back to his. They were the same hazel color as mine, and they twinkled with mischief. "Naomi."

"That's her." He nodded. "She's good for you and frantic right about now over something beyond her control. She doesn't know where you are, and she's pleading to the Almighty for you to come home. I won't lie to you. Ellie's curled up in a ball in that other girl's arms, nearly out of her mind. That's not even mentioning how worried sick your friends are. You're gonna be all right, that I can tell you, no matter what happens. If you decide to stay here, there's a seat up there on the stage for you, right among them greats. If you decide to go, there's a very special family waiting on you back at your church. They're prayin' up a storm, and I can tell you firsthand, God hears them." He pointed up. "And stop fretting about Ellie, she's going to be fine too. It's all about time, Rhebekka. Use it wisely."

"Will I get to come back?"

Grandpa grinned at me. "Someday." His hands clasped mine. "You've got more to do, young'un. It's time you get back to it. I love ya." He stood. "Give me a hug now. Ol' Chet up there is fixing to give me a guitar lesson."

He pointed to where the men I'd seen playing at the bar were now on stage. They were playing *Gentle on My Mind*. Country's crown prince, Glen Campbell, sat with the legendary Chet Atkins, who was waving at my grandpa to come up with him.

"Do you want your guitar?" I pointed to his Gibson sitting on the bench he'd vacated.

"That's not my guitar anymore. It belongs to one of the greats, like them." He pointed to the stage, then grinned at me. "I was just holding it for her for a little while."

He walked away, and Chet Atkins handed him a guitar at the edge of the stage. Together, they turned to me and began to play *House of the Rising Sun*. The greatest guitar master who ever strummed across a set of strings stood playing with the man I admired and loved above all others.

Sister Rosetta came to my side. "Pick up that guitar, chil'. It's time to get on that stage or go home." She smiled at me with teeth so white, they hurt my eyes. I put a hand up to block the pain it caused. The light became brighter and brighter, until I couldn't hold my eyes open anymore. I felt something. Warm flesh touched my neck. I heard mumbled voices all around me, and still I stared at that piercing white light. I couldn't tell if this was the end or not.

I tried to clear my muddled brain, to make out what was being said. Were these angels here to guide me on to heaven? I squinted and blinked rapidly, trying to clear the fog. I could finally make out shapes and colors. The shield reading *Search and Rescue* was so close, it almost blurred. The bright light continued to stab into my skull. A voice, louder now, screamed something I couldn't make out. When I didn't think I could take another second, my ears opened up. I heard the voice clearly.

"Rhebekka, it's Chance. We're going to get you out of here. Stay with me."

Try as I might, I couldn't stay with her. I tried to scream, the effort like yelling under water. All the air escaping, the sound was muffled and unintelligible. The white suddenly wasn't so bright anymore. All I saw was darkness, total and utter darkness, but I wasn't afraid.

Chapter Twenty-Eight

BEEP—BEEP—BEEP. CONSTANTLY, a repetitive beeping noise. It was like being in the studio to mix edit tracks. *Damn, I hurt all over.* I tried to listen, through the infernal beeping, to hear any of the incredible artists I'd seen as I walked around The Confluence with Sister Rosetta. Freaking Elvis had been in the room. My grandpa had been getting a lesson from Mr. Guitar himself. They played the song I'd used to name my church. All so unbelievable, and that was the problem. It was unbelievable. There was no way any of that could have been true. *Could it?*

Everything I'd experienced was beyond belief. How could the bar I'd built exist on another plane, where so many music greats met up to jam in some kind of purgatory? I was stunned. Beep—beep—beep. That infernal beeping. Maybe it was an alarm clock. I swung my arm out and tried to find the damn thing. Cool fingers wrapped my hand, followed by warm flesh meeting my fingertips. I traced the softness with the pad of my index finger. *Lips.*

I continued to follow the contours, hoping to find what I was looking for. I'd know it when I felt it, even without my eyes. There it was, on the left corner, just off center. A small, raised bump just under my fingertips. I'd kissed Naomi's beauty mark so many times. I took a deep breath, relieved that I'd get the chance again. Those soft lips kissed my palm, and I finally heard the one voice I needed to turn the light back on.

"Rhebekka, it's time to wake up. Please, honey. I need you to wake up."

I struggled back to a murky surface, back to that constant steady beep that now seemed like a marker beacon in my fog. I pried my gritty eyes open to see the most beautiful sight in my life, my Naomi. I tried to speak through a voice broken from lack of use. "Hey."

I watched her tears come.

"Hey yourself. Welcome back."

"Someday, remind me to tell you about where I've been. It involves Elvis."

Her laughter was a balm to my soul, as were the lips I felt on my cheek.

"Elvis, huh? Jesus I would have believed. Elvis, on the other hand." She wagged her hand back and forth.

"Where am I?" I tried to look around to get oriented. Robin's egg walls. Curtains on tracks that ran near the ceiling like our shower curtain. *Hospital, has to be.*

"You're at Garrett Memorial."

"What—" My voice croaked, and I tried to clear it. "What happened?"

Naomi leaned down and kissed me.

"Let me call for the doctor, and I'll tell you everything. I'll get you a drink of water."

I nodded, too weak to do much more. I must have drifted off, because I didn't hear her come back in. A touch to my bare arm caused me to startle.

"Sorry, Rhebekka. The doctor will be here in a minute. I've never been so scared in my life. I couldn't get in touch with you. I don't know where your phone is, but there are likely a hundred voice mails." She wiped her eyes.

"No service on Back Hollow Road. Tried to text. Weather was bad." I couldn't make detailed sentences. My throat felt like I'd gargled a glass of Drano filled with thumb tacks. "Throat sore."

She nodded and gave me a small drink. "When you didn't show up at Redemption's Road, Tank thought you'd skipped because you were still mad. I tried calling that night without an answer. I fell asleep after dinner from the long day and didn't realize you hadn't let me know you were back home. When I woke up the next morning, I filled up your mailbox, thought maybe your phone died. When the after-school kids found the door locked, Amanda texted Lynn, who got in touch with Tank. She went to the house looking for you. Tank called me and said she found the Land Cruiser in the garage, but not the truck."

Naomi was interrupted when a woman entered the room in a set of blue scrubs covered by a white lab coat. Her blonde hair was pulled away from her face in a high ponytail. She extended her hand. "Welcome back, Rhebekka. I'm Dr. Amy Halston. You gave us quite a scare for a while there. How do you feel?"

I tried to take inventory of the aches and pains, what I could feel and what I couldn't. Naomi held a straw extending out of the cup for me. I took a long drink and thanked Naomi, trying not to cough as I answered the doctor's question. "Head still feels a little muddled. I ache all over. I can wiggle my fingers and toes."

Naomi fiddled with her engagement ring. The woman I was deeply in love with wouldn't meet my gaze.

Dr. Halston moved to the side of my bed. "Let's check you over good, and we'll talk about what's been going on the last few days."

"Days?"

Naomi took my hand again, leaning on the bed close to my head. "You've been unconscious for two days, honey."

The curtain swished out of place, and my beautiful sister threw herself into the bed with me, sobbing.

"Bek!"

I put my arms around her. "Hey, hey. I'm all right. Settle down now. I'm right here."

She trembled in my arms, as I looked into Naomi's tear-filled eyes. *There's obviously much more to the story of how I came to be here.*

"How about you all fill me in on what happened?" I looked at Dr. Halston, as I stroked Ellie's back.

"Let's check everything out first, then explain. Okay?" Dr Halston took her stethoscope from around her neck.

"As long as you can do what you need to without extricating this growth." I kissed Ellie on the head.

My doctor smiled at me. "I'll try to work around it."

For the next few minutes, she listened, probed, and examined me. When she'd finished, she stood at my bedside. Ellie was quiet, her tears drying on her cheeks. Naomi still held my hand.

"First off, your fitness level, along with the clothes you had on, helped keep you alive. We've treated you for severe hypothermia. As of now, all your vitals are stable. You have a grade three concussion, which means it's severe, accompanied by a prolonged loss of consciousness. Can you remember anything about what happened?"

I searched my memory. The last thing I clearly remembered was getting fuel oil. "Victoria mentioned Mr. Slawbaugh was probably running out of fuel, so I took some out to him. After that, not much."

Naomi drew close to me. "You were in an accident coming back up out of Carr's Camp Road. The truck rolled down into Red Creek."

Another voice entered the room, as a woman in a black shirt drawn tight over a protective vest, stepped to my bed.

"Sheriff, nice to see you again."

"Lay still there, Pastor. You've got your hands full. Let me fill you in on what we know. Maybe that will help. Naomi contacted me, saying you'd missed a few of your normal activities. That didn't seem like you, so we started to backtrack. Naomi said, at last contact, you were going to Victoria's to shovel snow."

"And she told you I was headed to Mr. Slawbaugh's?"

"Yes. When we checked with him, he told us you'd delivered the fuel and left around three thirty. My search-and-rescue team fanned out from his place. One of my squad members, Sarah Ryker, spotted a disturbance where you went off the road and down about forty feet into Red Creek. With near whiteout conditions, you were pretty hard to spot. Nobody goes down that road regularly. I'll spare you the details of how we got you out. We put your ass in a Humvee ambulance and brought you here. We'll work on reports and such when you're feeling better. You gave us all a pretty good scare. Rest and get well. It's my understanding you're supposed to be getting married in a few weeks. Try not to hurt yourself before then, deal?"

I extended my hand, and she shook it. "Deal. Thank you, Chance. If there's ever anything I can do for you, name it."

"I'll keep that in mind. Jax is anxious to meet again for the community action team. You get better soon, you hear?"

"It would be my pleasure."

After the goodbyes, my attention turned back to Dr. Halston. "Okay Dr. Halston, I know there's something that you and this one"—I wiggled Naomi's hand—"don't' want to tell me. Spit it out."

"How about you call me Amy? Part of your body was in the water. In addition to your head injury, you were suffering from severe hypothermia. At its warmest, the ambient air temperature during that period never got above seventeen degrees. Your left foot was crushed in the accident and submerged in thirty-six-degree water. It probably kept you from bleeding to death. The surgeons did everything they could. Unfortunately, it was beyond repair and suffered from full-thickness frostbite. We couldn't save it."

She pulled the blankets back from over my feet. What I was looking at made no sense. Where my left foot should have been, all I could see was a rounded shape swathed in white gauze and covered by beige elastic wrap. I gasped at the sight. I could swear I'd felt my toes curl and flex, earlier, when I was trying to catalog my pain and mobility. Naomi clutched my hand. A calm came over me.

Now I knew why the two women in my life were acting as if I'd come back from the dead. It sounded as if, in some ways, I had. I needed to count my blessings. I was alive and would likely be able to do ninety-five percent of what I could before. By the grace of God, I was still here with my family. I turned to meet Naomi's eyes. "Well, this puts a damper on our first dance at the wedding."

Naomi laughed and wiped at the tears in her eyes. "We'll figure something out. Didn't you tell me Jax had a walking boot when she married Chance?"

I chuckled. "That's right, I did."

Ellie's words were muffled by her head being snuggled into my side. "You never were a very good dancer anyway."

"No commentary from the peanut gallery." I kissed her head again. "Okay, Doc Amy, where do we go from here?"

Amy put her stethoscope back around her neck and picked up my chart. "We keep you here for a few more days to monitor that concussion and watch for infection. After that, we'll get you set up with physical therapy and release you to the capable hands of your family." She finished writing in the chart. "I won't lie to you, Rhebekka, you could have died. You've apparently got a guardian angel watching out for you. Another night in those conditions, and this could have been a lot worse. I'd rather come and listen to you play at Redemption's Road instead of visiting here."

"You've been to hear me play?" I couldn't remember seeing her. That wasn't unusual. I didn't always see everyone in the bar when I performed. Room lighting played a big part of that. If I struck up a "fishing" conversation, I remembered them.

"A few times. The place has some incredible beer, and the women there are easy on the eyes. Your friend, Tank, is always great to talk with. By the way, she's outside waiting to see you. Want me to send her in?"

"Sure. Thanks, Doc. Not many know this, but I co-own that place with Tank. You're welcome anytime, and your tab is on the house from now on. No arguments."

She cupped her chin and rubbed under her lip. "You drive a hard bargain. We'll see about the argument part. God willin' and the creek don't rise, I'll be there."

"Trust me on this, I have it on good authority that God's willin'."

She gave me a thumbs up and walked out. When she'd gone, Ellie sat up.

"You scared the shit out of me, Bek. We couldn't find you. Siobhan and Tank organized everything, trying to figure out what happened, because we couldn't get back with the weather."

I looked at her with alarm. "Tank and Siobhan?"

She wiped her nose with her shirt sleeve. "Hard to fucking believe, but yes. They found a way to put their hard feelings aside, because they both care about you. They had half the bar patrons and your church signed up to search. Thank God, the sheriff's search-and-rescue team found you."

I heard work boots thud against the tile, as Tank stepped to the edge of my hospital bed. She wrapped white knuckles around the edge of the footboard.

I released Naomi's hand and held up my fist for Tank to bump. "I'm okay."

Instead, she moved up the side of the bed until she could weave her fingers in mine, palm to palm, as tears streamed down her normally stoic and unflappable game face.

"My God, Bek."

"My friend, trust me, God certainly played a major role. Don't ever doubt that."

She shook her head. "I'm so sorry."

"Water under the bridge. I hear you've buried the hatchet with Siobhan." I watched her eyes and body language, trying to see any form of anger when I said Ellie's girlfriend's name. Seeing none, I went on. "So, you rallied the troops?"

She nodded.

"Then you called Siobhan, didn't you?"

Tank took a deep breath and nodded again. "And Karmen."

"Thank you for going the extra mile."

"We were going to find you if we had to walk side by side from one end of Tucker County to the other."

I squeezed her hand. "Thank God you didn't have to. Blackwater Canyon would have been a bitch to span."

Tank laughed. "I'll be outside. Siobhan is probably upping the ante. She's a damn card shark. Don't play poker with her; you'll lose your ass."

This time I laughed. I couldn't' help it, even though it hurt. "I'll keep that in mind."

Tank leaned over and hugged me. "Welcome back, Bek. Don't ever fucking do that to me again."

I crossed my heart. "I promise."

Chapter Twenty-Nine

I DRAGGED MY ASS up the steps to our loft, one tread at a time. Despite my exhaustion, I was determined to get up there unassisted. Eventually, when I got my prosthetic foot, this wouldn't be an issue. We had a carpenter coming to install a second handrail on the opposite wall. That simple addition would allow me to balance with my arms, while I used my good leg to ascend.

My stump wouldn't be healed in time to fit a prosthetic foot for the wedding this week. That would happen in a few months. I'd been out of the hospital for three days and had experienced my first physical therapy session with Attila the Hun. Allana was a slave driver, who would help me retrain my body to use different muscles without hurting myself. I also knew her to be an angel of mercy in disguise. Every ounce of effort I had was now being directed into getting strong enough to handle what was coming. More immediately, my focus was on making my wedding day the happiest it could be for my bride. Operation wedding was at full hurricane force.

Naomi and Franklin had led the Easter Service the previous Sunday. My after-school kids had just left, after fussing over me like mother hens. I had great kids, and I laughed, remembering something they'd done for me earlier.

"Pastor Rhebekka? We have something to show you. Can we go boot up ArchAngel?"

I nodded. "I think we can manage that."

When they started playing, I could see the wide smiles and hear the whispers throughout the group. We got to the boss fight. I flew in as Vulgate, the winged book. Legs had been added to the book. The left one was decorated with steampunk designs. I stared at it and pulled off my headset to see seven sets of eager eyes looking back at me.

Amanda stepped to my side. "We asked Naomi to put us in touch with Daniel, while you were in the hospital."

I opened my arms to all of them.

Those kids knew something was gravely wrong when they met a

locked door after school the day after my accident. Amanda and Alton had alerted help immediately. The whole group started looking for me and contacted Sheriff Fitzsimmons, insisting something was off. I'd never missed a day with them without giving advanced notice. They were as dedicated to me as I was to them.

At the top of the stairs, I used the railing to stand. Naomi, who'd followed behind me, stepped up and handed me a mobility assistance knee walker. This was the apparatus Allana and I had worked with. This equipment strapped to my leg, cradling the amputation, and allowed me to put my weight on the knee instead of using crutches. Naomi was making me keep my forearm crutches until I got used to the knee walker. I'd adjusted fairly quickly, with Allana's help and guidance.

"This thing is going to be a lifesaver."

Naomi smiled at me, as she helped adjust the straps. "Go sit down and let me bring you something to drink. You've done enough for now. Get off that thing and rest."

"Honey, I'm all right, I promise." I pulled her close. She clung tightly to me. I'm not sure I'd been out of her sight for more than the two minutes it took me to go pee in the morning. I felt her nod against my chest.

I made my way into the living room and plopped down ungracefully on the couch. I removed the walker and rolled it to the side. Blank staff paper, my Bible, and a notebook sat around the area of my encampment. Since coming home from the hospital, this was where I'd spent the majority of my time. I was still sore in some places, but the cut on my head was healing.

Naomi handed me a cup of coffee. "The weather looks good for Saturday. I have rooms booked at Canaan Valley State Park for the crew from Regal Crimson and the attendees from Colorado. Karmen has the menu ready. Make sure you call Tank about setting up The Confluence the way we planned it."

I reached out and stroked my thumb across Naomi's cheek. "I promise, everything is going to be perfect. Even the weather looks like it's going to cooperate. What time will Ellie and Siobhan be here for dinner?"

"They ran to Morgantown to pick up a few things, said they'd be back by seven."

"We need to meet with Pastor Pegi. She wanted to go over the ceremony with us to see if there was anything in particular we wanted."

"I really like her."

I nodded in agreement. Pastor Pegi was what I liked to call "salt of the earth," someone who cared deeply about those around her and went out of her way to help others.

"Senna is working with Karmen on the catering, before she goes to Austin. She hates that she's going to miss the wedding." Naomi picked up her to-do list and touched a few items with her finger.

"I know. She has to be there by Wednesday with all her stuff to avoid another trip. We'll send her pictures, and she's promised to come visit when she finishes school. I nixed chairs for the ceremony. There isn't any way to set them up that looks right in that small space. We'll ask everyone to form a circle around us, if that's okay?"

"That works for me." I was so thankful for the second, no, third chance I was getting to have my best life. I remembered Grandpa telling me that he and MaMaw liked Naomi. "Did I ever tell you what I dreamed while I was trapped?"

"A few things. It sounds like it was an amazing place to be."

For the next few minutes, I went through the musicians I'd encountered and the songs they were playing. It had all seemed so real. "Sister Rosetta Tharpe led me around. Did you know the Godmother of Rock 'N' Roll had a relationship with another woman, Marie Knight?"

"I didn't know that."

"I researched her after you brought my laptop to me in the hospital. They were together until Marie's children and mother tragically died. I'm sure the grief was overwhelming. From what I read, their relationship was the worst kept secret around. I take comfort in thinking that they found each other again after they passed."

Naomi reached out and pulled my hand into hers. "Is your head hurting again?"

Apparently, I'd been rubbing my head without realizing it. "A little, it's not bad." The grade three concussion had left me with occasional headaches.

She moved all the detritus from around me and pulled off my boot. "Lay down and rest for a bit, while I start supper. Ellie and Siobhan will be back in a little while. We'll eat and have a quiet movie night, okay?

I relaxed and covered my eyes. "Not a bad idea. Thanks for knowing what I need when even I can't see it."

She leaned over and kissed me before drawing a blanket off the back of the couch and covering me. "It's all part of loving you."

"I thank God every day that you do." I drifted off and let the headache fade into the security that surrounded me.

***

After dinner, the four of us found our way back into the living room. With a stomach full of baked steak, mashed potatoes, and cherry pie, I wasn't sure I'd make it to the end of the movie. That would be all right too. I'd fall asleep with Naomi sifting her fingers through my hair, lulling me into rest. Seconds after we sat down, there was a knock at the loft door. Anyone who made it that far obviously had a key to the outside door. That meant it was either Karmen or Tank. Naomi got up and let our visitor in, and she wasn't alone. Tank brought Doc Amy in by the hand.

I sat up a little straighter. "Well, this is a pleasant surprise. Good to see you, Doc." She held Tank's hand and gave me an appraising look with a practiced, clinical eye.

"You're looking better than the last time I saw you. How are you?"

"Better every day. I started physical therapy today, to learn how to maneuver with this until I get my prosthetic." I pointed to the knee walker.

"Simply amazing. No more crutches causing sore armpits or hands." Amy touched the walker with a finger.

Naomi stepped to my side, as Tank turned her head to speak to Siobhan and Ellie. It was truly miraculous how the group had come to a truce over my accident. In one of her many days of babysitting me in the hospital, Ellie had filled me in on the talk she'd had with Tank. It hadn't been easy. More than one time out was called when the volume rattled the windows in the loft. Somewhere in the middle of the stream, they'd found a high spot they both could occupy and coexist.

From the looks of it, Tank might have truly turned the corner about my sister, if the way she was holding Amy's hand was any indication. I'd have to needle that information out of my best friend when we were alone.

"Sit down, you two." I pointed to the empty love seat. "What brings you to Thomas, Doc?"

Amy looked at Tank and blushed slightly. "Uh, I came over to fill a few growlers with your Savior's Red and to see if this one"—she pointed to Tank—"had time for dinner."

I chuckled, knowing Tank would be blushing to her toes on the inside. "Good thing we hired a few more bar keeps so she has more free time on her hands. Where are you taking her, Tank?"

The blush finally made it to the outside, and my best friend's face pinked. "I thought I'd take her out to the Golden Anchor. She likes seafood." Tank fiddled with her keys, flipping them back and forth on the ring. "Well, we'd better get going. We have a reservation in twenty minutes. Amy wanted to stop and see you."

I couldn't help grinning from ear to ear at Tank's discomfort. It had been a long time since she'd put herself out there. Naomi pinched me on the side, indicating for me to go easy on her. "Have a great time. You did give her the beer for free, right?"

"She certainly tried." Amy jammed her hands on her hips. "Look, Rhebekka, you don't owe me a thing other than to take care of yourself and get back to full strength. I wouldn't be opposed to a little time off for this one to do some exploring." She nodded her head in Tank's direction. "I've been working in Maryland for a few years. Somehow, I still haven't made it over here much."

"Deal." I held out my hand and we shook. I watched a peace come over Tank when her hand settled into Amy's. *Yes, this is going to be interesting to watch.*

Tank pointed back toward the door. "We need to head out. I'll call tomorrow so we can set the raw material order."

Naomi walked them out. I had a suspicion that Tank wanted to talk about much more than malted oats and barley. The outside door banged shut, and Naomi joined us again.

"I think Tank is smitten," Ellie declared.

Siobhan snorted. "Doc there was practically stripping the poor woman down to her knickers with her eyes."

That made me howl with laughter. I'd seen the smoldering look Amy had given my friend. "Yeah, exploring, that's what she called it."

Naomi smacked me on the arm and pointed at the other two. "All of you stop. Be happy for her. I think Amy is exactly the right medicine for what ails Tank."

The group collectively groaned at the pun.

"What?" Naomi smirked.

I pulled the budding comedian into my arms. "Be happy for her my ass. You're enjoying this as much as we are."

"I won't lie and tell you I'm not." Naomi melted into my embrace. "Having everyone happily attached has cut the tension around here down to nothing other than my aggravation that you won't rest the way you should."

"Okay, okay. Can we watch the movie now? I'd like to rest and watch Gal Gadot kick some Nazi ass, if you please."

"Just lay your head in my lap, and I'll be happy to let you ogle Gal. Remember, in a few days, you'll be marrying me."

I lay down and looked up at the most beautiful woman in the world. "I have my own Wonder Woman. Soon you'll have something even more powerful than that golden lasso."

"What's that?"

I held up her hand and kissed her knuckles, where her engagement ring sat. "A platinum band of eternity."

Chapter Thirty

SATURDAY MORNING, I WAS a nervous wreck. Within a few hours, I'd be marrying my soulmate, the woman who'd shown me more grace than I deserved. I wore a pair of snug-fitting jeans, with a midnight-blue tuxedo vest and tie to match. The vest's finely detailed and overlapping feathers looked like wings from the back. My solitary boot was so shiny, I could see myself in it, thanks to Siobhan. I hoped my prosthetic would fit the left shoes I still owned.

When I woke up, I saw my prayer had been answered. A fresh layer of wet snow had fallen overnight. A pristine white blanket covered the brown of winter's exit. Snows around Easter weren't unheard of. As expected, this wasn't the fluffy white snow that happened when the air was frigid. It would likely all be gone by late afternoon, with the rising temperatures. I wasn't worried, I knew the courtyard would be set up and ready to go. I had much to thank my friends for, as I was still trying to recover my strength.

My beautiful sister, Ellie, was fussing over me. Her maid-of-honor finery included a black leather outfit with a corset-like bodice in the same color blue as my tie and vest. Naomi had picked everything out with Ellie's help. I was happy to do whatever they asked. My after-school kids had applied a steampunk theme to my knee walker at our last meeting. It was now adorned with brass gears, watch faces, and more. It would be some time before I could be fitted for a prosthetic. The amputation site was still swollen and needed to heal.

Ellie smacked me on the arm. "Stand up straight, Bek. I can't get your tie right when you're leaning."

Pointing to the apparatus strapped to my leg, I raised an eyebrow at her and grinned. Our laughter broke the tension. I grabbed her hands and held them in mine. "As nervous as you are, you'd think you're getting married instead of me."

I felt her relax as I pulled her to me. She'd been instrumental in bringing me back together with Naomi. Regardless of the miles between us, neither of them gave up on me.

She clung to me. "I just want this to be perfect for you both."

"It is perfect. Everyone I love is here, and I'm marrying the center of my world. She's managed to put up with all my bullshit and say yes in spite of it."

Ellie fiddled with the buttons of my vest. "Naomi loves you so much, Bek, she always has. It's hard for me to think about how it took everything she had to keep it together when you were missing. She was a complete wreck. I don't know that I've ever seen anyone pray that much."

Naomi's complete breakdown in front of me had happened after we'd finally gotten home, once she had a chance to tell me everything. I'd never seen her cry like that, not even when we split up. My heart ached knowing how much pain she'd been in at the thought of losing me permanently.

"The fact that you two weren't together all those years never stopped her from knowing that, someday, you'd get your head out of your ass and realize how much you two were destined to be sharing a last name."

Every word she said was true. Regardless of the age gap between us, or the roads we had to travel to get to this place at this time, Naomi was destined to be my wife.

"How does she look?" I couldn't wait to see her. I'd been forbidden to go down into the sanctuary, even to pray. Naomi was using it as a giant dressing room, with Karmen and Ashley helping her.

"You're going to melt into a puddle of goo. I've never seen her look more beautiful."

Tank came in, struggling to button her shirt around her tie. "She's telling the truth. Naomi looks angelic, in a devilish sort of way."

Amy came out of the back bedroom and pointed to a spot on the floor in front of her.

"Stop fussing with that and come here."

"I think I'm allergic to this monkey suit." Tank pulled at the collar of her shirt.

The formidable doctor brushed Tank's hands away. Amy was stunning in a form-fitting, pinstriped suit. The wide lapels framed a light-blue, open-collared shirt. Her high-heeled boots poked out from underneath the flared pant legs. Tank couldn't take her eyes off Amy.

"Honestly, Tancy, you'd think you've never dressed up before." Amy buttoned the collar and slid the knot of Tank's tie up, before buttoning the vest, a shade darker than mine. Once she smoothed down the collar, Tank looked like she might be the one getting married.

Ellie and I both turned to our friend, a woman we'd known for almost two decades. We were well aware of her given name, as well as the fact that we were forbidden to ever use it. No one, and I do mean no one, ever called her Tancy.

Tank turned to glare at both of us. Ellie mimicked locking her lips and throwing away the key. I pretended to whistle and look over my shoulder. My friend was gut hooked and happier than I'd ever seen her.

Ellie walked over to the liquor cabinet and poured five tumblers of my best Scotch.

Siobhan walked out of the back room, threading a belt through her dark jeans. "Ah, I see the festivities have begun." She took the glass Ellie offered. "What are we toasting, lassies?"

I raised my glass and looked at the women in the room. "To faith, hope, and love. The greatest of which we will honor today, love."

Siobhan called out, "*Slàinte mhath*," before we sipped. The whiskey was so smooth, I barely felt the burn as it warmed its way into my stomach. Soon, I'd be pledging my mind and body to the woman who was the physical embodiment of all three of those sacred qualities, my Naomi.

***

We stood in the courtyard on the side of my church. Correction, *our* church. The House of the Rising Son, once again, was playing host to saints and sinners equally. Pastor Pegi stood to my right and Tank to my left. I looked out into the gathering, noting more people than we'd originally intended. All my kids from the after-school group were there with their parents. Alton was off to the side with Daniel, adjusting the video and sound equipment.

Roman grinned beside his handsome husband, Andre. Naomi and I had an appointment to have rings permanently tattooed on our fingers as well as the bands we'd wear to symbolize our union. Several members of Naomi's former church, including its new spiritual leader, Ashley, were gathered to my right. I was very happy to see that Chance and Jax had accepted our invitation. If Chance hadn't pulled me from that frigid water, I wouldn't have this opportunity to utter the two words I'd been longing to say since the day I fell in love with Naomi Layman—I do.

The members of Regal Crimson held their instruments ready, faces lit with joy. A long note across a violin signaled to all that the wedding was about to begin. I rolled my neck to relieve the tension that had been building since I woke. *This is it.*

Naomi had chosen Christina Peri's *A Thousand Years* for her wedding march. The lyrics reflected so much about our journey to this moment. After the opening piano refrains, my beautiful Ellie walked down the aisle. She stopped and kissed my cheek.

"Don't forget to breathe," she whispered to me. "I love you, big sister."

Love and worry for my little sparrow forced a tear from my eye. She brushed it away, before she moved to the other side of the pastor. I brought my gaze back to the space created by our guests as they'd parted for Ellie.

I was positive my heart completely stopped and jumped out of my chest. There, on Siobhan's arm, was an angel dressed all in white leather. Her skirt flared off the back into a train that barely dragged the ground. The front was cut above her white pirate boots. Tiny buttons traveled up the side of the bodice and across her shoulder to the neckline, while the sleeves draped elegantly over her hands, which held white lilies wrapped in lace. She'd never looked more beautiful. An angel sent from heaven.

Smoky shadows accentuated the glacial depths, and Naomi's blue eyes met mine. I was sure the alluringly seductive makeup was the work of Regal Crimson's artists. Her gaze sent my entire body into a clinch, as she glided to me.

Siobhan kissed her cheek before holding out Naomi's hand for me to take into my own. I couldn't resist, as I leaned in and softly kissed her lips.

I whispered to her. "Breathtaking."

Pastor Pegi cleared her throat. "The kiss comes later."

Naomi's hand shook as if she was shivering. "Cold?" I was worried we didn't have enough heaters out there to make this comfortable for her. She shook her head and side-eyed me from head to toe. She held her lower lip between her teeth. Now I knew what she was shivering about.

Pastor Pegi got everyone's attention. "Peace be with you."

"And also, with you." The crowd murmured.

She opened with a reading. "Ruth said to Naomi, 'Where you go I will go, and where you stay I will stay. Your people will be my people and your God my God.' These words are fitting, given the two people standing in front of us today. Naomi came to this place and made it her home with Rhebekka, the woman whom she helped to find God. I can speak for many in this community, as we are thankful for both of them. This union is certainly blessed."

I couldn't stop staring at the braided loops in the auburn locks that framed Naomi's face. I knew I should be listening to every word Pegi was saying, but my eyes and heart were locked onto the woman before me.

Pastor Pegi asked us to make the ceremonial pledge to each other. In answer to her question, we each said "I do," and I asked God to help me.

"The couple has chosen to speak their own vows before this assembly and God." She held out our rings and allowed us to take them to speak our truths.

Naomi held my hands in hers. "Rhebekka Lynn, I have loved you for so long, I can't remember when I didn't. Your love wraps me in complete safety and security. I will always believe God led you to my church, all those years ago, to show me that true love exists. From this day forth, all your days will be my days, all your struggles my struggles, and all your triumphs my triumphs. I will face this life and the prospect of our heavenly reward with you at my side, knowing God made you for me."

The ring bore a circle of crosses intertwined with treble clefs. She slid the platinum band onto my left ring finger. I squeezed my hand closed, sealing the words of her promise into my skin, before taking her hand in mine to speak my vows.

"Naomi Rainelle, in Jesus' time, the Pharisees were angry at him because he ministered to people they considered sinners. He told them a parable having a hundred sheep and how the shepherd would rejoice when he found one of the hundred that was lost. Jesus said there will be more joy in heaven over one sinner who repents, than over ninety-nine righteous persons who need no repentance. You found me."

"Though you had a congregation full of believers, you went after the lost sheep in me. I didn't make it easy on you, yet you never gave up. You never loved me less. Even when I was so lost I couldn't even find myself, you told me that you and God loved me. You shared His grace with me and proved to me that I, too, was worthy. I thank Him every day for the patience he gave you. Today, I faithfully pledge my heart, my mind, and my body to you and you alone."

"Together, we will show others grace, freely given through faith. I will love you all the days of my life, without fail." I slid the wedding band that matched her engagement ring onto her finger and locked us together in the unbreakable bond our union would be.

Pastor Pegi looked at the both of us, then spoke to the crowd. "Ellie, Rhebekka's sister, has something for the couple."

My little sparrow stepped over to the members of Regal Crimson and nodded. She'd promised me not to try any power ballads.

"This song is called *These Three Remain*, and it's for my two sisters. I love you both."

I didn't recognize the arrangement, until Ellie softly started to sing. I remembered a song I'd written long ago, in a roadside hotel somewhere out west. Ellie added the message from Corinthians to my melody and turned it into a song.

"'...and if I have a faith that can move mountains, but do not have love, I am nothing. If I give all I possess to the poor and give over my body to hardship that I may boast, but do not have love, I gain nothing. Love is patient, love is kind. It does not envy, it does not boast, it is not proud.'"

When she ran through a second verse that spoke of love and grace, I felt the tears come. Years of burden and guilt melted away. What washed over me was grace, full of promise. I admired the woman standing by my side, the one who'd always been there in one form or another, and I let every single regret go. They flowed down into the Blackwater River and drifted away on the muddy water. I was free. The shackles and yoke of my childhood, the indiscretion of my youth, and the stubbornness I developed as an adult were no longer the driving forces in my life.

I could finally accept what I'd known all along. God loved me and so did the woman who was taking my last name. We'd share the surname I'd chosen, not the one I'd been born with. As we carried MaMaw's maiden name, we'd honor the woman who'd taught me to heat up coffee in a small metal pan and whose love I still felt in my heart. I looked around the courtyard, saying a prayer of thanks for every single person there who had helped shape me. I was grateful for the lessons learned, no matter how hard they'd been. From simple mistakes to grave errors, those lessons had formed the person I became.

In the last few months, I'd lost more than just a piece of my flesh. I'd lost the weight of a life that existed on fractured purpose. I'd once been a follower, then a lost and confused sheep. I became a leader, a fisher of men, helping others find what Naomi had revealed to me. The best part was, I no longer had to do it all by myself. Naomi wiped tears from my cheeks and turned fully to me, as Ellie let the last note fade off.

Pastor Pegi began to speak again. "By the powers vested in me, I pronounce you wed. You each may kiss your bride. Ladies and gentlemen, let me be the first to introduce you to Mrs. and Mrs. Rhebekka and Naomi Deklan. Join with me in welcoming them to the joy of holy matrimony. What God has put together, let no one pull apart."

I drew Naomi into my arms, stumbling slightly on the knee walker, until I felt her arms steady me. I let her kiss permeate my soul and brand my heart. I returned the gift with all the passion I dared in front of an audience.

Siobhan amplified her Irish brogue by cupping her hands around her mouth. "Save some for the honeymoon!"

Everyone laughed and clapped, as my wife and I turned to the crowd, our clasped hands raised heavenward. This was the first time I could actually say those words, and it be real.

My wife.

Every day would be different now. I was tied to someone on a completely different level than ever before. Her needs would always come above mine; her happiness would always be more important to me than my own, and I would work every day to show her how grateful I was to have her as my wife. Only my devotion to a higher power would be stronger. With Naomi's help, even that would be more secure. She was my refuge and my stronghold; we would build our house on grace and faith. Together, we would make our way through this life.

***

The reception was in full swing at Redemption's Road. Our friends and family were enjoying an incredible feast provided by Karmen with Zandra's help. Siobhan's Trad Brigade and members of Regal Crimson were entertaining the crowd, while Naomi and I made our way around to greet and visit with everyone. Naomi insisted I get off my leg for a bit, because she wanted to dance with me later. I dutifully allowed her to wheel me around, happy to let her lead. She was deep in conversation with Ashley, when Tank handed me a Mason jar of Brimstone Stout.

She motioned toward Naomi. "Think you can keep up with her?"

I pointed to a chair beside me. I wasn't going to have a conversation looking up at her. Tank obliged and stretched out her legs, crossing them at the ankle.

"I'll do my best to try. Where's Amy?" I looked around for her.

"She had to take a call. It's too noisy in here, so I gave her the key to the office."

"Is that all she has the key to?" I couldn't help my smirk.

Tank let out what sounded like a contented sigh. "As a matter of fact, no. She also has one to the apartment."

I rolled my head toward her. "And?"

"She's working on the one in the armor around my stubborn side. Rest assured, she's whittling her own key to my heart."

I leaned in close. "Don't think I didn't hear her call you Tancy. I'd say she's already installed a new lock on that puppy."

Tank nodded slowly. "I'll give you that. Never met anyone like her. Takes no shit from me, period. When you were in the hospital, it started with coffee. If she couldn't meet me for a cup, I brought it to her. One night, I noticed she kept rubbing a muscle in her neck. I offered to massage her shoulders, while she wasn't needed by patients. She sat down in front of me in the lounge and fell asleep on me until her pager went off, calling her back to the ER."

"I'd say that means she's pretty comfortable with you."

"She's got that something you can't explain, you know? I'm all about the straight lines and edges. Amy's been helping me navigate the curves."

"I'll just bet she is." I couldn't help but laugh. I knew what went through my mind wasn't what Tank meant.

Tank glared and rolled her eyes. "Smartass."

"It's the company I keep." I held up my hand for her to bump my fist, which she did.

The kids from my group were all out dancing, trying to keep time to a style of music they weren't accustomed to. Traditional Irish music was filling The Confluence with joy. Amanda brought Kiersten, and by a twist of fate, her mother was home from her deployment. Sydney had been injured while on duty. She'd have to return at a later date. For the time being, the entire family was together. She and Lynn sat off to the side, watching Amanda interact with her very first girlfriend. I often wondered what it would have been like to have parents support me the way Amanda's did. They put no pressure on their daughter to be anything beyond who she was, continually encouraging her in so many ways.

"I'm happy for you, Bek. I really am." Tank took a drink from her jar.

"That goes both ways, my friend. I say we do all we can to keep it that way. I'm game if you are."

Tank slowly nodded in agreement. "Game on. Here comes your wife."

"I'll never get tired of hearing that."

"Good thing, she put a ring on that finger to match the one in your nose."

Amy joined us from behind and flicked Tank's ear. "Behave."

I nearly fell out of my wheelchair laughing. Tank blushed and looked so contrite. Naomi bent and kissed me softly.

"How are you, Mrs. Deklan?"

"I'm fine, Mrs. Deklan. I've missed you."

"Then I think it's time you dance with me." She reached around the back of the chair and handed me the knee walker. Once I strapped it on, I let her lead me to the floor. Ellie was standing on the stage, Siobhan by her side. I watched my sister's girlfriend pick up a guitar and join my old band, while Ellie stepped to the mic.

"It's time for the couple's first dance. Let's give both of our Mrs. Deklan a hand."

My wife gave a slight curtsey as she came into my arms. I kissed her softly and brought our left hands into my chest, right on the spot where her name was branded over my heart, as I wrapped my right arm around her waist. I knew my sister would be singing our song, the one I'd carried with me over the miles when I was with Naomi, and when I wasn't. The one I'd played more times in the wee hours of the morning than any other. Siobhan, along with my former base player and Ellie's lead guitarist, began Eric Clapton's, "Wonderful Tonight." It was slow enough that I could sway with her and not feel off balance. Her head nestled into my chest, and I held my lips to her hair, breathing in the scent that was so my wife—coffee beans and vanilla.

"I love you so much, Naomi."

She drew back to smile at me, that million-dollar wattage warming me inside and out. The twinkle in her eyes reminded me of Sister Rosetta.

"And I love you, Rhebekka. Now and forever."

We swayed to my sister's soft vocals and enjoyed the moment together. I hoped we'd repeat this dance a thousand more times in my life. She did look wonderful, and I was totally lost in loving her. The song ended, and I held her tightly. We were one, at last, my gratitude overwhelming that it didn't take a moment longer.

I remembered my dream, or maybe it would be better described as my vision from the accident. Grandpa had told me that he and MaMaw liked Naomi. I could feel them all around me and had no doubt they were there watching over us from above. We invited everyone onto the dance floor, including Ellie and Siobhan. One of her backup singers took over vocals, and we danced the night away.

We stood in the place I'd built to celebrate two things I loved, beer and music. The greatest gift was that I was able to do all that with my best friend, who'd finally found community in a place where she'd once felt like an outsider. It even looked as if she'd found love, as had Karmen and Ellie. The most important people in my life were all there, celebrating new life found on redemption's road.

Epilogue

I STOOD IN FRONT of my pseudo dominatrix, also known as Attila the Hun, learning how to walk up a set of steps. The prop was built in one corner of the room and led to a platform large enough for me to turn around and come back down the three steps. This was my fifth trip up and down this session. I wanted to be able to walk up the steps into my loft that night. It was all about balance and learning to trust the metal and fiberglass that replaced my foot and ankle.

Naomi stood at the side with Allana. "She's getting better at it."

"The fact she had a below the knee amputation is critical." Allana nodded. "Natural knee movement and fewer balance issues make the acclimation period much easier. Rhebekka's doing remarkably well."

"Of course, I'm crushing it like a rock star." I grinned at both of them.

Naomi rolled her eyes at me and pointed. "Focus, rock star."

We worked through several obstacles, including different surfaces around a small terrain area set up in a covered walkway. It was a beautiful day outside. Bright sunshine filled a cerulean sky dotted with cotton balls. The next day, there would be a parade through town followed by a fireworks show put on by the local fire department. Mountaineer Days, the area's Fourth of July celebration, was a big event. We'd planned a gathering on our rooftop, offering a front-row seat for the pyrotechnic display that brought people from far and wide. The streets would be full of people milling about, stopping in all the shops, while they enjoyed the food trucks and booths that lined the river walk.

Our church sanctuary would be open to all, and our small ensemble would play hymns and other music for festival goers. Our regular furniture had been moved to the side. We'd set up folding chairs to accommodate those who wanted to get out of the heat, rest, and enjoy music. There would be no sermon, only music. We had a good group of musicians to rotate in and out through the day, including some of the kids.

In summer, the after-school program transitioned into a twice-weekly gathering with music lessons. Alton was playing drums, while Amanda had continued to show incredible guitar talent for her age. Siobhan was giving Irish fiddle lessons to Holly, who could play her way through several of the simple hymns. It was good to see how much closer their small group had become. Sunday services during the festival were set for later in the day than normal.

There was much to be done, and I wanted to finish my rehab on a positive note. I stepped over repurposed railroad ties, across a section of river stone, and through five feet of sand in a long box.

Allana held the door open, leading back into the facility. "Great job. The sand is harder to navigate because it shifts. You can't feel it with your prosthesis the way you would your natural foot, requiring a bit more attention. I think you're doing great. Before long, you'll notice it less and less. You'll tire easily for a while, and if you gain or lose weight, your socket may fit differently. Be aware of sore spots or irritation. I'll see you next week."

Naomi gave her a hug. "Thank you for all you've done for us. Rhebekka's a work in progress, but I expect the end result to be worth the effort."

"I'm trying to figure out if that was a backhanded reprimand or a compliment." I squinted at my wife as she cupped my jaw. "I do agree with her though. Thank you for everything."

Allana leaned over and whispered in my ear. "Let me help you out before you dig yourself into a hole. Smile and hug your wife."

I saluted and did exactly as she suggested, pulling the woman I was so proud to call my wife into my arms. We stopped at the front desk and made an appointment for the next week. On our way home, we popped into Karmen's store. Zandra was working on a laptop over at a small table in the café section. Karmen came out of the back, holding a large box with our order for the gathering. The town was already starting to fill with tourists coming in for the event.

I took the box from her and set it down on a small counter near the register. "I'll bet you've been busy today."

"Every year. I can't keep enough cupcakes in the case. Zandra's updates to our website have made a big difference. People can order online ahead of time, which helps me keep enough stock on hand for the walk-ins."

"She's been so good for you." Naomi squeezed Karmen's hand.

"I'll second that. We fit. Having her move here permanently will give us so much more time together than a weekend here and there. That move should be completed by next month."

Seeing Karmen happy warmed my heart. The bell rang, and Amy walked in. "Hey folks, are you having a secret meeting without me?"

I still marveled at how Amy had breezed in and completely turned Tank's life upside down. The changes I'd seen in my best friend were remarkable. She was considerably less snarky and certainly less restless.

"Nope, just gathering sustenance for tomorrow's festivities. Are you going to be able to make it?"

"Unfortunately, no. The holiday weekend always means a lot of alcohol-related accidents. It's all hands on deck in the ER. I'll be there for church on Sunday though. Wouldn't want to miss my weekly dose of the dynamic duo dispensing faith with a side of musical bliss. Hey Karmen, our order ready?"

Karmen beamed at her. I was beyond pleased that Karmen and Amy had become close friends as well. Their relationship was helping to bridge the gap that had grown between Karmen and Tank over the previous months.

"It is. Nice to see you can get that blockhead to eat more than a bag of chips for dinner." Karmen gathered the order for her.

Naomi hooked her arm in Amy's, locking their elbows together. "It's a challenge loving these hardheads. I promise they're worth the effort."

Amy's laughter was the joyous kind. "I agree. I'm working tonight and she's bartending, as usual. I figure if I get her to eat now, she has enough fuel on board to make it through the night. I saw Siobhan's group is playing this evening."

I couldn't help but shake my head. The turnaround from Tank wanting to drag Siobhan into the street and beat her ass, to being friends was wonderfully strange. "They are. With Ellie's encouragement, Siobhan's been taking more of a backseat over at Beanders and concentrating on music. We'll probably come up to see them."

Karmen finished packaging our order, and then hit on an open wound. "Have you made any decision about Pittsburgh?"

I sighed. Ellie's voice had only marginally improved, even with seeing one of the premier doctors who specialized in vocal issues for musicians. The anniversary concert was the following weekend. Ellie and Siobhan were leaving Sunday night to go up and start rehearsals.

"We're still in the process of the come-to-Jesus discussions about that." Naomi pointed her thumb. "Hardhead. Remember?" She narrowed her eyes at me.

The bell rang over the door again, as I rubbed a hand over the back of my neck. "No one wants to hear a washed-up former rock 'n' roll singer turned reverend. Especially when Ellie's been the lead singer for years."

Tank stepped to Amy's side and pointed a finger at me. "That's bullshit, and you know it. You're running out of time to get your head out of your ass and be there for your sister. Just a thought, but you need to get the hell out of your own way and do the right thing. Humm, that sounds like something I've heard a few thousand times from a voice that can still carry a tune."

I was feeling outnumbered and held up my hands. "Guys, please?"

"Whatever." Tank turned to Amy. "If you're going to get to work on time, we'd better go eat now. I don't like you cutting it close and having to rush."

My best friend's protective nature was always present, even in her personal life.

Amy kissed her cheek. "I've got my marching orders, ladies. See you Sunday."

Tank and Amy left, as we picked up the supplies and said our goodbyes. When we got home, Naomi made me wait while she carried everything upstairs. She returned to walk behind me in my first attempt at getting into our loft using my new leg.

The flight of stairs seemed more daunting than I'd thought they'd be. *What if I stumble and fall backward? Naomi would try to catch me and possibly be injured in the process. What if my leg fails halfway up? What if I get too tired? What if—*

A soft hand firmly encircled mine and spoke the words I needed to hear. "Truly I tell you, if you have faith as small as a mustard seed, you can say to this mountain, 'Move from here to there,' and it will move. Nothing will be impossible for you." Naomi kissed my cheek. "Have a little faith in yourself, my love."

I closed my eyes and said a little prayer. I let my faith and Naomi's words serve as a driving force. With each step, I became more confident and more at ease. With Naomi's hand on my back, I took each tread, one at a time. When I pushed off the last one and up into our loft, I turned and looked at the passageway. *Through faith, all things are possible.*

Naomi kissed me and squeezed me tightly. "I knew you could do it. Now come on. Help me cook dinner, I'm starving."

***

Thursday evening, I paced the loft with the guitar over my shoulder. Ellie was on speakerphone. I could hear the anxiety in her voice. Stage AE, on Pittsburgh's North Shore, wasn't the largest concert arena in the area, by any means. The nice part was every ticket holder would have visuals to the stage. The grassy outdoor arena offered standing room for over 5000 people. Stuart had booked the venue for the anniversary concert, two years ago. Fan club members were given first option on tickets, before sales were opened to the public. The concert was sold out.

"They're going to be disappointed, Bek, I can't give them what they're coming to hear."

"They won't be disappointed. You're going to give the fans all you have, and that will be enough."

"Bek," Ellie's voice grew small. "How would you feel if the last sermon you ever gave was a flop?"

I stopped for a moment. She'd said *last* sermon. This was it for her. Though she may not have said it out loud until that moment, my sister was telling me she was retiring. "So, this is it?"

There was a long pause. Her soft sniffles broke my heart. That did it. I wanted nothing more than to already be in Pittsburgh. "Ellie?" I heard her blow her nose.

"Bek, I'm way past my prime. Since the surgery, my voice is shit. The other thing is I'm exhausted from this life. Do you know, the last few months I've spent with you is the longest amount of time I've spent in any one place in years?"

"I do. Naomi and I've loved you being with us."

"And then there's Siobhan. I've never felt the way I do about her. I've had so many people come in and out of my life. For the first time, I feel completely safe and so loved. Do you remember telling me about Naomi the first time? How your heart knew her before your mind did?"

"I do. It scares me to think about how I almost lost her."

"And that's my point. I don't want to miss a single moment with Siobhan. I want all the moments, all the days, weeks, and years."

I couldn't help the smile that came over my face and the warmth in my heart. My sister had fallen hopelessly in love with someone who could allow Ellie to be her feisty self and yet comfort the scared little girl right under the surface. "I'm so happy for you."

"I have to get through this concert. I'll be making my retirement announcement during the opening remarks. It's time. I want more to life than a night in a city with a name I have to write on my hand to remember and another hotel bed in a room that has nothing personal in it other than my clothes. I want a home, and I want it with Siobhan."

Somewhere in the back of my mind, I heard Grandpa speaking to me. *Don't hide your light under a bushel basket.* Decision made.

My wife was sitting on the couch with a book in her lap, watching me intently. I nodded to her. "Naomi and I will be there in four hours. We have a few things to arrange. We'll get packed and on the road as soon as we can."

Naomi smiled as she came to stand in front of me. She moved my guitar and wrapped her arms around me. She silently mouthed that she was proud of me. That was more than I deserved, but I was grateful. There had been many discussions about me performing with Ellie, though not since she'd left for Pittsburgh. I suspected my wife knew me better than I knew myself and believed I would eventually come to the right conclusion on my own. Letting Ellie down at this point in my sister's life was not in my DNA.

I put my forehead against my wife's and spoke softly to my sister. "I love you, Ellie, no thanks necessary. We'll be there soon."

***

Saturday night, I stood stage right in faded blue jeans, with no shoes. My black T-shirt was stenciled with Ephesians 2:8. *For it is by grace you have been saved, through faith.*

I was listening to the opening act, as they finished their set. Strings and Silk reminded me of Regal Crimson's early days. Two sisters with guitars had made their way in the music world, taking every opportunity as if it would be our last. With Ellie's new interest in producing and representing new artists, these siblings had an incredible ally.

I high fived the girls when they came off stage. "Go do an encore, you've earned it."

Kelly and Kira looked wide-eyed at me. "Really?"

I turned to Ellie, who stood beside me nodding.

"Go. I'm the boss, remember?"

The two women ran back out and waved to the clapping crowd that was still clamoring for more. I looked to my sister and pointed to the duet.

"The sky is the limit for those two. With you handling them, I see a long career."

Ellie shrugged. "We'll see. I feel it's important to give artists like them a shot, the same way we got ours. Though, the way we did it was insane."

I hugged her. "And we loved every minute of it. You ready for this?"

"I have been for a long time. To be honest, I'm looking forward to reliving a bit of the past. When you sang lead, all I had to do was follow you and add the harmony. I'll never be able to thank you for this, Bek. We started this dream together. Now that we're at its sunset, I wouldn't want to do it without you."

I squeezed her tightly then held up my pinky. "Together?"

A single tear dropped off her lashes. "Together. I do want the privilege of welcoming you back, so stay here, okay?"

"This is your show, little sparrow. Whatever you want."

"Wrong, big sister. This is our show."

With that, my incredibly talented sibling turned to hug Siobhan one last time, before she walked to center stage to greet the crowd. I stood in awe as I watched her. Naomi slid an arm around my side. Many years ago, she'd accompanied me to a few concerts and did this same thing. The difference now was that she did it as my wife. When we closed this last show, we'd be going home and not to the next tour stop. I kissed her, tethering us together in the very marrow of our bones.

She touched my face, radiating confidence in me with those ice-blue eyes. "This is it. The closing of one chapter in the story of your life."

"One chapter, with the best part of the story left to come." We watched my sister adjust the mic and look into the crowd.

"For the last twenty years, you fans have made this ride well worth taking. It all started right here in Pittsburgh, in a club that doesn't even exist anymore. When my sister and I came out of the Fort Pitt tunnel and crossed that bridge into the city, we had grand dreams. We had no idea we would sleep in cheap hotels and survive on ramen noodles to pay the bills. Pittsburgh became our home base. We built a following here that stayed with Regal Crimson for the twenty years we've traveled the globe."

The crowd whistled and clapped. Ellie stopped to compose herself.

"I need to take a moment to say a few things, if you'll indulge me. I'm sure you heard I had to cancel a few tour stops recently. To squash any rumors, yes, it was because of cancer. I had to have my thyroid removed." She raised her arms at the gasps. "The good news is they got it all. I'm cancer free."

A thunderous cheer went up from the fans scattered around the lawn, and I smiled.

"This year makes twenty years since Regal Crimson first took the stage."

I projected all my strength into the beautiful young woman standing center stage. Siobhan beamed at her as she addressed the crowd.

"This will be our last show. No farewell tour, just today with you, the incredible fans who have supported us through good times and bad. You've made being a musician fun, because you've stuck by us through it all. We realized there was no way to close out this incredible ride without bringing along someone who made every single song possible. If you've been a fan for over ten years, you know that I wasn't always the lead voice of Regal Crimson."

I heard the restlessness in the crowd as they anticipated her next words.

"When we started this long and winding road, my sister, Bek, stood beside me with a guitar slung over her shoulders, melting you with her powerful voice and incredible guitar skills. Tonight, Regal Crimson is complete again. For the first time in a decade, please welcome my sister, Bek, back to the stage."

A deafening roar came up from the crowd. My heart thudded in my chest. My body was cemented to a piece of the floor, until Naomi softly kissed my lips.

"I'd tell you to break a leg, but you only have one good one. Instead, I'll say I love you."

I took a second to ask God for strength and did my best not to limp, as I walked onto the stage with my guitar in my hands. I waved to the audience and clasped my sister's hand in mine, as I leaned in and kissed her temple.

I adjusted the mic to my taller frame. I'd told Ellie I wanted old school, a mic stand on the floor and an amp to plug into. I would need a stool before the night was over, and one had been provided. "What a road this has been. First, I want to say, we couldn't have done this without all of you. It's my privilege to be back here with my partner in crime, the incredible Ellie McNally. When I stepped away from the stage, she roared into the lead and did it better than I ever did. Enjoy yourselves tonight, because we plan to."

The band started into *We're One Step Away*, one of our very first songs. Within minutes, it was as if I'd never stepped away. The crowd sang with us. The lyrics to the song came easily, as did the music that flowed through my soul and into my hands playing my grandpa's guitar. I could see the tears in Ellie's eyes. I shook my head. *No tears tonight.* We played every song we'd done together and many more I'd written for the band after I'd quit. I lost myself in the music and in giving our fans their money's worth. I checked in on Ellie more than once, as we let each of our incredible band members have their moment in the sun. I leaned in close to her.

"You okay?"

"Stop worrying. This is the best I've felt in months. Thank you. How's the leg?"

"If I sit my ass on the stool for the next one, we'll be good for the remainder. I want to do that song I showed you yesterday. You remember the chorus?"

She nodded, and I moved back to center stage. Reston finished her keyboard solo, and we wrapped up the song. I took a deep drink of water and adjusted the mic out of habit.

"You guys are definitely getting a great show tonight, don't you think?" I waved my arm back to Ellie and the rest of the band. "We're going to slow this down a little and play something completely new. I can't say it will ever be recorded, so if you want to hear it again, get your phones out." I laughed, when I watched most of the crowd do just that. "I won't go into detail about how this song came about, but I'll give you a little background. A few months ago, something life-changing happened to me. During the dark of night, I walked into a bar where I got the opportunity to watch some of the world's guitar greats play together. From that experience, I wrote this song. It's called *Radio Stars in the Guitar Bar*." I looked back to Ellie and started the count.

"One, two, three, four."

The band didn't know this song, so they stayed silent. This was for me, Grandpa's Gibson, and Ellie. While I sang the tale of a bar full of guitar greats, all playing a center stage, I pictured my MaMaw singing in a heavenly choir. Grandpa stood beside Chet Atkins, playing for a packed house of angels. I could see him smiling at me, offering me a vision of what the future held.

To the side of the stage, I saw Naomi, the living angel I was privileged to walk through this world with. I was blessed to be married to a woman who showed me I was worthy. Somehow, she'd gotten through all my doubts and showed me that grace was for all. Inside every sinner existed a saint. My shirt said it all, by grace, you have been saved, through faith. Somewhere on redemption's road, I'd begun to believe that I too was worthy of that grace.

A Sovereign Chance

(Five Point Series Book 4)

Chapter One

CHANCE SAT AT HER desk feeding her godson, Jace, his afternoon bottle. She and Jax had been so honored that his parents had named their child after them. They'd settled on calling him Jace to give him his own unique name. Taylor sat across from her; dark shadows evident under her eyes. She looked down that the cherubic little face that ate greedily. "Little guy, you've got to start sleeping at night. Your mommas need the rest."

Taylor scrubbed a hand down her face. "I wish he'd listen to you. We've tried everything, and the most he sleeps is in three-hour increments. You'd think at seven months he'd be sleeping through the night. We've asked his pediatrician if something's wrong, but she can't find anything. Penny's mom is coming tomorrow to give us a break. She hasn't been very supportive of our relationship. With Jace's birth, she's finally turned the corner about our marriage. I basically have no family since my brother made a lewd suggestion to Penny when we first got together. The guy practically raised me, after I turned fourteen and our parents decided they didn't want kids anymore."

Chance knew Taylor's story and found herself eternally grateful she'd landed with mom-squared instead of in the foster system. With no living grandparents, she couldn't imagine where she'd have ended up after her father's death. "Definitely their loss, my friend. I'm grateful for her change of heart. It's sad that it took four months after his birth for her to realize what she was missing out on."

Taylor yawned and shook her head. "Penny's dad will be coming with her this trip. He wants to do some fishing now that he's allowed to come without repercussions. He always found a way to be in Penny's life, even when his wife wasn't happy about it."

Chance put the bottle down and wiped the milk from tiny plump lips. She hated to disturb him when he was almost asleep, but it was a necessary evil if she didn't want to be wearing his lunch in a few minutes. "Jace, it's time for you to burp, little man. We can't let all that goodness from Mommy go to waste."

Penny leaned in the doorway. "You'd better not, if he actually ate, then I want it to stay down." She came in and sat on Taylor's lap. "I called Maggie, and she wants you to drop Jace off with her. You need to sleep if you're coming back out at midnight. Even Midas is looking like he could use some uninterrupted downtime."

Taylor kissed Penny's cheek and pointed to Chance. "Your mother is a godsend as his oma. The fact that she'll take Jace anytime of the day or night is a lifesaver."

"Mom knows she's going to have to wait for Kendra to provide grandchildren. You guys filled the void, and she's going to take full advantage. Thank you for letting her choose what she wanted to be called." Chance put the baby to her shoulder and rubbed gentle circles on his back until she felt him release the built-up gas in his tummy. "There you go, that has to feel better."

Penny stood. "I'll take him. It's not long after he eats before that diaper will need changed. I'll spare you that chore. I'll get him ready to go."

Chance kissed the downy hair that went every different direction and handed the baby to Penny. "I'll take him every chance I can, and I know Jax feels the same."

"That I do." Jax walked in and held her arms out. "Oh, can I hold him for a minute?" Jax took him from Penny. "I can't believe how big he's getting. How much does he weigh?"

"The pediatrician says he's almost seventeen pounds. Some days, it feels like fifty." Penny put her hands on her back.

"You guys look exhausted. He's still not sleeping?" Jax cooed at the baby. "Hey little Jace, how are you? Auntie Jax loves you."

Penny yawned. "Taylor's dropping him with Maggie in a bit, then she's going home to sleep. My mom will be here soon. I'll get some rest as well. Small price to pay for the blessing that he is. Come on, let's go change him before we have to call out the hazmat team from that diaper. Taylor and Midas are going to get this little guy up the mountain."

Chance watched them take the baby into the other room and looked back at her chief deputy. "While they're gone, this came in the mail today." She passed over an informational sheet sent out by the ATF office out of Clarksburg. "It seems a few of our new county residents have made claims of sovereign citizenship. The article describes a run-in between a Department of Natural Resource officer and one of them who refused to produce a valid fishing license."

Taylor perused the pages. "If I remember right, these folks don't think they need a license for anything, not even to drive a car. Most are pretty harmless; they tie up the courts with frivolous lawsuits and try to scam the IRS."

"Not all of them. If you recall, Timothy McVeigh and Terry Nichols were convicted and executed for the Oklahoma City bombing. Both had declared that they were sovereign citizens. According to my research, as of two years ago, forty-two law enforcement officers have lost their lives to domestic extremists. Sovereign citizens are part of those groups and have been involved in several horrific incidents that I don't want our people unprepared for. I'm going to bring in a friend of mine from the FBI to do a seminar for all of us, including the communications center. They have to be able to recognize the signs if one of our officers calls in with confusing information."

Taylor nodded as if in agreement. "It certainly can't hurt. If we can get a class outline beforehand, I can check with the Sheriff's Association to make sure we can get law enforcement continuing-ed credits. Knowledge is always critical in our job. It's what we don't know that can really hurt us, and there's too much of that already."

Penny and Jax reappeared with Jace, who was happily babbling and grabbing at Jax's hair. Penny ran a hand across Taylor's shoulders.

"It's time for you to take this little guy to Maggie and for you to get to bed. Will you be alright to drive?"

Chance stood. "I need to see Mom anyway. How about I drive you guys in your vehicle? Daniel and Carl can drop mine at her office on their way to do some work with the horses and the dogs."

Taylor took a wiggling Jace and secured him in his car seat, while Midas and Zeus licked and sniffed the delighted boy. "Not a bad idea. I can make it home from Maggie's office. My cargo is too precious to take a risk. Come on, Midas."

Penny and Taylor left the office, while Chance walked over and softly kissed Jax. "I'm going to assume you came to take me to lunch?"

Jax wrapped her arms around Chance's neck. "That was my original idea. I had to stop in at our attorney and sign some papers, making sure your name is on all the right documents. After the hell we went through last year, I don't want anything up in the air in reference to our property or the clinic."

"How about I run Taylor to Maggie's and stop at Big Belly Deli for three specials. I'll meet you back at your office in about an hour?"

"I like that idea. Any chance we can go for a ride later? I need to scope out a course for that upcoming trials ride the Saddlebacks are hosting."

"I think that can be arranged as well. I'll tell Penny, after lunch I'm off duty."

Jax rolled her eyes. "Honey, if there is one thing I've learned since coming back here, you're never off duty."

Chance kissed her again. "I can't argue with that."

***

"We're here." Chance nudged Taylor who startled as if she'd just barely been under.

Taylor sat up, rubbing her eyes. "Sorry, I really hope he starts sleeping through the night on his own soon."

"Me too. Don't be afraid to take time off, Taylor. You can't be at the top of your game if you're exhausted. How about you let me take your midnight shift tonight? I'll be honest, if you don't get some sleep soon, it's going to start affecting your reaction time. We've got the bluegrass festival next week, and you know that's an all-hands-on deck event."

Taylor nodded and let her head fall back on the seat. "I knew parenthood wasn't for the faint of heart, but I thought after that first few months he'd sleep. We're up with him every night. He's got acid reflux, so we had to start giving him meds. I know this is a little on the TMI side, but he never did get the hang of breast feeding, which was extremely hard on Penny. She felt like it was something she'd done wrong. After we talked with our pediatrician, she told us it isn't uncommon. Some babies just don't. It's taken a while for Penny to deal with the emotional side of it and get over feeling like a failure. I can't do anything but support her. She suggested we alternate with cereal to keep him satisfied. Soon, we'll start him on some baby food. Dr. Yarnell says he's thriving, and the breast milk that Penny pumps is the best thing we could be giving him to build his immune system. Now, if he'll sleep more than three hours a night, life would be pretty damn perfect."

Chance put a hand on her friend's shoulder. "You and Penny are great parents. I think you two need a good night's sleep and a weekend to yourselves. Why don't you talk about it? If you're open to it, Jax and I will take him for a night. If that goes well, you two plan a weekend away or at home, and we'll watch Jace for you. With Penny being able to supply the milk, that takes care of one issue. It will be good practice for when Kendra and Brandi have kids and want some alone time."

"Are they getting married? I knew it was serious but didn't have any idea it was that close."

Chance sighed. "It's taking everything to get Kendra to wait until they've graduated. Her heart and mind are set. Brandi has several more years of vet school to go, but if Kendra stays on track with all the extra classes she's been taking, she can graduate this fall. She even took online classes to get ahead. Her plan is to start applying to agencies as soon as she has that degree." A wave of sadness washed over Chance, as she once again realized she couldn't offer her sister a position. It was even possible the first position would be out of state.

"Stop beating yourself up. A position will open up with us eventually. If that kid wants it, there's nothing that will stand in her way. Kendra has to forge her own path. This can't be something handed to her. It wasn't for you or me. We earned it. She needs to feel like that too. You can't protect her from everything. She's going to be an outstanding law enforcement officer, no matter where she lands."

Chance took a deep breath. "I know you're right but the idea of her learning from someone who doesn't share the same values as we do scares the shit out of me."

Taylor turned in her seat and pointed to the gold star on Chance's uniform. "Do you honestly think the lessons you've been teaching her about what that star stands for have meant nothing? She can recite those five points and sound like a recording of you. Those standards aren't just words you've said to her, Chance. They're words you've embedded in her heart and on her spirit. She won't forget them, no matter who her training officer is. She knows right from wrong and good from bad. You've taught her that, and she won't forget that lesson, ever. I haven't."

Chance nearly choked up at her friend's words. She was right, Kendra had been brought up with the values of honor, duty, courage, integrity, and empathy. The values Chance's father had instilled in her, she'd passed to Kendra and every officer that served under her, less one. Her mind was relieved that Brad was no longer of consequence. She looked up and saw Maggie standing at the office window, with her hands on her hips. Taylor unbuckled her seatbelt. "I think we better get this little guy inside. Oma looks like her patience is running thin."

"Oma loves having this baby around, so I imagine us sitting out here with him for ten minutes has been agonizing. The boys back there have managed to keep Jace entertained." Chance turned around to see Midas licking the baby's head. "Well, at least he's been bathed now."

*   *   *

Jax used a tablet to enter the patient notes into the electronic chart. "Keep the cone on her a few days and let the incision heal. If not, she'll start pulling at the stitches. She's going to be groggy for a while, from the anesthesia, which should help you keep her quiet too." The cat meowed weakly, as Jax picked her up and placed her in the carrier.

Naomi Deklan put her fingers through the wire mesh door and stroked the tuxedo cat's foot. "Anything special we should feed her?"

"We can stop on the way home if we need to, Doc." Rhebekka leaned against the wall, hands driven deep into the pockets of her jeans.

"Lindsey will give you a can of food we recommend after surgery. For the next few days, give her some of that and water. They don't always like it, but if they get hungry enough, they'll eat it. I'm so glad you gave this gal a home. Maddie found her wandering around up in Davis. She was such a mess when she came in. She'd been hit by a car and had some pretty serious internal injuries but has bounced back really well. Did you decide on a name yet?"

Rhebekka pushed off the wall and accepted the carrier from Jax. "We have. Meet Marlena Dietrich. Marley for short."

Jax let a true belly laugh go. "Well, she already has the tuxedo on. I guess we'll have to consider the cone her top hat."

"The kids are going to love her. She can join Janice Joplin, better known as JJ, at home. She enjoys walking across the kid's homework to get attention during the after-school program. Now they'll have two to share." Naomi slid her purse up on her shoulder and followed Jax out the door.

"I think the kids are a little more excited about having you join Rhebekka than anything else. How's the leg doing, Rhebekka?"

Rhebekka pulled up her pant leg to reveal a bit of the prosthesis. "I never forget it's gone, but I no longer need any arm crutches or a cane. We keep adjusting it to perfect my gait. I think, all things considered, my guardian angel was flying pretty close that night."

Jax nodded. "I know finding you shook Chance up. She was worried she hadn't gotten to you in time."

Jax watched, as Naomi visibly shivered. Her hands trembled as she handed Lindsey her credit card.

"By the grace of God, and the efforts of Chance's team, she's still with us. Not that we fear where we're going, but I'm planning on a lot more years together before that happens. She promised me a lifetime. I'm holding her to it."

Rhebekka leaned over and kissed Naomi's temple. "Count on it."

Lindsey held out a small bag that contained Marley's medicines and two cans of food. "You're all set. The instructions are on your printout attached to your receipt. If you have any questions, call us."

Jax hugged Naomi and whispered in her ear. "If you ever need to talk, I'm someone who understands. I've been told I'm a pretty good listener."

Naomi hugged her back. "I might take you up on that some time. Thanks for everything."

Jax held her at arm's length. "You two need to come to the house for dinner next week."

Rhebekka reached out and took Naomi's hand in hers. "You name the day and we'll bring the beer."

"I'd say that's a deal. Don't hesitate to call if you have questions about Marley's care."

"Will do, Doc. Let's get this girl home." Rhebekka took Naomi's hand in hers and stepped through the door Jax held open.

"See you two next week." Jax waved and turned back to Lindsey. "What time is your class tonight?"

"Six. I have a test, then a lecture. Should be an easy evening." Lindsey busied herself behind the counter. "Oh, I have a message from your candidate. He's looking forward to his interview and asked if it would be all right to come a bit early. His wife looked over the entertainment in the area and noticed one of their favorite bands is going to be in Elkins tonight. He said it was not a big deal, but it would certainly help his cause for scheduling an interview on his anniversary."

Jax grinned and shook her head. "Call him back and tell him that's fine. We don't have anything else on the books except for a few routine shots. Have him come in whenever he's ready. Chance is supposed to be on her way with some lunch for all of us, after she drops off Taylor and Jace. That little guy still isn't sleeping, and his mommas are exhausted."

"I can imagine. He's so adorable."

The door opened, and Chance walked in with two bags dangling from one hand and a drinks carrier in the other. Zeus followed close behind. "He certainly is. He's got his two omas wrapped around his little finger. Thank God for friends with babies who can ease that need for grandchildren."

Jax unconsciously put her hand on her stomach, feeling a slight pang of envy that she'd never fill that need for Maggie and Dee. That ache didn't even begin to block out the larger one she felt at never having a child with Chance. In her heart, she knew she was beyond the practical age to be pregnant. It made her think about all the years she'd wasted with Lacey in a loveless marriage. She felt strong arms wrap around her from behind.

"Let it go, honey. I know exactly where your mind went. The past is gone. All we can do is look forward. I will tell you that I would have loved to watch you go through pregnancy. We'll just have to spoil Jace as if he was ours."

Jax reached a hand up and cupped the back of Chance's neck, pulling her closer. "You always could read my mind." Jax's stomach growled.

"Right now, I'm reading your body. Let's go eat. I love you."

Jax turned in Chance's arms and looked in the eyes that were so unique to her wife. "And I love you."

Available in Fall 2020

About CJ Murphy

I began to create lesbian fiction after my wife suggested I write her a story as a personalized gift. I was privileged to be mentored by another published author who helped turn a raw manuscript, into an actual novel. Upon completion, she encouraged me to submit to Desert Palm Press. DPP offered me a contract for my first novel, 'frame by frame' in 2017. My second novel, The Bucket List, was published in late 2018. I credit my story telling ability to being an avid reader and having an adventure filled occupation for twenty-five years as a career firefighter.

Connect with CJ:
Email: cptcjldypyro@gmail.com
Facebook: CJ Murphy (Murphy's Law)
Blog: Murphy's Law Ink

Note to Readers:

Thank you for reading a book from Desert Palm Press. We have made every effort to edit this book. However, typos do slip in. If you find an error in the text, please email lee@desertpalmpress.com so the issue can be corrected.

We appreciate you as a reader and want to ensure you enjoy the reading process. We would like you to consider posting a review on your preferred media sites and/or your blog or website.

For more information on upcoming releases, author interviews, contest, giveaways and more, please sign up for our newsletter and visit us as at Desert Palm Press: www.desertpalmpress.com and "Like" us on Facebook: Desert Palm Press.

Bright Blessings

www.ingramcontent.com/pod-product-compliance
Lightning Source LLC
Chambersburg PA
CBHW051632260626
47170CB00004B/1144